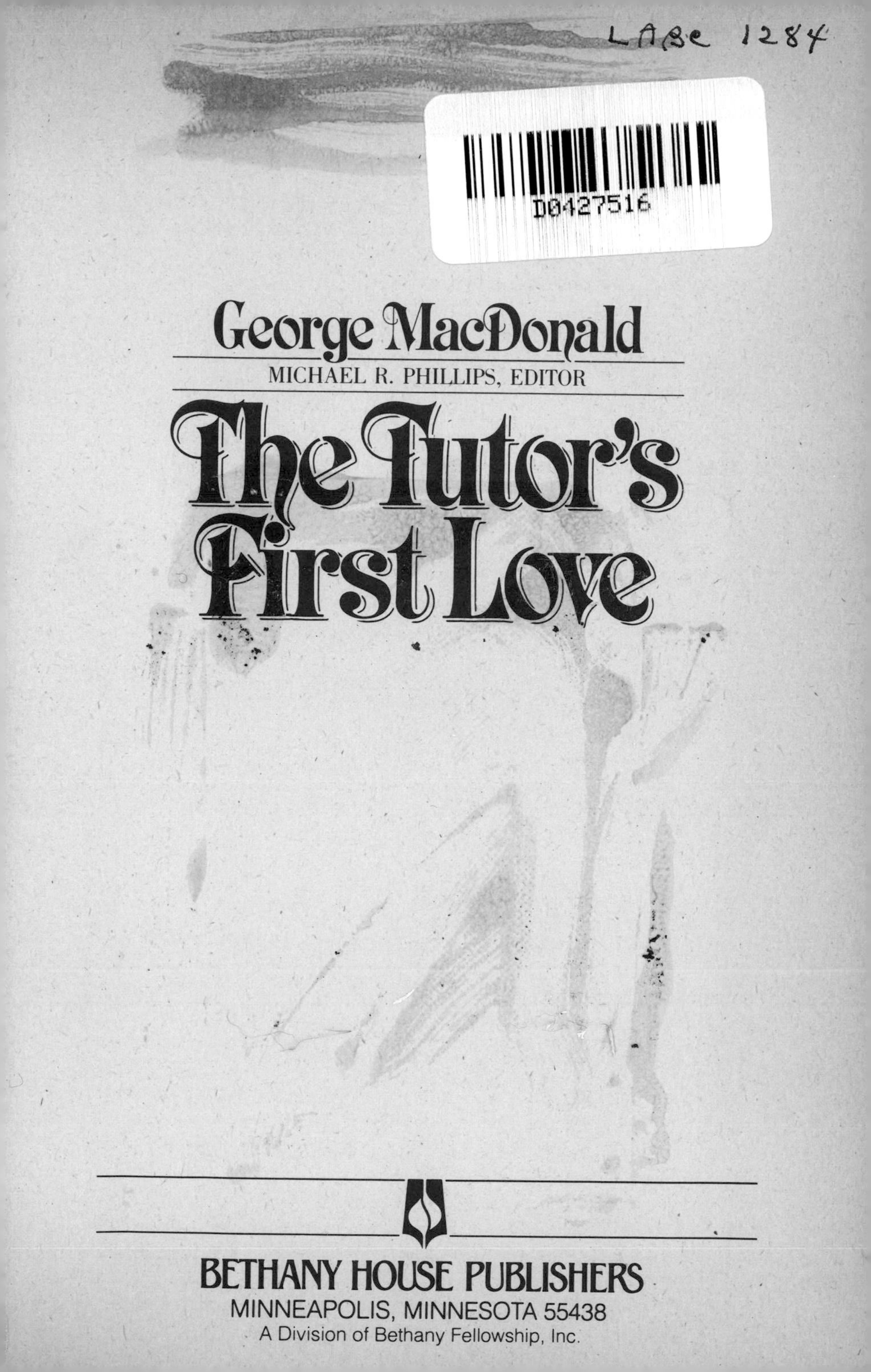

George MacDonald

MICHAEL R. PHILLIPS, EDITOR

The Tutor's First Love

BETHANY HOUSE PUBLISHERS
MINNEAPOLIS, MINNESOTA 55438
A Division of Bethany Fellowship, Inc.

Originally published in 1863 by Hurst & Blackett, London, under the title
David Elginbrod

Published by Bethany House Publishers
A Division of Bethany Fellowship, Inc.
6820 Auto Club Road, Minneapolis, MN 55438

Printed in the United States of America

Library of Congress Cataloging in Publication Data
Macdonald, George, 1824–1905.
The tutor's first love.

Originally published in 1863 under title: David Elginbrod.
I. Phillips, Michael, 1946– . II. Title.
PR4967.D3 1984 823'.8 84–6481
ISBN 0–87123–596–X

BETHANY HOUSE PUBLISHERS
Minneapolis, Minnesota 55438

The Novels of George MacDonald Edited for Today's Reader

Edited Title	**Original Title**
The two-volume story of Malcolm:	
The Fisherman's Lady	*Malcolm*
The Marquis' Secret	*The Marquis of Lossie*
Companion stories of Gibbie and his friend Donal:	
The Baronet's Song	*Sir Gibbie*
The Shepherd's Castle	*Donal Grant*
Companion stories of Hugh Sutherland and Robert Falconer:	
The Tutor's First Love	*David Elginbrod*
The Musician's Quest	*Robert Falconer*
The Maiden's Bequest	*Alec Forbes of Howglen*
Companion stories of Thomas Wingfold:	
The Curate's Awakening	*Thomas Wingfold*
The Lady's Confession	*Paul Faber*
The Baron's Apprenticeship	*There and Back*
Stories that stand alone:	
A Daughter's Devotion	*Mary Marston*
The Gentlewoman's Choice	*Weighed and Wanting*
The Highlander's Last Song	*What's Mine's Mine*
The Laird's Inheritance	*Warlock O'Glenwarlock*
The Landlady's Master	*The Elect Lady*
The Minister's Restoration	*Salted with Fire*
The Peasant Girl's Dream	*Heather and Snow*
The Poet's Homecoming	*Home Again*

MacDonald Classics Edited for Young Readers

Wee Sir Gibbie of the Highlands
Alec Forbes and His Friend Annie
At the Back of the North Wind
The Adventures of Ranald Bannerman

George MacDonald: Scotland's Beloved Storyteller by Michael Phillips
Discovering the Character of God by George MacDonald
Knowing the Heart of God by George MacDonald
A Time to Grow by George MacDonald
A Time to Harvest by George MacDonald

Contents

Introduction

What do you want in a hero?

We all have different men and women we admire, respect, and want to model our lives after. Today's society tends to choose its heroes from Hollywood and the television screen, disdaining the values of the past and looking down on biblical standards of goodness and moral decency.

George MacDonald, however, was a champion of such values, and the personalities in his novels upheld right, justice, and honesty, laying down their lives if necessary in their dauntless fight to maintain virtue and integrity.

Thus when I make acquaintance in one of MacDonald's books with a man or woman who stands for truth and goodness in everything he or she does, I am drawn to the ultimate role model in my life—Jesus. And I cannot but look up to such characters, fictional though they may be. They provide a solid image of how we were meant to live.

As a result, men like Malcolm (in *The Fisherman's Lady*) and Donal (from *The Baronet's Song* and *The Shepherd's Castle*) have become friends who are influential in my life. They continue to affect me, long after the actual reading of a particular book is over. I find myself wondering, "If Malcolm were facing this dilemma, what would he do . . . what would Donal say to this person?"

I consider this an evidence of the gift George MacDonald's writing has given me. I am a wiser man, a more confident person, a stronger Christian because of my association with the men and women he has brought to life. They raise a pure and uncompromising standard that I can look toward and aspire to. They accompany me through life in much the same way real flesh-and-blood friendships do, if only in my mind and heart—they teach me, encourage me, they make me laugh, they make me cry, and they support me when I am in need.

One of the striking aspects of this is the diversity of personalities one encounters. Not only do we meet strong, masculine knights of justice like Donal, Robert Falconer and Malcolm, we also find ourselves enriched by the quiet lives of MacDonald's elderly saints—Graham the schoolmaster, Janet Grant, and old Andrew the cobbler.

A contemporary magazine in MacDonald's time, reviewing his writing in general, made these comments: "The books are of their own kind. One cannot read them without being stimulated to something nobler and purer, for they may honestly be called both. . . . Their deep perceptions of human nature are certainly remarkable. . . . Let it stand to Mr. MacDonald's credit that, in an age of loose literature, he is, like Scott, Dickens, and Thackery, pure-minded and . . . he will merit and receive distinguished praise."

Another reviewer wrote, "In George MacDonald's company the very air seems impregnated with love, purity, and tenderness."

In 1863, George MacDonald's first conventional novel, *David Elginbrod* (from which *The Tutor's First Love* has been taken), was published. It was an immediate success and established MacDonald thereafter as a skilled novelist, popular both in Great Britain and the United States. Undoubtedly one of the features which made *David Elginbrod* such a popular book (prompting the *London Times* to call it "the work of a man of genius") was that its author brought such a wealth of personalities into the tale. The title character, David himself, provides the classic example of a wise, stalwart, virtuous, spiritual man. And we also come to love his wife in her own unique way, while his daughter Margaret grows to occupy a prominent role in the narrative.

However, it is Hugh Sutherland who attracts the main focus of our attention, but for reasons different than one might at first think. Hugh is not MacDonald's typical hero. He is genuine and down-to-earth; he struggles throughout the entire book—unsure about many things, falling frequently, hounded by immature judgments and poor decisions. Often he must repent, learn, and grow—helped by saintly David and his family—before he gains a solid footing of his own.

Hugh is, therefore, typical of us all. While Falconer or Gibbie may present "role models" to me, Hugh *is* the person I am—groping, questioning . . . yet persevering. He too is looking for that standard and finds it—not in perfect heroes but in the simple lives of a man and a woman whose love for the Lord is uncompromising.

Along the way, however, Hugh becomes involved in some rather questionable proceedings. As a writer, George MacDonald did not fear letting his author's pen probe into some of life's dark corners. Not because he in any way condoned occult activity nor would want any of his readers to dabble in it, but because his faith was so confidently founded in the light of God's truth that he wanted to expose Satan's deceit.

The sense of oppression surrounding the middle portion of this narrative is MacDonald's method of exposing the conflict between the forces of light and the forces of darkness, exemplified by Fenkelstein and Margaret. It is critical to remember that his use of séance, hypnotism, and even a crude Ouija board is intended to bring to light the evil source from which such things come.

Standing in the middle of the spiritual warfare being waged, Hugh senses the dark and evil oppression coming from one side and feels the warmth of light and goodness emanating from the other. In the end, his growth and persistence and desire for right is rewarded—not with a fairy tale ending, but with the dignity that comes from having endured his quest to discover life's truths, and finding himself and his true love in the process.

—Michael Phillips
Eureka, California

1 / The Primrose

It was, of course, quite by accident that Hugh Sutherland met Margaret Elginbrod in the fir wood. The wind had changed during the night and swept all the clouds from the face of the sky. And when he looked out in the morning he saw the fir tops waving in the sunlight and heard the sound of a southwest wind sweeping through them with the tune of running waters.

Hugh dressed in haste and went out to greet the spring.

He wandered into the heart of the wood. The sunlight shone as a sunset upon the red trunks and boughs of the old fir trees, yet as a sunrise upon the new green fringes that edged the young shoots of the larches. High up hung the memorials of past summers in the rich brown tassels of the clustering cones. The ground was dappled with sunshine on the fallen fir needles, and the great fallen cones which had opened to scatter their autumnal seed now lay waiting for decay. Overhead, the treetops waved in the wind as if to welcome spring.

The wind blew cool, but not cold, and was filled with a delicious odor from the earth, which Sutherland took as a sign that she was coming alive at last. At the foot of a tree he spied a tiny primrose peeping out of its rough, leaflike nest. He wondered how such a leafless stem could produce such a delicate flower. He bent to pluck it gently and continued on, the yellow primrose like a candle in his hand.

Deeper into the wood he went—it could hardly, despite its grandeur and height, be called a forest—when suddenly he saw another form of approaching spring. He spotted, a little way off, the same young girl he had glimpsed twice before, leaning against the trunk of a Scotch fir. Margaret (for this was her name) was looking up to its top swaying overhead. He went up to her with some shyness, partly from the fear of startling her shyness, as one feels when drawing near a crouching fawn. But when she heard his footsteps, she dropped her eyes slowly from the treetop and awaited his approach.

He said nothing at first but offered her, instead of speech, the primrose he had just plucked. She received it with smiling eyes and the sweetest "Thank you, sir" he had ever heard. But while she held the primrose in her hand, her eyes wandered to the book which, according to his custom, Sutherland had caught up as he left the house. It was the only well-bound book in his possession, and to Margaret that could mean only entrancing pages within such beautiful cover-boards. In this case her expectation was not in vain, for the volume was of Coleridge's poems.

Seeing her eyes fixed upon the book, he said, "Would you like to read it?"

"If you please, sir," she answered, her eyes brightening with the expectation of delight.

"Are you fond of poetry?"

Her face fell. She had hoped for stories. "I don't know much about poetry," she answered. "There's an old book on my father's shelf. But the letters are old-fashioned and I don't care for it."

"But this is quite easy to read, and very beautiful," said Hugh.

The girl's eyes glistened for a moment.

"Would you like to read it?" Hugh offered again.

She held out her hand for the volume. When he, in turn, held it toward her hand, she almost snatched it from him and ran toward her home with neither a word of thanks nor a good-bye—whether from eagerness or from doubt as to how to accept the offer, Hugh could not guess.

He stood for some moments looking after her, and then retraced his steps toward the house.

2 / David Elginbrod

While Margaret had been thus occupied, her mother stood at the cottage door looking for her daughter. And although she could not see her, she knew the little forest of fir trees the likeliest place for her daughter to be. For an aimless wandering among and through the trees was the ordinary occupation at the first hour of almost every day in Margaret's life. As soon as she woke in the morning, the fir wood drew her toward it, and she rose and went. Through its crowd of slender pillars she strayed hither and thither.

"Where have you been so long, lassie?" her mother asked the moment she became visible.

Margaret approached her mother with a bright, healthy face. "I didn't know it was so late, Mother."

"No doubt, no doubt," said her mother with no small discomposure. "We're waiting breakfast for you."

"Hoots! Let the bairn be, Jeanette, my woman," called Margaret's father from inside.

"What book have you got there, Meg?" asked Jeanette, "and where did you get it?"

Had it not been for the handsome binding of the book in her daughter's hand, it would neither have caught Jeanette's eye nor roused her suspicions. David glanced at the book, in his turn, and a faint expression of surprise crossed his face.

"I got it from Mr. Sutherland," said Margaret, sitting down at the white deal table with a steaming pot of oatmeal porridge in its center.

Jeanette's first response was an inverted whistle, her next another question: "Mr. Sutherland? Who's that?"

"You know well enough," interposed David. "He's the new tutor lad up at the house.—Let me look at the book, lassie."

Margaret handed it to her father.

"*Coleridge's Poems*," read David.

"Take it back immediately," commanded Jeanette.

"No, no," said David. "All the apples of the tree of knowledge aren't strewn with iniquity. And if this one is, she'll soon know by the taste of it.—It's not a bad book that you'll read, Maggie, my doo." Her father rarely called Margaret anything but his little "dove."

"God preserve us, man!" exclaimed Jeanette. "I'm not saying it's a bad book. But it's not right to make appointments with stranger lads in the woods so early in the morning.—Is it now, Meg?"

"Mother," said Margaret, "you know yourself I had no appointment with him or any man."

"Well, well," said Jeanette; and, apparently satisfied, she turned to her bowl and said no more.

David, finishing his porridge and handing the book to his daughter, rose and left the cottage by the path that led from its door toward a road that could be seen at a little distance through the trees. Before long Margaret was busy with her share of the household duties. But it was some minutes before the cloud caused by her mother's hasty words entirely disappeared from her countenance.

Meantime, David emerged upon the more open road and bent his course toward a large house, for whose sake alone the road seemed to have been constructed. The House of Turriepuffit stood about a furlong from David's cottage. It was the house of the laird for whom David filled several offices. The estate was a small one and almost entirely farmed by the owner himself, who, with David's help, managed to turn it to a modest profit. David was his steward, his administrator to oversee the laborers on the estate, to pay them, and to keep the farm accounts. In addition he was the laird's head gardener, but little labor was expended in that direction, seeing that the mistress of the house was no patroness of useless flowers.

The laird's family, besides his wife, consisted only of two boys, aged eleven and fourteen. He wished them to enjoy the same privileges he had himself possessed; therefore, he was giving them a classical and mathematical education with a goal of the university before them. Their private tutors had been many—since the salary was of the smallest—and the present one was Hugh Sutherland.

The young tutor was just entering a side door of the house when David approached him. "That's a fine book of ballads you lent my Maggie this morning, sir."

Sutherland was not old enough to keep from blushing at this sudden revelation of the girl's name and family; but, having a good conscience, he was ready with a good answer. "It's a good book, Mr. Elginbrod. It will do her no harm, though it be ballads."

"I'm not afraid of that, sir. Young girls must have their ballads. And to tell you the truth, I'm not much more than a child in that respect myself. You must come over to the cottage some time and enlighten me about your friend Coleridge."

"I'll stop in some evening and we'll have a chat about it," replied Sutherland. "I must go to my work now."

"Well, I'll be very happy to see you, sir," said David with a smile. "Good morning to you!"

David went to the garden, where there was not much to be done at this time of the year; and Sutherland went to the schoolroom, where he was busy all the rest of the morning and part of the afternoon, with Caesar and Virgil, algebra and Euclid—food upon which intellectual babes are reared to the stature of college youths.

Sutherland was himself only a youth, for he had gone early to college. He was now filling up with teaching the recess between this third and fourth winter at one of the Aberdeen universities. Despite strained circumstances, his father and mother had resolved, cost what it might in pinching and squeezing, to send their son to college before turning him out to shift for himself. And so they had managed to keep their boy at college for three sessions, after the last of which, instead of returning home as he had done on previous occasions, he had looked about for a temporary engagement as tutor. He soon found the situation he now occupied in the family of William Glasford, Esq., of Turriepuffit, where he intended to remain no longer than the commencement of his fourth and last session. To what he should devote himself afterward he had not made up his mind.

His pupils were rather dull and rather good-natured; so their temperament operated to confirm their intellectual condition, and rendered the labor of teaching them considerably irksome. But Hugh did his work tolerably well and was not so much interested in success for its own right as he was pained at the slowness of any visible results. At the time, however, the probability of his success was scarcely ascertainable, for he had been only two weeks at the task.

It was the middle of the month of April, in a rather backward season. The weather had been stormy, with frequent showers of sleet and snow. Old winter was doing his best to hold young spring back, and very few of the wild flowers had yet ventured to look out of their warm beds in the mould. Sutherland, therefore, had made few discoveries in the neighborhood.

Not that the weather would have kept him to the house had he had any particular desire to go out. But, like many students, he preferred the choice of his own weather indoors, namely his books, to an encounter with the keen blasts of the north, charged as they often were with sharp bullets of hail. When the sun did shine out between the showers, its cold glitter upon the pools of rain or melted snow and on the wet evergreens always drove Hugh back from the window with a shiver. The house stood in the midst of vast clumps of Scotch firs and larches, some very old and of great growth. There was very little to be seen from the windows except these woods, which at the present was cheerless enough. And Sutherland had found it dreary indeed, exchanged for the wide view from his own home on the side of an open hill in the Highlands.

In the midst of circumstances so uninteresting, it is not to be wondered at that the glimpse of a pretty maiden should occasion him some welcome excitement. Passing downstairs to breakfast, a week before their meeting in the wood, he had observed the drawing-room door ajar. Looking in, he saw a young girl peeping into a small, gilt-leaved book with mingled curiosity and reverence. He watched her for a moment with some interest; then she looked up, blushed deeply, put the book on the table, and proceeded to dust some of the furniture. It had been his first sight of Margaret.

Some of the neighbors were expected for dinner, and her aid had been requested to get the grand room of the house prepared for the occasion. Hugh supposed her to belong to the household, till one day, feeling compelled to go out for a stroll, he caught sight of her so occupied at the door of her father's cottage that he perceived at once it must be her home. She was seated on a stool peeling potatoes. She saw him as well, and, apparently ashamed at the recollection of having been discovered idling in the drawing room, rose from her place and went in. Hugh had met David once or twice about the house, and, attracted by his appearance, had had some conversation with him. But he had not then known where David lived, nor that he was the father of the girl whom he had seen.

3 / The Cottage

There was one great alleviation to the various discomforts of Sutherland's tutor life. It was the fact that except during school hours he was expected to take no charge whatever of his pupils. They ran wild all other times, which was far better both for them and for him. Consequently he was entirely his own master beyond the fixed margin of scholastic duties, and he soon found that his absence, even from the meal table, was a matter of no interest to the family. To be sure, it involved his own fasting till the next mealtime came round, for the lady was quite a household disciplinarian. But that was his own concern.

That very evening, following David's invitation, he asked directions from another of the servants of the house and proceeded to make his way to David's cottage. It was a clear, still, moonlit night, with just a hint of frost. There was light enough for him to see that the cottage grounds were very neat and tidy. A light was burning in the window, visible through the inner curtain of muslin and the outer one of frost. As he approached the door he heard the sound of a voice, and from the even pitch of the tone he concluded at once that its owner was reading aloud. The measured cadence soon convinced him that it was verse being read, and the voice was evidently that of David. He knocked at the door. The voice ceased, chairs were pushed back, and a heavy step approached.

"Eh, Mr. Sutherland," greeted David. "You're welcome! Come in. Our place is small, but I'm sure you'll not mind.—Jeanette," he said, turning to his wife, "this is Mr. Sutherland.—Maggie, my doo, he's a friend of yours of a day already.—It's very kind of you to come and see us, Mr. Sutherland."

As Hugh entered, he saw his own bright volume lying on the table, evidently that from which David had just been reading. Margaret drew up for him a cushioned armchair, the only comfortable one in the house; and presently, the table being drawn back, they were all seated around the peat fire on the hearth. On the crook, the hooked iron chain suspended within the chimney, hung a three-footed pot in which potatoes were boiling away merrily for supper. By the side of the wide chimney hung an iron lamp, from the beak of which projected almost horizontally the lighted wick. The light perched upon it was small but clear, and by it David had been reading. Margaret sat right under it on a small, three-legged stool. Sitting thus, with the light falling on her from above, Hugh could not help thinking she looked very pretty indeed.

"Well, Mr. Elginbrod," said the tutor, after they had been seated a few minutes, and had had some talk about the weather, "how do you like the English poet?"

"Ask me that this day next week, Mr. Sutherland. Maybe then I'll have an answer for you. But not tonight yet."

Therewith followed a good deal of conversation, mostly between David and Hugh, beginning with the meaning of some of Coleridge's work but ranging at times as far afield as the meaning of meaning itself. Hugh began before long to feel as if, notwithstanding David's ignorance as to specifics, he were in the presence of a superior.

By this time the potatoes were considered to be cooked and were accordingly lifted off the fire. The water was then poured away, the lid put aside, and the pot hung once more upon the crook, hooked a few rings further up in the chimney, in order that the potatoes might be thoroughly dry before they were served. Margaret was now very busy spreading the cloth and laying spoons and plates on the table. Hugh rose to go.

"Won't you stay," invited Jeanette in a most hospitable tone, "and have some potatoes with us?"

"I'm afraid of being troublesome," he answered.

"No fear of that if you can just put up with our homely meal."

"Make no apologies, Jeanette," said David. "A hot potato's plenty good fare, for simple or grand folk.—Sit down again, Mr. Sutherland.—Maggie, my doo, where's the milk?"

"I thought Hawkie would have a good supply of warm milk by this time," said Margaret, "and so I put off milking her to the last. But I'll have it drawn in two minutes." And away she went with a jug in her hand.

"That's hardly fair play to Hawkie," said David to Jeanette with a smile.

"I hope," said Hugh, "that this is the last time you will consider me a stranger—that is, if you don't tire of me visiting you."

"Give us the chance," said David. "It's a privilege for us to have a friend with as much book learning as you have, sir."

"I'm afraid it seems more to you than it really is," said Hugh.

With the true humility that comes of revering the truth, David had not the smallest idea that he was nearer the stars than Hugh, with all his knowledge.

"Nevertheless," David went on, "I envy your education. It's not many chances I get, at my age, to improve on mine. Maybe you can help from time to time."

Before Hugh could voice his consent, Maggie returned with her jug full of frothy milk. The potatoes were heaped up in a wooden bowl in the middle of the table, sending the fragrance of their hospitality to thc rafters. Jeanette placed a smaller wooden bowl filled with the delicious, yellow milk of Hawkie's latest gathering for each individual of the company, with an attendant horn-spoon by its side. They all drew their chairs to the table. David, asking no "blessing" as such, but nevertheless giving thanks for the blessing already bestowed in the perfect gift of food, then invited Hugh to take supper. In primitive but not ungraceful fashion, each took a potato from the dish with the fingers and ate it, using the horn-spoon for the milk. Hugh thought he had never feasted more pleasantly, and could not help observing how far good breeding is independent of the forms and refinements of society.

Soon after supper was over it was time for him to go. David accompanied him to the road, where he left him to find his way home by the starlight. It seemed to the young student a wonderful fact that the communion which was denied him in the laird's family should be afforded him in the family of a simple man who had once followed the plough. He certainly felt, on his way home, much more reconciled to the prospect of his sojourn at Turriepuffit than he would have thought possible only the day before.

4 / The Students

Hugh visited the cottage regularly after that; and at length David made a request which led to their even greater frequency.

"Do you think, Mr. Sutherland," he said, "that as past my prime as I am, I could learn anything of mathematics? I understand well enough how to measure land and such things. I just follow the rules. But I would like to understand the principles behind the rules."

"I have no doubt you could learn fast enough," replied Hugh, who had already, from the discussions they had had, come to regard David as something of a scholar in peasant's clothing. "I would be happy to help you with it if you like."

"No, no, I'm not going to trouble *you*. You have enough teaching to do already. But if you could just spare me one or two of your books for a while, any of them you think suitable?"

The result was that before long, both the father and daughter were seated at the kitchen table every evening busy with algebra and some geometry. And on most evenings Hugh was present as their instructor. It was quite a new pleasure to him. Few delights surpass those of imparting knowledge to the eager recipient. And few lessons had passed before David began to put questions to Hugh which the latter could not answer. Meantime, Margaret, though forced to lag a good way behind her father, remembered all she learned, and that is great praise for any student. She was not by any means remarkably quick. But she knew when she did not understand; and that is a sure and indispensable step toward understanding. The gratitude of David was too deep to be expressed in any formal thanks.

During the lesson, which often lasted more than two hours, Jeanette would be busy about the room, in and out of it, with a manifest care to suppress all unnecessary bustle. At times her remarks would seem to imply that she considered it rather absurd of her husband to trouble himself with book learning, but evidently on the ground that she felt he knew everything already that was worthy of the honor of his acquaintance. With regard to Margaret, however, Jeanette was full of pride at the idea of her daugther's education coming from the laird's own tutor.

Now and then she would stand still for a moment and gaze at them with her bright black eyes, brown arms bare to the elbows, and a look of pride on her equally brown, honest face. Her clothing consisted of a short, loose jacket of printed calico and a blue winsey petticoat. Margaret's was ordinarily like her mother's, but every evening when Hugh was expected she replaced the jacket with a dress of the same material, a cotton print. David made no other preparation than to wash his large, well-formed hands. He sat down at the table in his usual rough, blue coat with plain brass buttons. His pants were of broad striped corduroy; he wore blue-ribbed socks and leather gaiters. His sturdy shoes—with five rows of broad-headed nails in the soles—projected from beneath the other side of the table, for he was a tall man, about six feet—though at sixty-five he was considerably bent in the shoulders from hard work. Sutherland's style was that of a country gentleman—Norfolk jacket and knitted argyle vest, wool pants and boots. His sandy hair topped a pleasant face and serious gray eyes.

Such was the group which, three or four evenings a week, could be seen in David Elginbrod's cottage seated around the white deal table with their books and slates upon it, their only light a tallow candle.

The length and frequency of Hugh's absences, careless as she was of his presence, had attracted the attention of Mrs. Glasford; and very little trouble had to be expended to discover his haunt. For the servants knew well enough where he went and had come to their own conclusions as to the objects of his visits. So the lady chose to make it her duty to expostulate with Hugh on the subject. Waiting for the opportunity, therefore, one morning after breakfast Mrs. Glasford folded her hands on the tablecloth, drew herself up yet a little more stiffly in her chair, and addressed Hugh: "It's my duty, Mr. Sutherland, seeing you have no mother to look after you—"

Hugh expected something matronly about his linen or his socks, and with a smile put down the paper he had been reading. But to his astonishment, she went on: "—to point out to you the impropriety of going so often to David Elginbrod's. They're not company for a young gentleman like you, Mr. Sutherland."

"They're good enough company for a poor tutor, Mrs. Glasford," replied Hugh.

"Hardly," insisted the lady. "With your connections—"

"Good gracious! Who ever said anything about my 'connections'? I have never pretended to have any." Hugh was growing angry already.

Mrs. Glasford nodded her head significantly, as much as to say, "I know more about you than you imagine," and then went on: "Your mother would never forgive me if you get into a scrape with that smooth-faced hussy; and if her father hasn't eyes enough in his head, other people have—ay, and tongues too, Mr. Sutherland." Her head continued to bob.

Hugh was at the point of forgetting his manners altogether, but he managed to restrain himself and merely said that Margaret was one of the finest girls he had ever known and that there was no possible danger of any kind of scrape with her. This mode of argument, however, was not calculated to satisfy Mrs. Glasford. She returned to the charge.

"She's a sly one, with her shy airs and graces. Her father's just daft with conceit over her, and it's hardly surprising that she's cast her spell over you as well."

Though he had seen enough of Margaret's character to know her heart of gold, Hugh was still immature enough to consider her hardly his equal. His youthful pride presented as absurd any alliance with a lassie who tended cows barefoot, however pretty and bright she might be, and he resented the entertainment of such a degrading idea in the mind of Mrs. Glasford.

"It's not for lack of company that you're driven to seek theirs," Mrs. Glasford went on. "Them's two as fine lads and good scholars as you'll find in the whole countryside, not to mention the laird and myself."

Hugh could bear it no longer. But he would not condescend to excuse or explain his conduct.

"Madam," he said, "I beg you not to mention this subject again. I am accountable to you for my conduct in your house, and for the way in which I discharge my duty to your children—but no further."

"Do you call *that* 'discharging your duty,' to set them the example of hanging about with that girl and filling her head with idle promises?"

"I never see the girl but in her father's or mother's presence," he returned in as even a tone as he could manage.

"Well, well," said Mrs. Glasford in a final tone, trying to smooth Hugh's obvious anger, "we'll not talk about it any more at present. But I'll just have to talk to the laird himself and see what he says."

And with this threat she walked out of the room in what she considered a dignified manner.

Hugh remained very annoyed for some time afterward but calmed by degrees.

Meanwhile, the lady sent for David, who was at work in the garden. He was shown into the drawing room where Mrs. Glasford was sitting under the revered portraits of the laird and herself. When David had carefully wiped the shoes he had already wiped three times on the way up, she ordered him to shut the door and be seated, for she sought to mingle condescension and conciliation with severity.

"David," she began, "I am informed that you keep your door open to our Mr. Sutherland, and that he spends most of his evenings in your company."

"Well, ma'am, it's quite true," was David's forthright answer.

"David, I'm surprised at you," responded Mrs. Glasford, forgetting her dignity and becoming confidentially remonstrative. ''Here's a young gentleman with every prospect of a pulpit some day, and you're helping him to idle away his time. I thought you had more sense!''

David, with an almost paternal smile, looked out of his clear, blue eyes upon the ruffled countenance of his mistress.

''Well, ma'am, I must say I don't think the young man's in the worst of company. And as for idling away his time, he's well rewarded for his efforts if the holy words be not lies.''

''What do you mean?'' said the lady rather sharply, for she hated riddles.

''I mean that if it indeed be more blessed to give than to receive, as Saint Paul says that the Master said, then the young man'll be receiving plenty because of all the learning he imparts to us.''

''Are you saying, David, that the young man, who's overpaid to instruct my children, neglects them while he lays himself out for other folk who have no right to anything but the station in which their Maker put them?'' This was uttered with almost a religious fervor, for she was indignant at the thought of Meg Elginbrod having lessons from her boys' tutor, notwithstanding the fact that she was cowed beneath the quiet, steady gaze of Meg's father.

''I hardly think he's neglecting his duty to you, ma'am. For it was only yesterday the laird himself said to me that the boys had never got on so well with any of their other tutors.''

''The laird's too quick with compliments,'' she retorted, nettled to find herself in the wrong. ''But,'' she pursued, ''all I can say is that I consider it very improper of you, with a young lass in your home, to encourage the nightly visits of a young gentleman who's so far above her station, and doubtless will some day be further yet.''

''He visits her no more than me,'' interposed David.

''Be that as it may,'' she went on, with dignified disregard of his words, ''as long as my tutor visits her, for the sake of my own children and the morals of my household, I can't employ her about the house as I have before. Good morning to you, David. I'll simply have to speak to the laird since you'll not heed me.''

Upon these words, David withdrew, rather anxious about the consequences to Hugh of this unpleasant interference on the part of Mrs. Glasford. His Maggie would keep busy at home with Jeanette.

The lady's wrath kept warm without much nursing till the laird came home, when she turned it upon him. But he had more common sense than his wife in some things and saw at once how ridiculous it would be to treat the affair as of importance. So the next time he saw David, he addressed him half playfully from astride his horse, ''Well, David, you and my wife have been having a bit of a dispute, eh?''

"Well, sir, we weren't altogether of one mind," answered David with a smile.

"We must humor her, you know," said the laird, bending toward him familiarly, "or it might be the worse for us." He then winked and nodded with humorous significance.

"I'd be most happy to," said David, "except this is no small matter for my Maggie and me. We're getting food for our very souls from Mr. Sutherland and his books."

"Couldn't you be content with the books without the man, David?"

"We'd make but small and slow progress that way."

The laird began to get a little nettled himself at David's stiffness over such a small matter, but he held his peace.

"Besides, sir," David went on, "that's a matter for the young gentleman to decide. It would hardly be gracious of me, after all he's done for us, to lock the door in his face. No, as long as I have a door to hold open, it's not to be closed to him."

"But the door's mine after all, David," reminded the laird.

"As long as I'm in your service, sir, the door's mine." David's quiet voice was respectful but boded no argument.

Tha laird turned and rode away without another word. What further transpired between him and his wife never was known. Nothing more was said to Hugh. But afterward Margaret was never sent for to the house.

5 / Hugh and Margaret

The lessons went on as usual, and happy hours they were. Often, in later years and in far different circumstances, the thoughts of Hugh reverted, with a painful yearning, to the dim-lighted cottage with its clay floor and deal table and homely fireplace. And especially to the earnest pair seated with him, and to the thickset but active form of Jeanette. Indeed, it was wonderful what a share the motherhood of that woman, incapable as she was of entering into the intellectual occupations of the others, had in producing that sense of home-blessedness which wrapped Hugh in the folds of its hospitality. Certainly not one of the three would have worked so well without the sense of the presence of Jeanette, here and there about the room, or in the immediate neighborhood of it—love watching over labor. Once a week, always on Saturday nights, Hugh stayed to supper with them. And always on these occasions Jeanette contrived to have something better than ordinary in honor of their guest. Still it was of the homeliest country fare, such as Hugh could partake of without the least fear of inconvenience or economic distress to his hosts.

Nor was Hugh the only source of soul food. In addition to the rich gifts of human affection which grew more pleasant to him daily, many things were spoken into Hugh's mind and heart by the simple wisdom of David. They would have enlightened Hugh far more than they did had he been sufficiently advanced spiritually to receive them. But their very simplicity was often far beyond the grasp of his thoughts; for the higher we rise the simpler we become. And David was one of those of whom is the kingdom of heaven. Thus, beyond David's mere words, his very being, his presence, had deep impact on the spirit of Hugh and the direction of his development—though at the time Hugh remained unaware of the extent to which this process was taking place. There is a childhood into which we have to grow, just as there is a childhood which we must leave behind. Hugh was just leaving the one and as yet had scarce an inkling of the existence of the other, with which David was already well acquainted. One is a childishness from which but few of those who are counted wisest among men have freed themselves. The other is a childlikeness, which is the highest gain of humanity.

Meantime, the genuine interest Hugh felt for his girl-pupil deepened. The expression of her face usually remained inferior to the intelligence and power of thought inside. It was a still face; she seemed to have a peculiar faculty of retiring inside herself. But now and then, while he was talking to her and doubting, from her lack of expression, whether she was even listening, suddenly her face would light up with a radiant smile of intelligence. At such times, when the light shone through the forms and contours in her face, her countenance seemed absolutely beautiful. Hence it grew into an almost haunting temptation with Hugh to try to produce this expression, to unveil the delicate light of the beautiful soul. Often he tried, often he failed, but sometimes he succeeded. Had they been alone, it might have become dangerous—I mean for Hugh; I cannot tell for Margaret.

When they first met she had just completed her seventeenth year. But at an age when a town-bred girl is all but a woman, Margaret's manners and habits remained those of a child. This childishness, however, gradually began to disappear and the peculiar stillness of her face made her seem older than she was.

It was now early summer, and all the trees had put on their fresh leaves. In the morning the sun shone so clear upon them that, to the eyes of one standing beneath, the light seemed to dissolve them away to the most ethereal forms. Margaret continued to haunt the wood nearly every morning; Hugh less often. Occasionally they met.

Hugh continued to teach the two Glasford boys, with limited success. But Margaret's mental interests and facilities deepened noticeably. She began to read Wordsworth and others, and found herself introduced to nature in altogether new aspects which had hitherto been unknown to her. Not only was the fir wood now dearer to her than before, but its mystery seemed more sacred. And the purple hillside grew as dear as the wood, and her morning walks took her farther and farther from the cottage. Now taller and more graceful, the lasting quiet of her face began slowly to blossom into a constant expression of loveliness.

By and by Hugh began to lend her more difficult books, and Margaret found frequent occasion to apply to Hugh for help. One evening, toward the end of summer, Hugh climbed a waste heathery hill that lay behind the house of Turriepuffit and overlooked a great part of the neighboring country, the peaks of some of the greatest of the Scottish mountains being visible from its top. Here he intended to wait for the sunset. He threw himself on the heather, that most delightful and luxurious of all couches, and there he lay in the great slumberous sunlight of the late afternoon with the blue heavens closing down upon him. He fell fast asleep. When he awoke, the last of the sunset was dying away; and between him and the sunset sat Margaret, book in hand, waiting patiently for his waking. He lay still for a few minutes, to come to himself before she should see he was awake. But she rose at the moment and, drawing near very quietly, looked down upon him with her sweet sunset face to see whether or not he was beginning to rouse, for she feared to let him lie much longer after sundown. Finding him awake, she drew back again without a word, and sat down as before with her book.

At length he rose and, approaching her, said, "Well, Margaret, what book are you reading now?"

"One of Wordsworth's, sir," she replied, "but I had a difficulty I couldn't get past without your help."

He offered his hand; she took it, not without some timidity, it is true, but firmly, and he pulled her up. They turned, as by common consent, to go down the hill together.

"Tell me how Mr. Wordsworth confused you," Hugh began.

Then followed a lengthy discussion as they walked. It was dark before they reached home, at least as dark as it ever is at that season of the year in the North. They found David looking out with some slight anxiety for his daughter's return, for she was seldom out so late as this. In nothing could the true relation between them have been more evident than in the entire absence of any embarrassment when she met her father. She went up to him and told him all about finding Mr. Sutherland asleep on the hill, and waiting beside him till he woke, that she might walk home with him.

Turning to Hugh, David said, "I don't mean to be troublesome, but you might as well help the old man as the young lass. And I'm puzzled about a small matter on my slate. Would you mind coming in and giving me a hand?"

Hugh entered the cottage and laid on the table the fine sprig of heather he had carried down the hill.

After he had helped David out of his difficulty, he took up the heather, stripped off the bells, and shook them in his hand at Margaret's ear. He was proud of small discoveries, and this one he had made just that afternoon. A half smile dawned on her face. She listened with something of the same expression with which a child listens to the message from the sea, enclosed in a twisted shell. He repeated the exhibition at David's ear next.

"Eh, man! that's a bonny wee sound," said David lapsing into Scotch. "It's just like small sheep bells—fairy sheep, I reckon, Maggie, my doo."

"Let me listen as well," said Jeanette.

Hugh obliged.

Jeanette laughed. "It's nothing but a rustling. I would rather hear real sheep baaing."

"Eh, Mr. Sutherland," said David. "You've a keen eye and a sharp ear. The world's full of bonny sights and sounds, down to the very smallest. I wouldn't doubt there are thousands of such things, too small for human ears, just as there are creatures as perfect in beauty as any we can see that are too small for our own eyes.''

''I suppose you could easily believe with Plato,'' said Hugh, ''that the planets make a grand choral music as they roll about the heavens, only that as some sounds are too small, so that one is too loud for us to hear?''

''I could well believe that,'' was David's unhesitating answer. Margaret looked as if she not only could believe it, but would be delighted to know that it was true. Jeanette gave no indication of feeling on the matter.

6 / Harvest Time

Hugh had watched the green grain grow, and ear, and turn dim; then brighten to yellow, and ripen at last under the declining autumn sun. The long threads, on each of which hung an oat grain, had become dry and brittle, and the grains began to spread out their chaff-wings as if ready to fly. They rustled with sweet sounds against each other as the wind swept gently and tenderly over the fields. The harvest here was mostly of oats, and they hung most gracefully of all; next bowed the bearded barley; and stately and strong stood the fields of wheat, of a rich, ruddy, golden hue. Above the yellow harvest rose the purple hills, and above the hills the pale blue antumnal sky.

At length the day arrived to put the sickle to the barley, to be followed by the scythe in the oats. And then came the joy of labor. Books were thrown utterly aside. Everything was abandoned for the harvest field. For even when there was no fear of a change in the weather to urge labor on into the night, there was weariness enough in the work of the day to prevent the reading of anything that necessitated mental labor.

Jeanette and Margaret took to the reaping hook. The laird was in the fields from morning to night, and the boys would not stay behind. Hugh, though he was quite helpless at the sickle, thought he could wield the scythe and so joined the harvest. It was desperate work for him for a while, and he lagged far behind the others. But seeing the tutor dropping behind, David, who was the best scyther in the whole countryside, put more power into his arm, finished his first row and brought up the remainder of Hugh's before the others had done sharpening their scythes for the next.

"Be careful not to push yourself too fast," David warned him. "You'll be up with the best of them in a day or two. Take a good sweep with the scythe and let its weight pull right through the straw, and don't be at all ashamed to be last.—Here, Maggie, my doo, come and gather behind Mr. Sutherland. One of the young boys can take your place with the binding."

The work of Jeanette and Margaret had been to form bands for the sheaves, by cunningly folding together the heads of two small handfuls of the grain so as to make them long enough together to go around the sheaf. This they laid down for the gatherer to place enough of the mown grain upon. Then lastly they bound the band tightly around so as to form a completed sheaf. From this David had called his daughter, thinking to give Hugh a gatherer who would not be disrespectful of his awkwardness.

This arrangement, however, was far from pleasing to some of the young men in the field, and brought down on Hugh many sly hints of country wit and human contempt. There had been for some time great jealousy of his visits to David's cottage, for Margaret, though she had very little acquaintance with the young men of the neighborhood, was greatly admired among them, and not regarded so above their working station as to render aspiration useless.

At first Hugh could not hear them. But their remarks to each other got louder and louder till he at last began to perceive they were intended for him and he could not help but be annoyed. He gave no sign of hearing their remarks other than increasing his exertion. Looking round, however, he saw that Margaret was embarrassed, evidently not for her own sake. He smiled to her, to console her for his own part, and then put his shoulder to the work all the more and recovered much of the ground between himself and the others. But the smile that had passed between them did not escape unobserved and served to arouse all the more the wrath of the youths, especially as he now threatened soon to rival them in the work itself. They had regarded him as an interloper, who had no right to captivate one of their rank by arts beyond their reach. But it was still less pardonable to dare them to a trial of skill with their own weapons. To the fire of this jealousy the admiration of the laird added fuel, for he was delighted with the spirit with which Hugh laid himself to the scythe. But all the time nothing was further from Hugh's thoughts than the idea of rivalry with them.

Ordinarily, the laborers would have had sufficient respect for Sutherland's superior position to prevent them from giving such articulate utterance to their feelings. But they were stirred up and led by a man of doubtful character from the neighboring village. Roused by the liveliness of his genius, they went on from one thing to another, till Hugh saw it must be put a stop to somehow. They would not have dared to go so far if David had been present, but he had been called away to superintend an operation in another part of the estate. And they paid no heed to the expostulations of some of the other older men.

At the close of the day's work, therefore, after Jeanette and Margaret had left the field, Hugh walked up to this ringleader fellow and said, "I hope you will be satisfied with insulting me all of today and will leave it alone tomorrow."

The man replied with an oath and gesture of rude contempt, "I don't care the dirt in my fingernails for anything you may wish of me!"

Hugh's Highland blood flew to his brain, and before the rascal had finished the sentence he had laid him out on the stubble. The man sprang to his feet in a fury, threw off the coat he had just put on and darted at Hugh, who had by this time recovered his coolness and was the more agile of the two, the other being heavier and more powerful. Hugh sprang aside, as he would have done from the rush of a bull, and again with a quick blow felled his antagonist. Beginning rather to enjoy punishing him, he now went in for it, and before the other would yield he had rendered his next day's labor somewhat doubtful. He withdrew with no more injury to himself than a little water would remove.

Hugh went home and to bed—more weary than he had ever been in his life. When he made his appearance the following morning, he felt very stiff. But the best treatment for stiffness is more work of the same, and he had soon restored the elasticity of his muscles and had lubricated his aching joints. His antagonist of the foregoing evening was nowhere to be seen and the rest of the young men were respectful enough.

Hugh wielded the scythe the whole of the harvest, and Margaret gathered behind him. By the time it was over, he measured an inch less about the waist and an inch more about the shoulders and was as brown as the grain itself. ''Strong as an ox,'' David said while describing Mr. Sutherland's progress to Jeanette; for he took a fatherly pride in the youth, to whom at the same time he looked up with submission as his master in learning.

7 / The New Room

Had Sutherland been in love with Margaret, those would have been happy days. But though he could not help feeling the pleasure of her presence, he was not in love with her. Anyone would have been the better for having her near; but there was nothing about her quiet, self-contained being to rouse the feelings commonly called love in the mind of an inexperienced youth like Hugh Sutherland. I say "commonly called" because I believe that within the whole sphere of intelligence there are no two loves the same. That is not to say he was less easily influenced than other youths. A designing girl might well have caught him at once; but Margaret's womanhood kept so still in its pearly cave that it rarely met the glance of neighboring eyes.

At length the harvest was finished. Thereafter the fields lay bare to the frosts of morning and evening, and to the wind that grew cooler and cooler with the breath of winter, who lay behind the northern hills and waited for his time to come. But many lovely days remained, of quiet and slow decay, of yellow and red leaves, of warm noons and lovely sunsets. Finally every leafless tree sparkled in the morning sun, encrusted with fading gems, while the ground became hard under foot. Winter had laid the tips of his fingers on the land, soon to cover it deep with the flickering snowflakes shaken from the folds of his outspread mantle.

But long before this, David and Margaret had returned with renewed diligence and powers strengthened by the harvest intermission, to their mental labors; and Hugh was as constant a visitor at the cottage as before. The time, however, drew nigh when he had to return to his studies at Aberdeen. David and Margaret, and Jeanette too, were facing with sorrow the loss of their friend.

But several days before Hugh was to leave for the university, a letter came from home informing him that his father was dangerously ill. Hugh hastened to him, but could do nothing but comfort his last hours by all that a son can do, and support his mother by his presence during the first hours of her loneliness.

Now that her husband's military pension was gone, all that remained for Mrs. Sutherland was a small annuity secured by her husband's payment into a certain fund for the use of officers' widows. From this she could not spare but a trifle for Hugh's education, and the salary he had received at Turriepuffit was too small to be of any use. He therefore came to the resolution to write to the laird and offer himself through the winter, if they were not yet provided with another tutor. It was next to impossible to spend money there, and he judged that before the following winter he should be quite able to meet the expenses of his residence at Aberdeen.

Whether Mrs. Glasford was altogether pleased at the proposal I cannot tell, but the laird wrote a very gentlemanlike letter, condoling him and his mother upon their loss, and ending with a hearty acceptance of Hugh's offer. And with it, strange to tell, the unsolicited promise of an increase of salary to the amount of five pounds. Hugh, therefore, left his mother as soon as circumstances would permit and returned to Turriepuffit.

He reached the place early in the afternoon, received from Mrs. Glasford a cold, "I hope you're well, Mr. Sutherland," and a hearty shake of the hand from the laird. Straightaway he told his pupils to get their books and sat down with them at once to commence their winter labors. He spent two hours thus; and, after a substantial tea, walked down to David's cottage where a welcome awaited him worth returning for.

David stood in the middle of the floor. "Come in, my bonny lad," was his only greeting as he held out a great fatherly hand to the youth, grasping his in the one and clapping him on the shoulder with the other. Hugh thought of his own father and could not restrain his tears. Margaret searched his face, and, seeing his emotion, did not even approach offering him any spoken welcome. She hastened instead to place a chair for him as she had done when first he had entered their cottage.

"And how's your poor mother, Mr. Sutherland?" asked David.

"She's pretty well," was all Hugh could answer.

"It's a hard thing to live with," said David, "but it's a grand thing when a man's won through it. When my father died, I missed him. But I was so proud to see him lying there in the cold grandeur of death that I gloried right in the midst of my crying. He was but a poor old shepherd, Mr. Sutherland, with hair as white as the sheep that followed him. And he followed the great Shepherd, and followed and followed, till he just followed him home, where all his sheep are bound."

With that David rose and got down their Bible. He opened it reverently and read with a solemn, slightly tremulous voice the fourteenth chapter of John's Gospel.

When he had finished, they all rose and knelt down, and David prayed, "O God, we know that you take that you may give again the same thing better than before—more of it and better than we could have received otherwise. Come and abide in us and let us abide in you. Lord, help us to do our work like your men and maidens downstairs, reminding us that those we miss have only gone up the stairs to be with you, where we hope to be called before long to see you and your Son, whom we love above all. And in his name we say, Amen."

Hugh rose from his knees with a sense of solemnity and spiritual reality he had never felt before. Little was said that evening; supper was eaten, if not in silence, yet with nothing that could be termed conversation—in its usual sense. And, almost in silence, David walked home with Hugh.

If Hugh looked a little more into his Bible and tried a little more to understand it after his father's death, it is not to be wondered at. It is but another instance of the fact that we are usually ready, in times of profound trouble, to feel as if a solution or refuge lies somewhere in the sounds of wisdom in the best of the world's books. But David never sought to influence Hugh to this end. David read the Bible to his family, but he never in words urged the reading of it on others.

After a few days, Hugh began to encounter a source of suffering that caused him a very sufficient degree of distress. His room had no fireplace, and he could not pursue his studies in private without having to endure a most undesirable degree of cold. In summer this mattered little, for then the whole universe might be his room. But in a Scottish spring or autumn, not to say winter, a bedroom without a fireplace was not a study in which thought could operate to much satisfactory result. Indeed, pain is a far less hurtful enemy to thinking than cold. After the way in which Mrs. Glasford had behaved to him, Hugh was far too proud to ask of her a favor, even if he had had hopes of receiving his request. The prospect, therefore, of the coming winter in a country where there was scarcely any afternoon and where the snow might lie feet deep for weeks was not at all agreeable. He had begun to suffer already, for the mornings and evenings were cold enough now, although it was a bright, dry October.

One evening Jeanette remarked upon the fact that he had caught cold, and this led Hugh to state the discomfort he was experiencing at the house.

"Well," said David, after some silent deliberation, "that settles it. We must set about it immediately."

Of course Hugh was quite at a loss to understand what he meant and asked him to explain.

"You see," replied David, "we have very little extra room in this cottage. Except for the kitchen and Maggie's little corner, we have only the room where Jeanette and I sleep. And so last year I spoke to the laird to allow me what timber I'd need to build a small room onto the back of the cottage for a kind of parlor or a room any of us might go to if we wanted to be by ourselves. He had no objections, but somehow or other I never set my hand to it. But now seems like the time, and we must get the walls up before the wet weather sets in. So I'll be at it tomorrow morning, and maybe you'll lend me a hand, Mr. Sutherland, and take out your wages with spending evenings there with us after it's done. You're welcome to use it at other times as you wish."

"Thank you heartily!" said Hugh. "That would be delightful. It seems too good to be possible. But won't wooden walls be rather poor protection against such winters as you have in these parts?"

"Hoot, Mr. Sutherland, give me credit for more gumption than that. Wood was the only thing I needed to ask for. The rest lies free to whoever needs it—a few cartfuls of sod from the hill behind the house, and some handfuls of stones for the chimney from the quarry. We'll saw the wood ourselves and once we have the walls up we can finish the inside at our leisure. That's the way the Maker does with us—he gives us the walls and the materials, and then it takes a whole lifetime, maybe more, to furnish the house."

Hugh and David went out in the moonlight to choose the best spot for the room and soon came to the resolution to build it so that a certain back door, which added more cold in the winter than convenience in the summer, should be the entrance to the new chamber. The chimney was the chief difficulty, but all the materials being in the immediate neighborhood, and David capable of turning his hands to anything, no obstruction was foreseen. Indeed, he set about that part first, while, under his direction, the walls made progress at the same time by the labor of Hugh and two or three of the young men at the farm. They worked very hard, for if the rain should set in before the roof was on, their labor would be almost lost from the soaking of the walls. They built the walls of very thick turf from the upper and coarser part of the peat moss which was plentiful in the neighborhood. The thatcheaves of the cottage itself projected over the joining of the new roof so as to protect it from the drip, and David soon put a thick thatch of new straw upon the little building. Secondhand windows were procured at the village. They sawed thin planks of deal at the saw-pit on the estate, to floor and line the interior of the room. The roof had not been thatched two days before the rain set in; but now they could work quite comfortably inside, and they had it quite finished before the end of November. David bought an old table in the village, and two chairs. He mended them, made a kind of rustic sofa, put a few bookshelves against the wall, and at length one Saturday evening they had supper in the room, and the place was consecrated henceforth to friendship and learning.

From this time, every evening, as soon as lessons and the meal which immediately followed them were over at the estate, Hugh walked down to the cottage, on the shelves of which all his books by degrees collected themselves. There he spent the whole evening, generally till ten o'clock—

the first part alone, reading or writing, the last in company with his pupils, who now made more rapid progress than ever, inasmuch as the lessons were both longer and more frequent. Little would the passerby imagine that beneath that roof there sat, in a snug little homely room, such a youth as Hugh, such a girl as Margaret, such a grand peasant king as David, and such a truehearted mother to them all as Jeanette. There were no pictures and no music, for Margaret kept her songs for solitary places. But the sound of verse was often present. The thatch of that shed-roof was like the grizzled hair of David, beneath which lay the temple of holy, wise and poetic thought.

8 / David and Hugh

Of course the even more lengthened absences of Hugh from the house were subjects of remark, but Hugh had made up his mind not to trouble himself the least about that. For some time Mrs. Glasford took no notice verbally, but one evening, just as tea was finished and Hugh was rising to go, her restraint gave way.

"You're a day laborer it seems, Mr. Sutherland, and go home every night."

"Exactly so, madam," rejoined Hugh. "You have done your best to convince me that it is impossible for me to feel that this house is in any sense my home."

He left the room, and from that day till the time of his final departure from Turriepuffit, there was not another allusion made to the subject.

He soon reached the cottage. When he entered the new room, which was always called Mr. Sutherland's study, the welcome of the glowing fire and the outspread arms of the elbow-chair made ample amends to him for the unfriendliness of Mrs. Glasford. Going to the shelves to find the books he wanted, he saw that his had been carefully arranged on one shelf, and that the others were occupied with books belonging to the house. He looked at a few of them. They were almost all old books, and such as may be found in many Scottish cottages. He turned from them, found his own, and sat down to read.

By and by David came in. "I'm too soon, no doubt, Mr. Sutherland. Am I disturbing you?"

"Not at all," answered Hugh. "Besides I'm not much in a reading mood this evening; Mrs. Glasford has been annoying me again."

"Poor woman. What's she been saying now?"

Thinking to amuse David, Hugh recounted the short passage between them. David, however, listened with a very different expression from what Hugh had anticipated.

"Well," he said with a sigh when Hugh had finished, "it's not altogether her fault; she hasn't really had a fair chance. She doesn't come from a good family."

"I thought she brought the laird a sizeable piece of good property," said Hugh, not quite understanding David.

"Oh, she did. She brought him plenty of money. But how was it gotten? It's not riches that make good character. The richer the cheese the more the maggots. The mistress's father was well known to have made his money in creeping and crafty ways. He was a merchant in

Aberdeen and kept his thumb behind the yardstick, so he made an inch or two with every yard he sold. He took from his soul and put it into his money bag and had little to give his daughter but that. Now, I know nothing about *your* family, Mr. Sutherland, but you seem to me to come from good breed. I'm not flattering you, but just telling you that if you had an honest father and grandfather, and especially a good mother, you have a lot to answer for. And you ought never to be hard on them that's smaller than you, those who have lacked training and good example, for they can't help it so well as you and me can."

Hugh turned full round and looked at David. On his face lay a solemn quiet. What he had said about signs of breeding in Hugh's exterior certainly applied to himself as well. His carriage was full of dignity and a certain rustic refinement. His voice was wonderfully gentle, but deep, and slowest when most impassioned. He seemed to have come of some gigantic antediluvian stock; there was something of the Titan slumbering about him. He would have been a stern man but for an unusual amount of reverence that seemed to overflow the sternness and change it into strong love. No one had ever seen him thoroughly angry; his simple displeasure with any of the laborers, the quality of whose work was deficient, would go further than the laird's oaths.

At length Hugh said, "I wish I had known your father, David."

"My father was such a one, as I told you the other day. A pure, simple, God-fearing shepherd that never gave his dog an ill-deserved word or took the skin of any poor little lamb whose wool he was slipping between the shears. And my mother was compassionate and gentle. They're her books mostly up on the shelf there behind you. I honor them for her sake, though I seldom trouble with them myself."

"Looking at them, I wondered if they could be your books," said Hugh.

"But I have one old book that brings me upon my pedigree, Mr. Sutherland. For the poorest man has a pedigree just as long as the greatest, only he knows less about it. For all the finery of the lords and ladies, it's not always to their credit what's told in their ancestry. A willful sin in the father may be a sinful weakness in the son."

So saying, David went to his bedroom, whence he returned with a very old-looking book, which he laid on the table before Hugh. He opened it, discovered it to have been printed in 1612, and turned to the title page. Written either in German or in Old English character, he was not sure which, was the name *Martin Elginbrodde*.

"This book has been in our family far longer than I know," said David. "I can't read a word of it. But I can't help telling you a curious thing, Mr. Sutherland, in connection with the name on the title page; there's a gravestone, a very old one—how old I can't well make out, though I went all the way to Aberdeen to see it—and the name on the gravestone is *Martin Elginbrodde*. But the saying on the stone is strange, rather fearsome when you hear it for the first time, It says:

Here lie I, Martin Elginbrodde:
Hae mercy o' my soul, Lord God;
As I wad do, were I Lord God,
And ye were Martin Elginbrodde.

Hugh could not help a slight shudder at what seemed the irreverence of the epitaph. But he made no remark, and after a moment's pause, David resumed, "I certainly wasn't pleased with it at first, as you can suppose. But after a while, as I turned it over in my mind, it took on less the look of pride or presumption and instead began to sound to me like maybe a childlike way of saying that if he, Martin Elginbrodde, would have mercy, surely the Lord was not less merciful than he was. He felt that the mercy in himself was a good thing, and he couldn't think that there would be any less of it in the Father of Lights from whom comes every good and perfect gift."

"But aren't we in danger," said Hugh, "of thinking too lightly and familiarly of the Maker when we judge him by ourselves?"

"I don't think there's much danger of that. For I know that I would be a horse in a field or a pig in a stye, not merely if it was his will but if it was for his glory. For the glory of God, Mr. Sutherland, I would die the death. For the will of God I'm ready for anything he likes. I surely can't be in much danger of thinking lightly of him."

The almost passionate earnestness with which David spoke would alone have made it impossible for Hugh to reply at once. After a few moments, however, he ventured to ask the question: "Would you do nothing that other people should know God, David?"

"Anything that he likes. But I wouldn't take to interfering. He's at it himself from morning till night, from year's end to year's end."

"But you seem to make out that God is nothing but love."

"Ay, nothing but love. And why not?"

"Because we are told he is just."

"Would he be just for long if he didn't love us?" asked David.

"But doesn't he punish sin?"

"It would hardly be kindness if he didn't punish sin, not to use every means to put the evil thing far from us. Whatever may be meant by the place of misery, depend upon it, Mr. Sutherland, it's only another form of his love. Love shining through the fogs of evil, and thus made to look very different. Man, rather than see my Maggie—and you'll have no doubt that I love her—rather than see my Maggie do some wicked thing, I'd see her lying dead at my feet. But suppose once the wickedness is past, it's not at my feet I would lay her, but upon my heart with my old arms around her, to hold further wickedness away from her all the better. And shall mortal man be more just than God? Shall a man be more pure than his Maker?''

The entrance of Margaret would have prevented the completion of this conversation, even if it had not already drawn to a natural close. Not that David would not have talked thus before his daughter, but simply that minds, like instruments, need to be brought up to the same pitch before they can "atone together." One feels this instinctively on the entrance of another who has not gone through the same immediate process.

Their books and slates were got out and they sat down to their work; but Hugh could not help observing that David, in the midst of his lines and angles and algebraic computations, would every now and then glance up at Margaret with a look of tenderness in his face, yet deeper and more delicate in its expression than ordinary.

At supper, for it happened to be Saturday, Hugh said, "I've been busy while you were at work inventing, or perhaps discovering, an etymological pedigree for you, David."

"And what would that be?" inquired David.

"First, do you know that the old volume with your ancestor's name on it was written by an old German shoemaker, Jacob Boehman?"

"I've seen his name on the book, but knew nothing about him."

"He was a wonderful man. Some people think he was almost inspired. At all events, though I know nothing about it myself, he must have written wonderfully for a cobbler," said Hugh.

"I see no wonder in it," said David. "Why shouldn't a cobbler write as well as anyone else? My grandfather was a cobbler, as you call it, and they say he was no fool in his way either."

"Then it does go in the family!" cried Hugh triumphantly. "I am now quite convinced that Martin or his father was a German, who received the book from old Jacob Boehman, who gave him the book himself and was, besides, of the same craft. Coming to this country with a name hard to pronounce, they found a resemblance in the sound of it to his occupation, and so gradually the name was corrupted into *Elsynbrod, Elshinbrod,* thence Elginbrodde, with a soft *g*, and lastly Elginbrod, as you pronounce it with a hard *g*. The cobbler is in the family, David, descended from Jacob Boehman himself, by the mother's side."

This heraldic blazon amused them all very much, and David declared it to be incontrovertible. Margaret laughed heartily.

9 / Winter

Winter was fairly come at last. A black frost had bound the earth for many days, and at length the smell of snow in the air indicated an approaching storm. The snow fell at first in a few large, unwilling flakes that fluttered slowly and heavily to the earth, where they lay like a foundation of the superstructure that was to follow. Faster and faster they fell till the whole air was obscure and night came on, hastened by an hour from the gathering of their white darkness. In the morning all the landscape was transfigured. The snowfall had ceased but the whole earth was covered with its whiteness.

The most wonderful were the trees—every bough and twig thickened and bent with its own individual load of the fairy ghost birds. Each retained the semblance of its own form, magically altered by its thick garment of radiant whiteness, shining gloriously in the sunlight. Again at night the snow fell; and again and again, with intervening days of bright sunshine. Every morning the first fresh footprints were a new wonder to the living creatures, to the young-hearted among them at least. Paths had to be cleared in every direction, and again cleared every morning, till at last the walls of solid rain stood higher than the heads of the two young Glasford boys. It was a great delight to them to wander through the snow avenues, and great fun it was to both, when they were tired of snowballing each other and every living thing about the place, except their parents and tutor, to hollow out mysterious caves and vaulted passages.

There was no pathway cut to David's cottage, no track trodden except what David, coming to the house sometimes, and Hugh going every afternoon to the cottage, made between them. Hugh often went to his knees in the snow, but was well dried and warmed by Jeanette's care when he arrived. She always had a pair of stockings and slippers ready for him at the fire, to be put on the moment of his arrival and exchanged again for his own, dry and warm, before he traversed once more the ghostly waste. When neither moon was up nor stars were out, there was a strange eerie glimmer from the snow that lighted the way home. He thought there must be more light from it than could be accounted for merely by the reflection of every particle of light that might fall on it from other sources.

Margaret was not kept to the house by the snow, even when it was falling. She went out as usual—not of course wandering far, for walking was difficult now. But she was in little danger of losing her way, for she knew the country as well as anyone. Though its face was greatly altered by the filling up of its features and uniformity of the color, those features were yet discernible to her experienced eye through the sheet that covered them. It was only necessary to walk on the tops of dykes and other elevated ridges to keep clear of the deep snow.

There were many paths between the cottages and the farms in the neighborhood in which she could walk with comparative ease and comfort. But she preferred wandering away through the fields toward the hills. Sometimes she would come home like a creature of the snow, so covered was she from head to foot with its flakes. David smiled at her with peculiar complacency on such occasions. It was evident that it pleased him she could be the playmate of nature. And whatever her mother might think of it, Margaret was in this way laying up a store, not only of bodily and mental health, but of resources for thought and feeling, of secret understandings and communions with nature.

This kind of weather continued for some time. Gradually the frost grew harder, and the snow, instead of falling in large, adhesive flakes, fell in small dry ones. One day David heard that a poor old man of his acquaintance was dying. He immediately set out to visit him, at a distance of two or three miles. He returned in the evening.

The following afternoon, David set out to see him again. Before his return the wind rose rapidly and began to blow a snowstorm of its own making. When Hugh opened the door to take his usual walk to the cottage, just as darkness was starting to fall, the sight he saw made his young heart dance with delight. The snow that fell made but a small part of the wild, confused turmoil and uproar of the tenfold storm. For the wind, raving over the surface of the snow which lay nearly as loose as dry sand, swept it up in thick, fierce clouds and then cast it down again, no one could tell where. A few hours of this would alter the face of the whole country, leaving some parts bare and others buried beneath heaps upon heaps of snow. There was no path before him. Hugh could see nothing but the surface of a sea of froth and foam, whirled in all shapes and contortions and driven in every direction.

Hugh plunged into it with a wild sense of life and joy. In the course of his short walk, however, he realized that he needed not a stout heart only, but sound lungs and strong limbs as well to battle with the storm, even for such a short distance.

When he reached the cottage he found Jeanette in considerable anxiety, not only about David, who had not yet returned, but about Margaret as well. She had not seen her for some time, and she presumed her out in the storm. Hugh suggested that she might have gone to meet her father.

"The Lord forbid!" exclaimed Jeanette. "The road lies over the top of the Halshach, as eerie and bare a place as there is. The wind there is fierce, and there's many a pit along there that if you fell into you'd never come to the bottom. The Lord preserve us! I wish David was home."

"How could you let him go, Jeanette?"

"Let him go, laddie! It'd be a strong rope that would hold David once he's bound to do something. But I'm not afraid about him. I know he's under special protection if ever such could be said of a man. He's no more afraid of the storm than if the snow was angels' feathers fluttering from the wings all about him. But I'm not so easy in my mind about Maggie. If she be meeting her father, and chances to miss him, the Lord knows what may come of her."

Hugh tried to comfort her. But all that could be done was to wait David's return. The storm seemed to increase rather than abate its force. The footprints Hugh had made had all but vanished already at the very door of the house, which stood quite in the shelter of the fir wood. As they looked out, a dark figure appeared within a yard or two of the house.

"The Lord grant it be my bairn!" prayed poor Jeanette. But it was David, and alone. Jeanette gave a shriek.

"David, where's Maggie?"

"I haven't seen the bairn," replied David. "She's not out tonight, is she?"

"She's not home, David, that's all I know."

"Where'd she go?"

"The Lord only knows. She's buried in snow by this time." Jeanette's trembling hands covered her face.

"She's in the Lord's hands, Jeanette, even if she's covered beneath a huge snowdrift. Don't forget that. How long has she been gone?"

"An hour or more—I don't know how long . . . I'm clean out of my mind with dread!"

"I'll go look for her. Just hold her heart together till I come back, Mr. Sutherland."

"I won't be left behind, David. I'm going with you," said Hugh.

"You don't know what you're saying, Mr. Sutherland. I would soon have two of you to look for instead of only one."

"Don't fear for me. I'm going on my own account, come what may."

"Well, I'm not going to argue. I'm going up the creekside. You go over to the farm and ask if anybody's seen her. The lads'll be out to look for her in a jiffy.—My poor lassie!"

The sigh that must have accompanied the last words was lost in the wind as they vanished in the darkness. Jeanette fell on her knees in the kitchen, with the door wide open and the wind drifting in the powdery snow. A picture of more thorough desolation can hardly be imagined. She soon came to herself, however. She reflected that if the lost child was found, there should be a warm bed to receive her. She rose and shut the door and added wood to the fire. It was as if the silent attitude of her prayer was answered. For strength was gradually restored to her distracted brain. When she had made every preparation she could think of, she went to the door again, opened it and looked out. It was a region of howling darkness, tossed about by pale snowdrifts, out of which it seemed hardly hopeful that welcome faces would emerge. She closed the door once more and, knowing nothing else to be done, sat down on a chair, with her hands on her knees and her eyes fixed on the door. The clock went on with its slow swing, and she heard the sound of every second in the midst of the uproar in the fir trees, which bent their tall heads hissing to the blast, swinging about in the agony of their strife.

The minutes went by till an hour was gone, and there was no sound but of the storm and the clock. Still she sat and stared, her eyes fixed on the doorlatch. Suddenly without warning it was lifted and the door opened. Her heart bounded, but alas, the first words she heard were, "Is she not come yet?" It was her husband followed by several of the farm servants. He had made a circuit to the farm, and finding that Hugh had never been there, hoped that Margaret had already returned home. The question fell upon Jeanette's heart like the sound of the earth on a coffin lid, and her silent stare was the only answer David received.

But at that very moment, like a dead man burst from the tomb, Hugh entered from behind the party at the open door, silent and white with rigid features and fixed eyes. He stumbled in, leaning forward, dragging something behind him. He pushed and staggered through them, and as they parted, horror-stricken, they saw that it was Margaret—or was it her dead body that he dragged after him? He dropped her at her mother's feet and fell himself on the floor. David, who was quite calm, got the whiskey bottle out and tried to administer some to Margaret first. But her teeth were firmly set, and to all appearances she was dead.

One of the young men succeeded better with Hugh, whom at David's direction they took into the study while he and Jeanette got Margaret undressed and put to bed, with hot bottles all about her; for in warmth lay the only hope of restoring her. After she had lain thus for a while, she gave a sigh; and when they had succeeded in getting her to swallow some warm milk, she began to breathe normally and soon seemed to be only fast asleep. After half an hour's rest and warming, Hugh was able to move and speak. David would not allow him to say much, however, but got him to bed, sending word to the house that he could not go home that night. He and Jeanette sat by the fireside all night, listening to the storm that still raved outside, thanking God for the lives spared. Every few minutes a tiptoe excursion was made to the bedside, and now and then to the other room. Both the patients slept quietly. Toward morning Margaret opened her eyes and faintly called her mother. But she soon fell asleep once more and did not awaken again till nearly noon.

When sufficiently restored, the account she gave was that she had set out to meet her father. But, the storm increasing, she had thought it more prudent to turn around. It grew in violence, however, so rapidly that she was soon exhausted and benumbed with the cold. The last thing she remembered was dropping, as she thought, into a hole and feeling as if she were going to sleep in bed, yet knowing it was death, and thinking how much sweeter it was than sleep.

Hugh's account was very strange, and he was never able to add much to it. He said that when he rushed out into the dark the storm had seized him like a fury, beating him about the head and face till he was almost stunned. He took the road to the farm, which lay through the fir wood, but soon became aware that he had lost his way and might well tramp about in the woods till daylight, if he lived that long. Then, thinking of Margaret, he lost his presence of mind and rushed wildly along. He thought he must have knocked his head against the trunk of a tree, but he could not tell. He remembered nothing more but that he found himself dragging Margaret, with his arms round her, through the snow, and nearing the light in the cottage window. Where or how he had found her, or what the light was that he was approaching, he had not the least idea. He had only a vague notion that he was rescuing Margaret from something dreadful.

Margaret for her part had no recollection of reaching the fir wood. And, as long before morning all traces were obliterated, the facts remained a mystery. The only thing certain was that Hugh had saved Margaret's life. He seemed quite well the next day. She recovered more slowly, and perhaps never altogether overcame the effects of death's embrace that night. From the moment Margaret was brought home the storm gradually died away, and by morning all was still. But many starry and moonlit nights glimmered and passed before that snow was melted away from the earth, and many nights Jeanette awoke from her sleep with a cry, thinking she heard her daughter moaning deep in the smooth ocean of snow and could not find where she lay.

The occurrences of this dreadful night added to the interest and kinship his cottage friends felt in Hugh, and a long winter passed with daily and lengthening communion both in study and in general conversation. Whether Hugh and Margaret had begun to fall in love it would be impossible to tell. Certainly the bonds drawing them toward one another grew stronger each day. Yet who could dare to understand such a sacred mystery as the heart of Margaret, who continued to keep her own feelings very much her own.

Mrs. Glasford, however, would easily answer the question. Notwithstanding that she had heard the facts of the story correctly from the best of authorities, as often as the incident was alluded to in her hearing, she remarked, "They had no business to be out together."

10 / Transition

The long Scottish winter passed by without any interruption to the deepening friendship. But the spring brought a change, and Hugh was separated from his friends six months sooner than he had anticipated. His mother wrote to him in great distress because of a claim being made upon her for some debt which his father had contracted, probably for Hugh's own schooling. Hugh therefore requested from the laird the amount due him and sent all of it for the liquidation of this debt. In consequence he was now completely unprovided for with respect to the expenses of the coming winter's session at Aberdeen.

About the same time a fellow student wrote to him with news of a situation for the summer worth three times as much as his present one. Having engaged himself to the laird only for the winter (although he had intended to stay till the commencement of the fall session), Hugh felt that, although he would rather remain where he was, he ought not hesitate to accept his friend's offer. He therefore wrote at once.

I will not attempt to describe the parting. It was very quiet, but solemn and sad. Jeanette showed far more distress than Margaret, for she wept outright. The tears stood in David's eyes as he grasped the youth's hand in silence. Margaret said little, but was very pale. As soon as Hugh disappeared with her father, who was going to walk with him to the village through which the coach passed, she hurried away to the fir wood for comfort.

Hugh found his new situation in Perthshire very different from the last. He had more to do; but his work left him plenty of leisure. He wrote to David after his arrival, telling him all about his new situation, and received in return a letter from Margaret, written at her father's dictation. Three or four more passed between them, at lengthening intervals. Then they ceased—on Hugh's side first. By the summer's end, when on the point of leaving for Aberdeen and feeling somewhat conscience-stricken at not having written for so long, he scribbled a note to inform them of his approaching departure and promised to let them know his address as soon as he found himself settled.

Yet the entire session went by without the redemption of this pledge. Hugh was as yet unaware of the amount of obligation he was under to his humble friends. He may have thought that the obligation was principally on their side; as it would have been if intellectual assistance could outweigh heart-kindness and spiritual enlightenment. But of course it could not. Besides this, a thousand seeds of truth surely remained in his mind, dropped there by David's tongue of wisdom, waiting the friendly aid of a hard winter to break up the cold clods of clay before the loveliness of a new spring, as they became perfected in the beauty of a new summer.

However this may have been, he forgot his old friends far more than he could have thought possible. Spending his evenings in the midst of merry faces and ready tongues, surrounded by the vapors of whiskey-toddy and the smoke of cutty-pipes till late into the night, then hurrying home and lasping into unrefreshed slumbers over intended study or sitting up all night to prepare the tasks which had been neglected—it is hardly to be wondered that he would lose the finer consciousness of higher powers and deeper feelings. This came not from any behavior in itself wrong, but from the hurry, noise, and tumult in the streets of life that dazed and stupefied the silent and lonely watcher in the chamber of conscience. He had no time to think or feel.

The session drew to a close. He put away his idleness, shut himself up after class hours with his books, ate little, studied hard, slept irregularly, passed his exams, and at length breathed freely but with a dizzy brain, pale cheeks, and red, weary eyes. Proud of his success, he sat down and wrote a short note, with a simple statement of his achievement, to David. He hoped in his secret mind that he would attribute his previous silence to an absorption in study, which in reality had not existed before the end of the session was quite at hand. Now that he had more time for reflection, he could not bear the thought that the noble rustic face should look disapprovingly, or worse, coldly upon him. He could not help feeling as if the old ploughman had taken the place of his father as the only man of whom he must stand in awe and who had a right to reprove him. But David was delighted at having such good news from him, and the uneasiness which he had felt was almost entirely swept away in the conclusion that it had indeed been unreasonable to expect the young man to give his time to letter-writing when he had been occupied to such good purpose as this letter signified. Hugh received from him the following letter in reply to his, dictated as usual to his secretary, Margaret.

My Dear Sir:

You'll be a great man someday, if you keep at it. But there's better things than being a great man, after all. Forgive the liberty I take in reminding you of what you know well enough yourself. But you're a brave lad and you've been a good friend to me and mine; and I pray the Lord to thank you for me, for you have done wonderful good to his children—meaning me and my family. It's very kind of you to write to us in the moment of your victory. But you must know that amongst all your friends there's no one who would rejoice more over your success than Jeanette or Maggie, my doo, or your own obliged friend and servant,

David Elginbrod

P.S.—We're all well and excited by the arrival of your letter.

P.S. 2.—Dear Mr. Sutherland—I wrote all the above at my father's dictation, just as he said it. My mother and I are rejoiced at the good news that you are at last through with college successfully. My mother cried outright. I went out to the tree where I first met you. I sometimes wonder if you were an angel I met in the fir wood. I am

Your obedient servant,
Margaret Elginbrod

The letter touched Hugh. But he could not help feeling rather offended that David should write to him in such a warning tone. As for David's uneasiness about Hugh, he did not know his weakness very thoroughly and did not take into account the effect of the falling away which he dreaded—namely, an increase in Hugh's pride. The result, therefore, was that yet a longer period elapsed before he again wrote to David. He meant to do so, but as often as the thought occurred to him he was checked by both conscience and pride. The evil, and the good also, contributed to hold him back from doing the very thing he ought to have done.

It now remained for Hugh to look about for some occupation. The state of his funds made immediate employment absolutely necessary. For the moment there was but one way he could earn money without further preparation. This he could do while he took the time to make up his mind for the future. He was hopeful that his reputation at the university would stand him in some stead, and he hoped to find a tutorial position more desirable than either of those he had occupied before. With this expectation, he looked toward the South. Nor did he have to look long before he heard of just such a situation as he wanted in the family of a gentleman of fortune in the county of Surrey, not much more than twenty miles from London. Writing to present himself, he was fortunate enough to obtain it without difficulty.

Margaret was likewise on the eve of a change. She stood like a young fledged bird on the edge of the nest, ready to take its first long flight. It was necessary that she should do something for herself, not so much from the compulsion of immediate circumstances as in prospect of the future. Her father was getting on in years and at best could leave only a trifle at his death. If Jeanette outlived him she would probably require all of that. Margaret was anxious, too, not to be independent yet not to be burdensome. Both David and Jeanette saw that by her peculiar tastes and habits she had separated herself so far from the circle around her that she could never hope to be quite comfortable in that neighborhood. It was not that by any means she despised or refused the labors common to the young women of the country. But all things considered, they thought something more suitable for her might be procured.

David was much respected by the gentry of the neighborhood, with whom his position as the laird's steward brought him into frequent contact. And to several of them he mentioned his desire of finding some situation for Margaret. Jeanette could not bear the idea of her lady-bairn leaving them to encounter the world alone. But David, though he could not help sometimes feeling a similar pang, was able to take hearty comfort from the thought that if there were any safety for her in her father's house, there could not be less in her heavenly Father's. He felt that anxiety in this case, as in every other, would simply be a lack of confidence in God. Jeanette admitted all this, but sighed nevertheless. So did David at times. For he knew that though no sparrow could fall to the ground without him, sometimes the sparrow must fall. He knew that many a divine truth is hard to learn, all blessed as it is when learned, and that sorrow and suffering must come to Margaret before she could be fashioned into the perfection of a child of the kingdom.

An elderly lady of fortune, a Mrs. Elton, was on a visit to one of the families in the neighborhood. She was in want of a lady's maid, and it occurred to the housekeeper that Margaret might suit her. This was not quite what her parents would have chosen, but they allowed her to go and see the lady. Margaret was delighted with the benevolent-looking gentlewoman; and she, on her part, was quite charmed with Margaret. It was true she knew nothing of the duties of the office. But the maid who was leaving presently would soon initiate her into its mysteries. David and Jeanette were so much pleased with Margaret's account of the interview that David himself went to see the lady. The sight of him only increased her desire to have Margaret, whom she said she would treat like a daughter if only she were half as good as she looked. Before David left her, the matter was arranged. And within a month Margaret was borne in her mistress's carriage away from her father and mother and cottage home.

11 / A New Home

Hugh left the North dead in the arms of gray winter and found his new abode already alive in the breath of the west wind. As he walked up the avenue to the house, he felt that the buds were breaking all about, though, the night being dark and cloudy, the green shadows of the coming spring were invisible.

He was received at the hall door and shown to his room by an old, but certainly important, butler. Refreshment was then brought him with the message that, as it was late, Mr. Arnold would defer the pleasure of meeting him till the morning at breakfast.

Left to himself, Hugh began to look around him. Everything suggested a contrast between his present position and that which he had first occupied about the same time two years earlier at Turriepuffit. He was in an old, handsome room of dark wainscot, furnished like a library, with bookcases about the walls. A fire was burning cheerfully in an old, high grate, but its light failed to show the outlines of the room, it was so large and dark. The ceiling was rather low in proportion, and a huge beam crossed it. At one end an open door revealed a room beyond, likewise lighted with fire and candles. Entering, he found the bedroom to be an equally old-fashioned room, to which his luggage had already been taken.

''As far as creature comforts go,'' thought Hugh, ''I have fallen on my feet. This is beyond any wild expectation!'' He proceeded to examine the bookcases and found them to contain much of the literature with which he was most desirous of making an acquaintance. The sense of having good companions in the authors around him added greatly to his feeling of well-being, and he retired for the night filled with pleasant anticipation of his sojourn at Arnstead. All the night, however, his dreams were of wind and snow and Margaret out in them alone.

When he awoke, the budding twigs on the trees were waving in a network-tracery across the bright sunshine on his window curtains. To amuse himself before he was called down to breakfast, he proceeded to make another survey of the books. He concluded that these must be a colony from the mother library and that the room must be intended for his personal occupation, since his bedroom opened out of it. Next, he looked from all the windows to discover what kind of place it was. He could see only trees. As well as he could judge, his rooms seemed to occupy the end of a small wing at the back of the house. Then he resolved to test his faculty for discovery by seeing whether he could find his way to the breakfast room without a guide. In this he would have succeeded without much difficulty—for it opened from the main entrance hall to which the huge, square-turned oak staircase by which he had ascended led—had it not been for the somewhat intricate nature of the passages leading from his wing to the main staircase itself. After opening many doors, he became convinced that instead of finding a way on, he had lost his way back. At length he came to a small stair which led him down to a single door. This he opened and immediately found himself in the main library—a long, low, silent-looking room. Every foot of the walls was occupied with books in varied and rich bindings. The paned windows, with thick, stone dividing bars, were much overgrown with ivy, throwing a cool, green shadowiness into the room. One of them, however, had been altered to a more modern taste, and opened with folding doors onto a few steps which descended into an old-fashioned terraced garden.

To approach this window he had to pass a table, and on it he saw a paper with verses on it, evidently in a woman's hand and apparently just written, for the ink of the corrective scores still glittered. Just as he reached the window, which stood open, a lady had almost reached it from the other side coming up the steps from the garden. She gave a little start when she saw him, looked away momentarily, and then back toward him. Approaching him through the window, for he had retreated to allow her to enter, she bowed with a kind of studied ease and a slight shade of something French in her manner. Her voice was very pleasing, almost bewitching. All this Hugh sensed in the two words she said—merely, ''Mr. Sutherland?''

Hugh bowed and said, ''I am glad you have found me, for I had quite lost myself. I doubt whether I should ever have reached the breakfast room.''

''Come this way,'' she replied.

As they passed the table on which the verses lay, she stopped and slipped them into a writing case. Leading him through a succession of handsome, evidently modern passages, she brought him across the main hall to the breakfast room, which looked in the opposite direction to the library, namely, to the front of the house. She rang the bell; the urn was brought in, and she proceeded at once to make the tea. Before Hugh had time, however, to reflect on her appearance or her position in the family, Mr. Arnold entered the room with a slow, somewhat dignified step, and a dull outlook of gray eyes from a gray head balanced on a tall, rather slender frame. The lady rose, addressing him as uncle, and bade him good morning, a greeting he returned cordially with a kiss on her forehead. Then he turned to Hugh, with a manner which seemed the more polite and cold after the tone in which he had spoken to his niece, and bade him welcome to Arnstead.

"I trust you were properly attended to last night, Mr. Sutherland? Your pupil wanted very much to sit up till you arrived, but he is altogether too delicate, I am sorry to say." Then turning to the man in waiting, "Jacob, isn't Master Harry up yet?"

The boy's entrance at that moment rendered reply unnecessary.

"Good morning, Euphra," he said to the lady, and kissed her on the cheek.

"Good morning, dear," was the reply, accompanied by a pretense of returning the kiss. She smiled at him with a kind of confectionary sweetness, and dropping an additional lump of sugar into his tea at the same moment, placed it for him beside herself. The boy then shook hands with his father, and glancing shyly up at Hugh from a pair of large dark eyes, extended his hand. Taking his place at the table, he trifled with his breakfast, and after making pretense of eating for a while, asked Euphra if he might go. She gave him leave, and he hastened away.

Mr. Arnold took advantage of his retreat to explain to Hugh what he expected of him with regard to the boy.

"How old would you take Harry to be, Mr. Sutherland?"

"I should say from his size about twelve," replied Hugh. "But from his evident poor health and intelligent expression—"

"Ah, you perceive the state he is in," interrupted Mr. Arnold with some sadness in his voice. "You are right. He is nearly fifteen. He has not grown half an inch in the last twelve months."

"Perhaps that is better than growing too fast," said Hugh.

"Perhaps—perhaps. We will hope so. But I cannot help being uneasy about him. He reads too much and I have not yet been able to help it. For he seems miserable and without any object in life if I make him leave his books."

"Perhaps we can manage to get him over that in a little while."

"Besides," Mr. Arnold went on, paying no attention to what Hugh said, "I can get him to take no exercise. He does not even care for riding. I bought him a second pony a month ago, and he has not been twice on its back."

Hugh could not help thinking that to increase the supply was not always the best way of increasing the demand; and that one who would not ride the first pony would hardly be likely to ride a second.

Mr. Arnold concluded with the words, "I don't want to stop the boy's reading, but I can't have him a feeble effeminate."

"Will you let me manage him as I please, Mr. Arnold?" Hugh ventured to ask.

Mr. Arnold looked full at him, and Hugh was aware that the eyes of the lady, called by the boy "Euphra," were likewise fixed upon him.

"I will do my best for him," Hugh continued, "if you will trust me. For my part, I think the only way is to make the operation of the intellectual tendency on the one side reveal to the boy himself his deficiency on the physical. Once this is done, all will be well."

As he said this, Hugh caught sight of a cloud of dissatisfaction slightly contracting the eyebrows of the lady. Mr. Arnold, however, seemed not altogether displeased.

"Well," he answered, "I have my plans. But let us see first what you can do with yours. If they fail, perhaps you will oblige me by trying mine."

This was said with the decisive politeness of one who is accustomed to having his own way and fully intends to have it. But he seemed at the same time somewhat impressed by Hugh and not unwilling to yield.

Throughout the conversation the lady had said nothing but had sat watching, or rather, scrutinizing Hugh with a far keener and more frequent glance than he was aware of. Whether or not she was satisfied with her conclusions she allowed no sign to disclose. But breakfast now over, she rose and withdrew, turning, however, at the door and saying, "When you wish, Mr. Sutherland, I shall be glad to show you what Harry has been studying with me. For till now, I have been his only tutor."

"Thank you," replied Hugh, "but for some time we shall not be using any schoolbooks. He can read, I presume, fairly well?"

"Reading is not only his forté, but his fault," replied Mr. Arnold, while Euphra, fixing one more piercing look upon him, withdrew. "But now I must bid you good morning. You will, in all probability, find Harry in the library."

12 / Harry and Euphrasia

Hugh made no haste to find his pupil in the library, thinking it better not to pounce upon him. He went to his own room instead, got his books out and arranged them, then arranged his small wardrobe. After looking about a little, he finally went to seek his pupil.

He found him in the library, as he had been given to expect, coiled up on the floor in a corner.

"Well, Harry," said Hugh, "let me see what you are reading."

Harry had not heard him come in. He started and then looked up, hesitated, rose, and handed the book to Hugh. Hugh knew nothing about it, but glancing over some of the pages could not help thinking it could hardly be very interesting to the boy.

Setting the book down, Hugh approached the bookshelves and said to Harry, "You've read enough for the present, haven't you?"

"Yes. I have been reading since breakfast."

"Ah! There's a splendid book," said Hugh, reaching out to take an old-looking volume down. "Have you ever read it—*Gulliver's Travels*?"

"No. The outside looks so uninteresting."

"So did the binding on what you were just reading. But, come along, I will read it to you."

"Oh, that will be delightful! But must we not go to our lessons?"

"I'm going to make a lesson of this. I have been talking to your papa, and we're going to begin with a holiday instead of ending with one. I must get better acquainted with you, Harry, before I can teach you aright. We must be friends, you know."

The boy crept up close to him on the couch. Before an hour had passed Harry was laughing heartily at Gulliver's adventures among the Liliputians. Having arrived at this point of success, Hugh ceased reading and began to talk to him.

"Is that lady your cousin?"

"Yes. Isn't she beautiful?"

"I hardly know yet. I haven't got used to her enough to be able to tell. What is her name?"

"It's such a pretty name—Euphrasia."

"Is she the only lady in the house?"

"Yes. My mama is dead, you know. She was ill for a long time, they say, and she died when I was born."

Tears came into the poor boy's eyes. Hugh thought of his own father and put his hand on Harry's shoulder.

"But," he went on, "Euphra is so kind to me. And she knows everything!"

"Have you no brothers or sisters?"

"None. I wish I had."

"Well, I'll be your big brother. Only you must mind what I say. Is it a bargain?"

"Yes!" cried Harry in delight, and springing from the couch where they sat, he began hopping about the room to express his pleasure.

"Well, then, that's settled. Now, you must come and show me the horses and the pigs."

"I don't like pigs. I don't know where they are."

"Well, we must find out. Perhaps I shall make some discoveries for you. Have you any rabbits?"

"No."

"A dog though, surely?"

"No. I had a canary, but the cat ate it, and I have never had a pet since."

"Well, get your cap and come out with me. I will wait for you here."

Harry walked away; he seldom ran. He soon returned and they sallied out together. Happening to look back at the house, Hugh thought he saw Euphra standing at the window of a back staircase. They made the round of the stables, the cow-house, and the poultry-yard. And even the pigs, as proposed, came in for a share of their attention. As they approached the sty, Harry turned away his head with a look of disgust. They were eating out of the trough.

"They make such nasty noises!" he said.

"Yes, but just look. Don't they enjoy it?" commented Hugh.

Harry looked down at them. The notion of their enjoyment seemed to dawn upon him as something quite new. He went nearer and nearer to the sty. At last a smile broke out over his face.

"How tight that one curls his tail," he said, and burst out laughing.

By this time they had been wandering about for more than an hour, and Hugh saw by Harry's paleness that he was getting tired.

"Here, Harry, get on my back, my boy, and have a ride." Hugh knelt down. "You're tired."

"I shall get your coat dirty with my shoes."

"Nonsense. Rub them well on the grass there. And then get on my back."

Harry did as he was bid and found his tutor's broad back and strong arms a comfortable saddle. So away they went, wandering about for a long time in their new relation of horse and rider. At length they got into the middle of a long, narrow avenue, quite neglected, overgrown with weeds and obstructed with rubbish. The trees were beeches of considerable age. One end led far into a wood, and the other toward the house, a small portion of which could be seen at the end.

"Don't go down this," said Harry.

"Well, it's not a very good road for a horse certainly," replied Hugh, "but I think I can make it. What a beautiful avenue. Why is it so neglected?"

"Don't go down there, please, dear horse."

"Why?" asked Hugh.

"They call it the Ghost's Walk, and I don't much like it. It has a strange look."

"Very well, Harry," agreed Hugh and proceeded to leave the avenue by the other side. But Harry was not yet satisfied.

"Please, Mr. Sutherland, don't go on that side either. Ride me back, please, the way we came. It is not safe, they say, to cross her path. She always follows anyone who crosses her path."

Hugh laughed. "Very well, my boy," and returning, left the avenue by the side of which he had entered it.

"Shall we go home to lunch now?" said Harry.

"Yes," replied Hugh.

Approaching the front of the house, Hugh beheld it in its completeness for the first time. Though not imposing, the long front and the architectural style resulted in a somewhat mysterious and eminently picturesque appearance. All kinds of windows, all kinds of projections and recesses, a room here joined to a hall there, here a pointed gable, the very bell on the top overgrown with ivy, there a wide front with large bay windows, the next a turret of old stone, multitudes of roofs of all shapes and materials combined to make up the outside appearance of the house to Hugh's first inquiring glance. And even as he looked at the house of Arnstead, from one of the smaller windows Euphra was looking at him with the boy on his back.

"You are as kind to me as Euphra," said Harry, as Hugh set him down in the hall. "I've enjoyed my ride very much, thank you. I am sure Euphra will like you. She likes everybody."

Harry led Hugh to the dining room, a large oak hall with gothic windows and an open roof supported by richly carved woodwork. Over the high stone carving above the chimney hung an old piece of tapestry representing a hunting party of ladies and gentlemen just starting out. The table looked very small in the center of the room, though it would have seated twelve or fourteen. It was already covered for luncheon, and in a minute Euphra entered and took her place without a word. Hugh sat on one side and Harry on the other. Euphra, having helped both to soup, turned to Harry and said, ''Well, Harry, I hope you have enjoyed your first lesson.''

''Very much,'' answered Harry with a smile. ''I have learned pigs and horseback.''

The boy is positively clever, thought Hugh to himself.

''Mr. Sutherland,'' he continued, ''has begun to teach me to like animals.''

''You seem to have quite gained Harry already,'' murmured Euphra, glancing at Hugh and then looking away quickly.

''We shall be good friends, I think,'' replied Hugh.

Harry looked at him and then, turning to the lady, said, ''Do you know, Euphra, he is my big brother?''

''You must mind how you make new relations, Harry; for you know that would make him my cousin.''

''Well, you will be a kind cousin to him, won't you?''

''I will try,'' replied Euphra, looking up at Hugh with an expression of shyness and the slightest possible blush.

Hugh began to think her pretty, almost handsome. His next thought was to wonder how old she was. But about this he could not make up his mind. She might be twenty-two; she might be thirty. She had black hair and eyes to match. They could certainly sparkle and probably flash upon occasion. She was rather tall and of a pretty enough figure.

''Thank you,'' he replied. ''I shall do my best to deserve it.'' Then turning to Harry, he said, ''Now, Harry, you have had a rather tiring morning. I would like you to go and lie down a while.''

''Very well, Mr. Sutherland . . . in my bedroom?''

''No, have a change. Go to my room and lie on the couch.''

Harry went, and Hugh told Euphra what they had been about all the morning, ending with some remark on the view of the front of the house.

''It is a rather large house, is it not, for three—I beg your pardon—for four persons to live in, Mr. Sutherland?''

''It is indeed.''

''To tell you the truth, I don't quite know more than half of it myself.''

''You have not lived here long, then?''

''Not long for such a great place. A few years. I am only a poor relation.''

She accompanied this statement with another swift glance, but this time her eyes rested for a moment on Hugh's, with something of a pleading expression. Hugh could not quite understand her. A vague suspicion crossed his mind that she was bewitching him, but vanished instantly.

He replied with a smile and the remark, "Then you have all the more freedom. Did you know Harry's mother?" he added after a pause.

"No. She died when Harry was born. She was very beautiful and, they say, very clever, but always in extremely delicate health. Between ourselves, I doubt there was much sympathy on my uncle's part. But that is an old story."

A pause followed. Euphra resumed, "As to the freedom you speak of, Mr. Sutherland, I do not quite know what to do with it. I live here as if the place were my own and give what orders I please. But Mr. Arnold shows me little attention. So except when we have visitors, which is not very often, the time hangs rather heavily on my hands."

"But you are fond of reading—and writing too, I suspect," Hugh ventured to say.

She gave him another of her glances, in which the apparent shyness was mingled with something for which Hugh could not find a name. Nor did he suspect that it was in reality *slyness*.

"Oh, yes," she said. "One must read a book now and then, and if a verse should come up from nobody-knows-where, one may as well write it down. But please do not take me for a literary lady. I would not make the slightest pretensions of being such. I don't know what I should do without Harry. And indeed, Mr. Sutherland, you must not steal him from me."

"I should be very sorry to do so," replied Hugh. "Let me ask you to join us as often and for as long as you please. And that reminds me, I should go and see how he is."

He went to his room where he found Harry fast asleep on the sofa. He took care not to wake him, but sat down beside him to read till the nap should be over. But a moment later the boy opened his eyes with a start and gave a slight cry.

"What is the matter, dear Harry?"

"I had a dreadful dream."

"What was it?"

"I don't know. It always comes. It is always the same—I know that. And yet I can never remember what it is."

Hugh soothed him as well as he could, and when he had grown calmer he went and fetched *Gulliver's Travels*, and to the boy's great delight read to him till dinnertime. Before the first bell rang he had quite recovered, and indeed seemed rather interested in the approach of dinner.

Dinner was an affair of some state at Arnstead. Almost immediately after the second bell had rung, Mr. Arnold made his appearance in the drawing room where the others were already waiting for him. This room had nothing of the distinctive character of the parts of the house which

Hugh had already seen. It was merely a rather handsome, modern room. Mr. Arnold led Euphra to dinner, and Hugh followed with Harry.

Mr. Arnold's manner to Hugh was the same as in the morning—studiously polite, without the smallest approach to cordiality. He addressed him as an equal, but an equal who could never be in the smallest danger of thinking he meant it. Hugh soon discovered that he was one of those men who, if you will only grant their position and acknowledge their authority, will allow you to have much your own way in everything. His servants had found this out long ago, and almost everything about the house was managed as they pleased, and nothing went very far wrong. They all waited on Euphra, however, with a diligence that showed she could be quite mistress when and where she pleased. Perhaps they had found out that she had great influence with Mr. Arnold, and he seemed very fond of her indeed, in a stately fashion. Harry never asked for anything but always looked to Euphra, who gave the necessary order. Hugh saw that the boy was quite dependent on her.

"Do you find Harry very much behind with his studies, Mr. Sutherland?"

"I have not yet attempted to find out," replied Hugh.

"Not?" said Mr. Arnold with surprise.

"No. If he is behind, I am confident it will not be for long."

"But," began Mr. Arnold pompously, and then he paused.

"You were kind enough to say, Mr. Arnold, that I might try my own plans with him first. I have been doing so."

"Yes—certainly. But—"

Here Harry broke in with some animation. "Mr. Sutherland has been my horse, carrying me about on his back all the morning. He has been reading *Gulliver's Travels* to me—oh, such fun! And we have been to see the cows and the pigs; and Mr. Sutherland has been teaching me to jump. Do you know, Papa, he jumped right over the pony's back without touching it."

Mr. Arnold stared at the boy with lusterless eyes and hanging cheeks. These grew red as if he were going to choke. Such behavior was quite inconsistent with the dignity of Arnstead and its tutor, who had been recommended to him as a thorough gentleman. But for the present he said nothing; probably because he could think of nothing to say.

"Certainly Harry seems better already," interposed Euphra. "I cannot help thinking Mr. Sutherland has made a good beginning."

Mr. Arnold did not reply, but the cloud wore away from his face by degrees. Assessing Hugh across the table, he looked so very much like a gentleman, and stated his own views with so much independence that

Mr. Arnold judged it safer to keep him at arm's length for a season—at least till he should thoroughly understand his position: not that of a guest, but that of his son's tutor, belonging to the household of Arnstead only on approval.

13 / A Straw Cave and Two Flowers

The following morning dawned in a cloud, and there was gloomy weather indoors as well, for poor Harry was especially sensitive to variations of the barometer, without being in the least aware of it himself. Again Hugh found him in the library.

"Time to put away your book, Harry," he said. "Come, let's have a bit of Gulliver again."

Hugh read for an hour and then made Harry put on his coat, notwithstanding the rain—a slow, thoughtful, spring shower. Taking the boy again on his back, Hugh carried him into the woods. There he told him how the drops of wet sank into the ground and then went running about through it in every direction looking for seeds, which were all thirsty little things that wanted to grow, and could not, till a drop came and gave them a drink. And he told him how the raindrops were made up in the skies and then came down, like millions of angels, to do what they were told in the dark earth. The good drops went into all the cellars and dungeons of the earth to let out the imprisoned flowers. And he told them how the seeds, when they had drunk the raindrops, wanted another kind of drink next, which was much thinner and much stronger, but could not do them any good till they had drunk the rain first.

"What is that?" said Harry.

"It is the sunlight," answered his tutor. "When a seed has drunk of the water and is not thirsty anymore, it wants to breathe next. And then the sun sends a long, small finger of fire down into the grave where the seed is lying, and it touches the seed, and something inside the seed begins to move instantly and to grow bigger and bigger till it sends up two green blades out of it into the earth, and through the earth into the air. And then it can breathe. And then it sends roots down into the earth. And the roots keep drinking water, and the leaves keep breathing the air, and the sun keeps them alive and busy. And so a great tree grows up, and God looks at it and says, 'It is good!' "

"Then they really are living things?" said Harry.

"Certainly."

"Thank you, Mr. Sutherland. I don't think I shall dislike rain so much anymore."

They went into the barn where they found a great heap of straw. Recalling his own boyhood, Hugh made Harry take off his coat, and together they made a tunnel into the heap. Harry was delighted—the straw was so nice and bright and dry and clean. They drew it out by handfuls and thus excavated a round tunnel to the distance of six feet or so. Before it was time to go to lunch, they had cleared half of a hollow sphere, six feet in diameter, out of the heart of the heap.

After lunch, for which Harry had been very unwilling to relinquish the straw hut, Hugh sent him to lie down for a while where he fell fast asleep as before.

After he had left the room, Euphra said, "How are you getting on with Harry, Mr. Sutherland?"

"Perfectly to my satisfaction," answered Hugh.

"Do you not find him slow?"

"Quite the contrary."

"You surprise me. But you have not given him any lessons yet."

"I have given him a great many, and he is learning them very fast."

"I fear he will have forgotten all my poor labors before you take up the work where we left it. When will you give him any book lessons?"

"Not for a while yet."

Euphra did not reply. Her silence seemed intended to express dissatisfaction.

"Master Harry is a very peculiar child," Hugh went on after a moment, "and may turn out to be a genius or a weakling, just as he is managed. At least so it appears to me at present. May I ask where you left the work you were doing with him?"

"He was going through the Eton grammar for the third time," answered Euphra with a defiant glance at Hugh. "But I need not enumerate his studies, for I dare say you will not take them up at all after my fashion. But I can assure you I have been a very exact disciplinarian. What he knows, I think you will find he knows thoroughly."

So saying, Euphra rose and left the room with a flush on her cheeks. Hugh felt he had offended her. But to tell the truth he did not much care, for her manner had rather irritated him. He retired to his own room, wrote to his mother, and when Harry awoke carried him again to the barn for an hour's work in the straw. Before it grew dusk, they had finished a little, silent, dark, cozy chamber in the heart of the heap.

The next morning was still rainy, and when Hugh found Harry in the library as usual, he saw that the clouds had again gathered over the boy's spirit. He was pacing about the room in a very odd manner. The carpet was divided by colors in a regular pattern of diamonds. Harry's steps were, for the most part, planted on every third diamond as he slowly crossed the floor in a variety of directions. But every now and then the boy would make the most sudden and irregular change in his progression, setting his foot on the most unexpected diamond, at one time nearest to him, at another the farthest in his reach. When he looked up and saw his tutor watching him, still retaining the perplexed expression Hugh had noticed, Harry said, "How can God know on which of these diamonds I am going to set my foot next?"

"If you could understand how God knows, Harry, then you would know yourself. But before you have made up your mind, you don't know which you will choose, and even then you only know on which you intend to set your foot, for you have often changed your mind after making it up."

Harry looked as puzzled as before.

"Why, Harry, to understand how God understands, you would need to be as wise as he is. So it is no use trying. You see, you can't quite understand me, though I have a real meaning in what I say."

"I see it is no use. But I can't bear to be puzzled."

"But you need not be puzzled. You have no business to be puzzled. You are trying to get into your little brain what is far too grand and beautiful to get into it. Would you not think it very stupid to puzzle yourself how to put a hundred horses into a stable with twelve stalls?"

Harry laughed and looked relieved.

"It is a thousand times more unreasonable to try to understand such things. It would make me miserable to think that there was nothing but what I could understand. I should feel as if I had not room anywhere. Shall we go to our cave again?"

"Oh, yes, please!" cried Harry, and in a moment he was on Hugh's back once more, cantering joyously to the barn.

After various improvements, Hugh and Harry sat down together in the low, yellow twilight of their cave to enjoy the result of their labors. The rain was falling heavily out-of-doors, and they could hear the sound of the multitudinous drops of the broken cataract of the heavens like the murmur of the insects in a summer wood. They knew that everything outside was rained upon, and was again raining on everything beneath it, while they were dry and warm.

"This is nice!" exclaimed Harry after a few moments of silent enjoyment.

"This is your first lesson in architecture," replied Hugh.

They lay for some time in silence, listening to the rain. At length Harry spoke, "I have been thinking about what you told me yesterday, Mr. Sutherland, about the rain going to look for the seeds that were thirsty for it. And now I feel just as if I were a seed, lying in its hole in the earth and hearing the raindrops pattering down all about, waiting for some kind drop to find me out and give me itself to drink. I wonder what kind of flower I should grow up to be," he added, laughing.

"There is more truth than you think in your pretty fancy," remarked Hugh. Then he fell silent, for the memory of David came back upon him, recalled by the words of the boy. David, whom he loved and honored, and whom yet he had neglected and seemed to forget—the old man whose thoughts were like those of a wise child.

David had once said, "We have no more idea what we're growing up to be than that little turnip seed who doesn't know what a turnip is, though a turnip it will surely be. The only difference is that we *know* that we don't know, while the turnip seed knows nothing about it at all. But one thing, Mr. Sutherland, we may be sure of: whatever it be, it will be worth God's making and our growing into."

A solemn stillness fell upon Hugh's spirit as he recalled these words, broken finally by his young companion.

"Wouldn't this be a nice place for a story, Mr. Sutherland? Do you ever tell stories?"

"I was just thinking of one, Harry. But it is as much yours as mine, for you sowed the seed of the story in my mind."

"Do you mean a story that never was in a book—a story out of your own head? Oh, that will be grand!"

"Wait till we see what it will be, Harry, for I can't tell yet how it will turn out."

After a little pause, Hugh began. "Long, long ago, two seeds lay beside each other in the earth waiting. It was cold and rather wearisome.

" 'What are you going to be?' said the one.

" 'I don't know,' answered the other.

" 'For me,' rejoined the first, 'I mean to be a rose. There is nothing like a splendid rose.'

" 'It's all right,' whispered the second; and that was all he could say, for somehow when he had said that he felt as if all the words in the world were used up. So they were silent again for a day or two.

" 'Oh, dear,' cried the first. 'I have had some water. I never knew till it was inside me. I'm growing! I'm growing! Good-bye!'

" 'Good-bye,' repeated the other. He lay still and waited.

"The first grew and grew, pushing itself straight up, till at last it felt that it was in the open air, for it could breathe. And what a delicious breath that was! It was rather cold, but so refreshing. The flower could see nothing, for it was not quite a flower yet, only a plant. Still it grew and grew and kept its head up very steadily, meaning to see the sky the first thing once the eyes of its blossoms opened. But somehow or other, though it could not tell why, it felt very much inclined to cry. At length it opened its eye. It was morning, and the sky was over its head. But, alas, itself was no rose—only a tiny white flower. It felt yet more inclined to hang down its head to cry, but still it resisted and tried hard to open its eye wide and to hold its head upright and to look full at the sky.

"Its head felt very heavy, and a cold wind rushed over it and bowed it toward the earth. And the flower saw that the time of the singing birds was not come, that the snow covered the whole land, and that there was not a single flower in sight but itself. And it half closed its leaves in the terror and the dismay of loneliness. But that instant it remembered what the other flower seed used to say, and it said to itself: 'It's all right. I will be what I can.' And then it yielded to the wind, drooped its head to the earth, and looked no more to the sky, but on the snow. And immediately the wind stopped, and the cold died away, and the snow sparkled like pearls and diamonds. And the flower knew that it was the holding of its head up that had hurt it so; for its body came of the snow, and for that reason its name was Snowdrop. And so it said once more, 'It's all right!' and waited in perfect peace. All the rest it needed was to hang its head after its nature."

"And what became of the other?" asked Harry, eyes wide in fascination.

"I haven't done with this one yet," answered Hugh. "I only told you it was waiting. One day a pale, sad-looking girl with thin face, large eyes, and long white hands came, hanging her head like the snowdrop. She spied the little flower in the snow, smiled joyously, and saying, 'Ah, my little sister, are you come at last?' stooped and plucked the snowdrop. It trembled and died in her hand, which was a heavenly death for a snowdrop, for had it not cast a gleam of summer, pale as it had been itself, upon the heart of a sick girl?"

"And the other?" repeated Harry.

"The other had a long time to wait, but it did grow into one of the loveliest roses ever seen. And at last it had the highest honor ever granted to a flower: two lovers smelled it together and were content with it."

Harry was silent, and so was Hugh. For all the time he was speaking, he felt as if he were listening to David instead of talking himself. The fact was that he was only expanding, in an imaginative soil, the living seed which David had cast into it.

"What a delightful story, Mr. Sutherland," said Harry at last. "Euphra tells me stories sometimes. But I don't think I ever heard one I liked so much. I wish we were meant to grow into something like the flower seeds."

"So we are, Harry."

"Are we indeed? How delightful it would be to think that I am only a seed, Mr. Sutherland."

"I do believe it's true, Harry."

"Then please, let me begin to learn something. I haven't had anything disagreeable to do since you came."

Poor Harry, like so many thousands of good people, had not yet learned that God is not a hard taskmaster.

"I don't intend that you should have anything disagreeable to do if I can help it. We must learn things as they come to us and when we want to. Otherwise there will be little remembering. You can never *make* yourself like anything."

Harry was silent. They returned to the house through the pouring rain, Harry, as usual, mounted on the back of his big brother.

As they crossed the hall, Mr. Arnold came in. He looked surprised and rather annoyed. Hugh set Harry down, who ran upstairs to get dressed for dinner, while he himself half stopped and turned toward Mr. Arnold. But Mr. Arnold did not speak, and so Hugh followed Harry.

14 / More Learning

For a time there was very little interaction between Hugh and Euphra, whose surname Hugh still did not know. Her recent behavior had impressed him with the notion that she was proud and had made up her mind to keep him at a distance. For several days the rain continued. But seated in their straw bed, Harry and tutor cared not about rain. They were safe from the whole world and all the tempers of nature.

Finished with *Gulliver's Travels*, Hugh began to read about some of the chief stories of early Roman history with Harry. He told him tales of their battles and conquests, their grand men and their various contributions to the world's culture. This went on for some time, until Harry's own fascination with the period took over from Hugh as his tutor.

When the rain finally broke, Hugh suggested to Harry one morning after breakfast, "Let's go out to explore the woods. Perhaps we shall meet spring, if we look for her—perhaps hear her voice, too."

As they went across the lawn toward the shrubbery, on their way to the woods, Euphra joined them in walking dress. It was a lovely morning.

"I have taken you at your word, you see, Mr. Sutherland," she said. "I don't want to lose my Harry yet."

"You dear, kind Euphra," said Harry, going round to her side and taking her hand.

"You are most welcome," said Hugh. "We were just going on a hunt for spring."

"I dare say it comes sooner here than in your northern country."

"Indeed," replied Hugh. "My mother is probably still looking at a foot of snow."

"I have Scottish blood in me, you know," said Euphra. "I was born in Scotland, though I left it before I was a year old. My mother, Mr. Arnold's sister, married a gentleman who was half Scottish, and I was born while they were on a visit to his relatives, the Camerons of Lochnie. His mother, my grandmother, was a Bohemian lady, a countess with sixteen quarterings.* I haven't been to Scotland in years. But Mr. Arnold maintains many of his contacts there, some not far from where you lived for a time, I understand."

The ice of her recent constraint had suddenly thawed into this torrent of genealogical information and Hugh had no idea how to account for

*Divisions of coat of arms on a shield.

it. And how did she come to be so apparently familiar with his sojourn at Turriepuffit? He had not an inkling that the university friend who had persuaded him to write to Mr. Arnold was a family friend and had, on a previous trip to London, spent considerable time in the company of Euphra and Arnold Cameron. Further, it was odd that she should all at once volunteer so much about herself.

Hugh responded with a question. "Do I know your name then, at last? You are Miss Cameron?"

"Euphrasia Cameron, at your service." And she dropped a gay little curtsy to Hugh, looking up at him with a flash of her black diamond eyes.

By this time they had reached the woods in a different quarter from that which Hugh had gone through the other day with Harry. And here indeed, spring met them with a profusion of richness to which Hugh was quite a stranger. The ground was carpeted with primroses, the loveliest of all flowers, and other spring flowers. They were drinking in the sunlight, which fell upon them through the budded boughs.

"Do look at this beauty, Mr. Sutherland!" exclaimed Euphra suddenly as she bent at the root of a great beech tree where grew a large bush of rough leaves, with one tiny but perfectly formed primrose peeping out between. All about in shady places, the ferns were busy untucking themselves from their grave clothes, unrolling their mysterious coils of life, adding continually to the hidden growth as they unfolded the visible. All the wild, lovely things were coming up—orchis-harlequins, cuckoo-plants, wild arums. At last the wanderers came upon a whole company of bluebells—wild hyacinths growing in a damp and shady spot in wonderful luxuriance. They were quite three feet in height, with long, graceful, dropping heads. Euphra went into ecstasies over these.

"Look, Harry," she said, "they are all sad at having to go down there again so soon. They are looking at their graves so ruefully.—You have nothing like this in your country, have you, Mr. Sutherland?"

"No, indeed," answered Hugh.

And he said no more. For a vision rose before him of the rugged pine wood and the single primrose, and of the thoughtful maiden with unpolished speech and rough hands. And he thought of the grand old gray-haired David and of Jeanette with her quaint motherhood and all the blessedness of that past time.

As they walked, Harry was both surprised and delighted with Euphra's apparent joy. He could not help wondering, however, that she had never shown him such things before and had never said anything half so pretty to him about the flowers. Had Mr. Sutherland anything to do with it? Was he giving Euphra a lesson in flowers, such as he had given him in pigs?

Euphra had much of one element that goes into the making of a poet—namely, surface impressibility. She could laugh or cry in a moment, or call a mountain or flower a darling or a beauty. But her appreciation for the things about her was limited by the shallowness of her roots. Margaret would have walked through all this infant summer without speaking at all, but with a deep light far back in her quiet eyes. Perhaps she would not have had many thoughts *about* the flowers; rather, she would have been at home with them, in a delighted oneness with their life and expression.

But Euphra presently drew Hugh into conversation again, and the old times of David and Margaret and the pine and fir trees of the North were once more forgotten.

Many walks followed this, extending farther and farther from home, as Harry's strength gradually improved. It was quite remarkable how his interest in everything external increased in proportion as he learned to see into the inside life of it. With most children, the interest in the external comes first and, with many, ceases there.

As often as Mr. Arnold was away from home, which happened not infrequently, Miss Cameron accompanied them in their rambles. She did so only on such occasions, because, she said, she never liked to be out when her uncle might want her.

On one occasion, when Harry had run a little way after a butterfly, Hugh said to her, "What did you mean, Miss Cameron, by saying you were only a poor relation? You are certainly mistress of the house."

"But I have no fortune of my own."

"But Mr. Arnold does not treat you as such."

"Oh, no. He likes me. He is very kind. He gave me this ring on my last birthday. Isn't it beautiful?"

She pulled off her glove and showed a very fine diamond on a finger worthy of the ornament.

"It is more like a gentleman's, is it not?" she added, drawing it off. "Let me see how it would look on your hand."

She gave the ring to Hugh, who, laughing, got it with some difficulty just over the first joint of his little finger.

"I see I cannot ask you to wear it for me," she said. "I don't like it myself. I am afraid, however," she added, "that my uncle would not like it either—on your finger. Put in on mine again."

As she held her hand toward Hugh, he took it and did according to her request, feeling the slightest flutter in his chest as he slipped the ring back onto the tiny finger and released the smooth, dainty hand from his own.

15 / On Horseback

Mr. Arnold was busy at home for a few days after this, and Hugh and Harry went for their walks alone. One day, when the wind was rather cold, they took refuge in the barn. It was part of Hugh's care that Harry should be rendered hardy by being exposed to no more than he could bear without suffering. As soon as the boy began to feel fatigue, his tutor took measures accordingly.

On this day, inside their straw cave, the talk turned to horses.

"Will you teach me to ride, Mr. Sutherland?" asked Harry.

"Perhaps I will."

That evening at dinner, Hugh said to Mr. Arnold, "Could you let me borrow a horse tomorrow morning, Mr. Arnold?" Mr. Arnold stared a little, as he always did at anything new. But Hugh went on. "Harry and I want to have a ride tomorrow, and I expect we shall like it so much that we shall want to ride very often."

"Yes, that we shall!" cried Harry.

"Well, Harry," said Mr. Arnold, reconciled at once to the proposal and seeing an opportunity to be facetious, "don't you think your little Welch dray horse could carry Mr. Sutherland?"

"Ha, ha, ha! Papa, do you know Mr. Sutherland set him up on his hind legs yesterday and was going to lift him? But he kicked about so when he felt himself leaving the ground that he tumbled Mr. Sutherland into the horse trough."

Even the solemn face of the butler relaxed into a smile, but Mr. Arnold's clouded instead. His boy's tutor ought to be a gentleman.

"Wasn't it fun, Mr. Sutherland?" Harry asked.

"It was to you, you little rogue," said Hugh, laughing.

"And how you did run home, dripping like a water cart—and all the dogs after you!"

Mr. Arnold's monotonous solemnity soon checked Harry's prattle. "I will see, Mr. Sutherland, what I can do for a mount for you."

"I don't care what it is," assured Hugh, who, though by no means a thorough horseman, had been from boyhood in the habit of mounting everything in the shape of a horse that he could lay hands upon, from a cart horse upward and downward. "There's an old bay that would carry me very well."

"That is my own horse, Mr. Sutherland."

This stopped the conversation in that direction. But next morning after breakfast, an excellent chestnut horse was waiting at the door along with Harry's new pony. Mr. Arnold would see them off. This did not exactly suit Miss Cameron, but if she frowned it was when nobody saw her. Hugh put Harry up himself, told him to stick fast with his knees, and then mounted his chestnut.

Harry returned from his ride rather tired but in high spirits. "Oh, Euphra," he cried, "Mr. Sutherland is such a rider! He jumps hedges and ditches and everything. And he has promised to teach me and my pony to jump too."

The little fellow's heart was full of the sense of growing life and strength, and Hugh was delighted. He caught sight of a serpentine motion in Euphra's eyebrows as she bent her face again over the work from which she had lifted it on their entrance. He addressed her. "You will be glad to hear that Harry has ridden like a man."

"I am glad to hear it, Harry."

Why did she reply to the subject of the remark, and not to the speaker? At luncheon she spoke only in reply and then so briefly as to not afford the smallest peg on which to hang a response.

What can the matter be? wondered Hugh to himself. *What a peculiar creature she is.*

When dinner was over that evening, she rose as usual and left the room, followed by Hugh and Harry. But as soon as they were in the drawing room, she left it and returned to the dining room and resumed her seat at the table.

"Take a glass of claret, Euphra dear," said Mr. Arnold.

"I will, if you please, Uncle. I seldom have a minute with you alone now." Evidently flattered, Mr. Arnold poured out a glass of claret, handed it to his niece, and then took a chair beside her. "Thank you, dear Uncle," she said with one of her bewitching flashes of smile.

"Harry has been getting on bravely with his riding, has he not?" she continued.

"So it would appear . . . I am only a little fearful, Uncle, that Mr. Sutherland will urge the boy to do more than his strength will allow. He is exceedingly kind to him, but he has evidently never known what weakness is himself."

"True, there is danger of that. But you see he has taken him so entirely into his own hands. I don't seem to be allowed a word in the matter of his education anymore." Mr. Arnold spoke with the peevishness of weak importance. "I wish you would take care that he does not carry things too far, Euphra."

This was just what Euphra wanted.

Breakfast was scarcely over the next morning when the chestnut and pony headed out from the house, this time, however, accompanied by a lovely little Arab mare, white as snow with keen dark eyes. Euphra was clad in a well-fitted riding habit of black velvet, with a belt of dark red leather clasping a waist of the roundest and smallest. Her little hat, likewise black, had a single long, white feather, laid horizontally within the upturned brim, and drooping over it at the back. Her white mare was just the right pedestal for the dusky figure—black eyes, tawny skin and all.

Away they went, Euphra's mare Fatima infusing life and frolic into the equine as Euphra into the human portion of the cavalcade. Having reached the meadow, out of sight of the house, Euphra scampered about like a wild girl, jumping everything in sight, and so exciting Harry's pony that it was almost more than he could do to manage it, till at last Hugh had to ask her to go more quietly. She drew up alongside of them at once and made her mare stand as still as she could, while Harry made his first essay upon a little ditch. After crossing it two or three times, he gathered courage, and setting his pony at a larger one, bounded across it beautifully.

"Bravo, Harry!" cried both Euphra and Hugh. Harry galloped back, and over it again; then he came up to them with a glow of proud confidence on his pale face.

"You'll be a horseman yet, Harry," encouraged Hugh.

"I hope so," said Harry, in an aspiring tone which greatly satisfied his tutor. The boy's spirit was evidently reviving. Euphra must have mismanaged him. Yet she was not in the least effeminate herself. It puzzled Hugh a good deal. But he did not think about it long.

With Harry cantering away in front, he had an opportunity of saying to Euphra, "Are you offended with me, Miss Cameron?"

"Offended with you! What *do* you mean? A girl like me offended with a man like you?"

She looked twenty-two as she spoke. But even at that she was older than Hugh. He, however, certainly looked considerably older than he really was.

"What makes you say so?" she added, turning her face toward him.

"You would not speak to me when we came home yesterday."

"Not speak to you?—I had a little headache. And perhaps I was a little sullen, from having been in such bad company all the morning."

"What company had you?" asked Hugh in some surprise.

"My own," she answered, with a lovely laugh thrown full in his face. Then after a pause, "Let me advise you, if you want to live in peace, not to embark on that ocean of discovery."

"What ocean? What discovery?" asked Hugh, still bewildered.

"The troubled ocean of ladies' looks," she replied. "You will never be able to live in the same house with one of our kind if it be necessary to your peace to find out what every expression that puzzles you may mean."

"I did not intend to be inquisitive. It truly troubled me."

"There it is. You must never mind us. We show so much sooner than men; but take warning, there is no making out what it is we do show. Your faces are legible. Ours are so scratched and interlined that you had best give up at once the idea of deciphering them."

Hugh could not help looking once more at the smooth, simple, seemingly naïve countenance shining upon him. "There—you are at it again," she said, blushing a little, and turning her head away. "Well, to comfort you, I will confess I was rather cross yesterday—because—because you seemed to have been quite happy with only one of your pupils."

As she spoke the words, she gave Fatima the rein and bounded off, overtaking Harry's pony in a moment.

Hugh's heart bounded, like her Arab steed. He gave his chestnut the rein to overtake her. But Fatima's canter quickened into a gallop, and, inspirited by her companionship and the fact that their heads were turned stablewards, Harry's pony—one of the quickest of its race—laid itself to the ground and kept it up. Thus Hugh never got within three strides of the other two horses till they drew rein at the hall door, where the grooms were awaiting them. Euphra was off her mare in moment and had almost reached her own room before Hugh and Harry had crossed the hall.

She came down to luncheon in a white muslin dress, and taking her place at the table seemed to Hugh to have put off not only her riding habit but the self that was in it as well. For she chatted away in the most casual and lighthearted manner possible, as if she had not been out of her room all the morning. She had ridden so hard that she had left her last statement in the middle of the common, and its mood with it. There seemed now no likelihood of either finding its way home.

16 / The Picture Gallery

Luncheon over and Harry dismissed to lie down, Miss Cameron said to Hugh, "You have never been over the older part of the house yet, I believe, Mr. Sutherland. Would you like to see it?"

"I should indeed," said Hugh. "I have long hoped to do so."

"Come then; I will be your guide." She rose and rang the bell. When it was answered, she said, "Jacob, get me the keys of the house from Mrs. Horton."

Jacob vanished and soon reappeared with a huge bunch of keys. As she took them, she said, "Now, Mr. Sutherland.—Jane, will you come with us?" she said to one of the maids.

She unlocked a door in the corner of the hall, which Hugh had never seen open. Passing through a long, low passage, they came to a spiral staircase of stone, which they ascended, arriving at another wide hall, very dusty but in perfect repair. Hugh asked if there was not some communication between this hall and the great oak staircase.

"Yes," answered Euphra, "but this is the more direct way."

As she said this, he felt somehow as if she cast on him one of her keenest glances. But the place was very dusty, and he stood in a spot where the light fell upon him from an opening in a shutter, while she stood in deep shadow.

"Jane, open that shutter." The girl obliged, and the entering light revealed the walls covered with paintings, many of them apparently of no value, yet adding much to the effect of the place. Seeing that Hugh was at once attracted by the artwork, Euphra said, "Perhaps you would like to see the picture gallery first?" Hugh assented.

Euphra chose key after key, and opened door after door, till they came to a long gallery well lit from each end. The windows were soon opened.

"Mr. Arnold is very proud of his pictures," she continued, "especially of his family portraits. But he is content with knowing he has them, and never visits them except to show them—or perhaps once or twice a year when something or other keeps him home for a day without anything particular to do."

In glancing over the portraits, some of them by famous masters, Hugh's eyes were arrested by a blonde lady of great beauty in the dress of the time of Charles II. There was such a reality of self-willed boldness as well as something worse in her face that, though arrested by the picture, Hugh felt almost ashamed of looking at it. The woman almost put him out of countenance, and yet at the same time fascinated him. Drawing his eyes from it, he saw that Jane had turned her back upon it, while Euphra regarded it steadily.

"Open that opposite window, Jane," she said. "There is not enough light on this portrait." Jane obeyed.

While she did so, Hugh caught a glimpse of her face, and saw that the formerly rosy girl was deadly pale. He said to Euphra. "Your maid seems ill, Miss Cameron."

"Jane, what is the matter with you?" She did not reply, but leaning against the wall, seemed ready to faint.

"The place is confined," said her mistress. "Go into the next room there"—she pointed to a door—"and open the window. You will soon be well."

"If you please, Miss, I would rather stay with you. This place makes me feel strange." She had joined the household only recently and had never been over the house before.

"Nonsense!" said Euphra, looking at her sharply. "What do you mean?"

"Please, don't be angry, Miss. But the first night I was here I saw that very lady—"

"Saw that lady!"

"Well, Miss, I mean, I dreamed that I saw her. And I remembered her face the moment I saw her portrait. It gave me a turn, like . . . I'm all right now, Miss."

Euphra fixed her eyes on her again. The girl seemed as pale as before and began to breathe with difficulty.

"You silly goose!" said Euphra, and withdrew her eyes. The girl eventually began to breathe more freely.

Euphra turned to Hugh and began to tell him that the portrait was of her three- or four-times great-grandmother, painted by Sir Peter Lely just after she was married. "Isn't she fair?" she said. "She turned a nun at last, they say."

She is more fair than honest, thought Hugh. *It would take a great deal of nun to make her into a saint.* But he only said, "She is more beautiful than lovely. What was her name?"

"If you mean her maiden name, it was Halkar—Lady Euphrasia Halkar—for whom I am named. She had foreign blood in her, of course. And to tell the truth, there were strange stories told of her, of more sorts than one."

All the time Euphra was speaking, Hugh was perplexed with that most annoying of perplexities—the flitting phantom of a resemblance which he could not catch. He was forced to dismiss it for the present, utterly baffled. "Were you really named after her?"

"No. It is a family name with us. But then, maybe I *was* named after her, for she was the first of us who bore it. You don't seem to like the portrait."

"Not really. But I cannot help looking at it."

"I am so used to the lady's face," said Euphra, "that it makes no impression on me. But it is said," she added, glancing at the maid who stood at some distance looking uneasily about her—and as she spoke she lowered her voice to a whisper—"it is said she cannot lie still."

"Cannot lie still . . . what do you mean?"

"I mean down there in the chapel," she answered.

The Celtic nerves of Hugh shuddered. Euphra laughed and her voice echoed in silvery billows that broke on the faces of the men and women of ancient time whose lives had ebbed and flowed through the old house.

Ashamed of his feeling of passing dismay, Hugh changed the subject. "What a strange ornament that is. Is it a brooch or a pin? No, it looks like a ring—large enough for three cardinals, and worn on her thumb? It seems almost to sparkle in the picture. Is it a ruby or carbuncle or what?"

"I don't know—some clumsy old thing," answered Euphra carelessly.

"Now I see," said Hugh, "it is not a red stone. The glow is only a reflection from part of her dress. It is as clear as a diamond. But that would be impossible for such a size. There seems something curious about it. And the longer I look at it the more strange it appears."

Euphra stole another of her piercing glances at him but said nothing.

"Surely," Hugh went on, "a ring like that would hardly be likely to be lost out of the family. Your uncle must have it somewhere."

Euphra laughed, but it was very different from her last. It seemed to rattle rather than ring. "You seem quite taken with a trifling piece of finery—for a man of letters, that is, Mr. Sutherland. The stone may have been carried down any one of the hundred streams into which a family river is always dividing."

"It is a very remarkable ornament for a lady's finger, notwithstanding," said Hugh, smiling in his turn.

"But we shall never get through the pictures at this rate," remarked Euphra; going on, she directed Hugh's attention now to this, now to that portrait, saying who each was and mentioning anything remarkable in the history of their originals. Having gone nearly to the other end of the gallery—"This door," she said, stopping at one, and turning over the keys, "leads to one of the oldest portions of the house, the principal room of which is said to have belonged especially to the lady over there." As she said this, she fixed her eyes once more on the maid.

"Oh, don't ye now, Miss," implored Jane. "Hannah do say as how a white-blue light shines in the window of a dark night, sometimes—that lady's window, ye know, Miss. Don't ye open the door—pray, Miss.'' Jane seemed on the point of falling into the same terror as before.

''Really, Jane,'' rebuked her mistress, ''I am ashamed of you and of myself for having such silly servants about me.''

''I beg your pardon, Miss, but—''

''So Mr. Sutherland and I must give up our plan of going over the house because my maid's nerves are too delicate to permit her to accompany us!''

''Oh, do ye now go on without me!'' cried the girl, clasping her hands.

''And you will wait here till we come back?''

''Oh, don't ye leave me here. Just show me the way out.'' And once more she turned pale as death.

''Mr. Sutherland, I am very sorry, but we must put off the rest of our ramble till another time. I am, like Hamlet, vilely attended as you see. Come then, you foolish girl,'' she added more mildly.

The poor maid was in a pitiable condition and seemed almost too frightened to walk behind them. They returned as they came, and Jane, receiving the keys to take to the housekeeper, darted away. When she had reached Mrs. Horton's room, she sank on a chair in hysterics.

''I must get rid of that girl,'' said Euphra, leading the way to the library. ''She will infect the whole household with her foolish terrors. We shall not hear the last of this for some time to come. We had a fit of it the same year I came, and I suppose the time has come round for another attack of the same epidemic.''

''What is there about the room to terrify the poor thing?''

''Oh, they say it is haunted. Was there ever an old house anywhere in Europe, especially an old family house, but was said to be haunted? Here, the story centers in that room, or at least in that room and the avenue in front of its windows.''

''Is that the avenue called the Ghost's Walk?''

''Yes. Who told you?''

''Harry would not let me cross it.''

''Poor boy. This is really too bad. He cannot stand anything of that kind, I am sure. Those servants!''

''Well, I hope we shall soon get him too well to be frightened at anything. Are these places said to be haunted by any particular ghost?''

''Yes. By Lady Euphrasia.''

Had Hugh possessed a keener perception of resemblance, he would have seen that the phantom-likeness which haunted him in the portrait of Euphrasia Halkar was that of Euphrasia Cameron. But the mere difference of complexion was sufficient to throw him off. Euphra herself was perfectly aware of the likeness but had no wish that Hugh should discover it.

Their midday walk completed, Euphra retired, and Harry soon joined Hugh.

Euphra had another glass of claret with her uncle that evening in order to give her report of the morning's ride. ''Really, there is not much to be afraid of, Uncle,'' she stated carelessly. ''He takes very good care of Harry.''

''I am glad he has your good opinion so far, Euphra,'' said Mr. Arnold. ''I confess there is something about the youth that pleases me. I was afraid at first that I might be annoyed by his overstepping the true boundaries of his position in my family. But your assurance lessens my apprehension considerably.''

''I think, however, if you approve, Uncle, that it will be prudent for me to keep watch over the riding for a while. I confess, too, I should be glad of a little more of that exercise than I have had for some time. I found my seat not very secure today.''

''Very desirable on both considerations, my love.''

17 / Nest Building

In a short time, Harry's health was so much improved and consequently the strength and activity of his mind so much increased that Hugh began to give him more exacting mental operations to perform. They began to read Shakespeare together and study geometry—the latter not from books just yet but from Harry's interest in measuring the house and areas about it. For the reading of Shakespeare, Euphra always joined them.

One afternoon, when Harry had waked from his siesta, upon which Hugh still insisted, they went for a walk in the fields. The sun was halfway down the sky, but very hot and sultry.

"I wish we had our cave of straw to creep into now," said Harry. "Now that it is used up, we have no place to go for our own private place. And the consequence is that you have not told me any stories about the Romans for a whole week!"

"Well, Harry, is there any way of making another?"

"There's no more straw lying about that I know of," answered Harry.

"But don't you think it would be pleasant to have a change now? And as we have lived underground, we might now try living in the air."

"Delightful!" cried Harry. "A balloon?"

"Not quite that high. I was thinking of a nest."

"Up in a tree?"

"Yes."

Harry darted off for a run as the only means of expressing his delight. When he came back he said, "When shall we begin, Mr. Sutherland?"

"We will go and look for a place at once. But I am not quite sure when we shall begin. Tomorrow perhaps."

They left the fields and went into the woods in the neighborhood of the back of the house. Here the trees had grown to a great size, some of them being very old indeed. They soon fixed upon a grotesque old oak as a proper tree in which to build their nest; and Harry, who as well as Hugh had a good deal of constructiveness in his nature, was so delighted he could hardly contain himself.

The following afternoon they went again to the woods and found the tree they had chosen. To Harry's intense admiration, Hugh scrambled up the tree. Just one layer of foliage above the lowest branches, he came to a place where he thought there was a suitable foundation for the nest. From the ground Harry could scarcely see him while with an axe he cut away several smaller branches from three of the principals ones. Assessing these three as the rafters and making some necessary measurements, he descended. Then they walked to the workshop, where they procured some boards and tools and together carried them back to the tree. Ascending again with the materials by use of a piece of rope and Harry's help, Hugh soon had a fairly level floor, four feet square, in the middle of the oak tree. It was quite invisible from below, buried in a cloud of green leaves. For safety he fastened ropes as handrails all around it from one branch to another. And now nothing remained but to construct a bench to sit on and a stair up which Harry could easily climb. The boy was quite restless with anxiety to get up and see the nest; he kept calling out constantly to know if he might not come up yet. At length Hugh allowed him to try, but the poor boy was not half strong enough to climb the tree without help. So Hugh descended, and with his aid Harry was soon standing on the newly built platform.

"I feel just like an eagle!" he cried. But here his voice faltered, and he was silent.

"What is the matter, Harry?" said his tutor.

"Oh, nothing," he replied; "only I didn't know where we were until I got up here."

"Where are we then?"

"Close to the end of the Ghost's Walk."

"But you don't mind that now, surely, Harry?"

"Not as much as I used to."

"Shall I take all this down and build our nest somewhere else?"

"Oh, no, if *you* don't think it matters. Besides, I shall never be here without you. And I don't think I should be afraid of the ghost herself if you were with me." Yet Harry shuddered involuntarily at the thought.

"Very well, Harry, my boy; we will finish it here." Hammer and nails were soon busy again, and shortly they sat down on the bench to enjoy the cool breeze blowing through all the leaves about them. Harry was highly contented. He drew a deep breath of satisfaction as, looking above and beneath and all about him, he saw that they were folded in an almost impenetrable net of foliage.

"Now I must build you a stair, Master Harry," said Hugh. "So why don't you just sit here till I fetch you."

Nailing a little rude bracket here and there on the trunk of the tree, just where Harry could avail himself of its natural handholds as well, Hugh had soon finished a strangely irregular staircase, which took Harry two or three times of trying to quite master.

The next day after dinner Mr. Arnold said to the tutor, "Well, Mr. Sutherland, how is Harry getting on with his geography?"

"We have not done anything with that yet, Mr. Arnold."

"Not done anything at geography! I am astonished, Mr. Sutherland. Why, when he was a mere child he could repeat all the counties of England."

"Perhaps that may be the reason for the decided distaste he shows for it now. But I will begin to teach him at once if you desire it."

"I do desire it, Mr. Sutherland. A thorough geographical knowledge is essential to the education of a gentleman."

"We shall begin tomorrow then," said Hugh.

"What books do you have?"

"Oh, no books, if you please, just yet. If you are satisfied with Harry's progress so far, let me have my own way in this too."

"But geography does not seem your strong point."

"Granted. But I may be able to teach it all the better from feeling the difficulties of a learner myself."

The following morning Hugh and Harry went out for a walk to the top of a hill in the neighborhood. When they reached it, Hugh took a small compass from his pocket and set it on the ground, contemplating it and the horizon alternately.

"What are you trying to do, Mr. Sutherland?" asked Harry.

"I am trying to find the exact line of direction that would go through my home," he said.

"Is that funny little thing able to tell you?"

"Yes. Isn't it curious, Harry, to have in my pocket a little thing with a kind of spirit in it that understands the spirit that is in the big world, and always points to the North Pole?"

"Explain it to me."

"It is nearly as much a mystery to me as to you."

"Let me hold it, please. I will turn it away—oh, it won't go! It goes back and back, do what I will."

"Yes, it will always point north if you turn it away all day long. Look, Harry, if you were to go straight in this direction, you would come to a Laplander harnessing his broad-horned reindeer to his sledge. He's at it now, I dare say. If you were to go in this line exactly, you would go through the smoke and fire of a burning mountain in a land of ice. If you were to go this way, straight on, you would find yourself in the middle of a forest with a lion glaring at your feet, for it is dark night there now, and so hot. And over there is such a lovely sunset. And there—there is a desert of sand and a camel dying, and all his companions just disappearing on the horizon. And over there is an awful sea, without a boat to be seen on it, dark and dismal, with huge rocks all about it and waste borders of sand."

"How do you know all this, Mr. Sutherland? You have never walked along those lines. I know, for you couldn't."

"Geography has taught me."

"No," said Harry incredulously.

"Well, shall we travel along this line, just across that crown of trees on the hill?"

"Yes, do let us."

"Then," said Hugh, drawing a telescope from his pocket, "this hill is henceforth Geography Point, and all the world lies round about it. Do you know we are in the very middle of the earth?"

"Are we indeed?"

"Yes. Any point you like to choose on a ball is the middle of it."

"I see."

"And what lies at the bottom of the hill down there?"

"Arnstead, to be sure."

"And what beyond that?"

"I don't know."

"Look through here."

"Oh, that must be the village we rode to yesterday—I forgot the name." Hugh told him the name; then he had him look with the telescope all along the receding line to the trees on the opposite hill.

Just then a voice behind them said, "What are you doing, Harry?" Hugh felt a glow of pleasure as Euphra's voice fell on his ear.

"Oh," replied Harry, "Mr. Sutherland is teaching me geography with a telescope. It's such fun!"

"He's a wonderful tutor, that tutor of yours, Harry."

"Yes, isn't he? But," Harry went on, turning to Hugh, "what are we to do now? We can't see farther than that hill."

"We'll have to ask your papa to lend us some of his maps. They will teach us what lies beyond it. And then we can read in some of his books about what lies farther still, and so go on and on till we reach the wide, beautiful, restless sea, over which we must sail, in spirit of wind and tide, straight on till we come to land again. But we must make a great many journeys before we really know what sort of a place we are living in, and we shall have ever so many surprises."

"Oh, that sounds like fun!" exclaimed Harry.

After a little more geographical talk, they put away their instruments and began to descend the hill. Harry was in no need of Hugh's back now, but Euphra was in need of his hand. In fact, she reached for its support.

"How awkward of me! I am stumbling over the heather." She was in fact stumbling over her own dress, which she would not hold out of the way. Hugh offered his hand; her small one seemed quite content to be swallowed up in his large one.

"Why do you never let me put you on your horse?" said Hugh.

"You always manage to prevent me somehow or other."

"It's only a trick of independence, Hugh—Mr. Sutherland—I beg your pardon." Though she had never once heard him called Hugh, her slip of the tongue—or was it intentional?—sounded as if she had been saying his name over and over to herself.

"I beg your pardon," repeated Euphra hastily; for, as Hugh did not reply, she feared her arrow had swerved from its mark.

"For a sweet fault, Euphra—I beg your pardon—Miss Cameron."

"You punish me with forgiveness," she returned with one of her sweetest looks. Hugh could not help pressing the little hand.

Was the pressure returned? So slight, so airy was the touch that it might have been only the throb of his own pulse, all consciously aware of the wonderful woman-hand that rested in his. If he had claimed it, she might easily have denied it, so ethereal and uncertain it was. He never dreamed that she was exercising her skill upon him.

Meantime, this much is certain, that she was drawing Hugh closer and closer to her side, that a soothing dream of delight had begun to steal over his spirit, soon to make it toss in feverous unrest—as the first effects of some poisons are like a dawn of tenfold strength. The mountain wind blew from her to him, sometimes sweeping her garments about him and bathing him in their faint, sweet odors. Sometimes so kindly strong did it blow that it compelled her, or at least gave her excuse enough, to leave his hand and cling to his arm.

But though love be good, a tempest of it in the brain will neither ripen the fruits like a soft, steady wind nor waft the ships home to their desired haven.

Perhaps what enslaved Hugh most was the feeling that the damsel stooped to him. She seemed to him in every way above him. She knew so many things of which he was ignorant, could say such lovely things, could write lovely verses, could sing like an angel, was mistress of a great, rich, wonderful house, and more than all was a beautiful woman. It was true that his family was as good as hers. But his father had disowned the rest of the family on grounds of principle. And Hugh's pride was now increasingly causing him gradually to despise his present position and look upon a tutor's employment as others looked upon it, as rather contemptible for one such as he.

The influence of Euphrasia was not of the best upon him from the first, for it had greatly increased this feeling about his occupation. It set him upon a very unprofitable kind of castle-building. He would become a soldier like his father. He would leave Arnstead, to return with a sword by his side and a Sir before his name. Sir Hugh Sutherland would be somebody of importance and worth in the eyes of the master of Arnstead. Yes, a six-foot fellow, though he may be sensible in most things, is not free from small vanities, especially if he is in love.

18 / Hugh and Euphra

With so many shafts opening into the mountain of knowledge, it soon became necessary for Harry and his tutor to spend more time working the mine than they had given previously. This made a considerable alteration in the interaction of the youth and the lady, for although Euphra was often present during school hours, Hugh and Harry spent most of their time at their books. She sat beside them in silence, occupied with her needlework, and saving up her glances for use. Now and then she would read, taking an opportunity sometimes, but not often, when a fitting pause occurred, to ask him to explain some passage. It must be conceded that such passages were well chosen for the purpose; for she was too wise to do her own intellect discredit by feigning a difficulty where she saw none.

But by and by she began to discontinue these visits to the schoolroom.

One morning, in the course of their study, Hugh had to leave his room—where for the most part they carried on the more difficult portions of their labors—to go to the library for a book. As he was passing an open door, Euphra's voice called him. He entered, and found himself in her private sitting room. He had not known where it was before.

"I beg your pardon, Mr. Sutherland, for calling you, but I am at this moment in a difficulty. I cannot manage this line in Dante's *Inferno*. Do help me."

She moved the book toward him as he came by her side. As he looked at it he was compelled to confess his utter ignorance of Italian.

"Oh, I am disappointed," said Euphra.

"Not so much as I am," replied Hugh. "But could you spare me one or two of your Italian books?"

"With pleasure," she answered, rising and going to her bookshelves.

"I only want a grammar, a dictionary, and a New Testament."

"There they are," she said, taking them down one after the other and bringing them to him. "I dare say you will soon be past poor, stupid me."

"I shall do my best to get within hearing of your voice at least, which in Italian must be lovely."

There was no reply, but a sudden droop of her head.

"But," continued Hugh, "let me hear you read a little first . . . just give me one lesson in pronunciation."

"With all my heart!"

Euphra began and read delightfully, for she was an excellent Italian scholar. It was necessary that Hugh should look over the book. This was difficult while he remained standing. Gradually, therefore, he settled into a chair by her side. Half an hour went by like a minute as he listened to the silvery tones of her voice, breaking into a bell-like sound on the double consonants of that sweet lady-tongue. Then it was his turn to read and be corrected, and read again and be corrected again. Another half hour glided away, and yet another.

It must be confessed that he made good use of the time, for at the end of it he could pronounce Italian very tolerably.

Suddenly he came to himself and looked up as if from a dream. Had she been bewitching him? He was in Euphra's room—alone with her. And the door was shut—how or when he couldn't remember. And—he looked at his watch—poor little Harry had been waiting his return from the library for the last hour and a half. He was conscience-stricken. He gathered up the books hastily, thanked Euphra in the same hurried manner, and left the room, closing the door very gently, almost guiltily, behind him.

I am afraid that Euphra had been perfectly aware that he knew nothing about Italian. Did she see her own eyes shine in the mirror as he closed the door? Was she in love with him?

When Hugh returned with the Italian books, instead of the encyclopedia he had gone to seek, he found Harry sitting where he had left him, with his arms and head on the table, fast asleep.

Poor boy, said Hugh to himself. But he could not help feeling glad he was asleep. He stole out of the room again, passed the fatal door with a longing pain, found the volume of his quest in the library, and returned with it. He sat down beside Harry till he awoke.

When he did awake at last, it was nearly time for lunch. The shamefaced boy was penitent, but Hugh reassured him. "It was my fault, Harry. I stayed away too long. You were so nicely asleep I did not want to wake you. You will now not need a siesta." He was ashamed of himself as he uttered the less-than-honest words to the truehearted child. But this, alas, was not the end of it.

Desirous of learning the language, but far more desirous of commending himself to Euphra, Hugh began in downright earnest, while Harry was left to his own resources. In itself there was no harm in this. Hugh had a right to part of every day for his own uses. But up till then he had been with Harry almost every evening, and the boy missed him very much, for he was not yet self-dependent. So he took refuge in the library, and some of the old books began once more to exercise their former dreary fascination upon him. At length, bored and lonely, he crept to Hugh's room and received an invitation to enter. But Hugh was so absorbed in the first day of his new study that he hardly took notice of him, and Harry found it almost as dreary there as in the library. He would have gone out, but a drizzling rain was falling, and he shrank into himself at the thought of the Ghost's Walk. The dinner bell was a welcome summons.

Hugh, inspired by the close presence of Euphra and the desire to make himself generally agreeable, talked almost brilliantly, delighting Euphra, overcoming Harry, and even interesting slow Mr. Arnold with whom he was gradually becoming a favorite.

Hugh pursued his Italian studies with a singleness of aim and effort that carried him on rapidly. He asked no assistance from Euphra and said nothing to her about his progress. But he was so absorbed in it that it drew him still further from his pupil. Of course he went out with him, walking or riding every day the weather would permit; and he had regular school hours with him indoors. But during the latter, while Harry was doing something on his slate, or writing, or learning some lessons, Hugh would take up his Italian. And notwithstanding Harry's quiet hints that he had finished what had been set before him, remained buried in it for long periods of time. When he woke at last to the necessity of taking some notice of the boy, he would only appoint him something else to occupy him again, so as to leave himself free to follow his new bent.

Now and then he would become aware of his blamable neglect and make a feeble struggle to rectify what seemed to be growing into a habit, and one of the worst for a tutor. But he gradually sank back into the mire, for mire it was, comforting himself with the resolution that as soon as he was able to read Italian he would let Euphra see what progress he had made; then he would return with renewed energy to Harry's education.

At the end of a fortnight he thought he might venture to request Euphra to show him the passage which had perplexed her. This time he knew where she was—in her own room. For his mind had begun to haunt her whereabouts. He knocked at her door, heard the silvery, thrilling, happy sound, "Come in," and entered trembling.

"Would you show me the passage in Dante that perplexed you the other day?"

Euphra looked a little surprised but got the book and pointed it out at once.

Hugh glanced at it. His superior acquaintance with the general forms of language enabled him, after finding two words in Euphra's larger dictionary, to explain it to her immediate satisfaction.

"You astonish me," said Euphra.

"Latin gives me an advantage, you see," said Hugh modestly.

‘‘It seems to me very wonderful, nevertheless.’’ These were sweet words to Hugh’s ear. He had gained his end. And she hers.

‘‘Well,’’ she said, ‘‘I have come upon another passage that perplexes me greatly. Will you try your powers upon that for me?’’ So saying, she proceeded to find it.

‘‘It is schooltime,’’ said Hugh. ‘‘I fear I must not wait now.’’

‘‘Don’t make such a strict schoolmaster of yourself. You know you are here more as a guardian—big brother, you know—to the dear child. I am, in fact, afraid you are working him a little too hard at his studies.’’

‘‘Do you think so?’’ returned Hugh, quite willing to be convinced.

‘‘This is the passage,’’ said Euphra.

Hugh sat down, once more at the table beside her. He found this morsel considerably tougher than the last. But at length he succeeded in pulling it to pieces and reconstructing it in a simpler form for the lady. She was full of thanks and admiration. Naturally enough they went on to the next line, and the next stanza, and the next, and the next. Euphra knew a great many more words than Hugh, so that with her knowledge of the words and his insight into the construction, they made rapid progress.

‘‘What a beautiful passage it is,’’ said Euphra.

‘‘It is indeed,’’ responded Hugh. ‘‘I never have read anything more beautiful.’’

‘‘I wonder if it would be possible to turn that into English. I should like to try.’’

‘‘You mean in verse?’’

‘‘To be sure.’’

‘‘Let us try then. I will bring you mine when I have finished it. I fear it will take some time, though, to do it well. Shall it be blank verse or what?’’

‘‘Oh, don’t you think we should keep the rhyming pattern of the original?’’

‘‘It will add much to the difficulty.’’

‘‘Cowardly knight,’’ teased Euphra playfully, ‘‘will you shrink from following where your lady leads?’’

‘‘Never, so help me my good pen!’’ answered Hugh, and took his departure with a trembling in his heart. Alas, the morning was gone. Harry was not in his study. He sought and found him in the library, buried in an old book he could not possibly understand.

‘‘I am so glad you have come,’’ said Harry. ‘‘I am so tired.’’

‘‘Why do you read that stupid book then?’’

‘‘I don’t know—I wanted to try it.’’

‘‘Nonsense! Put it away,’’ said Hugh, his dissatisfaction with himself making him cross with Harry, who in consequence felt ten times more desolate than before. He could not understand the change.

If it went poorly before, it went worse now. Hugh seized every gap of time, and widened their margins shamefully, in order to work at his translation. He found it very difficult. But he would not back down. The thought of her praise, and of the yet better favor he might gain, spurred him on. And Harry was the sacrifice. But he would make it all up to him when this was once over. Indeed he would.

The boy's spirit sank; but Hugh did not, or would not, see it. His step grew less elastic. He became more listless, more like his former self—sauntering about with his hands in his pockets. And Hugh, of course, found himself caring less and less about him; for the thought of him, rousing as it did the sense of his own neglect, had become troublesome. Sometimes he even passed poor Harry without speaking to him.

Gradually, however, he grew still further into the favor of Mr. Arnold, who would go out riding with them sometimes and express great satisfaction for the way Harry sat his pony, for which he accorded Hugh the credit. Mr. Arnold was a good horseman, and his praise was always grateful to Hugh, because Euphra was always near and always heard it. I fear, however, that his progess in the good graces of Mr. Arnold was the result of the greater anxiety to please, which sprang from the consciousness of not deserving approbation. Pleasing is an easy substitute for well-doing. Not acceptable to himself, he had the greater desire to be acceptable to others, and so reflect the side-beams of a false approbation on himself. The necessity to Hugh's nature of feeling right drove him to this false mode of producing the false impression. If one only wants to feel virtuous, there are several roads to that end.

The reaction in Hugh's mind was sometimes torturing enough. But he had not strength to resist Euphra and so reform.

Well or ill done, his translation at length was finished. So was Euphra's. They exchanged papers for a private reading first and arranged to meet afterward in order to compare criticisms.

19 / Alone at Midnight

One morning at breakfast, the mail having just been brought in, Mr. Arnold opened the post bag and found, among other letters, one in an old-fashioned, female hand, which, after reading, he passed to Euphra.

"You remember Mrs. Elton, Euphra, from up north?"

"Quite well, Uncle—a dear old lady."

But the expression which passed across her face seemed rather to Hugh to say, *I hope she is not going to bore us again.*

Euphra read the letter, after which Mr. Arnold said, "Poor, dear girl. You must try to make her as comfortable as you can. There is consumption in the family, you see."

"Of course I will, Uncle," she said. But as she spoke, an irrepressible flash of displeasure broke from her eyes and then vanished. Mr. Arnold rose from the table and left the room. As soon as he was gone, Euphra gave the letter to Hugh. He read:

My Dear Mr. Arnold:

Would you be so kind as to extend the hospitality of your beautiful house to me and my young friend, who has the honor of being your relative, Lady Emily Lake? For some time her health has been failing, and it is considered desirable that she have some change in climate. Remembering the charming month I passed at your house and recalling that Lady Emily is cousin only once removed from your late, most lovely wife, I hope there to be no impropriety in writing to ask you whether you could, without inconvenience, receive us as your guests for a short time.

We shall bring only our two lady's maids (mine whom I've had only for a short time, acquired while visiting a mutual friend we share not far from here) and a steady old manservant who has been in my family for many years.

I trust you will not hesitate to refuse my request should I happen to have made it at an inopportune time. In all events, I trust you will excuse what seems—now that I have committed it to paper—a great liberty.

I am, my dear Mr. Arnold,

Yours most sincerely,
Hannah Elton

Hugh refolded the letter and laid it down. Harry had left the room.

"Isn't it a bore?" inquired Euphra.

Hugh answered only by a look. A pause followed. ''Who is Mrs. Elton?'' he said at last.

''Oh, a good-hearted creature enough. But, frightfully dull,'' she added.

''And what sort of person is Lady Emily?''

''I have never seen her. Some blue-eyed milkmaid with a title, I suppose. And in consumption too! I presume the dear girl is as religious as the old one . . . Good heavens! What shall we do?'' she burst out at length.

''Dear Euphra,'' Hugh ventured to say, ''never mind. Let us try to make the best of it.''

She turned toward him, smiled as if ashamed and delighted at the same moment, then rose and slid out of the room.

That morning he sought her again in her room. They talked over their versions of Dante. Hugh's was certainly the better. But at the same time there were individual lines and passages in hers which he considered better than any part of his version. This he was delighted to say, and she seemed just as pleased that he should think so. A great part of the morning was thus spent.

''I cannot stay longer,'' said Hugh.

''Let us read together, then, after we come upstairs tonight.''

''With more pleasure than I dare to say,'' replied Hugh.

''But you mean what you do say?'' she asked.

''You can doubt it no more than myself.''

Yet Hugh did not like Euphra's making the proposal. Neither did he like the flippant, almost cruel way in which she referred to Lady Emily's illness. But he put it down to annoyance, got over it somehow, and began to feel that even if she were a devil, he could not help loving her and would not help it if he could. The hope of meeting her alone that night gave him spirit and energy with Harry, and the poor boy was more cheery and active than he had been for some time.

In the course of the day Euphra took an opportunity of whispering to him, ''Not in my room—in the library.''

After dinner that evening Hugh did not go to the drawing room with Mr. Arnold, but out into the woods about the house. It was early in the twilight. The month was June, and the sun set late. Strange to tell, at that moment, instead of the hushed gloom of the library toward which his soul was leaning, there arose before him the vision of the bare, stern pine wood, with the chilly wind of a northern spring morning blowing through it. And beneath a lofty, gaunt, and huge fir tree, there was Margaret sitting on one of its twisted roots, the very image of peace.

The vision came and passed, for he did not invite its stay; it rebuked him to the deepest soul. He strayed in troubled pleasure, restless and dissatisfied. No peace was resting on his face—only a false mask, at best. Had he been doing his duty to Harry, his love for Euphra, however unworthy she might be, would not have troubled him thus.

He came upon an avenue. At the farther end the boughs of the old trees met in a perfect pointed arch. A kind of holy calm fell upon him as he regarded the dim, dying colors of the sunset through the trees, while the spirit of the night sank into his soul and made a moment of summer twilight there. He walked along the avenue for some distance and then passed on through the woods. Suddenly it flashed upon him that he had crossed the Ghost's Walk. A slight cold shudder passed through the region of his heart. Then he laughed at himself and turned to cross it once again, in spite of his tremor.

He went to his own study, where he remained till the hour had nearly arrived. He tried to write some verses but found the attempt useless. At length he rose, much too preoccupied, and went to the library. There he seated himself and tried to read. But it was scarcely even an attempt, for every moment he was looking up to the door by which he expected her to enter.

Suddenly an increase of light warned him that she was in the room. How she had entered he could not tell. One hand carried her candle, the light of which fell on her pale face, the other was busy trying to secure a stray lock of hair which had escaped its coiffure.

"Let it alone," said Hugh. "It's beautiful."

But she gently repelled the hand he raised to hers and persisted in confining the hair, then seated herself at the table. Again they went over their work, their faces almost meeting as they followed the lines, sitting close beside one another. They had just finished and were about to commence reading from the original when Hugh, who missed a sheet of Euphra's translation, stooped under the table to look for it. He discovered her foot to be upon it. He asked her to move a little but received no reply. Looking up he saw that she was either asleep or in a faint. By an impulse he went to the windows and drew the green blinds. When he turned to her again, she was reviving.

"How stupid of me to go to sleep," she said. "Let us go on with our reading."

They had read for about half an hour when they were suddenly startled by three taps upon a window—slight but peculiar. Hugh turned at once toward the windows, but of course could see nothing, having just lowered the blinds. He turned again toward Euphra. She had a strange, wild look; her lips were slightly parted and her nostrils wide; her face was rigid and pale.

"What was it?" said Hugh. But she made no answer and continued staring toward one of the windows.

He rose and was about to advance to it when she caught him by the hand with a grasp of hers, of which she would have been incapable except under the influence of terror. At that moment, a clock in the room began to strike. It was a slow clock and went on deliberately, striking one . . . two . . . three . . . till it had struck twelve. Every stroke was a blow from the hammer of fear, and his heart was the bell. Hugh could not breathe for dread so long as the clock was striking. When it had ended they looked at each other again, and Hugh's breath escaped.

"Euphra!" he sighed. But she made no answer. She turned her eyes again to one of the windows. They were both standing. He sought to draw her to him, but she yielded no more than a marble statue.

"I crossed the Ghost's Walk tonight," he said in a hard whisper, scarcely knowing that he uttered it till he heard his own words. They seemed to fall upon his ear as if spoken by someone outside the room. She looked at him once more and kept looking with a fixed stare. Gradually her face became less rigid and her eyes less wild. She could move at last.

"Come, come," she said in a hurried whisper. "Let us go—no, no, not that way"—as Hugh would have led her toward the private stair—"let us go the front way, by the oak staircase."

They went up together. When they reached the door of her room, she said "Good night" without even looking at him and went in. Hugh went on, in a state of utter bewilderment, to his own apartment; he shut the door and locked it—something he had never done before. Then he lit both candles on his table and walked up and down the room, trying, like one aware that he is dreaming, to come to his real self.

"Pshaw!" he said aloud at last. "It was only a little bird or large moth. How can simple darkness make such a fool of me!"

As he said this in his mind, he went to one of the windows of his sitting room, which was nearly over the library, and looked into the wood.

Could it be?

Yes—he *did* see something white, gliding through the wood, away in the direction of the Ghost's Walk. It vanished, and he saw it no more.

The morning was far advanced before he could go to bed. Though troubled by fear's short reign, at length Hugh slept.

When he awoke, he found it so late that it was all he could do to get down in time for breakfast. Euphra was there before him. She greeted him in the usual way, quite circumspectly. But she looked troubled—her face was very pale and her eyes were red. When her uncle entered, she addressed him with more gaiety than usual, and he did not perceive anything amiss. But the whole of that day she walked as in a reverie, avoiding Hugh two or three times. As to the gliding phantom of the previous night, the day denied it all, telling him it was but the coinage of his own overwrought brain.

Although fear in some measure returned with the returning shadows, he yet resolved to try to get Euphra to meet him again in the library that night. But she never gave him a chance of even dropping a hint to that purpose. He could not help seeing she did not intend to let him speak to her. He could not understand her and was more bewitched, more fascinated than ever by seeing her through the folds of the incomprehensible, in which element she had wrapped herself. When they parted for the night, she shook hands with him with a cool frankness that put him nearly beside himself with despair. When he found himself in his own room, it was some time before he could collect his thoughts. Having succeeded, however, he resolved, in spite of growing fears, to go to the library and see whether it were not possible she might be there. He took up a candle and went down the back stair. But when he opened the library door, a gust of wind blew his candle out and all was suddenly dark inside. A horror seized him and, afraid of yielding to the inclination to bound back up the stair lest he should go wild with the terror of pursuit, he crept slowly back, feeling his way to his own room with a determined and steady pace. Had the library window been left open?

The next day, and the next and the next, he fared no better. Euphra's behavior continued the same, and she allowed him no opportunity of requesting an explanation.

20 / The Storm

At length, the expected visitors arrived. Hugh saw nothing of them until they assembled for dinner. Mrs. Elton was a benevolent elderly lady—not old enough to give in to being old. Rather tall and stout, her kindly gray eyes looked out from a calm face which seemed to have taken comfort from loving everybody in a mild and moderate fashion. Lady Emily was a slender girl, rather shy, with fair hair and a pale, innocent face. Mrs. Elton was solicitously attentive to her, and she received it all sweetly and gratefully, taking no offense at being treated as more of an invalid than she was. She ate nothing but chicken, custard pudding, or rice all the time she was at Arnstead.

"What sort of clergyman have you now, Mr. Arnold?" asked Mrs. Elton at the dinner table.

"Oh, a very respectable young gentleman."

"You know, Lady Emily and I"—here she looked at Lady Emily, who smiled and blushed faintly—"are very dependent on our Sundays, and—"

"We all go to church regularly, I assure you, Mrs. Elton; and of course my carriage shall always be at your disposal."

"I was in no doubt about either of those things, indeed, Mr. Arnold. But what sort of preacher is he?"

"He is quite a respectable preacher as well as a clergyman. He is an honor to the cloth."

"I am afraid you will not find him very original though," said Hugh, wishing to contribute to the conversation.

"Original!" interposed Mr. Arnold. "How is a man to be original on a subject that is all laid down in plain print?"

"Very true, Mr. Arnold," responded Mrs. Elton. "We don't want originality, do we? It is only the gospel we want. Does he preach the gospel?"

"How can he preach anything else? His text is always out of some part of the Bible."

The conversation veered into a discussion of the inspiration of the Scriptures, after which, dinner over, the ceremony of tea was observed.

The next day was Sunday, and the morning was spent in church. At luncheon Lady Emily was forced to confess that she had not been much interested in the sermon. Mrs. Elton thought he had spoken plainly enough, but there was not much of the gospel in it. Mr. Arnold let his opinions flow freely, after which the conversation flagged noticeably, and the visitors withdrew to their respective rooms to comfort themselves with their private devotions.

The next day, and during the whole week, Mr. Arnold did all he could devise for the entertainment of the two ladies. There were daily rides in the open carriage, in which he always accompanied them to show them his estate. Euphra always made one of the party, and it was dreary indeed for Hugh to be left in the desolate house without her. But when she was at home, she still never permitted him to speak to her alone.

There might have been some hope for Harry in Hugh's separation from Euphra. But the result was that although he spent school hours more regularly with him, Hugh was yet more dull and uninterested in the work than he had been before. Instead of caring that his pupil should understand this or that particular, he would be speculating on Euphra's whereabouts. Meanwhile, Harry would be stupefying himself with work which he could not understand for lack of some explanation that ought to have been given him weeks ago. Still, however, Harry clung to Hugh with a worshipping love, never suspecting that the latter could be to blame. When Hugh would be wandering about the place seeking to catch a glimpse of the skirt of Euphra's dress as she went about with her guests, Harry would be following him at a distance, like a little dog that had lost its master and did not know whether this man would be friendly or not—not spying on his actions but merely longing to be with him. If Hugh could have once seen into that warm, true, pining little heart, he would not have neglected it as he did. He had no eyes, however, but for Euphra.

Still, it may have been that even then Harry was able to gather, though with tears, some advantage from Hugh's neglect. Nature found some channels, worn by his grief, through which her comforts might gently flow into him with their sympathetic soothing. Often he would creep away to the nest which Hugh had built. Seated there in the solitude of the wide-bourgeoned oak, he would sometimes feel for a moment as if lifted above the world and its sorrows, to be visited by an all-healing wind from God coming to him through the wilderness of leaves about him.

While Harry took to wandering abroad in the afternoon sun, Hugh on the other hand found the bright weather so distasteful that he generally trifled away his afternoons with some old romance in the dark library, or listlessly lay on his couch in his study. He could neither read nor write. What he felt he absolutely must do he did—but nothing more.

One day about noon the weather began to change. In the afternoon it grew dark, and Hugh, going to the window, perceived that a great thunderstorm was at hand. Harry was rather frightened, but under his fear lay a great delight. The storm came nearer and nearer, until at last a vivid flash broke from the mass of darkness over the woods, lasted for one brilliant moment, and vanished. The thunder followed, like a pursuing wild beast, close on the traces of the vanishing light. Without the usual prelude of a few great drops, the rain poured at once. Harry had crept close to Hugh, who stood looking out of the window; and as if the convulsion of the elements had begun to clear the atmosphere both within as well as without, Hugh looked down on the boy kindly and put his arm round his shoulder. Harry nestled closer and wished it would thunder forever.

But longing to hear his tutor's voice, he ventured to speak, looking up in his face. ''Euphra says it is only electricity, Mr. Sutherland. What is that?''

But before Hugh could make any reply, a flash, almost invisible from excess of light, was accompanied rather than followed by a roar that made the house shake. In a moment the room was filled with the terrified household, which by an unreasoning impulse, rushed to the neighborhood of him who was considered strongest. Mr. Arnold was not home.

''Come away from the window instantly, Mr. Sutherland. How can you be so imprudent?'' cried Mrs. Elton, her usually calm voice elevated in command, but tremulous with fear.

''Why, Mrs. Elton,'' asked Hugh, ''do you think the devil makes the thunder?''

Lady Emily gave a faint shriek, whether out of reverence for the devil or fear of God I hesitate to decide; and flitting out of the room she dived into her bed and drew the clothes over her head. Euphra walked up to the window beside Hugh, as if to show her approval of his rudeness, and stood looking out with eyes that filled their own night with little flashes, though her lips were pale and quivered a little. Mrs. Elton, confounded at Hugh's reply and perhaps fearing the house might in consequence share the fate of Sodom, notwithstanding the presence of a godly portion of the righteous, fled, accompained by the housekeeper, to the wine cellar. The rest of the household crept into various corners.

But there was one in the house, one whom Hugh had not yet seen, who, left alone, threw the window wide open and with gently clasped hands and calm countenance looked up into the heavens. The clearness of this one's eye seemed the prophetic symbol of the clearness that rose above the wild turmoil of the earthly storm.

Truly God was in the storm. But there was more of God in the clear heaven beyond, and yet more of him in the eye that regarded the whole with a still joy.

Euphra, Hugh, and Harry were left together looking out upon the storm. Hugh could not speak his heart in Harry's presence. At length the boy sat down in a dark corner on the floor, concealed from the others by a window curtain. Hugh thought he had left the room.

"Euphra," he began.

Euphra looked around for Harry and though not seeing him, glided away without making any answer to Hugh's invocation.

He stood for a few moments in motionless despair; then glancing round the room, caught up his hat and rushed out into the storm. It was the best relief his feelings could have had; for the sullen gloom, alternated with sudden bursts of flame and wailing blasts of tyrannous wind, gave him his own mood to walk in and met his spirit with its own element. His spirit flashed in the lightning, raved in the thunder, moaned in the wind, and wept in the rain.

But this could not last long, either without or within him.

He came to himself in the woods. How far he had wandered, or where he was, he did not know. The storm had died away, and all that remained was the wind and the rain. The treetops swayed wildly in the irregular blasts. It was evening, but what hour of the evening he could not tell. He was wet to the skin, but that to a young Scotsman is nothing.

He had no intention of returning home for some time and meant especially to avoid the dinner table—for in the mood he was, that seemed more than he could endure. So looking all about him and finding where the wood seemed thinnest, he went in that direction and soon found himself on the high road, within a quarter mile of the country town next to Arnstead—about three miles away. This little town he knew pretty well and, beginning to feel exhausted, resolved to go to an inn there, dry his clothes, then walk back in the moonlight; for he felt quite sure the storm would be over in an hour or so. The fatigue he now felt was proof enough that the inward storm had, for the time, spent itself, and now he wished very much for something to eat and drink.

He was soon seated by a blazing fire with a chop and a jug of ale before him.

21 / Meetings

The inn possessed a room of considerable size in which the farmers of the neighborhood were accustomed to hold their gatherings. While eating his dinner, Hugh learned from the conversation around him that this room was being readied for a lecture on hypnotism. Signs had been posted all over the town, and before he had finished his dinner the audience had begun to arrive. Partly from curiosity about a subject of which he knew nothing, and partly because it was still raining, Hugh resolved to be one of them. So he stood by the fire until he was informed that the lecturer had made his appearance. He then went upstairs, paid his shilling, and was admitted.

Scarcely even the hint of a theory showed itself in the mass of what the little, thickset man called facts and scientific truths. The lecturer depended chiefly for his success upon the manifestation of his art upon his consort, whom he proceeded to bring forward—a pale-faced, dull-looking youth who scrambled upon the platform beside his master. Upon this tutored slave a number of experiments were performed. But, aware that all this was open to the objection of collusion, the operator next invited any of the company to submit themselves to his influences. After a pause of a few moments, a stout country fellow, florid and healthy, got up and slouched to the platform. But in this case, as with the former, the operator was eminently successful, and the clown returned to his seat, looking remarkably foolish. Several others volunteered their services, but with none of them did he succeed so well.

"The blundering idiot," growled a voice close to Hugh's ear, in a foreign accent, as the proceedings developed.

He looked around sharply.

A tall, powerful, and eminently handsome man, with his face as foreign as his tone and accent, sat beside him.

"I beg your pardon," he said to Hugh. "I was thinking aloud."

"I should like to know," said Hugh quietly, "why you consider him a blunderer. I am quite ignorant of these matters."

"I have had many opportunities of observing them, and I see at once that this man, though he has some of the natural power, is excessively ignorant of the whole subject."

The brief conversation ended, Hugh once more fixed his attention on what was going on. But presently he became aware that the foreigner was scrutinizing him with the closest attention. He knew this, somehow, without having looked around. He could feel his stare, and the knowledge was accompanied with a feeling of discomfort that caused him to make a restless movement on his seat. Presently he felt that the annoyance had ceased; but not many minutes had passed before it again commenced. In order to relieve himself, he turned toward his neighbor so suddenly that it caught him off guard.

But the stranger recovered himself instantly with the question, "Will you permit me to ask what country you are from?"

Hugh thought he had made the request only to cover his rudeness, and so merely answered, "Why, an Englishman, of course."

"Yes, it is not necessary to be told that. But it seems to me, from your accent, that you are a Scotsman."

"So I am."

"A Highlander?"

"I was born in the Highlands. But if you want to know my pedigree, I am by birth half a Scotsman and half a Welchman."

The foreigner riveted his gaze once more upon Hugh, but for the briefest moment, and then with a slight bow of acquiescence, turned toward the lecturer.

When the meeting was over and Hugh was walking away in the midst of the withdrawing crowd, the stranger touched him on the shoulder.

"You said you would like to know more of this science. Will you come to my lodging?" he said.

"Certainly," said Hugh, though the look accompanying the words was one of surprise.

"You are astonished that a stranger should invite you. You English always demand an introduction. Here is mine."

He handed Hugh a card with only his name inscribed—*Herr von Fenkelstein*. Hugh provided him one of his in exchange.

The two walked out of the inn and through the town's irregular streets until they came to a court, down which Herr von Fenkelstein led the way. He let himself in with a key at a low door and then conducted Hugh up a narrow stair and into a modest room. The German—for such he seemed to Hugh—offered him a chair in the politest manner, and Hugh sat down.

"I am only in lodgings here," said the host, "so you will forgive the poverty of my establishment."

"There is no occasion, I assure you," answered Hugh.

"You wished to know something of the subject with which that lecturer was befooling himself and the audience at the same time."

"I shall be grateful for any enlightenment," said Hugh.

Von Fenkelstein began with generalities and commonplaces and for some time gave no sign of coming either to an end or to the point. All the time he was watching Hugh—or so Hugh thought—as if speculating on him in general. Then appearing to have come to some conclusion, he gave his mind more to his talk and encouraged Hugh to speak. The conversation lasted for nearly half an hour. At its close, though the stranger had touched upon a variety of interesting subjects, Hugh did not feel that he had gained any insight. During the course of the talk, his eyes had appeared to rest on Hugh with a kind of compulsion.

"Will you take a glass of—?"

"Of nothing, thank you," interrupted Hugh. "It is time for me to be going. Indeed, I fear I have stayed too long already. Good night."

"You will allow me the honor of returning your visit?"

Hugh felt he could do no less, although he had not the slightest desire to keep up the acquaintance. He wrote *Arnstead* on his card.

The next day Hugh was determined to find or make an opportunity of speaking to Euphra. She had that morning allowed the ladies and her uncle to go without her, and Hugh met her as he went to his study.

"May I speak with you for one moment?" he said hurriedly and with trembling lips.

"Yes, certainly," she replied, with a smile, and a glance in his face as of wonder to what could trouble him so much. Then turning and leading the way, she said, "Come into my room."

He followed her. She turned and shut the door which he had left open behind him.

"Euphra," he said, "what have I done to offend you?"

"Offend me! Nothing." Her tone was one of perfect surprise.

"How is it that you avoid me as you do and will not allow me one moment with you? You are driving me mad."

"Why, you foolish man!" she answered half playfully, pressing the palms of her hands together and looking up on his face. "How can I? Don't you see how those two dear old ladies swallow me up in their faddles? Oh dear, oh dear, I wish they would go! Then it would be all right again—wouldn't it?"

But Hugh was not to be so easily satisfied.

"Before they came, ever since that night—"

"Hush-sh," she interrupted, putting her finger on his lips, and looking round her with an air of fright which he could hardly tell whether was real or assumed.

Comforted wondrously by the hushing finger, Hugh would yet understand more.

"I am no child, dear Euphra," he said, taking hold of the hand to which the finger belonged and laying it on his mouth. "Do not make one of me. There is some mystery in all this—at least something I do not understand."

"I will tell you about it one day. But you must be careful how you behave to me. For if my uncle should for one moment entertain a suspicion . . . well, good-bye to you. All my influence with him comes from his thinking I like him better than anybody else. So you must not make him jealous. By the way," she went on, turning the current of the conversation, "what a favorite you have grown with him. You should hear him talk of you to the ladies. I might well be jealous of you. There never was a tutor like his!"

Hugh's heart smote him that the praise of this common man should be so undeserved. He was troubled too at the flippancy with which Euphra spoke. Yet not the less did he feel that he loved her passionately.

"But I must go," Euphra went on. "Bring your Italian to—to—" She hesitated.

"To the library. . . ?" suggested Hugh.

"No-o," she answered, looking quite solemn.

"Well, will you come to my study?"

"Yes, I will," she answered with a definitive tone.

She opened the door, and having looked out to see that no one was passing, told him to go. As he went he felt as if the oaken floor were elastic beneath his feet.

It was some time after the household had retired before Euphra made her appearance at the door of his study. She seemed rather shy of entering, and hesitated as if she felt she was doing something she ought not to do. But as soon as she had entered and the door was shut, she appeared to recover herself, and they sat down at the table with their books. They could not get on very well with their reading, however. Hugh often forgot what he was about in looking at her; and she did not seem inclined to avert his gazes or to check the growth of his admiration.

Rather abruptly, but apparently starting from some suggestion in the book, she said to him, "By the way, has Mr. Arnold ever said anything to you about the family jewels?"

"No," said Hugh. "Are there many?"

"Yes, a great many. Mr. Arnold is very proud of them, as well as of the portraits. So he treats them in the same way—keeps them locked up. Indeed, he seldom allows them to see daylight, except it be as a mark of special favor to someone."

"I should much like to see them. I have always been curious about stones."

Euphra gave him a very peculiar, searching glance as he spoke, but then it vanished as quickly as it had come.

"But what could have led me to talk about the jewels?" she said. "—Oh, I see. What a strange thing is the association of ideas."

She looked down again at the passage they had been reading.

"There is not a very obvious connection here, is there?" she said.

"No, but one cannot account for such things. The links in the chain of ideas are sometimes slender; yet the slenderest is sufficient to enable the electric flash of thought to pass along the line."

She seemed pondering for a moment.

"That strikes me as a fine simile," she said. "You ought to be a poet yourself."

Hugh made no reply.

"I dare say you have hundreds of poems in that old desk there?"

"I think they might be counted by tens."

"Do let me see them."

"You wouldn't care for them."

"Wouldn't I, Hugh?"

"I will, on one condition—two conditions, I mean."

"What are they?"

"One is that you show me yours."

"Mine?"

"Yes."

"Who told you I wrote verses? That silly boy?"

"No. I saw your verses before I saw you. Do you remember?"

"It was very dishonorable of you to read them."

"I only saw they were verses. I did not read a word."

"I forgive you then. But you must show me yours first, till I see whether I could venture to let you see mine. If yours were very bad indeed, then I might risk showing mine."

"I said two conditions."

"And the second?" asked Euphra, half suspecting and looking him full in the face.

"A kiss," said Hugh. But as he spoke the words he could not return her gaze.

Euphra did not reply at once, then said simply, "Let me see your poems then, Hugh."

He rose and took from the old escritoire a bundle of papers and handed them to Euphra. However, in getting these papers, Hugh had to open a concealed portion of the cabinet which his mathematical knowledge had enabled him to discover. It had evidently not been opened for many years before he had found it. He had made use of it to hold the only treasures he had—his writings.

When Euphra saw him open this place, she uttered a suppressed cry of astonishment.

"Ah," said Hugh, "you did not know of this hidden drawer, did you?"

"Indeed, I did not. I had used the desk myself, for this was a favorite room of mine before you came. But I never found that. Let me look!''

She put her hand on his shoulder and leaned over him as he pointed out the way of opening it.

''Did you find nothing in it?'' she asked with a slight tremor in her voice.

''Nothing whatever.''

''There may be more such places.''

''No. I have accounted for the whole bulk, I believe.''

''How strange!''

''But now you must give me my reward,'' Hugh reminded her timidly.

She turned her face toward him. He approached her slowly, trembling with mingled terror and ecstasy.

Suddenly three distinct knocks were heard on the window. They sprang apart and saw each other's face pale as death. Hugh leaped to the window, but could see nothing but the trees. Turning again toward Euphra, he found to his mortification that she had vanished and had left the bundle of poems behind her.

He replaced them in their old quarters in the escritoire, and his vague dismay at the unaccountable noises was drowned in the bitter waters of miserable humiliation. He slept at last from the exhaustion of disappointment.

He was generally the first in the breakfast room—that is, after Euphra, who was always the first. She went up to him as he entered the next morning and said, almost in a whisper, ''Have you got the poems for me?''

Hugh hesitated.

''No,'' he said. ''I thought you didn't want them.''

''That it very unkind when you know I was only frightened out of my wits.''

''They are not worth giving you.''

''I have a right to them,'' she said, looking up at him slyly and shyly.

''You shall have them then, or anything else I have—the brain that made them, if you like.''

''Was it only the brain that had to do with the making of them?''

''Perhaps the heart too, but you have that already.''

Her face flushed like a damask rose.

At that moment, Mrs. Elton entered and looked a little surprised. Euphra instantly said, ''I think it is rather too bad of you, Mr. Sutherland, to keep the boy so hard at his work when you know he is not strong. Mrs. Elton, I have been begging a holiday for poor Harry.''

The flush, which she could not get rid of all at once, was thus made to do duty as one of displeasure. Mrs. Elton was thoroughly deceived and united her entreaties to those of Miss Cameron. Hugh was compelled to join in the deception, and to pretend to yield a slow consent.

Thus a day off was extemporized for Harry, subject to the approval of his father. This was readily granted; and Mr. Arnold, turning to Hugh, said, "You will have nothing to do, Mr. Sutherland. Had you not better join us?"

"With pleasure," he replied, "but the carriage will be full."

"You can take your horse."

"Thank you very much. I will."

The day was delightful, one of those gray summer days that are far better for an excursion than bright ones. In the best of spirits, riding alongside the lady who was everything to him and who would contrive to throw him a glance now and then, Hugh would have been overflowingly happy but for a quiet, distressed feeling which all the time made him aware of a sick conscience somewhere within. Mr. Arnold was exceedingly pleasant. For he was much taken with the sweetness and modesty of Lady Emily who, having no strong opinions upon anything, received those of Mr. Arnold with attentive submission. On their way home he made, with evident earnestness, entreaties for an extension of their visit to a month, so rapidly did Lady Emily seem to be advancing in his good graces. Euphra gave Hugh one look of misery and then turned again with increased warmth to their immediate consent. It was gained without much difficulty before they were back at Arnstead.

Harry, too, was captivated by the gentle kindness of Lady Emily and hardly took his eyes off her all the way. On the other hand, his delicate little attentions had already gained the heart of good Mrs. Elton, who from the first had noticed and pitied the sad looks of the boy.

22 / Herr von Fenkelstein

As they drew near the house, Hugh saw the distinguished figure of Herr von Fenkelstein approaching them from it. Saluting as they met, the visitor informed Hugh that he had just been leaving his card for him and would call some other morning soon. Then turning to the rest of the party in the carriage, Fenkelstein exclaimed, in a tone of surprise, "What! Do I see Miss Cameron . . . here?" and he advanced with a profound obeisance, holding his hat in his hand.

Hugh thought he saw her look annoyed, but she held out her hand to him, and in a voice indicating some reluctance, introduced him to her uncle with the words: "We met at Sir Edward Laston's when I was visiting Mrs. Elkingham two years ago, Uncle."

The carriage now stopped and its inhabitants proceeded the rest of the way on foot. Ordinary civilities passed, marked by an air of flattering deference on Fenkelstein's part, the new visitor turned as if forgetful of his previous direction and accompanied them toward the house. Before they reached it, he had, even in that short space, ingratiated himself so far with Mr. Arnold that he asked him to stay and dine with them—an invitation which was accepted with manifest pleasure.

"Mr. Sutherland," said Mr. Arnold, "will you show your friend about the place? He has kindly consented to dine with us, and in the meantime I have some letters to write."

"Certainly," answered Hugh.

But all this time he had been inwardly meditating on the appearance of his friend, as Mr. Arnold called him, with the jealousy of a youth in love. For was not Fenkelstein an old acquaintance of Miss Cameron? What might have passed between them in that old hidden time? And he could not help seeing that Fenkelstein was one to win favor in ladies' eyes. Very regular features and a dark complexion were lighted up by eyes as black as Euphra's and capable of a wonderful play of light, while his form was remarkable for strength and symmetry. Hugh felt that in any company he would attract immediate attention. His long, dark beard, of which just the center was removed to expose a finely turned chin, blew over each shoulder as often as they met the wind in going round the house. He had just enough of the foreign in his dress to add to the appearance of fashion which it bore.

As they walked about the precincts of the house, Fenkelstein asked many questions of Hugh, which his entire ignorance of domestic architecture made impossible for him to answer. This seemed only to excite the questioner's desire for information to a higher pitch, and, as if the very stones could reply to his demands, he examined the whole range of the various buildings constituting the estate of Arnstead.

"This they call the Ghost's Walk," said Hugh off-handedly, as they approached the ancient avenue of trees.

"Ah, about these old houses there are always such tales. Germany is prolific with such stories."

"But surely you don't believe those things?"

"To me it is equal. And, confess, don't you like a ghost story?"

"Yes, if it is a good one."

"Hamlet?"

"Ah, but we don't speak of Shakespeare's plays as stories. His characters are too real for that."

"You islanders are always so in earnest about everything."

"I hope you can be in earnest about dinner, then, for I hear the bell."

When they entered the drawing room they found Miss Cameron alone. Fenkelstein advanced and addressed a few words to her in German, with which Hugh's limited acquaintance prevented him from catching. At the same moment, Mr. Arnold entered and Fenkelstein, turning to him immediately, proceeded, as if by way of apology for speaking in an unknown tongue, to interpret.

"I have just been telling Miss Cameron how much better she looks than when I saw her at Sir Edward's."

"I know I was quite a scarecrow then," said Euphra, attempting to laugh.

"And now you are quite a decoy duck, eh, Euphra?" said Mr. Arnold, laughing at his own joke, which put him in great good humor for the whole of dinner. "When did you rise on our Sussex horizon, Herr von Fenkelstein?" he went on.

"Oh, I have been in the neighborhood for a few days, but I owe my meeting with you to the coincidence of meeting Mr. Sutherland the other evening."

Just then dinner was announced. Fenkelstein took Miss Cameron by the arm; Hugh, Mrs. Elton, and Mr. Arnold followed with Lady Emily. Hugh tried to talk with Mrs. Elton, but with meager success. He suddenly felt a nobody. But just as they passed through the dining room door, Euphra looked around at him and, without putting into her face the least expression discernible to any of the others, contrived to banish for the time all Hugh's despair and to convince him that he had nothing to fear from the German intruder.

During dinner, Mrs. Elton was delighted with Fenkelstein's behavior and conversation. Without showing great originality, he yet had seen so much and knew so well how to bring it out that he was a most interesting companion.

"Had you and Mr. Sutherland been old acquaintances then, Herr von Fenkelstein?" asked Mr. Arnold, reverting to the conversation which had been interrupted by the announcement of dinner.

"Not at all. We met quite accidentally. I believe a thunderstorm and a lecture on hypnotism were the mediating parties between us."

"A lecture on what?" interposed Mr. Arnold, who did not like to confess his ignorance on any subject.

A discussion followed, in which Mr. Arnold and Fenkelstein took the greater share until, following dinner, Euphra—her face dreadfully pale—rose to go. This interrupted the course of the talk, and the subject was not resumed. Immediately after tea, which was served very soon, Fenkelstein took his leave of the ladies.

"We shall be glad to see you often while in this neighborhood," said Mr. Arnold as he bade him good night.

"I shall, without fail, do myself the honor of calling again soon," he replied, and bowed himself out.

Repairing to the drawing room where Euphra was recovering her complexion, Lady Emily first, followed by Euphra, each sang a selection from Handel. As the day had already been full, the guests and their hosts soon retired.

Later in his room, Hugh heard a tap on his door which made him start with the suggestion of the former mysterious noises about the house. He sprang to the door. But instead of looking out on a vacant hall as he expected, he saw Euphra standing there in the dark.

In a whisper she said, "Do you no longer love me because Lady Emily can sing psalms better than I can?"

Not replying to her question, he said, "Come in, Euphra."

"No—no, I shouldn't have come."

"Do come in. I want you to tell me something about Fenkelstein."

"What do you want to know about him? You're not jealous—?"

"I only want to know what he is."

"Oh, some twentieth cousin of mine."

"Does Mr. Arnold know that?"

"No. It's so far off I can't even count it. In fact, I doubt it altogether. It must date back centuries."

"His intimacy, then, is not to be accounted for by his relationship?"

"Ah, I thought so," she said; "you're jealous of the poor count!"

"Count?"

"Oh dear, what does it matter? He doesn't like to be called count, because all foreigners are counts or barons or something. I oughtn't to have let it out."

"Never mind. Tell me something about him."

"He is Bohemian. I met him first some years ago on the Continent."

"Then the meeting at Sir Edward Laston's was not your first."

"No . . . but if he is my cousin, he is yet more Mr. Arnold's. But he does not want it mentioned yet. I'm sure I don't know why."

"Is he in love with you?"

"How can I tell?" she shrugged her shoulder. "But even if he is, it does not follow that I am in love with him—does it? Besides, why should I answer all your impertinent, downright questions? They are as point blank as the church catechism—mind, I don't say rude. Yet, how can I be in love with two at—the—?"

She seemed to check herself. But Hugh had heard enough—as she had intended he should. She turned instantly and sped to the door, where she vanished noiselessly.

A few days passed. Euphra and he seemed satisfied without meeting in private, perhaps both afraid of carrying it too far and risking discovery. Mr. Arnold continued to be thoroughly attentive to his guests and became more and more devoted to Lady Emily. There was no saying where it might end, for he was not an old man yet, and Lady Emily seemed to have no special admirers. A reminiscence of his first wife seemed to haunt all Mr. Arnold's contemplations of Lady Emily and all his attentions to her. Hugh made some fresh efforts to do his duty by Harry, and so far succeeded that the boy made some progress. But what helped Harry more than anything was the motherly tenderness of Mrs. Elton who often had him sit with her in her own room. To her he generally fled now when he felt deserted or lonely.

23 / Ghost Hunting

A few days later, Hugh happened to meet his new acquaintance while walking in the neighborhood and joined him in a stroll. Mr. Arnold met them on horseback and invited von Fenkelstein to dine with them that evening, to which he willingly consented.

In the course of the dinner, Mr. Arnold said, "It is curious, Herr von Fenkelstein, how often, if you meet with something new, you encounter it again almost immediately. I found an article on hypnotism in the newspaper the very day after our conversation on the subject. But absurd as the whole thing is, it is quite surpassed by what I have read about spirits of the dead and mediums."

This observation at once opened the discussion toward the whole question of those physico-psychological phenomena to which the name of *spiritualism* has irreverently been applied. Mr. Arnold was profound in his contempt of the whole thing, but not necessarily on the basis of any profoundly "spiritual" grounds. Everyone had something to remark, except Fenkelstein, who maintained a rigid silence.

This silence at last attracted the attention of the rest of the party, upon which Mr. Arnold said, "You have not given us your opinion on the subject, Herr von Fenkelstein."

"I hesitate encountering the opposition of so many fair adversaries."

"We are in England, sir. Every man is at liberty to say what he thinks."

"I agree that a great deal that has found its way into print recently does seem ridiculous indeed. But yet I have seen more than I can account for on the basis of reason alone. There are strange stories connected with my own family which indeed incline me to believe in the supernatural. And without making the pretense of calling myself a *medium*, I would even tell you I have myself had some highly curious experiences."

"You rouse our curiosity," said Mr. Arnold. "But I fear, after our free statements in opposition to your greater experience, you will not be inclined to make us wiser by sharing your experiences, however much we may desire to hear it."

"I'm afraid, Mr. Arnold, that the repetition of some of the matters to which you refer would prove agitating to the ladies present."

"In that case, I must beg your pardon for pressing the matter."

"Well, Mr. Arnold, if you wish it, I am ready—although I rather dread the possible effects on the nerves of the ladies, especially as this is an old house—to repeat certain experiments which I have sometimes found only too successful."

"Oh, don't," said Euphra faintly.

An expression of the opposite desire followed, however, from the other ladies. Their curiosity seemed to strive with their fears and overcome them.

"I hope we shall have nothing to do with it in any way than merely as spectators." said Mrs. Elton doubtfully.

"It is not likely that you can remain simply spectators. But, that remains to be seen."

"Good gracious!" exclaimed Mrs. Elton.

"Then, if you will allow me," continued Fenkelstein, "all I need is a small drill and an earthenware plate—not china."

"I know where the tool chest is," offered Hugh.

"I can manage the plate," said Euphra.

Hugh soon returned with the drill and Euphra with the plate. The Bohemian, with some difficulty, drilled a small hole in the bottom of the plate. Then cutting off a small piece from a pencil, he fit it into the hole, making it just long enough to touch the table with its point when the plate lay in its ordinary position.

"Now I am ready," he announced. "But," he added, raising his head and looking all around the room, "I do not think this room will be quite satisfactory."

Hugh could not help thinking there was more or less of the charlatan about the man.

"Choose the room in the house that will suit you," said Mr. Arnold.

"The library?" suggested Lady Emily.

They adjourned to the library. The library would do. After some further difficulty they succeeded in procuring a large sheet of paper and fastening it down to the table by pins. Only two candles were in the great room, and it was scarcely lighted by them, yet Fenkelstein requested that one of these should be extinguished.

He then said solemnly, "Let me request silence—absolute silence and quiescence of thought."

After stillness had settled down the outspread wings of intensity, he resumed "Will any one, or better, two of you, touch the plate as lightly as possible with your fingers?"

All hung back for a moment. Then Mr. Arnold came forward.

"I will," he said, and laid his fingers on the plate.

"As lightlly as possible, if you please. If the plate moves, follow it with your fingers, but be sure not to push it in any direction."

"I understand," said Mr. Arnold; and silence fell again.

The Bohemian, after a pause, spoke once more, but in a foreign tongue. The words sounded first like an entreaty, then like command, and at last almost like imprecation. The ladies shuddered.

"Any movement of the vehicle?" he said to Mr. Arnold.

"No," said Mr. Arnold, solemnly. The ladies were glad for the pretext to attempt a laugh in order to get rid of the oppression which they had begun to feel.

"Hush," said Fenkelstein. "Will no one else touch the plate as well? It will seldom move with only one. It does with me. But I fear I might be suspect if I joined myself."

"Do not even hint at such a thing. You are beyond suspicion." What ground Mr. Arnold had for making such an assertion was no better known to himself than anyone else present.

Von Fenkelstein, without another word, put the fingers of one hand lightly on the plate beside Mr. Arnold's. The plate instantly began to move upon the paper. The motion was a succession of small jerks at first, but it soon tilted up a little and moved upon a changing point of support. Now it careened rapidly in wavy lines, sweeping back and forth, the men not appearing to influence its motion. After a minute or two the motion gradually ceased. Von Fenkelstein withdrew his hand and requested that the other candle should be lighted. The paper was taken up and examined. Nothing could be discovered upon it but a labyrinth of wavy and sweeping lines. Fenkelstein pored over it for some time, and then confessed his inability to make a single letter out of it, still less words and sentences as he had expected.

"But," he concluded, "we have been at least so far successful; it moves. Let us try again. Who will try next?"

"I will," said Hugh.

A new sheet of paper was fixed. The candle was extinguished. Hugh put his fingers on the plate, followed by Fenkelstein's. In a second or two it began to move.

Hugh grew quite cold and began to tremble. The oppression in the room had now grown quite thick. The plate careened violently, then went more slowly, making regular short motions and returns, as if trying to write. Could he be mistaken? Did he feel beneath his fingers the jerky formation of the letters D - A - V - I - D E - L . . .? Hugh shuddered, then withdrew his hand. The plate fell to the table and the writing ceased.

Hugh tried to speak to say he felt the dubious convocation should be stopped at once. But his tongue seemed immobilized in his mouth. It was clear Fenkelstein was no ordinary man and his powers over the others present greater than they had imagined. Where his power originated Hugh began to have a clear notion.

Suddenly, Mrs. Elton discovered that Lady Emily was either asleep or in a faint. The Bohemian had not been so intent on the operations with the plate as he had appeared to be and had been employing part of his energy mesmerizing Lady Emily. Unwilling to make a disturbance, Mrs. Elton rang the bell quietly and, going to the door, asked the servant who answered it to send her maid up with some eau-de-cologne. Meantime, Fenkelstein made efforts to re-interest Hugh—who remained silent, as if in a trance—and then the others in attempting to discover the plate's message. As this was going on, Hugh involuntarily raised his eyes toward the door of the room. In the near darkness between him and the door, he saw a pale, beautiful face—a face only. It was the face of Margaret Elginbrod.

A mist of darkness fell upon his brain, and the room swam round with him. But he was saved from falling to the floor in a faint by a sudden cry from Lady Emily, who had waked without warning.

''See, see!'' she cried wildly, pointing toward one of the windows.

These looked across to another part of the house, one of the oldest. One of its windows shone with a faint bluish light.

Hugh came to himself as all the company hurried to the window at Lady Emily's exclamation.

''Who can be in that part of the house?'' said Mr. Arnold angrily.

''It is Lady Euphrasia's window,'' said Euphra in a low voice, in a tone which suggested that she was very cold.

''What do you mean by speaking like that?'' said Mr. Arnold, forgetting his dignity. ''Surely you are above being superstitious!''

The light disappeared, fading out slowly.

''Is it possible the servants could be about some mischief?''

''Indeed, the servants are much too alarmed, after what took place last year, to go near that wing—much less that room,'' said Euphra. ''Besides, Mrs. Horton has all the keys.''

''Go yourself and get them for me, Euphra. I will see at once what this means.''

Hugh had now recovered sufficiently to recognize that the real source of the light in the window was merely the dim reflection of the moon through the trees on the neglected and dusty pane. He thought the others would have seen it to be such as well but for the effect of Lady Emily's sudden exclamation. Perhaps she was under the influence of the Bohemian at that moment.

''Will you all accompany me, ladies and gentlemen,'' said Mr. Arnold, ''that we may all see with our own eyes that there is nothing dangerous in the house?''

Of course Fenkelstein was quite ready, and Hugh as well, although he felt at this moment rather ill-fitted for ghost-hunting. The ladies hesitated; but at last, more afraid of being left behind alone than of going on with the gentlemen, they consented. Euphra brought the keys and they commenced their march of investigation. Up the grand staircase they went, Mr. Arnold first with the keys, Hugh next with Mrs. Elton and Lady Emily, and the Bohemian, considerably to Hugh's dissatisfaction, bringing up the rear with Euphra. They had to go through various doors, some locked, some open, following a different route from that taken by Euphra on the former occasion.

Mr. Arnold found the keys troublesome. He could not easily distinguish those he wanted and was compelled to apply to Euphra for assistance. But at last, by tortuous ways, across old rooms, and up and down abrupt little stairs, they reached the door of Lady Euphrasia's room. The key was found and the door opened with some perturbation—manifest on the part of the ladies, concealed on the part of the men.

The place was quite dark. They entered, and Hugh was struck with its antiquity. Lady Euphrasia's ghost had driven the last occupant out of it nearly a hundred years ago, but most of the furniture was much older than that, having probably belonged to Lady Euphrasia herself. Even the bedclothes were still folded down as the last occupant had left them. The fine linen had grown yellow. On the wall hung a portrait of a nun in convent attire.

"Some have taken that for a second portrait of Lady Euphrasia," said Mr. Arnold, "but it cannot be—Euphra, we will go back through the picture gallery—I suspect it of originating the tradition that Lady Euphrasia became a nun. I do not believe it myself. The picture is certainly old enough to stand for her, but it does not seem to me in the least like the other."

It was a great room, with large recesses and very irregular in form. Old chairs, with remnants of enamel and gilding, stood all about. The walls were entirely covered with rich tapestry.

"Come and see this strange piece of furniture," said Euphra to Hugh, who had kept by her side since they entered the room.

She led him into one of the recesses, almost concealed by the bed hangings. In it stood a cabinet of ebony, reaching almost to the ceiling, curiously carved in high relief.

"I wish I could show you the inside of it," she went on, "but I cannot now." This was said in almost a whisper. Hugh gazed at the carving, on whose black shadows his candle made little light.

"Explain it to me, Euphra," he said.

She proceeded to tell him what she fancied the carvings meant, still speaking in the low tone which seemed suitable to the awe of the place. Suddenly after some minutes, becoming aware of the sensation of silence, they looked up and saw that theirs was the only light in the room. They were left alone in the haunted chamber.

They looked at each other for one moment, then said, with half stifled voices, ''Euphra—''

''Hugh.''

Recovering herself, Euphra said, ''Come . . . come,'' and led the way to the door.

When they reached it, however, they found it closed and locked.

''This is a double door,'' she said. ''I fear it is already too late for us to knock and be heard. Mr. Arnold will have locked all the doors between this and the picture gallery. That is where I imagine they are now. What shall we do?'' She said this with an expression of comical despair.

''Never mind,'' Hugh said, pleased with the turn of events. ''Let us go on with our study of the cabinet. They will soon find we are left behind and come back to look for us.''

''Yes, but imagine being found here!'' She laughed, but it could not hide a genuine embarrassment.

''Let us put out the light,'' said Hugh, also laughing, ''and make no answer when they return.''

''Can you starve so happily?''

''With you.''

She murmured something to herself, then said aloud, ''But this won't do. I dare say they are still looking at the portrait. Come.''

So saying, she went into another recess, and lifting a curtain of tapestry, opened a door.

''Come quickly,'' she said.

Hugh followed her down a short stair into a narrow passage, nowhere lighted from the outside. The door behind them shut heavily, as if someone had banged it in anger at their intrusion. The passage smelled very musty, and was as quiet as death.

''Not a word of this, Hugh, as you love me. It may be useful yet.''

''Not a word.''

They came through a sliding panel into an empty room. Euphra closed it behind them.

''Now shade your light.''

He did so. She took him by the hand. A few more turns brought them in sight of the lights of the rest of the party. As Euphra had conjectured, they were looking at the picture of Lady Euphrasia, Mr. Arnold discoursing away in proof that the nun could not be she. They entered the gallery without being heard, and parting a little way, one pretending to look at one picture, the other at another, crept gradually round until they joined the group. It was a piece of most successful generalship. Euphra was, doubtless, quite prepared with her story in case it should be needed.

"Dear Lady Emily," she said, "how tired you look. Do let us go, Uncle."

"By all means. Take my arm, Lady Emily. Euphra, will you take the keys again and lock the doors?"

Mrs. Elton had already taken Hugh's arm and was leading him away after Mr. Arnold and Lady Emily.

"I will not leave you behind with the ghosts, Miss Cameron," said Fenkelstein.

"Thank you. They will not detain me long. They don't mind being locked up."

It was some time, however, before Euphra and the count presented themselves in the drawing room, to which the party had gone. They had had enough of horrors for that night.

Later, in the quietness of his own chamber, Hugh tried to reflect on the events of the evening. He could not tell what to make of the plate writing, but of one thing he was certain: Fenkelstein served a different master, whoever it be, than his friend David Elginbrod. And he also did not doubt for a moment that the vision he had seen of that man's daughter was only a vision—a homemade ghost, sent out from his own creative brain, prompted somehow from the stupefied state of his consciousness at that moment. Still, he felt that Margaret's face, wherever it had come from and why, was a living reproof to him. For he was losing his life in vain passion, sinking deeper in it day by day. His powers were slowly deserting him.

In point of actual fact, Hugh had seen Margaret that evening. But not as he had once known her. She was now a woman, and had grown into a lady as well. Her whole nature had blossomed into a still and stately beauty which accounted for the differences Hugh perceived and his taking the face for merely an imagined specter.

Ever since she had left the home of Jeanette and David, Margaret's womanhood had grown through service. She had served Mrs. Elton faithfully, little suspecting the lady's close acquaintance with Hugh's recent employer and even less imagining that it was to the very home of Hugh's hire that they were bound when Mrs. Elton announced their journey to the precincts of London. But long before she saw him, Margaret had known, from what she heard among the servants, that Master Harry's tutor could be no other than her own tutor of time past. By and by she learned a great deal about him from Harry's talk with Mrs. Elton and Lady Emily. But she did not give the least hint that she knew him nor betray her desire to see him.

Margaret had obeyed her mistress's summons to the drawing room that night and had entered while Hugh was stooping over the table. As the room was nearly dark, and she was dressed in black, her pale face alone caught the light and his eye as he looked up. Thus, in the exercise of his excited imagination, her face shown to him as a vision suspended in the midst of the surrounding blackness, a memory of a former and happier time.

As sleep overtook him, Hugh's thoughts were of Euphra's hand clasping his as they made their way to the picture gallery. But his dreams were of that radiant face appearing to him as out of a past life.

24 / Aftereffects

At breakfast the following morning, the influences of the past day on the family were evident. There was a good deal of excitement, alternated with listlessness. The moral atmosphere seemed unhealthy. Hugh was careful enough of Harry to try to divert the conversation entirely, knowing that it could have an injurious effect on him, and he took him away as soon as breakfast was over.

In the afternoon, Fenkelstein called to inquire after the ladies. Mr. Arnold, who had a full allowance of curiosity—its amount being frequently in an inverse ratio to that of higher intellectual gifts—begged him to spend the rest of the day with them. Renewed conversations that evening led to renewed experiments in the library. Hugh refused to have anything more to do with the plate writing, for he dreaded its influences. But Fenkelstein once more seemed to hold sway over those in the household. No one was inclined, for various reasons, to resist him; he begged absolute silence and solicited unknown prisoners in the aerial vaults whom he supposed capable of communicating with those in this earthly cell. Various raps were heard on the windows, and when the lights were extinguished several light articles seemed to move about the room on their own. Most of the activity seemed directed against Lady Emily. In terror she shrank back, but at this moment one of the doors opened and a dark figure passed through the room toward the opposite door. Everything that could be called ghostly ceased instantly.

Lady Emily, who had been on the point of hysterics, recovered herself slowly but by no means entirely. Mr. Arnold proceeded to light the candles, saying in a righteous tone, "I think we have had enough of this nonsense."

When the candles were lit, though several had observed the figure, no one else was in the room, and all took it for part of the illusive phantasmagoria. There was no renewal of the experiments. All were in a very unhealthy state of excitement. Vague fear and a certain indescribable oppression had dimmed for the time all the nobler faculties of the soul. Lady Emily was affected the most. Her eyes looked scared and her face was deathly pale. Mrs. Elton became alarmed and persuaded Lady Emily to go to bed.

But the contagion spread and indistinct terrors were no longer confined to the family itself. The rumor revived among the servants that the house was haunted. It was whispered that the very night after these occurrences, the Ghost's Walk had been in use as the name signified—

a figure in black garments had been seen gliding along the deserted avenue nearly at midnight.

Lady Emily remained in bed, but apparently more sick in mind than in body. She said she had tossed about all the previous night without once falling asleep. In the morning, Mrs. Elton, wishing to relieve the maid who had been up most of the night with her, sent Margaret to Lady Emily. Margaret arranged the bedclothes and pillows, which were in a very uncomfortable condition, sat down behind the curtain and began to sing to her. Before she had finished one song, Lady Emily was fast asleep. A sweet, peaceful, half-smile lighted her troubled face graciously. Finding her thus at rest, Margaret left the room to fetch some work. When she returned she found her tossing and moaning. As soon as she sat down by her, her trouble diminished by degrees until she lay in the same peaceful sleep as before. In this state she continued for two or three hours and awoke much refreshed.

She held out her hand to Margaret and said, "Thank you. Thank you. What a sweet creature you are!"

"Shall I send Sarah to you now, my lady?" said Margaret, "or would you like me to stay with you?"

"Oh, would you please—if Mrs. Elton can spare you?"

"I know she will only think of your comfort."

Mrs. Elton entered just then and confirmed what Margaret had said.

"But," she added, "it is time Lady Emily had something to eat. Go to the cook, Margaret, and see if the beef broth Miss Cameron ordered is ready."

Margaret went.

Soon Lady Emily began to toss about and show signs of discomfort.

"How long has Margaret been gone?" she moaned out, though she had hardly left the room two minutes.

"I am here," comforted Mrs. Elton.

"Yes . . . yes, thank you. But I want Margaret."

"She will be here presently."

"Please don't let Miss Cameron come near me. I just couldn't bear it right now."

"Of course, my dear, we will keep to ourselves."

"Is Mr.——, the foreign gentleman, I mean—in the house?"

"No. He is gone."

"Are you sure? It still feels like he is around."

"What do you mean, dear? I am sure he is gone."

Lady Emily did not answer. Margaret returned with the broth.

"You must not leave her ladyship, Margaret," whispered her mistress. "She has taken it into her head to care for no one but you."

"Very well. I shall be most happy to stay."

When Mrs. Elton left the room, Lady Emily said, "Read something to me, Margaret."

"What shall I read?"

"Anything you like."

Margaret got a Bible and read to her one of her father's favorite chapters, the fortieth of Isaiah.

"I have no right to trust God, Margaret," she murmured when the reading was finished.

"Why, my lady?"

"Because I do not feel any faith in him. And you know we cannot be accepted without faith."

"That is to make God as changeable as we are, my lady."

"But the Bible says so."

"I don't believe it does. I love God with all my heart, and I cannot bear you should think that way of him. You might as well say that a mother would go away from her little child, lying moaning in the dark, because it could not see her and was afraid to put its hand out into the dark to feel for her."

"Then you think he does care for us, even when we are very bad? But he cannot bear wicked people."

"Has he not been making the world go on and on with all the evil that is in it? If he cannot bear wicked people, then this world is hell itself and the Bible is all a lie."

"Oh, how happy I should be if that were true!"

"You are not wicked, dear Lady Emily. But if you were, God would bend over you, trying to get you back, like a father over his sick child. Will people never truly believe about the lost sheep?"

"Oh, yes, I believe that. But then—"

"Trust in God, then. Never mind the words."

Lady Emily was weeping as Margaret knelt and prayed beside her. When she had ceased, Lady Emily said, "You will not leave me, Margaret? I will tell you why another time."

"I will not leave you, my dear lady."

Margaret stooped and kissed her forehead. Lady Emily threw her arms around her neck. In another minute she was fast asleep, with Margaret seated by her side, every now and then glancing up at her from her work with a calm face.

That night, about midnight, Hugh was suddenly startled by the sudden opening of his door. There stood Harry in his nightshirt, pale as death, and scarcely able to articulate the words, "The ghost . . . the ghost."

He took the poor boy in his arms, held him fast, and comforted him.

When he was a little soothed, he said, "Harry, you must've been dreaming. Where's the ghost?"

"In the Ghost's Walk!" cried Harry, almost shrieking with terror.

"How do you know it is there?"

"I saw it out my window. I couldn't sleep. I got up and looked out—I don't know why—and I saw it. I saw it!"

The words were followed by a long, mournful cry.

"Come and show it to me," said Hugh, wanting to make light of it.

"No, no, Mr. Sutherland. I couldn't go back into that room."

"Very well, Harry. You shall sleep with me tonight."

"Oh, thank you, thank you, dear Mr. Sutherland. You will love me again, won't you?"

This touched Hugh's heart. He could hardly refrain from tears. His old love, buried before it was dead, revived. He clasped the boy to his heart, carried him over to the bed and lay down beside him.

Lady Emily's room also looked out upon the Ghost's Walk. Margaret heard Harry's cry as she sat by the sleeping Emily. Not knowing whence it came, she went to the window. From it she could see distinctly, for it was clear moonlight, a white figure gliding away along the deserted avenue. She was not very uneasy about it but resolved to be prepared for any possible recurrence. She was sure that any report of the ghost coming to Lady Emily's ears would greatly slow her recovery; for she instinctively felt that her illness had more than a little to do with the questionable occupations in the library with Fenkelstein. She watched by her bedside all the night, slumbering at times, but roused in a moment by any restlessness of the patient.

25 / The Ghost's Walk

Margaret sat watching the waking of Lady Emily. Knowing how much the first thought colors the feeling of the whole day, she wished that Lady Emily should at once be aware that she was by her side.

She opened her eyes and a smile broke over her face when she perceived her nurse. But Margaret did not yet speak to her. Every nurse should remember that waking ought always to be a gradual operation. And except in the most triumphant health is never complete on the opening of the eyes.

"Margaret, I am better," whispered Lady Emily at last.

"I am very glad, my lady."

"I have been lying awake for some time, and I am sure I am better. I don't see strange-colored figures floating about the room as I did yesterday. Were you not out of the room a few minutes ago?"

"Just for a moment, my lady."

"I knew it. But I did not mind it. Yesterday, when you left me, those figures grew ten times as many the moment you were gone. But you will stay with me today, too, Margaret?" she added with some anxiety.

"I will if you need me. But I may be forced to leave you a little while this evening."

When Harry woke, after a very troubled sleep, Hugh made him promise not to increase the confusion of the household by speaking of what he had seen. Harry promised, but begged that Hugh would not leave him all day. It hardly needed the pale, scared face of his pupil to enforce the request; he hardly let him out of his sight.

But although Harry kept his word, the cloud of perturbation gathered thicker in the kitchen and the servants' hall. Nothing came to the ears of their master and mistress; but gloomy looks, sudden starts, and side-long glances of fear indicated the prevailing character of the feelings of the household.

And although Lady Emily was not so ill, she had not yet taken a decided turn for the better but appeared to suffer from some kind of low fever. The medical man who was called in confessed to Mrs. Elton that he could say nothing very decided about her condition but recommended great quiet and careful nursing. Margaret scarcely left her room, and the invalid showed far more than the ordinary degree of dependence upon her nurse.

About noon, feeling much better, Lady Emily called Margaret and said to her, "That man haunts me. I cannot bear the thought of him, and yet I cannot rid my mind of him. Are you certain he is not here?"

"Yes, indeed, my lady. He has not been here since the day before yesterday."

"And yet, when you leave me for an instant, I always feel as if he were sitting in the very seat where you were the moment before, or just coming to the door and about to open it. That is why I cannot bear you to leave me."

"God is nearer to you than any thought or feeling of yours, Lady Emily. Do not be afraid. If all the evil things in the universe were around us, they could not come inside the ring that he makes about us. He always keeps a place for himself and his child into which no other being can enter."

"Oh, how you must love God, Margaret. You always speak of him as though he were your closest friend."

"Indeed I do love him, my lady. And that is just what he is. If ever anything looks beautiful or lovely to me, then I know at once that God is in it."

"Oh, you are a comfort to me, Margaret, " Lady Emily said after a short silence. "Where did you learn such things?"

"From my father, and from God himself showing them to me in my heart."

"Ah, that is why I often feel when you come into my room as if the sun were shining and the wind were blowing in the treetops and the birds were singing. You seem to make everything clear, and right and plain. I wish I were you, Margaret."

"But how much better, my lady, to be what God chooses to make of you. To be made by God, is that not the grandest, most precious thing in all the world?"

"It is," agreed Lady Emily, and was silent.

The shadows of evening came on. As soon as it was dark, Margaret took her place at one of the windows hidden from Lady Emily by a bed curtain. She raised a blind and pulled aside one curtain to let her have a view of the trees outside. She had placed the one candle so as not to shine either on the window or on her own eyes. Lady Emily was asleep. One hour and another passed, and still she sat there—motionless, watching, waiting.

Margaret did not know that at another window stood a second watcher. It was Hugh, in Harry's room. Harry was asleep in Hugh's bed. He had no light. He stood with his face close against the windowpane on which the moon shone brightly. All below him the woods were half dissolved away in the moonlight. The Ghost's Walk lay full before him, like a tunnel through the trees. He could see a great way down, by the light that fell into it from between the boughs overhead. He stood thus for a long time, gazing somewhat listlessly.

Suddenly he became all eyes as he caught the white glimmer of something passing up the avenue. He stole out of the room, down to the library by the back stair and through the library window into the wood. He reached the avenue sideways, at some distance from the house, and peered from behind a tree, up and down. At first he saw nothing. But after a moment, while he was looking down the avenue away from the house, a veiled figure in white passed noiselessly from the other direction. From the way in which he was looking at the moment it had passed him before he saw it.

It made no sound. Only some leaves on the ground rustled as they hurried away in uncertain eddies, startled by the sweep of its trailing garments.

On it went. Hugh's eyes were fixed on its course. He could not move and his heart labored so frightfully that he could hardly breathe. The figure had not gone far, however, before he heard a repressed cry of agony. It sank to the earth and vanished.

Just then, from where it disappeared, down the path came a second silent figure, turning neither to the right nor the left, veiled in black from head to foot.

It is the nun in Lady Euphrasia's room was Hugh's frantic thought.

This passed him too and, walking slowly toward the house, disappeared somewhere near the edge of the avenue. Turning once more, with reviving courage—for his blood had begun to flow more equably—Hugh ventured to approach the spot where the white figure had vanished. He found nothing there but the shadow of a large tree. He walked through the avenue to the end and then back to the house but saw nothing, although he often started at fancied appearances. Sorely bewildered, he returned to his own room. After speculating until his thoughts made him weary, he lay down beside Harry and fell fast asleep.

Margaret lay on a couch in Lady Emily's room, and slept likewise. But she started wide awake at every moan of her patient, who often cried out in her sleep.

26 / Count Halkar Versus the Spirit

When Euphra recovered from the swoon into which she had fallen—for I need hardly explain to my readers that it was she who walked the Ghost's Walk in white—she found herself lying in the wood. On seeing Margaret and taking her for the very being whom Euphra herself was impersonating, she had cried out and fainted. Coming to herself, she found Fenkelstein, whom she had gone out to meet, standing beside her. Her first words were of anger as she tried to rise.

"How long, Count Halkar, am I to be your slave?"

"Till you have learned to submit."

"Have I not done all I can?"

"You have not found it. You are free the moment you place that ring, belonging to my family, into my hands."

I doubt the man really was Count Halkar, although he had evidently persuaded Euphra that such was his name and title. It is far more probable that in the course of picking up a mass of trifling information about various families of distinction, he had learned something about the Halkar family and this particular ring, which, for some reason or other, he wanted to possess himself.

"What more can I do?" moaned Euphra, succeeding at length in raising herself to a sitting posture and leaning against a tree. "I shall be found out one day. I have already been seen wandering through the house at midnight with the heart of a thief. How I hate you!"

A low laugh was the count's only reply.

"And now Lady Euphrasia herself dogs my steps to keep me from the ring." She gave a low cry of agony at the remembrance.

"Miss Cameron—Euphra—are you going to give in to such folly?"

"Folly! Is it not far worse to torture me as you do—all for a worthless ring! What can you want with it? I do not know that he even has it."

"You lie! You know he has it. You cannot take me in so easily."

"You vile—you base man! You are a coward. You are afraid of Lady Euphrasia yourself. See there," she cried, glancing and pointing through the wood.

Fenkelstein looked about uneasily. It was only the moonlight on the bark of a silver birch. Conscious of having betrayed weakness, he grew spiteful.

"If you continue to behave so, I will compel you. I can, you know. Rise up, Euphra!"

After a moment's hesitation she rose.

''Put your arms around me.''

She seemed glued to the earth, then began to drag herself up from it one slow movement at a time. She came close up to the Bohemian and reluctantly put one arm half round him, looking to the earth all the time.

''Kiss me.''

''Count Halkar!''—her voice sounded hollow—''I will do what you please. Only release me.''

''Go then; but do not resist me any longer. I do not care for your kisses. You were ready enough once. But now I see that idiot of a tutor has taken my place.''

''Would to God I had never seen you—never yielded to your influence over me! Swear to me that I shall be free if I find you that ring.''

''You find me the ring first. Why should I swear it? I can make you. You know well enough that it was you yourself who first set out to entrap me with your arts, and I only turned upon you with mine. And now you are in my power. But you will be free—if you find me the ring!''

''You are cruel! You are doing all you can to ruin me.''

''On the contrary, I am doing all I can to save myself. If you had loved me as you allowed me to think once, I should never have made you my tool.''

''You would, all the same.''

''Watch your tongue. I am irritable tonight.''

For a few moments Euphra made no reply.

''To what will you drive me?'' she said at last.

''I will not go too far. I should lose my power over you if I did. I prefer to keep it.''

Euphra turned without another word and went, murmuring, as if in excuse to herself, ''It is for my freedom I do it . . . only for my freedom.''

Whether or not Euphra was actually in the man's power would be impossible to tell for certain. She at least believed herself compelled to do what the man pleased. She had yielded to his will once. Had she not done so he could not have compelled her. But having once yielded, she felt she had not strength sufficient to free herself again.

It is evident that he had come to the neighborhood of Arnstead for the sake of finding her and exercising his power over her for his own ends. He had made her come to him once, if not oftener, before fortune had smiled on him and he had met Hugh and by means of his acquaintance obtained admission to Arnstead. Once admitted, he had succeeded by his efforts to please and ingratiate himself with Mr. Arnold, so that now the door of the house stood open to him, and he even had his own recognized seat at the dinner table.

The next morning, Lady Emily wanted to get up. But her eyes were still too bright and Margaret would not hear of it. During the day she was better, but restless by fits.

When Hugh woke, the extraordinary experiences of the previous night appeared like a dream that now, in the light of day, seemed to have never happened.

Euphra did not appear at breakfast, sending a message to her uncle that she had a bad headache but hoped to take her place at the dinner table. When the dinner hour came, Euphra looked very pale. Her eyes had an unsettled look and there were dark hollows under them. She would start and look sideways without any visible cause and was very different from her usual self. Hugh was concerned. It did not diminish his discomfort that, about the middle of dinner, Fenkelstein was announced. Had Euphra been tremulously expectant of him?

"This is an unforeseen pleasure, Herr von Fenkelstein," Mr. Arnold greeted him.

"It is very good of you to call it a pleasure, Mr. Arnold," he said. "Miss Cameron—but, good heavens! How ill you look."

Hugh wondered what right he had to be so solicitous about Euphra's health. She muttered some commonplaces after which the subject of her headache was dropped.

As the gentlemen sat at their wine, Mr. Arnold said, "I am anxious to have one more trial of those strange things you have brought to our knowledge. I have been thinking about them ever since."

"Of course I am at your service, Mr. Arnold, only I am concerned for the ladies."

"That is very considerate of you, but they need not be present if they do not like it."

They adjourned once more to the library. This time only the men went.

"Margaret," said Lady Emily from her bed about this time, "I am certain that man is in this house."

"He is, my lady," answered Margaret.

"Are they about some more of those horrid experiments, as they call them?"

"I do not know."

Mrs. Elton entered the room at that moment, and Margaret said, "Do you know whether the gentlemen are—in the library again?"

"I don't know, Margaret. I certainly hope not. We have had enough of it. But I can go and find out."

"Will you take my place for a few moments first, please?" Margaret detained her. She had felt a growing oppression for some time, and had scarcely left the sickroom that day.

"Don't leave me, Margaret," said Lady Emily imploringly.

"Only for a short time, my lady. I need some fresh air. I shall be back in less than a quarter of an hour."

"Very well, then," she resigned herself.

Margaret went out into the moonlight and walked for ten minutes, seeking the open spaces where the winds were. She then returned to the sickchamber, refreshed and strong.

"Now, I will go and see what the gentlemen are about," said Mrs. Elton, as if on an errand of business.

The good lady did not like these proceedings, but she was irresistibly attracted by them notwithstanding. Having gone to see for Lady Emily, she now remained to watch the proceedings for herself.

After she had left, Lady Emily grew more uneasy. Not even Margaret's presence could make her comfortable. Mrs. Elton did not return after many minutes had elasped.

At last Lady Emily said, "Margaret, I am terrified at the idea of being left alone. But not so terrified as at the idea of what is going on in that library. I know it is evil. I do not think Mrs. Elton will come back. Would you go down and ask her to come to me?"

"Certainly," said Margaret. "But I don't want to be seen."

In truth, Margaret did not want to be seen by Hugh. Lady Emily, with her dislike of Fenkelstein, thought Margaret did not want to be seen by him.

"You will find a black veil of mine," she said, "in that wardrobe. Just throw it over your head and hold a handkerchief to your face. They will be so busy they will never see you."

Margaret yielded to the request of Lady Emily, who herself arranged the veil for her.

When Mrs. Elton had reached the library some twenty or thirty minutes earlier, she found it darkened and the three men seated at the table. She could not help watching with a curious dread.

In a minute or two, the table at which they were seated began to move up and down with a kind of vertical oscillation, and several things in the room began to slide about, by short, apparently purposeless jerks. Everything threatened to assume motion. Mrs. Elton declared afterward that several books were thrown about the room.

But now suddenly everything was as still as the moonlight. Every chair and table was at rest, looking as usual perfectly incapable of motion. Mrs. Elton felt that she dared not say they had moved at all. Not a sound was to be heard from corner or ceiling. After a moment's silence, Mrs Elton was quite restored to her sound mind, as she said, and left the room.

"Some adverse influence is at work," remarked Fenkelstein, with some vexation. "What is through that door?" So saying, he approached the door of the private staircase and opened it. They saw him start aside, and a veiled, dark figure passed him, crossed the library, and left by another door.

"I have my suspicions," said Fenkelstein with a rather tremulous voice.

"And your fears too, I think. Admit it now," said Mr. Arnold.

"Granted, Mr. Arnold. Let us go to the drawing room."

Just as Margaret had reached the library door at the bottom of the private stair, a puff of wind upset the arrangement of the veil and caused it to fall over her face. She stopped for a moment to readjust it. She had not quite succeeded when Fenkelstein opened the door. Without an instant's hesitation she let the veil fall and walked forward.

Mrs. Elton had gone to her own room, on her way to Lady Emily's. When she reached the latter, she found Margaret seated as she had left her, by the bedside.

"I did not miss you, Margaret," said Lady Emily, "half as much as I expected. But I don't think he can hurt me now."

"Certainly not. I hope he will give you no more trouble. But my advice is that you get well as soon as you can and leave this place."

"You frighten me, Margaret. And Mr. Arnold is most kind to me."

"This place quite suits Lady Emily," said Mrs. Elton.

"But she is not so well as when she came," answered Margaret.

"No; but that is no fault of the place," said Lady Emily. "I am sure it is all that horrid man's doing."

"How else will you be rid of him, then? What if he wants to get rid of you?"

"What harm can I be doing him—a poor girl like me?"

"I don't know. But I fear there is something not right going on."

"We will tell Mr. Arnold at once," said Mrs. Elton.

"But what would you tell him? Mr. Arnold is hardly one to listen to your maid's suspicions." Margaret turned to her patient. "Dear Lady Emily, you must get well and go."

"I will try," said Lady Emily, submissive as a child.

"I think you will be able to get up for a little while tomorrow."

A tap came to the door. It was Euphrasia, inquiring about Lady Emily.

"Ask Miss Cameron to come in," she called from her bed.

Euphra entered. Her manner was much changed—subdued and suffering.

''Dear Miss Cameron, you and I ought to change places. I am sorry to hear that you have been ill.''

''I have only had a headache all day. I shall be quite well tomorrow, thank you.''

''I intend to be so, too,'' said Lady Emily cheerfully.

After some small talk, Euphra went, holding her hand to her forehead. Margaret did not look up all the time she was in the room, but went on busily with her needlework.

That night was a peaceful one.

27 / The Ring

The next day, Lady Emily was nearly as well as she had proposed being. She did not, however, make an appearance downstairs. Mr. Arnold, hearing that she was now out of bed, immediately sent up his compliments with the request that he be allowed to visit her that afternoon. To this Lady Emily gladly consented.

He sat with her a long time, talking about various things. The presence of the girl, reminding him of his young wife, brought out the best in the man lying yet alive under the encrustation of self-importance. At length further conversation failed.

"I wonder what we can do to amuse you, Lady Emily?" he said to break the silence.

"Thank you, Mr. Arnold, but I am not bored."

"I have it! I know something that will interest you."

He went to his own room to get an ebony box of considerable size. Finding it rather awkward and heavy and meeting Euphra on the way, he requested that she take one of its silver handles and help him carry it to Lady Emily's room.

"Now, Lady Emily," he said setting down the box and taking out a curious antique key, "we shall be able to amuse you for a little while."

He opened the box and displayed such a glitter and show of jewelry as would have delighted the eyes of any lady. All kinds of ancient watches, cameo necklaces, pearls abundant, diamonds, rubies, and all colors of precious stones—every one of them having some history—lay before Lady Emily's wide and glistening eyes. But Euphrasia's eyes shone with a very different expression from that which sparkled in Lady Emily's. They seemed to search the box with invisible fingers of lightning. Mr. Arnold chose two or three and gave Lady Emily her choice of them.

As Lady Emily and Mr. Arnold spoke and tried various rings on her fingers, Euphrasia's eyes were not on them, nor did her ears hear their words. She gazed steadily at the jewels in the box.

At length a large gold chain, set with emeralds, was lifted from where it lay coiled up in a corner. A low cry, like a muffled moan, escaped from Euphrasia's lips and she turned her head away from the box.

"What is the matter, Euphra?" asked Mr. Arnold.

"A sudden shot of pain—I beg your pardon, dear Uncle. I fear I am not quite so well as I thought I was."

''Do sit down. I fear the weight of the box was too much for you. How stupid of me.''

''Nonsense. I do want to see the pretty things.''

''But you have seen them before.''

''No, Uncle. You promised to show them to me, but never did.''

The chain was examined, admired, and laid aside.

Where it had lain, the other two now observed what Euphra had spotted immediately, a huge stone like a diamond.

''What is this?'' asked Lady Emily, picking it up. ''Oh, it is a ring. But such a ring for size I never saw. Look, Miss Cameron.''

Euphra was not looking. She was leaning her head on her hand and her face was ash white. Lady Emily tried the ring on. Any two of her small fingers would go into the broad gold circle, and the stone projected far above it. Indeed, the ring was attached to the stone, rather than the stone being set in the ring.''

''This is curious, is it not?'' said Mr. Arnold. ''It can be of no value in itself; it is nothing but a crystal. But it seems to have been always highly thought of in the family. I presume it is the very ring painted by Sir Peter Lely in that portrait of Lady Euphrasia which I showed you the other day.''

Lady Emily was about to lay it down when she spied something that made her look at it more closely.

''What curious engraving is this upon the gold?'' she asked.

''I don't know, indeed,'' answered Mr. Arnold. ''I have never noticed it.''

''Look at it—all over the gold. The characters look like German. I wish I could read it. I am but a poor German scholar. Do look at it, please, Miss Cameron.''

Euphra glanced slightly at it without touching it and said, ''I am sure I could make nothing of it. But,'' she added as if struck by a sudden thought, ''as Lady Emily seems interested, I suppose we could send for Mr. Sutherland. I have no doubt he would be able to decipher it.''

''Oh, don't trouble yourself,'' said Lady Emily.

''No trouble at all,'' answered Euphra and her uncle almost in the same breath.

In a few minutes Hugh was at the door.

''Here's a puzzle for you, Mr. Sutherland,'' said Mr. Arnold as he entered. ''Decipher that inscription and gain the favor of Lady Emily forever.''

He put the ring in Hugh's hand. Hugh recognized it at once. ''Ah, Lady Euphrasia's wonderful ring,'' he said.

Euphra cast on him one of her sudden glances.

''What do you know about it?'' said Mr. Arnold.

Euphra flashed at him once more, covertly.

"I only know that this is the ring in her portrait. Anyone may see that it is a very wonderful ring indeed, by only looking at it," answered Hugh smiling.

"I hope it is not too wonderful for you to get at the mystery of it though, Mr. Sutherland?" said Lady Emily.

By this time Hugh was turning it round and round, trying to get a beginning to the legend. But the initial letter of the inscription could only be found by looking into the crystal, held close to the eye. The words seemed not altogether unknown to him, though the characters were a little strange, and the words themselves were undivided.

The dinner bell rang.

"Dear me, how time goes in your room, Lady Emily," said Mr. Arnold who was never known to keep dinner waiting a moment.

"Do please put these beauties away before you go," said Lady Emily. "I dare not touch them without you. And it is so much better to see them when I have you to tell me about them."

All this time Hugh had stood poring over the ring at the window, where he had taken it for better light. Euphra busied herself replacing the others in the box. When they were in she hastily shut the lid.

"Well, Mr. Sutherland?" said Mr. Arnold.

"I seem on the point of making it out, but I certainly have not succeeded yet."

"Confess yourself vanquished, then, and come to dinner."

"I am very unwilling to give in. I am convinced that if I had leisure to copy the inscription I could, with the help of my dictionary, supply the translation. I am very unwilling, as well, to lose a chance of the favor of Lady Emily."

"Yes, do read it if you can," said Euphra. "I too am dying to hear it."

"Will you trust me with it?" asked Hugh. "I will take the greatest care."

"Oh, certainly," replied Mr. Arnold, with only the slightest hesitation in his voice.

Hugh carried it to his room immediately and laid it beside his manuscript verses in the hiding place of the old writing desk. He was in the drawing room but a few moments later.

There he found Euphra and the Bohemian alone. Von Fenkelstein had, in an incredibly short space of time, established himself as *hausfreund* and came and went as he pleased. They looked as if they had been interrupted in a hurried and earnest conversation—their faces were so impassive. Yet Euphra's wore a considerably heightened color—a more articulate indication. She could school her features, but not her complexion.

28 / The Wager

Hugh had an immediate attack of jealousy which caused him, throughout dinner, to speak to everyone else but Euphra as often as there was the slightest pretext for doing so, while carefully abstaining from looking in her direction. To enable himself to keep this up, he drank wine freely. By the time the ladies rose, it had begun to affect his brain. It was not half so potent, however, in its influence as the parting glance which Euphra succeeded in sending through his eyes to his heart.

Hugh sat down to the table again with a quieter tongue. He drank still, without thinking of the consequences. A strong will kept him from showing any signs of intoxication; but he was certainly nearer to that state than he had ever been before in his life.

"How long is it since Arnstead was first said to be haunted?" asked Fenkelstein.

"Haunted!" exclaimed Mr. Arnold, who resented any such allusion.

"I beg your pardon. I thought it was an open subject of remark."

"So it is," broke in Hugh. "Everyone knows it."

Mr. Arnold was struck dumb with indignation. But before he had recovered himself sufficiently, the conversation between the other two had continued.

"You have seen it yourself, then?" said the Bohemian.

"I did not say that," answered Hugh. "But it is commonly reported among the servants."

"With a blue light?—such as we saw that night from the library window, I suppose."

"I did not say that," answered Hugh. "Besides, that was only the moon. But—"

He paused. Fenkelstein saw the condition he was in, and pressed him.

"You know something more, Mr. Sutherland."

Hugh hesitated again, but only for a moment.

"Well," he said, "I have seen the specter myself, walking in her white graveclothes in the Ghost's Avenue." He laughed.

"Were you frightened, then?" asked Fenkelstein.

"Frightened!" repeated Hugh in a tone of contempt. "I am of Don Juan's opinion with regard to such gentry."

"Bravo!" cried the count. "You despise all these tales about Lady Euphrasia, wandering about the house with a death candle in her hand, looking everywhere about as if she had lost something and couldn't find it?''

''Pooh! I wish I could meet her.''

''Then you don't believe a word of it?''

''I don't say that. There would be less of courage than boasting in talking so if I did not believe a word of it.''

''Then you do believe it?''

But Hugh was too much of a Scotsman to give a hasty opinion, or a direct answer—even when half tipsy. Especially when such was evidently desired. He only shook his head and nodded at the same moment.

''Do you really mean you would meet her if you could?''

''I do.''

''Then if all the tales are true, you may do so without much difficulty. For the coachman told me only today that you may see her light in the window of that room almost any night toward midnight. He told me also that one of the maids had once heard talking through the keyhole of a door that led into that part of the house and saw a figure dressed exactly like the picture of Lady Euphrasia wandering up and down, wringing her hands.''

''You think to frighten me, Fenkelstein, and make me tremble at what I said a moment ago. But I will even go further. I will sleep in Lady Euphrasia's room this very night, if you like.''

''I lay you a hundred guineas you won't!'' cried the Bohemian.

''Done!'' said Hugh, offering his hand. Fenkelstein took it, and so the bet was committed to the decision of courage.

''I presume,'' said Fenkelstein, looking toward his host, ''that Mr. Arnold has no objection.''

''Of course not. My house, ghost and all, is at your service, gentlemen,'' said Mr. Arnold, rising.

They went into the drawing room. Mr. Arnold was in good humor. ''These wicked men have been betting, Mrs. Elton.''

''What about?'' said Euphra, coming up to her uncle.

''Herr von Fenkelstein has laid a hundred guineas that Mr. Sutherland will not sleep in Lady Euphrasia's room tonight.''

Euphra turned pale.

''By *sleep*, I suppose you mean, *spend the night*?'' said Hugh to Fenkelstein. ''I cannot be certain of sleeping, you know.''

''Of course,'' answered the other and, turning to Euphrasia, continued, ''I must say I consider it rather courageous of him to dare the specter as he does. But come and sing me one of the old songs,'' he added in an undertone.

Euphra allowed him to lead her to the piano; but instead of singing a song for him she played some noisy music, through which he and she contrived to talk for some time without being overheard. He then left the room. Euphra looked round to Hugh and begged him with her eyes to come to her. He could not resist, burning with jealousy as he was.

"Are you sure you have nerve enough for this, Hugh?" she said, still playing music.

"I have had nerve enough to sit still and look at you for the last half hour," answered Hugh rudely.

She turned pale and glanced at him with a troubled look. Then, without responding to his answer, she said, "I dare say the count is not overanxious to personally hold you to your bet."

"Perhaps he wishes to have an interview with the ghost himself and grudges me the privilege."

She turned deadly pale this time and gave him one terrified glance, but made no other reply.

"You will arm yourself?"

"Against a ghost? Only with a stout heart."

"But don't forget the secret door we came through that night, Hugh. I distrust the count." The last words were spoken in a whisper.

"Tell him I shall be armed. But I tell you I shall meet him, if he comes, bare-handed. Betray me if you like." Hugh had taken revenge for his jealous heart.

But instead of the reaction he anticipated, she seemed on the point of bursting into tears. He had never seen her weep before. He would have fallen at her feet had he been alone with her. To hide his feelings, he left the room and then the house.

He wandered into the Ghost's Walk and finding himself there, walked up and down it. This was certainly throwing the lady a bold challenge, seeing he was going to spend the night in her room. The excitement into which jealousy had thrown him had been suddenly checked by the sight of Euphra's silent tears. And the sight of her emotion had given him a far better courage than jealousy or wine could afford. Yet after ten minutes passed in the shadows of the Ghost's Walk, he would not have taken the bet at ten times its amount.

But to lose now would be a serious affair. Not only would there be the disgrace of failure, but he had no hundred guineas to lose. Yet even now he had not the slightest thought of receding. The ambition of proving his courage to Euphra was quite sufficient to carry him on to the ordeal.

He walked up and down the avenue till he began to feel the night chilly. The walk became eerie, for cold is very antagonistic to physical courage. He returned to the drawing room. Fenkelstein and Euphra were there alone, but in no close proximity. Mr. Arnold soon entered.

''Shall I have the bed prepared for you, Mr. Sutherland?'' asked Euphra.

''Which of your maids will you persuade to that office?'' said Mr. Arnold, with a facetious expression.

''I will do it myself,'' answered Euphra, ''if Mr. Sutherland persists.''

Hugh saw, or thought he saw, the Bohemian dart an angry glance at Euphra, who shrank under it.

''Do not disturb the ghost's bed for me,'' said Hugh. ''It would be a pity to disarrange it after it has lain so for an age. Besides, I need not rouse the wrath of the poor specter more than can be helped. If I must sleep in her room, I need not sleep in her bed. I will lie on the old couch.—Herr von Fenkelstein, what proof shall you require that I have fulfilled my task?''

''Your word, Mr. Sutherland,'' replied Fenkelstein with a bow.

''Thank you. At what hour must I be there?''

''Oh, I don't know. By eleven, I think. Any time before midnight. That's the ghost's own time, is it not? It is now—let me see—almost ten.''

''Then I will go at once,'' said Hugh, thinking it better to meet the gradual approach of the phantom hour in the room itself than to walk there through the desolate house and enter the room just as the fear would be gathering thickest within it. Besides, he was afraid that his courage might have broken down a little by that time.

''I have one good cup of tea left, Mr. Sutherland,'' said Euphra. ''Will you not strengthen your nerves with that before we lead you to the tomb?''

Then she will go with me? wondered Hugh. ''I will, thank you, Miss Cameron.''

He approached the table at which she stood pouring the cup of tea. She said, low and hurriedly, without raising her head, ''Don't go, dear Hugh. You don't know what may happen.''

''I will go, Euphra. Not even you shall prevent me.''

''I will pay the wager for you.''

''Euphra!'' The tone implied many things.

Mr. Arnold approached. Other conversation followed. As half past ten chimed from the clock on the chimney-piece, Hugh rose to go.

''I will just get a book from my room,'' he said, ''and then perhaps Herr von Fenkelstein will be kind enough to see me make a beginning at least.''

''Certainly. My own recommendation would be that the book be Edgar Poe's tales.''

''Hardly. I shall need all the courage I have, I assure you.''

Hugh went to his room and washed his face and hands. Before doing so, as usual he pulled from his finger a ring of considerable value which had belonged to his father. As he was leaving the room to return to the company, he remembered he had left the ring on the washstand. He generally left it there at night, but now thought that as he was not going to sleep in the room it might be as well to place it in the escritoire. He opened the secret place and laid the diamond beside his poems and the crystal ring belonging to Mr. Arnold. This done, he picked up his book, returned to the drawing room, and found the whole party prepared to accompany him. Mr. Arnold had the keys. Von Fenkelstein and he went first. Hugh followed with Euphra.

"We will not contribute to your discomfort by locking the doors on the way, Mr. Sutherland," said Mr. Arnold.

"So you will not compel me to win the wager *in spite* of my fears," said Hugh.

"But you will let the ghost loose on the household," said the Bohemian, laughing.

"I will be responsible for that," replied Mr. Arnold.

Euphra dropped a little behind with Hugh.

"Remember the secret passage," she whispered. "You can get out when you will, whether they lock the door or not. Don't carry it too far, Hugh."

"The ghost, you mean, Euphra—I don't think I shall," laughed Hugh. But as he laughed, an involuntary shudder passed through him.

They reached the room and entered. Giving him the key of the door to lock from the inside, they bade him good night. They were just leaving when Hugh felt bound to say one thing more. "One word with you, Herr von Fenkelstein, if you please."

Fenkelstein followed him into the room. Hugh half-closed the door and then said, "I trust to your sympathy as a gentleman not to misunderstand me. I wagered a hundred guineas with you in the heat of after-dinner talk. I am not at present worth a hundred shillings, much less guineas."

"Oh," began Fenkelstein with a sneer, "if you now wish to get off on that ground—"

"Herr von Fenkelstein," interrupted Hugh in a very decided tone, "I pointed to your gentlemanly instincts. If you have difficulty accepting my statement on the ground, perhaps another may be found."

Hugh paused, but Fenkelstein did not seem to understand him. Hugh therefore went on, "Meantime, what I wanted to say was this. I have just left a ring in my room. I am uncertain of its exact value, yet it may be able to serve as a pledge of my good faith as it is of infinitely more value to me than can be reckoned by money. The ring is a diamond and belonged to my father.''

Von Fenkelstein merely replied, ''I beg your pardon, Mr. Sutherland, for misunderstanding you. The ring is quite an equivalent.'' And making him a respectful bow, he turned and left him.

29 / Lady Euphrasia

As soon as Hugh was alone, he locked the door by which he had entered. He then took the key from the lock and put it in his pocket. Looking to see if there were any other fastenings, he found an old tarnished brass bolt as well and succeeded in making it do its duty for the first time that century, which required some persuasion. He then turned toward the other door. As he crossed the room he found four candles, a decanter of port, and some biscuits on a table—placed there, no doubt, by the kind hand of Euphra. He vowed to himself that he would not touch the wine. But he lit the candles and then saw that the couch was provided with plenty of warm wraps for the night. One he recognized, to his delight, as a Cameron tartan, often worn by Euphra. He then went to the farthest recess, lifted the tapestry, and proceeded to fasten the concealed door. But to his dismay he could find no fastening on it.

"No doubt," he thought, "it must fasten in some secret way or other." But he could discover none. There was no mark of bolt or socket to show where one had been removed and no sign of friction to indicate that the door had ever been made secure. It closed simply with a spring.

As it was not yet the time when ghosts were to be expected, and as he felt very tired, he changed his mind and drank one glass of the wine, threw himself on the couch, drew Euphra's shawl over him, opened his book, and began to read. But the words soon vanished in a bewildering dance, and he slept.

He started awake in that agony of fear in which I suppose most people have awakened in the night once or twice in their lives. He felt that he was not alone. But the feeling seemed altogether different from that with which we recognize even the most unwelcome bodily visitor. The whole of his nervous skeleton seemed to shudder. Every sense was intensified, while his powers of movement were inoperative. He lay in mortal terror, unable to move a finger.

He saw, a few feet away, bending as if looking down upon him, a face which, if described as he saw it, would be pronounced far past the liberal boundary line of the human norm. It had passed beyond that degree of change at which a human countenance is fit for the upper world no longer and must be hidden away out of sight. The lips were dark and drawn back from the closed teeth, which were white as those of a skull. There were spots—in fact, the face corresponded exactly to the description given by Fenkelstein of the reported ghost of Lady Euphrasia. The dress was point for point the same as that in the picture. Had the portrait of Lady Euphrasia been hanging on the wall above, instead of the portrait of the unknown nun, Hugh would have thought, as far as the dress was concerned, that it had come alive and stepped from its frame—except for one thing: there was no ring on the thumb.

That he was able to recall all these particulars as he lay shivering in fear may seem strange. But the fact was that they burned themselves in upon his brain. They returned upon him afterward by degrees, as one becomes sensible of the pain of a wound.

But there was one sign of life. Though the eyes were closed, tears flowed from them and seemed to have worn channels for their constant flow down this face of death which ought to have been lying still in the grave, returning to its dust rather than weeping above ground instead. The figure stood for a moment as one who would gaze, could she open her heavy, death-rusted eyelids. Then, as if in hopeless defeat, she turned away. To crown the horror literally as well as figuratively, Hugh saw that her hair sparkled and gleamed, as the hair of a saint might if the halo of light were combed down into it.

She moved toward the door with a fettered pace, such as one might attribute to the dead if they walked. She dragged one limb after the other slowly and, to appearance, painfully as she moved toward the door which Hugh had locked.

When she had gone halfway to the door, Hugh, lying as he was on the couch, could see her feet, for her dress did not reach the ground. They were bare, as the feet of the dead ought to be which are about to tread softly in the realm of Hades. But how stained and mouldy and iron-spotted—as if the rain had been soaking through the spongy coffin—did the dress look beside the pure whiteness of those exquisite feet. Not a sign of the tomb was upon them as they lingered along the floor in their noiseless progress.

She reached the door, put out her hand, and touched it. Hugh saw it open outwards and let her through. It closed again behind her, noiseless as her footfalls.

The moment she vanished Hugh came to himself and the power of motion returned. He sprang to his feet and leaped to the door. With trembling hand he inserted the key. The lock creaked as he turned it. He recalled having heard that same creak a few moments before Euphra and he discovered they had been left alone in this very chamber. He had never thought of it before this moment.

Still the door would not open. It was bolted as well and the bolt was very stiff to withdraw. But at length he succeeded.

When he reached the passage outside, he thought he saw the glimmer of light, perhaps in the picture gallery beyond. Toward this he groped his way. Later he could never account for his having left the candles burning in the room behind him and going forward in the darkness, unless his wits had left him from the shock he had just suffered. When he reached the gallery, there was no light there; but somewhere in the distance he fancied he saw a faint shimmer.

The impulse to go toward it was too strong to be disputed with. He advanced with outstretched arms, groping his way. After a few steps he had lost all idea of where he was or how he ought to proceed. The light had vanished. He stood . . .

Was that a stealthy step he heard beside him in the dark?

He had no time to speculate, for the next moment he fell senseless.

30 / The Accident

Hugh came to himself slowly. His head ached. Had he fallen downstairs or had he struck his head against some projection and stunned himself? The last he remembered, he was standing quite still in the darkness and hearing something. Had he been knocked down? Where was he? Could the ghost have all been a dream and this headache be nature's revenge upon last night's wine? For he lay on the couch in the haunted chamber, and on his chest lay the book over which he had dropped asleep.

Mingled with all this doubt there was another. For he remembered feeling when his consciousness had first begun to return as if he had seen Euphra's face bending down close over his. Could it be possible? Had Euphra herself come to see how he had fared?

The room lay in the gray light of the dawn. Could she have been but a fantasy occurring when the last of sleeping and the first of waking are indistinguishably blended in a vague consciousness?

And what of the ghost? Was it not likely that she too was the offspring of his imagination—especially when considered that she corresponded exactly to the description given by the Bohemian? It was natural to expect an excited imagination to supply the missing details.

Hugh felt ghastly within. He raised himself on his elbow and looked into the room. Everything was the same as it had been the night before, only with an altered look in the dawn light. The dawn has a peculiar terror of its own, perhaps more real in character but very different from the terrors of the night. The room looked as if no ghost could have passed through its still, old, musty atmosphere. And yet it seemed as if some temporary cast-off body of the ghost must be lingering somewhere about it. He rose and peered into the recess where the cabinet stood. Nothing was there but the blackness. Having once yielded to the impulse, he could not keep from searching every moment, now into one, and now into another, of the many hidden corners. After all, even in the daylight there might be some dead thing there—who could tell? But he found nothing and remained manfully at his post till the sun rose, till bells rang, and till Fenkelstein came to fetch him. The count had clearly slept the night in the house, as he presented himself in a housecoat.

"Good morning, Mr. Sutherland. How have you slept?"

"So soundly that I woke quite early," answered Hugh.

"I am glad to hear it. But it is nearly time for breakfast, for which I am myself hardly ready yet, as you can see."

So saying he walked away. Hugh was a little surprised that he asked not a single question more as to how he had passed the night. Hugh hastened to his own room where he washed and dressed for breakfast.

"Well, Mr. Sutherland," said Mr. Arnold, greeting him, "how have you spent the night?"

"I slept with profound stupidity," answered Hugh, "a stupidity, in fact, quite worthy of the folly of the preceding wager."

This was true as it related to the time during which he had slept. But it was of course false in the impression it gave.

"Bravo!" exclaimed Mr. Arnold. "So you positively passed a pleasant night in the awful chamber? This is something to tell Euphra. You have restored the character of my house, Mr. Sutherland. I am greatly in your debt."

At this moment Euphra's maid brought the message that her mistress was sorry she was unable to appear at breakfast.

Mrs. Elton took her place.

"The day is so warm and still, Mr. Arnold, that I think Lady Emily might have a drive today. Perhaps Miss Cameron may be able to join us by that time."

"I cannot think what is the matter with Euphra," worried Mr. Arnold. "She never used to be affected in this way. But of course," he said, turning to Mrs. Elton, "you are most welcome to the carriage. I am sorry I cannot accompany you myself. But I must go to town today. You can take Mr. Sutherland with you if you like. He will take care of you."

"I shall be happy to," said Hugh.

"So shall we all," responded Mrs. Elton. "Will you favor us with your company as well, Herr von Fenkelstein?"

"I am sorry," replied Fenkelstein, "but I too must go to London today. Shall I have the pleasure of riding with you, Mr. Arnold?"

"If you can leave in ten minutes. I must go at once to catch the express train. I will go to the stable and order the ladies' carriage at once. I shall then be able to put a stop to these absurd rumors in person. I will, through the coachman, send a report of your courage, Mr. Sutherland, and its results all over the house."

This was a very gracious explanation of his measures. But Hugh had not expected such an immediate consequence of his less than truthful report of the night and could not help feeling rather uncomfortable about it.

While Mr. Arnold had been speaking, Fenkelstein had gone to a side table where he wrote out a check on a London banking house for a hundred guineas. He now handed this to Hugh. In his innocence, Hugh could not help feeling ashamed of gaining such a sum by such means.

But he felt that to show the least reluctance would place him at a great disadvantage with a man of the world like the count. He therefore thanked him and thrust the check into his pocket, as if a greater sum of money than he had ever handled before were nothing out of the ordinary. He then left for the schoolroom.

Harry was waiting for him, looking tolerably well and happy. This was a great relief to Hugh who had worried that he might have missed him in the night (they were still bedfellows) and thus had one of his dreadful attacks of fear. It was evident this had not taken place.

When Mrs. Elton left the breakfast table she went straight to Miss Cameron's room. Knocking, she received no answer and then went in search of Euphra's maid.

"Is your mistress going to get up today, Jane?" asked Mrs. Elton.

"I don't know. Has she not rung yet?"

"Have you not been to see her?"

"No, ma'am."

"How was it that you brought that message at breakfast then?"

Jane looked confused, then said, "She told me to say it."

"How did she tell you?"

Jane paused again.

"Through the door, ma'am," she answered at length. Then she muttered that they would make her tell lies by asking her questions she couldn't answer, and she wished she was out of the house, that she did.

Mrs. Elton heard this, and, of course, felt considerably puzzled by it.

"Will you not go and inquire after your mistress, with my compliments?"

"I daren't, ma'am."

"Dare not! What do you mean?"

"Well, ma'am, there is something about my mistress—" Here she stopped abruptly. As Mrs. Elton stood expectantly, she tried to go on. But all she could add was, "No, ma'am, I daren't."

"But there can be no harm in going to her room. Why won't you go now?"

"Why—why—because she told me—" Here the girl stammered and turned pale. At length she forced out the words, "She won't let me tell you why," and burst into tears.

With that she hurried out of the room, while Mrs. Elton turned in bewilderment. What this incident indicated I cannot say. It shows evidently enough that if Euphra had more than usual influence over servants in general, she had a great deal more over this maid in particular.

At one o'clock the carriage came round to the door, and Hugh, in the hope of seeing Euphra alone, was the first in the hall. Mrs. Elton and Lady Emily presently came and proceeded to take their places without seeming to expect Miss Cameron. Hugh helped them into the carriage, but instead of getting in, lingered, hoping that Euphra was yet going to make her appearance.

"I fear Miss Cameron is unable to join us," said Mrs. Elton.

"Shall I run upstairs and knock at her door?" said Hugh.

"Do," replied Mrs. Elton, who had remained curious all morning.

Hugh bounded upstairs. But just as he was going to knock, the door opened and Euphra appeared.

"Dear Euphra, how ill you look!" exclaimed Hugh.

She was pale as death and dark under the eyes. She had evidently been weeping.

"Never mind. It is only a bad headache. Don't take any notice of it."

"The carriage is at the door. Will you not come with us?"

"With whom?"

"Lady Emily and Mrs. Elton."

"I am sick of them."

"I am going, Euphra."

"Stay with me instead."

"I must go. I promised to take care of them."

"Oh, nonsense! What could happen to them? Stay with me."

"I wish I could. I am very sorry."

"Then I must go with you, I suppose." Yet her tone expressed annoyance.

"Oh, thank you!" cried Hugh in delight. "I will run down and tell them to wait."

He bounded away and told the ladies that Euphra would join them in a few minutes.

But Euphra was cool enough to inflict on them quite twenty minutes of waiting. When she did appear at last she was closely veiled and stepped into the carriage without once showing her face. She made a very pretty apology for the delay she had caused, which was certainly due, seeing it had been perfectly intentional. She made room for Hugh; he took his place beside her and they drove away.

Euphra scarcely spoke, but begged indulgence on account of her headache. Lady Emily enjoyed the drive very much and said a great many pleasant little nothings.

"Would you like a glass of milk?" Mrs. Elton said to her as they passed a farmhouse on the estate.

"I would—very much," answered Lady Emily.

The carriage was stopped and the servant sent to ask for a glass of milk. Euphra, feeling very uncomfortable for some time from riding backward with a headache, wished to get out while the carriage was waiting. Hugh jumped out and assisted her. She walked a little way, leaning on his arm, up to the house where she had a glass of water. She said she felt better, and they returned to the carriage.

In getting back in, either from carelessness or the weakness brought on by her illness, she slipped from the step and fell with a cry of alarm. Hugh caught her as she fell, and she would have been none the worse for it had not the horses started and sprung forward at that moment. As her foot hit the ground the hind wheel of the carriage jerked forward over it, crushing her ankle beneath it. Hugh, raising her in his arms, found she was unconscious.

He laid her down upon the grass by the roadside. In agony he ran to the house for a glass of water, but she showed no sign of recovering.

At length he lifted her back into the carriage, and they made what arrangements they best could to allow her to lie down. Blood was flowing from her foot, and it was already greatly swollen. Hugh would have walked home in order that she might have more room. But he knew he would be more useful there when they arrived. He seated himself so as to support the injured foot and prevent as best he could the torturing effects of motion of the carriage. When they had gone about halfway, she opened her eyes feebly, glanced at him, and closed them again with a moan of pain.

He carried her in his arms up to her own room and laid her on a couch. She thanked him by a pitiful attempt at a smile. He rushed back downstairs, mounted his horse, and galloped at full speed for a surgeon.

The injury was a serious one, but until the swelling could be reduced, it was impossible to tell how serious. The surgeon, however, feared that some of the bones of the ankle might be badly broken. The ankle seemed to be dislocated, and the suffering was great. She endured it well, however, so far as absolute silence constitutes endurance.

Hugh was miserable. The surgeon had required his assistance, but a suitable nurse soon arrived, and there was no further pretext for his presence in the sickroom. He wandered about the grounds. Harry haunted his steps like a spaniel. The poor boy felt it much, and the suffering abstraction of Hugh sealed up his chief well of comfort. At length he went to Mrs. Elton, who did her best to console him.

By the surgeon's express orders everyone but the nurse was excluded from Euphra's room.

31 / The Robbery

When Mr. Arnold came home to dinner and heard of the accident, his first feeling, as is the case with weak men, was one of mingled annoyance and anger. Hugh was the chief object of it, for had he not committed the ladies to his care? And the economy of his house being partially disarranged by it, had he not a good right to be angry? His second feeling was one of concern for his niece.

Still, nothing must interfere with the order of things; and when Hugh went into the drawing room at the dinner hour, he found Mr. Arnold standing there in tailcoat and white neckcloth looking as if he had just arrived at a friend's house for a party. And the party which sat down to dinner was certainly dreary enough. Mr. Arnold was considerably out of humor and though the subject of the accident filled the minds of all at the table, it was scarcely more than alluded to.

"By the way, Mr. Sutherland," Mr. Arnold said after dinner, "have you succeeded in deciphering that curious inscription yet? I don't like the ring to remain long out of my own keeping. It is quite an heirloom, I assure you."

Hugh was forced to confess that he had never thought of it again.

"Shall I go get it at once?" he asked.

"Oh, no," replied Mr. Arnold. "Tomorrow will do perfectly well."

After breakfast the next day, Hugh got together his German books and then went to his desk to take out the ring. He opened the secret place and stood in shock. The ring was gone!

His packet of papers was there, rather crumpled, but the ring was nowhere. It was not long before a conclusion suggested itself, flashing upon him all at once.

"The ghost has got it," he said half aloud. "It is shining now on her dead finger. It *was* Lady Euphrasia. She was going for it, then. It wasn't on her thumb when she went. She came back with it, shining through the dark—stepped over me, perhaps, as I lay on the floor in her way."

He shivered at his own words.

Again and again he searched the receptacle but in the end just stood gazing. Then a new thought stung him. Suddenly he shot his hand into the place once more, useless as he knew the search to be. He took up his papers and scattered them loose. It was to no avail. His father's ring was gone as well.

He sank on a chair for a moment. The loss of his own ring added to his perplexity. What could she want with *his* ring? Could she have carried with her such a passion for jewels as to come from the grave to appropriate those of others as well as to reclaim her own? Would it be better to tell Mr. Arnold of the loss of both rings or should he mention the crystal only? He came to the conclusion that it would only exasperate him the more and perhaps turn suspicion all the more on himself if he communicated the fact that he too was a loser and to such an extent. For Hugh's ring was worth twenty of the other.

Mr. Arnold returned from a day's horseback ride late in the afternoon. It did not prejudice him in favor of the reporter of bad tidings that he begged a word with him before dinner.

"Mr. Arnold," Hugh began, "I am sorry to say I have been robbed, and in your house too."

"In my house? Of what, pray, Mr. Sutherland?"

"Of your ring, Mr. Arnold."

"Of—my—ring?"

He looked at his ring finger, as if he could not understand the meaning of Hugh's words.

"Of the ring you lent me to decipher," explained Hugh.

"Do you suppose I do not understand you, Mr. Sutherland? A ring which has been in the family for two hundred years at least! Robbed of it? In my house? You must have been disgracefully careless, Mr. Sutherland. You have lost it!"

"Mr. Arnold," said Hugh with dignity. "I am above using such a subterfuge, even if it were not certain to throw suspicion where it was undeserved."

Mr. Arnold was a gentleman as far as his self-importance allowed. He did not apologize for what he had said, but he changed his manner at once.

"I am quite bewildered, Mr. Sutherland. It is a very annoying piece of news—for many reasons."

"I can show you where I laid it—in the safest corner in my room, I assure you."

"Of course, of course. It is enough you say so. We must not keep dinner waiting now. But after dinner I shall have all the servants up, and we will investigate the matter thoroughly."

So, thought Hugh to himself, *someone will be made a felon of because the dead go stalking about this infernal house at midnight. No, that won't do. I must at least tell him what I know of the doings of the night.*

Mr. Arnold was walking toward the door, and turned with some additional annoyance when Hugh addressed him again.

"One moment, Mr. Arnold, if you please."

Mr. Arnold merely turned and waited.

"I fear I will jeopardize your good opinion of me, but there is something more to the disappearance of the ring. I must tell you what happened the night I kept watch in Lady Euphrasia's room."

"You said you slept soundly."

"So I did, part of the time."

"Then you kept back part of the truth."

"I did."

"That was hardly worthy of you."

"I thought it best at the time. I doubted myself what I had seen."

"What has caused you to change your mind now?"

"The disappearance of the ring."

"What has that to do with it? How do you even know it was taken on that night?"

"I do not know; for till this morning I had not opened the place where it lay. I only suspect it."

"I am the local magistrate, Mr. Sutherland. I would rather not be prejudiced by suspicions."

"The person to whom my suspicions refer is beyond your jurisdiction, Mr. Arnold."

"I'm afraid I do not understand you."

Hugh went on to give Mr. Arnold a hurried yet circumstantial sketch of the apparition he believed he had seen.

"What am I to judge from all this?" he asked coldly.

"I have told you the facts and must leave the conclusions to yourself. But I confess, for my part, any disbelief I had in apparitions is almost entirely removed since—"

"Since you dreamed you saw one."

"Since the disappearance of the ring," said Hugh.

"Bah!" exclaimed Mr. Arnold with indignation. "Can a ghost fetch and carry like a spaniel? Mr. Sutherland, I am ashamed to have such a reasoner for tutor to my son. Come to dinner and do not let me hear another word of this folly. I beg you will not mention it to anyone."

"I have been silent till now. But circumstances, such as the charging of anyone else with stealing the ring, might compel me to mention the matter."

It was evident that Mr. Arnold was more annoyed at the imputation of ghostly nocturnal habits of his house than at the loss of the ring. He looked at Hugh for a moment as if he might break into a rage. Then his look gradually changed into one of suspicion, and turning without another word he led the way to the dining room. To have a ghost held in his face in this fashion was more than man could bear. He sat down to dinner in gloomy silence, breaking it only as often as he was compelled to do the duties of a host, which he performed with greater loftiness of ceremony than usual.

There was no summoning of the servants after dinner. Nor was the subject once more alluded to in Hugh's hearing. No doubt Mr. Arnold felt something ought to be done. But I presume he never could make up his mind what that something ought to be.

One thing is certain—from this time he ceased to behave to Hugh with that growing cordiality which he had shown him for weeks past. Hugh could not help associating it with that look of suspicion, the remains of which were still discernible on Mr. Arnold's face, although he could not determine the exact direction of his suspicions. Mr. Arnold, however, did not reveal his change of feeling so much by neglect as by ceremony, which sooner than anything else builds a wall of separation between those who meet every day.

As for Hugh's original deduction that his nocturnal visitor in Lady Euphrasia's bed chamber was now wearing the ring again, this idea was gradually replaced by the suspicion that a certain count now had *two* rings in his possession, one of which had more value to Hugh than could ever be described in monetary terms. He mentally chastised himself a dozen times a day for the socially approved instincts of a gentleman which had prodded him to risk his dearest possession to the grasp of Fenkelstein in a stupid wager.

32 / A Clandestine Meeting

Dreary days followed the accident. The reports concerning Euphra were mixed. Hugh heard that the swelling was reduced but that the final effect upon the use of the limb was doubtful. The pretty foot lay aching in Hugh's heart. Before Harry went to bed in the evening he would walk out through the grounds. As often as he dared he would pass under Euphra's window, for all he could have of her now was a few rays from the same light that lit her chamber.

When a week had passed she was sufficiently recovered as to be able to see Mr. Arnold, from whom Hugh heard, in a somewhat reproachful tone, that she was but the wreck of her former self. A fortnight passed, and she saw Mrs. Elton and Lady Emily for a few moments. Then one day, when the visitors were out with Mr. Arnold, Jane brought a message to Hugh that Miss Cameron wanted to see him. Hugh's heart fluttered as he rose, restraining his desire to dash through the house, and followed the maid. He entered the room and approached the bed. He stood over Euphra, pale and speechless. She lay before him wasted and wan, her eyes seemingly twice their former size but with half their former light. She had just raised herself with difficulty to a sitting posture and the effort had left her weary.

"Hugh," she said softly.

"Dear Euphra," he answered, kissing the thin hand he held in his.

She looked at him for a few moments, and the tears rose in her eyes.

"Hugh . . . I am a cripple for life."

"God forbid, Euphra!" was all he could reply.

She shook her head mournfully. Then a strange, wild look came into her eyes and grew till it seemed to overflow her whole face.

"What is the matter, dear Euphra?" asked Hugh in alarm. "Is your foot painful?"

She made no answer. She was staring at his hand.

"Shall I call Jane?"

She shook her head.

"Can I do nothing for you?"

"No," she answered in a strange tone.

"Shall I go, Euphra?"

"Yes . . . yes. Go."

He left the room. But a sharp cry of despair drew him back to her bedside in an instant. Euphra had fainted.

He rang the bell for Jane and waited until he saw signs of returning consciousness.

What could this mean? He was more perplexed with her than he had ever been. The next day Lady Emily brought him a message from Euphra—not to distress himself about her; it was not his fault. The bearer understood this message to refer to the original accident, as the sender intended she should. The receiver interpreted it in light of the occurrence of the day before, as the sender likewise intended. It comforted him.

It had become almost a habit with Hugh to ascend the oak tree in the evening and sit alone, sometimes for hours, in the nest he had built for Harry. One time he took a book with him, another he went without, and now and then Harry accompanied him.

One night after tea, when the house became oppressive to him from the longing to see Euphra, Hugh wandered out alone. In the shadows of the coming night he climbed the nest. An aging moon was feeling her path somewhere through the heavens, but a thin veil of cloud was spread like a tent under the dome where she walked. He did not know how long he sat in the oak nest. Light after light was extinguished in the house, and still he sat there brooding, dreaming.

All at once he became aware of human voices. He looked out from his leafy screen and saw once more at the end of the Ghost's Walk a form clothed in white. But there were voices of two. He sent his soul into his ears to listen. A horrible, incredible, impossible idea forced itself upon him—that the tones were of Euphra and Fenkelstein! The one voice was weak and complaining; the other firm, and strong.

"It must be some horrible ghost that imitates her," he said to himself, for he was nearly crazy at the very suggestion.

He would see nearer, if only to get rid of the frightful insinuation. He descended the tree noiselessly but lost sight of the figure as he did so. He drew near the place where he had seen it, but there was now no sound of voices to guide him. As he came within sight of the spot, he saw the white figure in the arms of another, a man. Her head was lying on his shoulder. A moment later and she was lifted in those arms and borne down the Ghost's Avenue toward the house.

A burning agony seized on Hugh. He had to know! He fled like a deer to the house by another path; he tried in his suspicion the library window. It was open and he was at Euphra's door in a moment. He hesitated. She *must* be inside.

Dare he knock? If she was there she would be asleep. He would not wake her. There was no time to lose. He would risk anything to be rid of this horrible doubt.

He gently opened the door. The night light was burning. He thought at first that Euphra was in the bed. He felt like a thief, but he stole nearer.

She was not there!

She was not on the couch. She was not in the room. Jane was fast asleep in the dressing room.

It was enough.

He withdrew. He would watch at his door to see her return, for she must pass his door to reach her own. He waited a time that seemed hours. At length, Euphra crept past him, appearing in the darkness to crawl along the wall against which she supported herself, scarcely suppressing her groans of pain.

Hugh was nearly mad. When she was in her own room, he rushed down the stair to the library and out into the wood. Why or where he was running to he did not know.

Suddenly he received a blow on the head. He staggered under it. Had he run into a tree? No, for there was the dim bulk of a man disappearing through the woods. Hugh darted after him. The man heard his footsteps, stopped, turned, and waited. As Hugh came up to him he made a thrust at him with some weapon. He missed his aim. The next moment Hugh had wrenched the sword-stick from him and grappled with the man himself. But, strong as Hugh was, the Bohemian was as strong, and the contest was doubtful.

"Give me my ring!" gasped Hugh as they struggled.

An imprecation of emphatic character was the only reply. The Bohemian got one hand loose and Hugh heard a sound like the breaking of glass. Before he could gain any advantage—for his antagonist seemed to have concentrated all his force in his other hand—a wet handkerchief was held firmly to his face. Hugh's fierceness died away. He was lapped in the vapor of dreams, and his senses departed.

33 / Changes

When Hugh came to himself, he was lying in the first gray of the dawn amidst the dews of the morning woods. He rose painfully and looked around him. The Ghost's Walk lay in long silence before him. Here and there a little bird moved and peeped. The glory of a new summer's day was climbing up the eastern coast of heaven. But for him the spirit was gone out of the world.

Perhaps had he overheard the conversation, he would now have thought more gently of Euphra. But it is to be doubted whether even then his deeper feelings toward her could have remained what they had been. Like many youths he had the loftiest notions of feminine grace and thought and action. Now he found that he had loved a woman who would creep from her own room, at the cost of great suffering, to meet in the night and in the woods a man no better than a thief. Had his emotions not been in the way, he would have realized that the very extravagance of the action demanded a deeper explanation than what seemed to lie on the surface.

Instead of being torn in pieces by storms of jealousy as one might expect, the effect on Hugh was that all the summer growths of his love were suddenly chilled by an absolute frost of death. A kind of annihilation sank upon the image of Euphra. There had been no such Euphra as he had thought he loved. She had been but a creation of his own brain. It was not so much that he ceased to love as that the beloved ceased to exist.

There were fleeting moments in which he seemed to love her still with a wild outcry of passion. But the frenzy soon vanished in the selfish feeling of his own loss. His love was not a high one—not such as thine, my Falconer. Thine was love indeed. Though its tale is too good to tell simply because it is too good to be believed. And we do men a wrong sometimes when we tell them more than they can receive.

Hugh soon began to look back upon his former fascination with a kind of wondering unbelief. He could hardly even recall the feelings with which he had regarded Euphra. He felt now just as he had felt in his earlier years on waking in the morning to find he had been in love with a dream lady all the night. It had been very delightful, and it was sad that the feeling was gone and could come back no more. He mourned bitterly over the loss of those feelings for Euphra, for they had been precious to him. But he could not help it. For his love had been fascination, and the fascination having ceased, the love was gone.

Had he *really* loved Euphra—herself—her own self, the living woman who looked at him out of those eyes, out of that face, such pity would have blended with the love as would have made it greater and permitted nothing to overwhelm it. As it was, his fault lay in the original weakness that submitted to be so fascinated that gave in to it in spite of the vague expostulations of his conscience that he was neglecting his duty to Harry in order to please Euphra and enjoy her society. Had he persisted in doing his duty, it would have kept his mind more healthy and lessened the absorption of his passion. But now the spell was broken.

All that day he walked in a dream of loss. Euphra was removed to a vast distance from him. An impassable gulf lay between them.

She sent for him. He went, filled with a sense of emptiness. She was much worse and suffering great pain. Hugh saw at once that she knew all was over between them. She knew he had seen her pass his door or had been in her room, for he had left her door a little open, and she had left it shut. One pathetic, pitiful glance of entreaty she fixed upon him after a few moments of silence. There were no words. He turned to leave the room.

She made no effort to detain him, but turned her face away and sobbed. Hardhearted, he did not turn to comfort her. Perhaps it was better. Some kinds of comfort are like the food on which the patient and the disease live together. Some griefs are soonest got rid of by letting them burn out. All the fire engines in creation can only prolong the time and increase the sense of burning. There is but one cure: the feeling of the human God, which converts the agony itself into the creative fire of a higher life.

The day went on, as days will go. After what lessons he was able to get through with Harry, he threw himself on the couch and tried to think. But though thoughts passed through him, he did not think them. He was powerless in regard to them. They came and went of their own will; he could neither say *come* nor *go*. Tired at length of the couch, he got up and paced about the room for hours. When he came to himself a little, he found that the sun was nearly setting. But there was no beauty for him in the going down of the sun, no glory in the golden light. The sun sank, and gradually a gray light rather than golden filled the room. The change had no interest for him. The aching of a lost passion tormented him.

As the next few days passed, Hugh took refuge with Harry. His pupil was now his consoler. The boy was again filled with delight at having his big brother all to himself and worked harder than ever to make the best of his privileges. For Hugh it was wonderful how soon his peace of mind began to return after he gave himself to duty. Painful thoughts about Euphra would still present themselves, but instead of becoming more sorrowful as the days went by, they grew more angry. He even began to wonder whether she knew all about the theft of both rings, for only to her had he divulged the secret place in the old desk.

Along with these feelings and thoughts of mingled good and bad came one feeling which he needed more than any other—repentance. As he sat alone one day on a fallen tree, the face of poor Harry came back to him as he first saw it that day in the library, poring sadly over a book he could never understand. The memory of that sickly little face smote him with a pang. *What might I not have done for the boy?* he thought. Alas, though he was now giving his best to Harry once again, much time and relational energy had been lost.

He did not see Euphra again for more than two weeks.

At length, one evening, entering the drawing room before dinner, Hugh found Euphra there alone. He bowed with embarrassment and mumbled some commonplace congratulation on her recovery. She answered him formally and coldly. She took his arm to go into the dining room and leaned upon it, as she was compelled to do. Her uncle was delighted to see her once more. Mrs. Elton addressed her with kindness and Lady Emily with sweet cordiality. As soon as dinner was over she sent for her maid and withdrew to her own room. It was a great relief to Hugh to feel that he was no longer in danger of encountering her eyes.

Gradually she recovered strength, though it was again some days before she appeared at the dinner table. The emotional distance between Hugh and her continued to increase.

The time drew near for Lady Emily's departure.

"What are your plans for the winter, Mrs. Elton?" asked Mr. Arnold one day.

"I intend to spend the winter in London," she answered.

"Then you are not going with Lady Emily to Spain?"

"No."

"I have in mind to spend the winter abroad myself, but the difficulty is what to do with Harry."

"Could you not leave him with Mr. Sutherland?"

"I choose not to do that."

"Then let him come with me. There will be plenty of room for Harry."

"A very kind offer. I will think about it."

"I fear we could hardly accommodate his tutor, though," she added. "Perhaps we could arrange for him to lodge elsewhere."

"Give yourself no trouble about that. I want Harry to have different tutors for the various branches he will study."

"But Mr. Sutherland is a very good tutor."

"Yes. Very. Still I feel he may have done all he can for my Harry."

Euphra gradually resumed her duties in the house, as far as great lameness would permit. She continued to show a quiet and dignified reserve toward Hugh. She made no attempt to fascinate him, but never avoided his look when it chanced to meet hers. However, Hugh's eyes always fell before hers. Her behavior to Mrs. Elton and Lady Emily showed a cordial indifference. When the time came for their departure, she did not appear to be much relieved.

One day toward the end of September, Mr. Arnold and Hugh were alone after breakfast. Mr. Arnold spoke, "Mr. Sutherland, I have changed my plans with regard to Harry. I wish him to spend the winter in London."

Hugh listened and waited.

Mr. Arnold went on, after a slight pause. "There I hope for him to reap such advantages as are to be gained in the metropolis. He has improved wonderfully under your instruction and is now, I think, to be benefited by a variety of teachers. Consequently, I shall be compelled to deny him your further services."

"Very well, Mr. Arnold," said Hugh. "When shall I take my leave of him?"

"Not before the middle of next month. But I will write you a check for your salary at once."

So saying, Mr. Arnold left the room for a moment and returned, handing Hugh a check for a year's salary. Hugh glanced at it and handed it again to Mr. Arnold.

"I can claim scarcely more than half a year's salary."

"Mr. Sutherland, you were hired for a year, and if I prevent you from fulfilling your part of it, I am still bound to fulfill mine."

"You are very kind, Mr. Arnold."

"Only just," rejoined Mr. Arnold with conscious dignity. "I am under great obligation for the way in which you have devoted yourself to Harry."

Hugh's conscience gave him a pang. But he persisted no longer in his refusal. He could not doubt that his dismissal was somehow or other connected with the loss of the ring; but he would not stoop to inquire into the matter. He hoped that time would set all right. At the moment he felt considerable indifference to the opinion of Mr. Arnold, or anyone in the house, except Harry.

The boy burst into tears when informed of his father's decision with regard to his winter studies and could only be consoled by the hope which Hugh held out to him—certainly upon a very slight foundation—that they might meet sometimes in London. For the little time that remained, Hugh devoted himself unceasingly to his pupil—not merely studying with him, but walking, riding, reading stories, and going through all sorts of exercises for the strengthening of his person and constitution. The best results followed for both Harry and his tutor.

34 / Departure

The last evening that Hugh was to spend at Arnstead inevitably arrived. He wandered out alone. He had been with Harry all day and now he wished a few moments of solitude. It was a lovely autumn evening and he sought the woods behind the house. The leaves were still thick upon the trees, but most of them had changed to gold, brown, and red, and the sweet faint odors of those that had fallen and lay thick underfoot ascended to perfume the air. As he strolled about, the whole history of his past life arose before him.

In this mood he could think of no time so golden as the memory of the cottage in which lived David, Jeanette, and Margaret. That kingly, gracious old man who had been a father to him was forgotten recently in the passion of a foolish love. He had allowed himself to neglect them. Not forget, for he loved them still. But yes, he had neglected them in his memory.

Musing sorrowfully and self-reproachfully, he came to the Ghost's Walk. Up and down it he walked, a fit place for remembering all that had taken place. The strange sight he had seen here on that moonlit night, of two silent wandering figures—or could it be that they were one and the same, suddenly changed in hue?—returned upon him. This vision had been so speedily followed by the second and more alarming apparition of Lady Euphrasia that he had hardly time to speculate on what the former could have been.

He was meditating upon all these strange events—remarking to himself that since his midnight encounter the house had been quiet as a churchyard at noon—when suddenly he saw before him, at some distance, a dark figure approaching. His heart bounded into his throat as he said to himself, "It is the nun again!" But the next moment he saw that it was Euphra. His first impulse was to turn aside, for indeed, Euphra had become almost like a ghost to him. But she had seen him and was evidently going to address him. She approached with painful steps and spoke first.

"I have been looking for you, Mr. Sutherland. I wanted very much to talk to you for a moment before you go. Will you allow me?"

Euphra's manner was collected and kind, yet showed her awareness that the relation which had once existed between them had passed away forever. In her voice there was something like the tone of wind blowing through a ruin.

With a hint of awkwardness, Hugh said, "I shall be most happy."

She smiled sadly. A great change had passed upon her.

"I am going to be frank with you," she said. "I am perfectly aware that the boyish fancy you had for me is gone. Do not be offended. You are manly enough, but your love for me was boyish. Most first loves are childish, quite irrespective of age."

Hugh could not help feeling hurt.

She went on, "But I cannot afford to lose *you*, the only friend I have."

Hugh turned toward her with a face full of manhood and truth.

"You shall not lose me, Euphra, if you will be honest to yourself and to me."

"Thank you. I can trust you. I will be honest."

At that moment, without the resurgence of a trace of his former feelings, Huge felt nearer to her than he had ever felt before. Now there seemed to be truth between them, the only medium through which beings can unite.

"I fear I have wronged you much," she went on. "I fear I am the cause of your having to leave Arnstead."

"You, Euphra? You must be mistaken."

"I do not think so. But I am compelled to disclose a secret to you—a sad secret about myself. Please, do not hate me . . . I am a sleep-walker.

She hid her face in her hands. Hugh did not reply.

She went on after a pause. "I did not think at first that I had taken the ring. But last night, and not till then, I discovered that I was the culprit."

"How?"

"That requires an explanation. Whenever I have been walking in my sleep, I have no recollection of it. Indeed, the utter absence of a sense of dreaming always makes me suspect that I have been wandering. But sometimes I have a vivid dream which I know to be a reproduction of some previous somnambulic experience. Do not ask me to recall the horrors I dreamed last night. Suffice it to say, I am sure I took the ring."

"Then you dreamed what you did with it?"

"Yes, I gave it to—"

Her voice sank and ceased.

"Have you mentioned this to Mr. Arnold?"

"No. I do not think it would do any good. But I will, if you wish," she added submissively.

"Not at all. Whatever you think best."

"I could not tell him everything. I cannot tell you everything. If I did, Mr. Arnold would turn me out of the house. I am a very unhappy girl, Mr. Sutherland."

From the tone of these words Hugh could not for a moment suppose that Euphra had any remaining design of trying to charm him.

"Perhaps he might want to keep you if I told him. But I doubt you could stay after the way he has behaved to you, for he would never apologize. Perhaps it is selfish of me, but I do not have the courage to confess it to him."

"Nothing could make me remain now . . . but what can I do for you?"

"If only I can depend on you, in case I should need your help, or—"

Euphra stopped suddenly and caught up Hugh's left hand.

"Where is your ring?" she said in a tone of suppressed anxiety.

"Gone, Euphra. My father's ring. It was lying beside Lady Euphrasia's."

Euphra again hid her face in her hands and sobbed. When she grew a little calmer she said, "I am sure I did not take your ring, dear Hugh—I am not a thief. I had a kind of right to the other. Although he said it ought to have been his, for his real name was Count von Halkar—the same name as Lady Euphrasia's before she was married. He took it, I am sure."

"It was he that knocked me down in the dark that night, then, Euphra?"

"Did he? Oh, I shall have to tell you it all. That awful man has a terrible power over me. I loved him once. But I refused to take the ring from your desk. He threw me into a hypnotic sleep and sent me for the ring. But I know I should have remembered if I had taken yours. Even in my sleep I don't think he could have made me do that. He promised to set me free if I would get the ring. But he has not done it, and he will not."

Sobs again interrupted her.

"I have been afraid your ring was gone," she went on. "I don't know why I thought so except that you didn't have it on when you came to see me. Or perhaps it was because I am sometimes forced to think what that wretch is thinking. He made me go to him that night you saw me, Hugh. I was so ill I don't think I would have been able, but I could not rest till I had asked him about your ring. He said he knew nothing about it."

"I am sure he has it," said Hugh. And he related to Euphra the struggle he had had with Fenkelstein and its result. She shuddered.

"I have been terrible to you, Hugh. I have betrayed you. I fear you will never see your ring again. Here, take mine. It is not as good as yours, but for the sake of the way you thought of me, take it."

"No, no, Euphra; Mr. Arnold would miss it. Besides, you know it would not be my father's ring, and it was not for the value of the diamond

I cared most about it. And I am not absolutely sure I shall not find it again. I am going to London where I plan to fall in with him once more.''

``Oh, but *do* take care of yourself! He has no conscience. God knows I have had little. But he has none.''

``What could he want that ring of Lady Euphrasia's for?''

``I don't know. He never told me.''

``It was not worth that much.''

``Next to nothing. There must be something about it, some power or advantage he feels it would give him. But do be careful.''

``Don't fear.''

She held out her hand as if to take leave of him, but withdrew it again with a sudden cry. ``Oh, Hugh, what shall I do? I am a slave, body and soul.''

She paused, thinking, then resumed in a calmer tone, ``Hugh, do you think there is a God?''

Her eyes glimmered with faint tears. And now Hugh's own spiritual poverty struck him with grief and humiliation. Here was a soul seeking her God, and he had nothing to offer. He had been told . . . she had been told, a million times. But he could not say that he *knew* it.

``I do not know. I hope so.''

``I think, if there were a God, he would help me. For I am nothing now; I hardly have a will of my own.'' The sigh she heaved told of a hopeless oppression.

``The best and wisest man I ever knew,'' said Hugh, ``believed in God with his whole heart. In fact, he cared for nothing but God; or rather, he cared for everything because it belonged to God. He was never afraid of anything, never troubled about anything.''

``Ah, I wish I knew him. I would go to that man and ask him to help me. Where does he live?''

``Alas, to my shame I do not even know whether he is alive or dead. He was aging when I knew him, and it has been some time. But if he lives, he lives far away in the north of Scotland.''

``I will write to him.''

``I will write down his address for you when I go in,'' said Hugh. ``But what can he save you from?''

``From no God,'' she answered. ``If there is no God, then I am sure there is a devil and that he has got me in his power.''

Hugh felt her shudder, for she was leaning on his arm.

``Oh, if I had a God, he would help me. I know it!'' she cried.

Hugh could not reply. A pause followed.

``Good-bye, Hugh,'' said Euphra, regaining control. ``I am sure we shall meet again, and my premonitions are generally true.''

Hugh kissed her hand with more real devotion than he had ever kissed it before.

She left him and hastened to the house as best she could. He was sorry she was gone. He walked up and down for some time until he heard the dinner bell. After dinner, Mr. Arnold wished him good night more kindly than usual. When he went up to his room he found that Harry had already cried himself to sleep.

He sat down at the desk, took his poems out of the fatal drawer, wrote, "Take them, please, such as they are. Let me be your friend," enclosed them with the writing, and addressed them to Euphra.

Then his thoughts turned toward his future. He would go to London. He would try to find Fenkelstein. He would write. He would make acquaintance with London life. Who could live more thriftily than he? He could give some private lessons or perhaps might get a situation in a school for a short time. At all events, he would see London and look about him for a little while before he settled into anything definite.

The next morning he bade adieu to Arnstead. I will not describe the parting with poor Harry. The boy's heart seemed ready to break, and Hugh could hardly refrain from tears. One of the grooms drove him to the railway station in the dog cart. As they came near the station, Hugh gave him half a crown. Enlivened by the gift, the man began to talk.

"He's a rum customer, that ere gem'men with the forin name. The color of his puss I couldn't swear to now. Never saw sixpence o' his'n. My opinin is that master had better look arter his spoons. And for missus—well, it's a pity! He's a rum un, as I say, anyhow."

The man here nodded several times, half importantly.

Hugh did not choose to inquire what he meant. They reached the station, and in a short time he was shooting toward London.

35 / London

Hugh felt rather dreary as he drew near to the London Bridge Station. Fog, drizzle, smoke, and stench comprised the atmosphere. Leaving his luggage at the office, he set out on foot to explore—to go and look for his future, which, even when he met it, he would not be able to recognize with any certainty. The streets, from garret to cellar, seemed muddy, moist and filthy. He had to wade through thin mud even on the pavements. Everybody looked depressed and hurried; the rain and general misery seemed a plague drawn down on the city. Nobody seemed to care for anybody or anything. And yet in reality the whole mass was so bound together, interwoven by the crossing and intertwisting threads of interest and mutual relationship of every kind, that Hugh soon found how hard it was to get within the mass at all, so as to be in any degree partaker of the benefits it shared within itself.

He did not wish to get lodgings in the outskirts, but he found none around him. Growing tired and hungry, he went at length into an eating-house and dined upon a cinder which had once been a steak. He tried to delude himself into the idea that it was a steak still by concentrating his attention instead on a newspaper two days old. He came upon some advertisements for lodgings and searched for one whose address might suit him. At last he found one and, with the assistance of the girl who waited upon him, located it on his map. Then, refreshed by his dinner, such as it was, he set out again. The rain was over, and an afternoon sun was trying, with some slight measure of success, to pierce the clouds of the London atmosphere. He found the house he sought and, notwithstanding its size and important look, rang the bell. A withered old lady came to the door, cast a doubtful glance at Hugh and, when he had stated his object, asked him to come in. He followed her and found himself in what seemed to him a sumptuous dining room.

He said at once, "I'm sorry. I can see at once that your rooms will not suit me. It is needless to trouble you further."

The old lady looked annoyed. "My apartments have always given satisfaction."

"I am sure of that," said Hugh. "But for a poor—"

He did not know what to call himself.

"Well?" said the landlady interrogatively after a pause.

"Well, I was a tutor last, but don't know what I may be next."

"You are respectable?"

"I hope so," said Hugh, laughing.

"Well . . . how many rooms are you looking for?"

"The fewer the better. Half a one if there were nobody in the other half."

"And you wouldn't give much trouble, I dare say?"

"Only for coals and water to wash and drink."

"And you wouldn't smoke indoors?"

"No. Or anyplace else."

"And you would wipe your boots before you came in?"

"Certainly." Hugh was beginning to be amused.

"Have you money?"

"For the present. But when I shall get more I don't know."

"Well . . . I have a room at the top of the house which I could make comfortable for you for, say four shillings a week—to you. Would you like to see it?"

"Yes, indeed; that is very kind of you."

She conducted him to the third floor and showed him a good-sized room, rather bare, but clean.

"This will be delightful," said Hugh. "Shall I pay a month in advance?"

"No, no," she answered with a grim smile. "I might want to get rid of you. A week at a time will be fine."

"Very well. I have no objection. I will go and fetch my luggage."

She led him back down the stairs, and Hugh hurried away, delighted that he had so soon succeeded in finding just what he wanted. As he went he speculated on the nature of his landlady, trying to account for the genuine kindness beneath her rough manner. In all probability some unknown sympathy had drawn her to Hugh, for certainly seldom had lodgings been rented so oddly or cheaply.

When he returned in a couple of hours with his boxes on the top of a cab, the door was opened by a tidy maid. She helped him carry his things upstairs, and when he reached his room he found a fire burning cheerily, a muffin on the table which was set with a nice white cloth in front of the fire, a teakettle singing on the hob, with an old-fashioned high-backed easy chair by its side—the very chair to go to sleep in over a novel. The high, old-fashioned bed in the corner had been made up since his earlier visit and now boasted a warm, knitted coverlet. The old lady soon made her appearance with a teapot in one hand and a plate of butter in the other.

"Oh, thank you," said Hugh. "This is most comfortable."

She answered only by compressing her lips until her mouth vanished altogether and by nodding her head as if to say, "I know it is. I intended it should be." She then poured water into the teapot, set it down by the fire, and vanished.

Hugh sat down in the easy chair in great contentment. After another few moments passed a knock came on his door. His landlady entered, laid a newspaper on the table and went away once more. This was just what he wanted to complete his comfort. He took it up and read while he ate his bread and butter. When he had had enough of tea and newspaper, he said to himself, "Now, what am I to do next?"

It is a happy thing for us that this is really all we have to concern ourselves with—what to do *next*. No man can do the second thing. He can only do the first. If he omits that, the wheels of time roll over him and leave him powerless behind. If he does it, he keeps in front and finds room to do the next thing and so is sure to arrive at something in due time. Let a man lay hold of something—anything—and he is on the high road toward success, though it is not always possible to foresee the characteristics that success will have.

In Hugh's case the difficulty was to make a beginning anywhere. He knew nobody. His eye fell on the paper. Why not? He could advertise. He rose immediately, found his writing materials, and wrote to the effect that a graduate of a Scottish university was prepared to give private lessons in the classics, mathematics, or in any other branch of education. This announcement he would take to the *London Times* the next morning.

As soon as he had done this, another writing duty lifted her head and called him. He obeyed, wrote to his mother, and then, with much trepidation and humiliation, began a letter to David Elginbrod.

My Dear Friend:

After much occupation of thought with other things, a period of silence has come upon my life, and my sins look me in the face. First of them all is my neglect of you, to whom I owe so much. Forgive me. You know it takes a child a long time to know its mother. He takes everything as a matter of course till suddenly, one day he lifts up his eyes and knows that a face is looking at him. I have been like the child toward you, but I am beginning to feel what you have been to me. I want to be good. I am very lonely now in great, noisy London. Do not suppose that I am in trouble of any kind. I am comfortable as far as external circumstances go. But I have a kind of aching inside. Something is not right, and I want your help. You will know what I mean. What am I to do? Please give my regards in the most kind and grateful manner to Mrs. Elginbrod and to Margaret. It is more than I deserve, but I hope they have not forgotten me as I have seemed to forget them.

I am, my dear Mr. Elginbrod,

Your old friend,
Hugh Sutherland

I may as well insert here another letter, likewise addressed to David, which arrived at Turriepuffit some six weeks after Hugh's:

Sir:

I have heard from one who knows you that you believe—really believe—in God. That is why I write you. It may seem strange for me to do so, but I am a very unhappy woman, for I am in the power of an evil man. I cannot explain it, nor will I attempt to. Sometimes I think it is all a delusion and I am out of my mind. But whether delusion or not, it is a dreadful reality in its consequences to me. No one can help me—but God. If there be a God, I am sure he can help me—that is, if you can *help* me believe he is there. And even if I am out of my mind, who can help me but him? Tell me what to do. Tell me there is certainly a God. My acquaintance said you knew about him better than anybody else.

I am honored to be

Your obedient servant,
Euphrasia Cameron

Hugh went to bed more happy than he had been for a long time. It was very pleasant to see the dying fire as he dozed off. The writing of the letters had removed a load from his heart. He soon fell asleep and dreamed that he was a little child lost in a snowstorm. Just as the snow had reached above his head and he was beginning to be smothered, a great hand caught hold of him and lifted him out. The storm had ceased, and the stars were sparkling overhead. And he saw that it was David, as strong as ever, who had rescued him as the little child and was leading him home to Jeanette. But he got sleepy on the way and fell asleep in David's arms. When the little child Hugh awoke and opened his eyes to look up at the one who bore him, it was David no longer. The face was that which had suffered more than any man's, because the soul within had lived more: it was the face of the Son of Man, and he was carrying him like a lamb in his bosom. He gazed more and more as they traveled through the cold night. And the joy of lying in the embrace of that man grew and grew, until it became too strong for the bonds of sleep, and Hugh the man awoke in the fog of a London morning. But his dream remained with him, and he thought often of the One who had carried him.

Hugh took his advertisement to the *Times* office and paid what seemed to him an awful amount for its insertion. Then he wandered about London till the middle of the day. He began thinking that he might try to write, possibly a novel, as a means of earning bread. He had always found spinning stories as easy as if he had been a spider. Before many days had passed he had made up his mind and had made a tolerable beginning.

His advertisement did not produce a single inquiry, but he continued to write regularly. His meager horde of savings dwindled, and his concern grew. He did not, however, forget about the rings. Frequent were his thoughts about the best means of recovering them. To proceed, it was clear that he must first find the count, but he could think of no plan, since any alarm would place the count on the defensive and the jewels at once beyond reach. He had never intended using the count's one hundred guinea check, especially since he felt it would be useless to present it anyway. To confirm this, however, he took it to the bank where it was confirmed there were no funds to cover it.

36 / A Sunday

For some time after his letter to David, Hugh received no reply. At length, however, a letter arrived. He knew the handwriting, but could not place it immediately. He opened it and found the following answer to his:

Dear Mr. Sutherland:

Your letter to my father has been sent to me by my mother, for what you will feel to be the sad reason that he is no more in this world. But it is not so very sad to me to think that he is now gone home. Nor indeed, dear Mr. Sutherland, must you be too troubled that your letter never reached him. My father was like God in this way, that he always forgave anything the moment there was anything to forgive. For when else could there be such a good time?—although, of course, the person forgiven could not know it till he asked for forgiveness. But, dear Mr. Sutherland, if you could but see me smiling as I write to say that I forgive you in his name for everything with which you reproach yourself, I am sure your heart would be eased. Ah! how much I owe you! And how much he used to say he owed you. We shall thank you one day, when we all meet.

I am, dear Mr. Sutherland,

Your grateful scholar,
Margaret Elginbrod

Hugh burst into tears on reading the letter. Not from an overpowering sense of conviction, for he felt he was forgiven. But he suddenly saw more of the grandeur of the man and something of the loveliness which had been transmitted to Margaret. Purposely or not, there was no address on the envelope. But to his surprise, when he examined the envelope, he discovered a London postmark.

"So," he said to himself, "in my quest of the devil Fenkelstein, I may cross the track of an angel—who knows? But how can she be here?"

To this of course he had no answer.

Meantime, one day his landlady—whose grim attentions had been increasing—addressed him—in itself an extraordinary event—after breakfast. "Have you got any pupils yet, Mr. Sutherland?"

"No, I'm sorry to say. Why, do you know of something?"

"Well, I can't exactly say, but I happened to mention to my grocer round the corner that you wanted pupils. Don't suppose, Mr. Sutherland, that I'm in the habit of talking about any young men of mine; but—''

''Not for a moment,'' Hugh interrupted, and Mrs. Talbot (for that was her name) resumed.

''Well, if you wouldn't mind stepping round the corner, I shouldn't wonder if you might make an arrangement with Mr. Appleditch. He said you might call on him if you liked.''

Hugh jumped up and got his hat, received the few necessary directions from Mrs. Talbot, and soon found the shop. There were a good many poor people in it, buying sugar, soap, and the like, and one lady apparently placing a large order with Mr. Appleditch himself. When she had departed, he approached Hugh from behind the counter and stood before him.

''My name is Sutherland,'' Hugh began.

''Sutherland? Seems I've heard the name somewhere, but I don't know your face.''

''Mrs. Talbot mentioned me to you, I believe, Mr. Appleditch.''

''Ah, yes. I remember. I beg your pardon. Will you step this way, Mr. Sutherland?''

Hugh followed him through a sort of drawbridge which he lifted in the counter into the back of the shop. ''So you want pupils, do you, sir?'' he said.

''Yes,'' answered Hugh.

''Well, pupils is scarce at this time of year. But I think Mrs. Appleditch could find you one, that is if you could agree with her about the price, you know, and all that.''

''How old is he?''

''My Jonathan is just ten, but a wonderful forward boy for his years—bless him.''

''And what would you wish him to learn?''

''Oh, Latin and Greek and all that. We intend bringing him up for the ministry. I hope your opinions are decided, sir.''

''On some points they are. But I don't know what you're referring to exactly.''

''I mean theological opinions, sir.''

''But I surely shall not have to teach your little boy theology!''

''Certainly not. That department belongs to his mother and me. Unworthy vessels, mere earthen vessels; but filled with the grace of God, I hope. But, Mr. Sutherland, I must get back to my customers. So if you'll do us the honor to dine with us next Lord's day, you will see little Jonathan and Mrs. Appleditch.''

''I shall be happy to. What is your address?''

''You had better come to Salem Chapel, Dervish Town, and we can go home together. Service commences at eleven. Mrs. Appleditch will be glad to see you. Ask for Mr. Appleditch's pew. Good morning, sir."

When Sunday came several days hence, Hugh found his way to Salem Chapel, and was shown to Mr. Appleditch's pew. The couple stood up, along with their son, and Hugh had to force his way between the front of each person and the next pew all the way to the end where there was room for him to sit. No other recognition was taken until after the service.

Meantime, the minister ascended the pulpit stair with all the solemnity of one of the self-elect, and a priest besides. He was just old enough for his intermittent attacks of self-importance to have become chronic. He stood up and worshipped his Creator aloud, in a manner which seemed to say in every tone: "Behold, I am he that worshippeth Thee." Then he read the Bible in a quarrelsome sort of way, as if he were a bantam and every verse were a crow of defiance to the sinner. Then they sang a hymn during which there was almost a complete absence of a modest self-restraint and tempering of the tones on the part of the singers, the result being what Hugh could only describe as a sort of scratching.

Then came the sermon. The text was the story of the good Samaritan. Some idea of the value of the sermon may be formed from the fact that the first thing to be considered was, "The culpable imprudence of the man in going from Jerusalem to Jericho without an escort."

It was a strange and grotesque medley, here and there the fragments of Scripture shining through like gold amidst the worthless ore of the man's own production. There are Indians who eat clay, and thrive on it more or less. The power of assimilation in a growing nature is astonishing. It will find its food in the midst of a whole cartload of refuse. On no other supposition would it be possible to account for the earnest face of Mrs. Talbot, which Hugh spotted turned up to the preacher as if his face were the very star in the east. It was well for Hugh's power of endurance that he had heard much the same thing in Scotland and in the church of Arnstead and so was used to it.

After the final prayer, the pastor spread abroad his arms and hands, as if he would clasp the world in his embrace, and pronounced the benediction in a style of arrogance that the Archbishop himself would have been ashamed of. The service being thus concluded, the organ absolutely blasted the congregation out of the church, so did it storm and rave.

When they reached the open air, Mr. Appleditch introduced Hugh to Mrs. Appleditch on the steps in front of the chapel. Hugh lifted his hat, and she made a curtsy. She was a very tall woman with a general air of greed and contempt, richly dressed. Master Appleditch, the future pastor, was a fat boy, dressed like a dwarf in a frock coat and man's hat, with a mean look in his eye. They walked home in silence—Mr. and Mrs. Appleditch apparently pondering either upon the spiritual food they had just received or the corporeal food for which they were about to be thankful.

The boy ran on ahead and when they reached the house rushed in, bawling, "Peter, Peter, here's the new apprentice! Papa's brought him home to dinner because he was at chapel this morning."

Hugh was shown into the dining room where the table was already laid for dinner. It was evident that the Appleditches were well-to-do people. The room was full of what is called handsome furniture in a high state of polish. In a few minutes the host and hostess entered, followed by a pale-faced boy some years younger than the youngster Hugh had met at church.

"Come here, Petie," said his mother, "and tell Mr. Sutherland what you have got."

Hugh imagined she referred to some toy, possibly a book.

Petie answered in a solemn voice. "I've got five bags of gold in the Bank of England."

"Poor child!" said his mother with a scornful giggle.

"Mr.——, I don't know your name," said Peter, whose age Hugh had just been trying in vain to conjecture.

"Mr. Sutherland," said the mother.

"Mr. Slubberman, are you a converted character?" resumed Peter.

"Why do you ask me that, Master Peter?" said Hugh, trying to smile.

"I think you look good, but Mamma says she don't think you are because you say Sunday instead of Sabbath, and she always finds people who do are worldly."

Mrs. Appleditch turned red and said quickly, "Peter shouldn't repeat everything he hears."

"I don't, Mamma. I haven't told what you said about—"

Here his mother caught him up and carried him out of the room, saying, "You naughty boy! You shall go to bed."

"Oh, no, I shan't!"

"Yes, you shall.—Here, Mollie, take this naughty boy to bed."

"I'll scream."

"Don't you dare, young man."

But with that there was suddenly heard such a yell as if ten cats were being cooked alive.

"Well, well . . . my Petie!" interposed the father. "He shan't go to bed if he'll be a good boy. Will he be good?"

"May I stay up to supper then? May I?"

"Yes, yes. Anything to stop such dreadful screaming," said Mrs.

Appleditch. "You are very naughty—very naughty indeed."

"No, I'm not naughty. I'll scream again."

"Just go and get your pinafore on and come down to dinner. Anything rather than a scream."

As the meal progressed, Hugh noted a certain liberality about the table and a kind of heartiness in Mrs. Appleditch's way of pressing him to have more than he could eat, which contrasted strangely with her behavior afterward in money matters. There are many people who can be liberal in almost anything but money.

After dinner was over and the children had been sent away, Mr. Appleditch proceeded to business.

"Now, Mr. Sutherland, what do you think of Johnny?"

"It is impossible for me to say yet; but I am quite willing to teach him if you like."

"He's a forward boy," said his mother.

"And very eager and retentive," added his father.

Hugh had seen the little glutton paint both cheeks to the eyes with a berry tart and render more than a quantity proportionate to the coloring invisible down his throat.

"Yes, I dare say," responded Hugh. "But much will depend on whether he has a will to study."

"Well, you will find that out tomorrow. I think you will be surprised, sir."

"What time would you like me to come?"

"You have said nothing yet about terms," interposed Mrs. Appleditch to her husband, "and that is of some importance, considering the rent and taxes we pay."

"Well, my love, what do you feel inclined to give?"

"How much do you charge a lesson, Mr. Sutherland? Only let me remind you that he is a very little boy, although stout, and that you cannot expect to put much Greek and Latin into him for some time yet. Besides, we want you to come every day, which ought to be considered in the rate of charge."

"Of course it ought," said Hugh.

"How much do you say then, sir?"

"I should be content with half a crown a lesson."

"I dare say you would!" replied the lady with indignation. "Half a crown! That's—six half crowns is—fifteen shillings. Fifteen shillings a week for that mite of a boy! Mr. Sutherland, you ought to be ashamed of yourself!"

"You forget, Mrs. Appleditch, that it is as difficult to teach one little boy—a great deal more difficult—than to teach twenty grown men."

"You, a Christian man, talking of the trouble in teaching such a little cherub as that!"

"But remember the distance I have to come and that it will altogether take nearly four hours of my time every day."

"Then you can get lodgings nearer."

"But I could not get any so cheap."

"Then you can the better afford to do it."

And she threw herself back in her chair as if she had struck the decisive blow.

Mr. Appleditch remarked gently, "It is good for your health to walk the distance, sir."

Mrs. Appleditch resumed, "I won't give a farthing more than one shilling a lesson!"

"Very well," said Hugh rising, "then I must wish you good day. We need not waste any more time in talking about it."

"Don't be in such a hurry, Mr. Sutherland," said the grocer mildly. "We tradespeople like to make the best bargain we can, you know. Now, dear," he said turning to his wife, "suppose we say to Mr. Sutherland—"

"You leave that to me," interrupted his wife. "I'll tell you what, Mr. Sutherland—I'll give you eighteen pence a lesson and your dinner on the Sabbath; that is if you attend the chapel with us in our pew and walk home with us."

"That I must decline," said Hugh. "I must have my Sundays for myself. I need my personal day of rest as well."

Mrs. Appleditch was disappointed. She had coveted the additional importance which the visible possession of a tutor would secure her at Salem Chapel.

"Ah, Mr. Sutherland," she said, "it seems I must trust my child, with his immortal soul, to one who wants the Lord's only day for himself—for *himself*, Mr. Sutherland!"

Hugh made no answer because he had none to make.

Again Mrs. Appleditch resumed, "Shall it be a bargain then, Mr. Sutherland? Eighteen pence a lesson—that's nine shillings a week—beginning tomorrow?"

Hugh's heart sank within him, not so much with disappointment as with disgust. But to a man who is making nothing, the prospect of earning ever so little is nevertheless attractive. Even on a shilling a day he could keep the hunger at arm's length. And a beginning is half the battle.

"Let it be a bargain, Mrs. Appleditch."

The lady immediately brightened up and at once put on her company manners again, behaving to him with great politeness. From this Hugh suspected that she had made a better bargain than she had originally hoped for. But the discovery was now too late. He hated bargain-making as heartily as the grocer's wife loved it.

He very soon rose to take his leave.

"Oh," said Mrs. Appleditch to her husband, "Mr. Sutherland has not yet seen the drawing room."

Hugh wondered what there could be so remarkable about the drawing room, but he soon found that it was the pride of Mrs. Appleditch's heart. She abstained from all use of it except upon great occasions—when parties of her friends came to drink tea with her. She made it a point, however, of showing it to everybody who entered the house for the first time. So Hugh was led upstairs, to undergo the operation of being shown the drawing room and fully aware that he was expected to be astonished at it. Portraits of Mr. Appleditch (in his deacon's uniform) and Mrs. Appleditch (in her wedding dress) hung over the hearth and over the piano. The piano was ornate and Mrs. Appleditch demonstrated that she could play psalm-tunes on it with one finger. The round table in the middle of the room had books in gilded red and blue covers symmetrically arranged all round it.

Having feasted his eyes on the magnificence of it all, Hugh walked home more depressed at the prospect of his new employment than he could have believed possible. On his way through Regent's Park, the sight of people enjoying themselves lifted his spirits. He kept as far as possible from the open-air preachers and was able to thank God that all the world did not keep the sort of Sunday Sabbath he had just left—a day neither Mosaic, nor Jewish, nor Christian. Not Mosaic inasmuch as it kills the very essence of the fourth commandment, which is rest; not Jewish inasmuch as it is in certain respects even more severe and legalistic; and unchristian inasmuch as it insists on the observance of times and seasons—abolished in the New Testament—and elevates one day as more holy than all the rest.

37 / Robert Falconer

It was dusk before Hugh turned his steps homeward. He wandered along thinking of Euphra and the count and the stolen rings. He greatly desired to clear himself to Mr. Arnold and, for Euphra's sake, to somehow gain power over Fenkelstein. If his own ring was beyond recovery, at least by proving him a thief he might hold such over him as would keep him from exercising his villainous influences on her again.

Deep in thought, he came upon two policemen. He recognized one of them from his speech as a Scotsman. It occurred to him at once to seek his advice.

"You are a countryman of mine, I think," he said as soon as the other had parted.

"If ye're a Scotsman, sir, whaur do ye come frae?"

"Near Aberdeen. My name's Sutherland."

"They call me John MacPherson," said the policeman and shook Hugh's hand with vehemence.

"I was after some advice," said Hugh.

"I'm fully at yer service, sir."

"When will you be off duty?"

"At nine o'clock."

Hugh asked him to come to his house and gave him directions.

Mrs. Talbot received her lodger with more show of pleasure than usual, knowing he had spent the day sanctified by the presence of one of the chapel's prominent deacons. But she was considerably alarmed and shocked later when the policeman called and requested to see him. Sally rushed to her mistress in dismay.

"Please 'm, there's a pleaceman wants Mr. Sutherland. Oh, lor'm!"

"Well, go and let Mr. Sutherland know, you stupid girl," answered her mistress, trembling.

"Oh, lor'm!" was all Sally's reply as she vanished to bear the awful tidings to Hugh.

"He can't have been housebreaking already," puzzled Mrs. Talbot to herself. "But it may be forgery or embezzlement."

"Please, sir, you're wanted, sir," said Sally out of breath and pale as her apron.

"Who wants me?" asked Hugh.

"Please, sir, the pleaceman, sir," answered Sally, bursting into tears.

Bewildered by the girl's behavior, he said, "Well . . . show him up then."

Notwithstanding the trepidation of Sally and her mistress, the two Scotsmen were soon seated at opposite corners of the fire having a long chat. They began about the old country and the places and people they both knew, and the ones they didn't know. At length Hugh referred to the object of their desired talk.

"What plan should I pursue, John, to find a man in London?"

"I could manage that for ye. I know most all the detectives."

"But I wish for the police not to have anything to do with it."

"Ay! hm! hm! Ye'll be after a stray sheep, no doot?"

Hugh did not reply.

"It's not that easy otherwise. Lon'on's a big city. Have ye ony clue to where to start?"

"Not the least."

The man pondered a while.

"I have it!" he exclaimed at last. "I should have thought o' that before. I tell ye what. There's a man, a countryman o' our own and a gentleman besides, that'll do more for ye in that way than all the detectives put together; and that's Robert Falconer. I know him well."

"Can you introduce me to him?"

"Certainly. He lives close by here, just around two corners. And I'm thinking he'll be at home now, for I saw him going there afore ye came up to me. And the sooner we go the better, for he's not easy to get hold of."

"But won't he consider it an intrusion?"

"Na, na. There's no fear o' that. He's any man's and every woman's friend. Come away, Mr. Sutherland, he's yer verra man."

Hugh rose and accompanied the policeman. He took him round rather more than two corners. But within five minutes they stood at Mr. Falconer's door. John rang. The door opened without visible service, and they ascended to the second floor. Here a respectable-looking woman awaited their ascent.

"Is Mr. Falconer at home, mem?" said Hugh's guide.

"He is; but I think he's going out again."

"Will ye tell him, mem, that John MacPherson the policeman would like to see him?"

She left them but returned in a moment and invited them to enter a large bare room behind her, in which there was just light enough for Hugh to see the figure of a large man. Six-foot Hugh felt dwarfed beside him. He was dressed in loose, shabby black which strangely combined with an expression of repose, strength, and quiet concentration.

"How are you, MacPherson?" said a deep, powerful voice out of the gloom.

"Verra well, thank ye, Mr. Falconer. I've a gentleman by the name of Sutherland here with me who wants your help with somebody or ither 'at he's interested in who's disappeared."

Falconer advanced and extended his hand. "I shall be most happy to help if I can." Then addressing Hugh he said, "Our friend MacPherson has rather too exalted an idea of my capabilities, however."

"Well, Mr. Falconer," said the policeman, "I just ask ye yourself if you was ever foiled with anything ye took in hand?"

Falconer made no reply. There was the story of a whole life in his silence.

"You can leave the gentleman with me then, John. I'll take care of him. I'm obliged to you for bringing him."

"The obligation's mine—and the gentleman's. Good night.—And good night to you, Mr. Sutherland."

"You know my quarters," said Hugh, shaking his hand. "I am greatly in your debt."

When he had left, Falconer said, "I have to walk to Somers Town tonight—no great way. We can talk as well walking as sitting. If you don't mind and have the time?"

"With pleasure," replied Hugh.

Their talk was nothing worth recording until they entered a narrow court in Somers Town.

"Are you afraid of infection?" Falconer said.

"Not in the least, if there is a reason for exposing myself to it."

"And there is none this time. You will not mind waiting for me till I come out of this house? There is typhus in it."

"I am glad to wait. I will go with you if I can be of any use."

"There is no occasion."

So saying, Falconer opened the door and walked in.

In a few minutes he rejoined Hugh, looking solemn, but with a kind of relieved expression on his face.

"The poor fellow is gone," he said.

"Ah!"

"What a thing it must be, Mr. Sutherland, for a man to break out of the choke hold of a typhus fever into the clear air of the life beyond!"

"Yes," said Hugh after a slight hesitation, "if he is prepared for the change."

"Where a change belongs to the natural order of things," said Falconer, "there must always be some preparedness for it. Besides, I think a man is generally prepared for a breath of fresh air."

Hugh did not reply, for he felt he did not yet fully comprehend his new acquaintance. But he had a strong suspicion that it was because he moved in a higher region than himself.

"We are perhaps," resumed Falconer, "too much in the habit of thinking of death as the culmination of disease. But I think rather of death as the first pulse of the new strength, shaking itself free from the old mouldy remnants of earth, that it may begin the new life that grows out of the old. The caterpillar dies into the butterfly. Who knows but that disease may be the coming of the keener life? And then disease would be but the sign of the salvation of fire, of the agony of the greater life to lift us to itself?"

"But surely all cannot fare alike in the new life?"

"Far from it. According to the condition. But what would be hell to one will be quietness and hope and progress to another. But perhaps you are not interested in such subjects, Mr. Sutherland, and I weary you."

"If I have not been interested in them up to now, I am ready to become so now."

"I have several other people I must see tonight," said Falconer, who had still not referred to Hugh's object in seeking his acquaintance. "I have to tell you, some of it will not be too pleasant. There is much pain and suffering in the more wretched parts of this city. For many, death is anticipated as the blessing."

"Let me go with you," said Hugh.

"With pleasure."

38 / Euphra

Meanwhile, Lady Emily had gone to Spain, and Mr. Arnold followed. Mrs. Elton, Harry, and Margaret had gone to London. Euphra was left alone at Arnstead.

A great alteration had taken place in this strange girl. The servants were positively afraid of her now, from the butler down to the kitchen maid. She was subject to violent fits of temper and long seasons of the deepest dejection, in which she would confine herself to her room for hours or—lame as she was—wander about the house and the Ghost's Walk, herself pale as a ghost, looking meager and wretched. Subject to frequent fainting fits and headaches, she was most evidently miserable.

For her misery there were very sufficient reasons. Her continued lameness gave her great cause for anxiety. But worse still, her mind had been thrown back upon itself as often happens in loneliness and suffering. She began to feel that she herself was a worse tyrant than the count.

Simple natures will often look up at once, lifting their eyes to the heavens whence comes their aid. Yet Euphra was of a nature that will endure an immense amount of misery before it feels compelled to look for help whence all help and healing comes. But even Euphra was cast down so low in her despair that she had begun to look upward, for the waters were about to close over her head. She had therefore taken herself to the one man of whom she heard knew God. She wrote, but no answer came. Days and days passed, but there was no reply.

In bitterness she said to herself, "If I cried to God forever I should hear no word of reply. What does he care for me?"

Yet even as she spoke, she rose and by a sudden impulse threw herself on the floor and cried out, for the first time, "O God, help me."

She rose slowly, with at least a little hope. For if she could cry to him, it might be that he could listen to her.

The days continued to pass wearily by. Dim, slow November days came on and went. The overarching boughs of the avenue of the Ghost's Walk were now bare, themselves living skeletons. From the ground she could now look straight up to the blue sky which had been there all the time.

The days crawled one after the other. She tried to read but could not. Gradually the realization became clearer to her that she had been leading a false and worthless life, that she had never been a true friend to anyone. She came to see that she must leave her former self behind her and rise into a purer life and reality. But these feelings were alternated with fierce bursts of passion during which her old self jumped up with feverish energy and writhed for life. She was attempting by sheer force of will to make improvements on herself.

One day a letter arrived. She had had no letter from anyone for weeks. Yet when she saw it was from old Mrs. Elton she flung it from her. It lay unopened until the next day. But finally, with the sun shining the following morning, Euphra took courage to read it while drinking her coffee. It contained an invitation to visit Mrs. Elton at her home in Hyde Park with the assurance that they had plenty of room for her.

Had this letter arrived a few weeks earlier, Euphra would have infused into her answer a skillful concoction of delicate contempt. Not for the amusement of knowing that Mrs. Elton would never discover a trace of it, but simply for a relief to her own dislike of her. Now, however, she would write a plain letter containing as brief and as true an excuse as she could find. But just as she was surveying her possible options for declining, a second little note, which had escaped her attention, fell from the envelope. It read:

Dear Euphra:

Do come and see us. I do not like London at all without you. There are no happy days here like those we had at Arnstead with Mr. Sutherland. Mrs. Elton and Margaret are very kind to me, but I wish you would come. Do, do, do. Please do.

Your Affectionate Cousin,
Harry Arnold

"The dear boy," said Euphra with a gush of pure and grateful affection. "I will go and see *him*."

Harry was doing his best with his studies, which was very good. Ever since Hugh had given his faculties a shove in the right direction, he had been making up for the period during which childhood had been protracted into boyhood. And now he was making rapid progress.

When Euphra arrived, Harry rushed to the hall to meet her. She took him in her arms and burst into tears. Her tears drew forth his.

He stroked her pale face and said, "Dear Euphra, how ill you look."

"I shall soon be better now, Harry."

"I was afraid you did not love me, Euphra. But now I am sure you do."

"Indeed I do. I am very sorry for everything that made you think I did not."

"That's all right. Now we shall be very happy."

And so Harry was. And Euphra, through means of Harry, began to gain a little of what is better than most kinds of happiness—peace. This foretaste of rest came to her from the devotedness with which she now applied herself to aid him. She took all his books when he had gone to bed and read over all his lessons that she might be able to assist him in preparing them. This produced in her quite new experiences. One of these was that in proportion as she labored for Harry, hope grew for herself. It was of the greatest benefit that her thoughts, instead of lying vacant to melancholy, were occupied by healthy mental exercise.

Still, however, she was subject to great changes in emotions. Her old self was sometimes only too ready to appear. But the pure forgiveness of the boy was wonderful. He was thus able to keep at bay the evil spirits, and find Euphra's former self once more on her face. But, her health continued to be very poor—she suffered often from headaches and at times from faintings.

39 / The New Pupils

After Hugh's first meeting with Falconer, which lasted so long that he had made a bed of Falconer's sofa, he felt a little good-natured anxiety as to his landlady's reception of him after being out all night. He made some allusion to it as he sat at his new friend's breakfast table.

"What is your landlady's name?" Falconer asked.

"Mrs. Talbot."

"Oh, little Mrs. Talbot. You are in good quarters—too good to lose, I can tell you. Just tell her you were with me."

"You know her, then?"

"Oh, yes."

"You seem to know everybody."

"If I have spoken to a person once I have never forgotten him."

"It must be hard to remember everyone."

"The secret of it is that I try not to forget that there is a deeper relation between myself and those I meet. I succeed worst in drawing rooms and so-called social situations. But even then I try to apprehend the true inner self. The consequence is, I never forget anybody, and I generally find that others remember me—at least those with whom I have had any real relationship."

"Is it not awkward sometimes?"

"Not in the least. I am never ashamed of knowing anyone."

Hugh found the advantage of Falconer's friendship when he mentioned to Mrs. Talbot that he had been his guest that night.

"You should have sent us word, Mr. Sutherland," was her only reply.

"I could not do so before you would all have been in bed. I am truly sorry, but I could not help it."

Mrs. Talbot turned away into the kitchen. The only other indication of her feeling in the matter was that she sent him up a delicious cup of chocolate for his lunch before he set out for Mr. Appleditch's.

When he arrived for his first day with the new pupils—the younger boy was included for the odd sixpence—Hugh was shown into the dining room, into which the boys were separately dragged to receive the first installment of the mental legacy left them by their ancestors. But Hugh was dismayed at the impossibility of interesting them in anything. He even tried without success telling them stories. They stared at him, but whether there was more speculation in the open mouths or in the fishy, overfed eyes, he found it impossible to determine. But he did his best, and before the two hours had expired he discovered that the elder had a turn for sums and the younger for drawing.

Though a mother's love is often more pure than most other loves, there is yet a class of mothers whose love is only an extended form of selfishness. Mrs. Appleditch did not in the least love her children, but she loved them dearly because they were *her* children.

One day, as the ultimate recourse, Hugh gave Master Appleditch a smart slap across the hand. The child screamed as he well knew how. His mother burst into the room.

"Johnny, hold your tongue!"

"Teacher's hurt me."

"Get out of the room."

She seized him by the shoulders and turned him out. Then, turning to Hugh, "Mr. Sutherland, how dare you strike my child?" she demanded.

"He required it, Mrs. Appleditch. I did him no harm. He will mind what I say another time."

"I will not have him touched. To strike a child is disgraceful."

Johnny behaved better after this, however, and the only revenge Mrs. Appleditch took for this interference with the dignity of her eldest-born was to impress Hugh with a due sense of menial position he occupied in her family. She always paid him his fee of one shilling and sixpence every day before he left the house. Once or twice she contrived that the sixpence should be in a handful of coppers. Hugh was too much of a philosopher, however, to mind this from such a woman.

After this, nothing went amiss for some time. But it was dreary work to teach such boys. Slow, stupid resistance appeared to be the only principle of their behavior toward him. They scorned him; their mother despised and yet valued him for the selfsame reason—namely, that she had acquired him so cheaply. The boys would have defied him had they dared, but he managed to establish an authority over them. Still, he could not rouse them to any real interest in their studies. Their eyes grew dull at a storybook, but greedily bright at the sight of toffee.

All went the same until subtle, doubtful symptoms of an alteration in the personal appearance of Hugh accumulated at last into a mass of evidence. The conviction was forced upon the mind of the grocer's wife that her tutor was actually growing a beard. Could she believe her eyes?

At length she suddenly addressed Hugh in her usual cold, thin, and cutting fashion of speech. "Mr. Sutherland, I am astonished that you, a teacher of babes, who should set them an example, should disguise yourself in such an outlandish way."

"What do you mean, Mrs. Appleditch?" asked Hugh.

"What do I mean? It is a shame for a man to let his beard grow like a monkey."

"But a monkey hasn't a beard," retorted Hugh, laughing.

"It's no joking matter, Mr. Sutherland, with my two darlings growing up to be ministers of the gospel."

What! both of them? thought Hugh. *Good heavens!*

But he said, "Well, you know, Mrs. Appleditch, the apostles themselves wore beards."

"Yes, when they were Jews. But they shaved as soon as they became Christians. It was the sign of Christianity. The Apostle Paul himself says that cleanliness is next to godliness."

Hugh restrained his laughter.

"But there is nothing dirty about them," he said.

"Not dirty? Now really, Mr. Sutherland, you provoke me. Nothing dirty in long hair all round your mouth and going into it every spoonful you take?"

"But it can be kept properly trimmed, you know."

"But who's to trust you to do that?"

Hugh laughed and said nothing. Of course his beard would go on growing, for he could not help it.

So did Mrs. Appleditch's wrath.

It was not long before Hugh repeated his visit to Falconer. But he went three times before he found him at home.

"I am very sorry. I am out so much," said Falconer.

"I ought to have taken the opportunity when I had it," replied Hugh, "but I was so caught up in your work the other evening. I wanted to ask your help. May I begin at the beginning and tell you all the story?"

"Be as detailed as you please. I will understand the thing the better."

So Hugh began and told the whole of his history insofar as it bore upon the story of the crystal ring.

"It is a remarkable story. I will think about what can be done," said Falconer when he had finished. "Meantime I will keep my eyes and ears open. I may find the fellow. Tell me what he is like."

Hugh gave as minute a description of the count as he could.

"I think I see the man. I am pretty sure I would recognize him."

"Have you any idea what he could want with the ring?"

"I ran across an article just yesterday on this very thing," answered Falconer. "I think it might give a correct suggestion as to his object. But you can judge for yourself."

So saying, Falconer went to a side-table, heaped up with books and papers, maps and instruments of various kinds. He selected the paper he wanted and handed it to Hugh who read the following:

> I have been for over thirty years in the habit of investigating the question by means of crystals. And I now have come into the possession of the celebrated crystal once belonging to Lady Blessington, in which many persons have seen visions of spirits of the deceased and other beings claiming to be such, and of numerous angels and other beings of the spiritual world. These have in all cases supported the purest and most liberal Christianity. The faculty of seeing in the crystal I have found to exist in about one person in ten. . . .

"Is it possible," said Hugh, pausing, "that people today believe such things?"

"There are more fools in the world, Mr. Sutherland, than there are crystals in the mountains."

Hugh resumed his reading. He came at length to this passage:

> The spirits which appear do not hesitate to inform us on all possible subjects, which may tend to improve our morals and confirm our faith in the Christian doctrines. . . . They warn against another class of spirits who are in the habit of communicating with mortals by rapping and such proceedings, and it behooves all Christian people to be on their guard against error and delusion.

"But," said Hugh, "I do not see how this is to help me as to the count's object in securing the ring. For certainly he is not likely to have committed the theft for the sake of instruction in doctrines and morals."

"No. But such a crystal might be put to other uses. Lady Blessington's crystal might be a pious crystal, and the other stolen one which belonged to Lady—"

"Lady Euphrasia."

"To Lady Euphrasia, might be a worldly crystal altogether. It might reveal demons and their satanic counsels."

"Ah, I see. I should have thought, however, that the count had been too much of a modern man of the world to believe such things."

"No amount of worldly wisdom can set a man above the inroads of the occult. In fact, there is but one thing that can free a man from the occult and that is faith in God."

"You remind me of a passage in my story which I omitted."

"Let me have it. It cannot fail to interest me."

Hugh gave a complete account of the experiments they had made with the plate.

"There was a moment, as the plate moved, that I felt I knew what it was trying to write."

"What was it?"

"A name. The name of the best man I ever knew."

Hugh was then compelled, in responding to the natural interest of

Falconer, to give a description of David. This led to a sketch of his own sojourn at Turriepuffit.

"And did it write his name?" asked Falconer.

"I am sure it would have," said Hugh. "I was trembling as I felt the letters forming beneath my fingers and released my hand from the plate. Several minutes later I saw a vision of the man's daughter."

"And that was the man the creatures dared to impersonate!" broke out Falconer, seemingly restraining his wrath with difficulty. "I hate the whole thing, Sutherland. It is full of impudence and irreverence. Perhaps the wretched beings may want another thousand years damnation. But of one thing you may be certain, and that is that the man you described would never write a copy at the order of a charlatan, or worse, such as you indicate the count is."

"But it could hardly be deception. How else could they have known what David signified to me?"

"A man like him could not get through them without being recognized."

"I don't understand you. By whom?"

"By swarms of low, miserable evil spirits and creatures that so lament the loss of their beggarly bodies that they would brood upon them in the shape of flesh-flies rather than forsake the putrefying remnants. After that, chair or table or anything they can come into contact with is sufficient for them. Don't you remember that once, rather than have nobody to go into, they leapt into the very swine? But the herd of pigs themselves could not stand it and preferred drowning."

"Then you do not think there was a message from David himself?"

"Not in the least. It required no great powers for the evil spirits to be aware that a great man of God was dead, and that you had known him well. It was nothing but an impudent forgery of that man's good name, trying to draw you under their influence—possibly through the count himself. He appears already to be a pawn in their hands. But you say during a later session there came an abrupt end to the apparent supernatural movements of things in the room and the faint visions you perceived, and that was the last of it?"

"Fenkelstein commented about adverse influences."

"I suspect there must have come into the house about that time something or someone strong in the power of God. They can never operate under such conditions. A man such as your David Elginbrod, just by walking into a room, would send them scurrying for their dark places."

Falconer put a good many other questions to Hugh, about Euphra and her relation to the count. Finally he said, "Now I have the material out of which to begin to construct a theory. But in the meantime, as I said before, I will make inquiry. Let us try to get together again next Sunday morning."

"My consolations are so few these days that I will look forward to it with pleasure."

They parted and Hugh went home to work on his novel.

40 / Questions and Dreams

Mrs. Elton read prayers morning and evening—elaborate compositions which would have instructed the apostles themselves in many things they had never anticipated. Likewise she read certain remarks in the form of a devotional homily, intended to impress the Scripture upon the minds of the listeners. Between the mortar of the homilist's faith and the dull blows from the pestle of his arrogance, the fair form of truth was ground into the powder of pious talk. The result was not pleasant either to Harry or to Euphra. Euphra, with her life threatening to go to ruin, was crying out for someone real. Harry had the natural dislike of all childlike natures to everything formal, exclusive, and unjust.

One morning the passage of Scripture which Mrs. Elton read was the story of the young man who came to Jesus and went away sorrowful because the Lord loved him so heartily that he wanted to set him free from his riches. A great portion of the homily was occupied with proving the evangelist could not possibly mean that Jesus *loved* the man in any full sense of the word but merely "felt kindly disposed toward him."

Harry's face was in a flame all the time she was reading. When the devotion was over he and Euphra left the room together. As soon as the door was shut, he burst out, "I say, Euphra. They would make Jesus out as bad as themselves. We shall have somebody writing a book next to prove that, after all, Jesus was a Pharisee."

"Never mind," said the heart-sore, skeptical Euphra. "Never mind, Harry. It's all nonsense."

"It's not nonsense. Jesus *did* love the young man."

"I hope so" was all she could reply, but she was comforted by Harry's vehement confession of faith.

The homily which Mrs. Elton read at prayers that evening bore upon the subject of election—a doctrine which in the Bible asserts God's choosing certain persons for the specific purpose of receiving spiritual truth first and so communicating the gifts of his grace to the whole world. However, in the homily it was taken to mean the choice of certain persons for ultimate salvation to the exclusion of the rest. They were sitting in silence after the close when Harry started up suddenly, saying, "I don't want God to love me if he does not love *everybody*." Then, bursting into tears, he hurried from the room. Mrs. Elton was shocked. Euphra hastened after him, but he would not return and went supperless to bed. She kissed him and tucked the quilts around him.

As she was about to leave he said, "If what that man said is true,

Euphra, I would rather not have been made."

"It is not true," said Euphra, in whom a faint glimmer of faith awoke for the sake of the boy she loved. "No, Harry dear, if there is a God at all, he could not be like that."

Later, Euphra knelt by her bedside and prayed more hopefully than she had many days before. She prayed that God would let her know he was not an idol of man's invention.

Until friendly sleep came and untied the knot of care, both Euphra and Harry lay troubled with things too great for them. Even in their sleep the care would gather again and body itself into dreams. The following morning's prayers only revived their troubles. Midway through the morning, Harry sought Euphra in her room.

"I have been trying very hard to be good. But I don't know if I'm *really* being good. It always seems to me it would be so much nicer of God to say, 'Come along, never mind. I'll make you good. I can't wait till you are good, I love you so much.' "

His own words were too much for Harry and he burst into tears at the thought of God being so kind. Euphra, instead of trying to comfort him, cried too. Thus they continued for some time. Harry was the first to recover.

"Just think, Euphra. What if, after all, I should find out that God is as kind as you are."

Euphra's heart smote her. "God must be a great deal kinder than I am. I have not been kind to you at all."

"Don't say that, Euphra. I shall be quite content if God is as kind as you."

"Oh, Harry. I hope God is like what I dreamed about my mother last night."

"Tell me what you dreamed."

"I dreamed I was a little child—"

"Were you a little girl when your mother died?"

"Oh, yes. I was so tiny. But I can just remember her."

"Tell me your dream, then."

"I dreamed I was a little girl, out all alone on a wild mountain moor, tripping and stumbling on my nightgown. And the wind was so cold. And somehow or other the wind was my enemy, and it followed me and caught me and tossed me about and then ran away again. I kept going, but I was barefoot, and the thorns went into my feet and the stones cut them and they bled."

"Then they would be like the feet I saw in my dream last night," said Harry.

"Whose feet were they?"

"Jesus' feet."

"Tell me about it."

"You must finish yours first, Euphra."

So Euphra went on. "I got dreadfully lame. And the wind ran after me and caught me again. It was very hard to go on but I couldn't stop and the wind was everywhere. Then suddenly I saw before me a great waterfall falling from a cliff, and I thought to myself, *I will go into the waterfall and it will beat my life out and then the wind will not get me anymore*. So I hastened toward it, but the wind caught me many times before I could get near it. At last I reached it and threw myself down into the basin it had hollowed out of the rocks. But as I was falling, something caught me gently and held me fast, and it was not the wind. I opened my eyes and, behold, I was in my mother's arms, and she was clasping me to her breast. For what I had taken for a waterfall falling into a gulf was only my mother, with her white graveclothes floating all about her, standing up in her grave to look after me. 'It was time you came home, my darling,' she said, and stooped down into her grave with me in her arms. And I was so happy, and her bosom was not cold or her arms hard, and she carried me just like a baby. And when she stooped down, a door opened somewhere in the grave; I could not find out where exactly, and in a moment afterward we were sitting together in a summer grove, with the treetops steeped in sunshine and waving about in a quiet, loving wind. Oh, how different from the one that chased me home. And I said, 'Mother, I've hurt my feet.' "

"Did you call her *mother* when you were a little girl?" asked Harry.

"No," answered Euphra, "I called her *mamma* like other children. But in my dreams I always call her *mother*."

"And what did she say?"

"She said, 'Poor child,' and held my feet to her bosom, and after that, when I looked at them, the bleeding was all gone, and I was not lame anymore."

Euphra paused with a sigh.

"Oh, Harry, I don't like to be lame."

"What happened then?" said Harry, intent only on the dream.

"Then I was so happy I woke up."

"What a pity. But if it should come true?"

"How could it come true, Harry?"

"Why, this world is sometimes cold and the road is hard—you know what I mean, Euphra."

"Yes, I do."

"I wish I could dream like that."

"But you dream dreams too, Harry. Tell me yours."

"Oh, no, I never dream dreams. The dreams dream me," answered Harry with a smile.

Then he told his dream. Each interpreted the other's with reverence.

They ceased talking and sat silent for a while.

Then Harry put his arms around Euphra's neck and his lips close to her ear and whispered, "Perhaps God will say 'my darling' to you some day, Euphra, just as your mother did in your dream."

She was silent. Harry looked round into her face and saw that the tears were flowing down it.

At that instant a gentle knock came to the door. Euphra could not reply to it. It was repeated. After another moment's delay the door opened and Margaret walked in.

41 / A Sunday with Falconer

It was not often that Falconer went to church, but he seemed to have some design in going oftener than usual at present. The following Sunday he went, and took Hugh with him, though to a far different church than Mrs. Elton's or Mrs. Appleditch's.

As they walked home afterward, Falconer said, "I seldom attend church. But when I do, I come here. I heartily trust that man. He speaks his heart."

"They say he is quite unorthodox."

"Granted."

"How can he remain in the church, then, if he is as honest as you say?"

"I like to think it is because he looks to life and the practice of the principles of the Bible rather than emphasizing formula and doctrines and creeds. He is a lover of the truth. I had a brief vision of him this morning as I sat and listened to his voice. Shall I tell you it?"

"Please do."

"I saw a crowd scrambling up a steep hill. Everyone was only for himself, fleeing to save their souls from the fires of hell which were rolling along below, moving toward the hill and threatening to devour it. Priests and preachers and elders and holy people and laymen all frantically trying to save themselves. But beneath them all, right in the course of the billowy flame, stands that man on a little rock, facing the approaching flames. He stands with eyes bright with faith in God, declaring the truth in holy defiance of the terrifying fire. The fugitives pause, looking back, and begin shouting at him, calling him names. 'False prophet,' they yell, 'liar . . .' But he pays no attention. In the name of God he rebukes the flames of hell. And be sure that, come what may of the rest, let the flames of hell ebb or flow, that man is safe. He trusts in God so absolutely that he leaves his salvation to him. He only sets himself to do the work that God has given him to do. Let God's will be done and all is well. To him God is all in all. If it be possible to separate such things, it is the glory of God, even more than the salvation of men, that he seeks. He believes entirely that God loves, yea, *is* love. Therefore hell itself must be subservient to that love and must be an embodiment of it. He believes that the grand work of Justice is to make way for a Love which will give to every man that which is right, even if it should be by means of awful suffering—a suffering which the love of the Father will not shun, either for himself or his children but will eagerly meet for their sakes, that he may give them all that is in his heart."

"Surely you speak your own opinions in describing the faith of the preacher."

"I do. He is accountable for nothing I say."

"How is it that so many good people consider him unorthodox and his ways suspect?"

"I do not mind that. To such well-meaning people with small natures, theology must be like a map—with plenty of lines in it. They cannot trust their house on the high tableland of this man's theology because they cannot see the outlines bounding his land. It is not small enough for them. They cannot take it in. Such people, one would think, can hardly be satisfied with creation, seeing there is no line of division anywhere in it."

"Does God draw no lines, then?"

"When he does, they are pure lines, without breadth and consequently invisible to mortal eyes, not walls of separation such as these definers would construct."

"But is it reasonable that a theory in religion be correct if it is so hard to see?"

"They are only hard to see for certain natures."

"But those people, those natures you speak of, are above average usually. And you have granted them good intentions."

"Generally good, but very narrow perspective."

"Is it not rather hard of you then to say that they cannot understand, cannot perceive truth in the high tableland?"

"Is it hard of me? Why? They will get to heaven, which is all they want. And they will understand one day, which is more than they pray for. Till they have done being anxious about their own salvation, we must forgive them that they can contemplate with calmness the damnation of a universe, all the while believing that God is yet more indifferent than they."

"But who is to say that you are right and they are the unenlightened ones? They could bring the same charge against you, of being unable to understand them."

"Yes. And so it must remain until the Spirit of God decides the matter, which I presume must take place by slow degrees. For this decision can only consist in the enlightenment of souls to see the truth. Till then, the Right must be content to be called the Wrong and—which is far harder—to seem the Wrong. There is no spiritual victory gained by a verbal conquest, or by any kind of torture. And even more, so long as the wicked themselves remain impenitent, there is mourning in heaven. And when there is no longer any hope over one last remaining sinner, heaven itself must confess its defeat, heap upon that sinner what plagues you will.''

Hugh pondered, and continued pondering till they reached Falconer's chambers. At the door, Hugh paused.

''Will you not come in?'' Falconer invited.

''I fear I shall be troublesome.''

''No fear of that. I promise to get rid of you as soon as I find you so.''

''Thank you. Just let me know when you have had enough of me.''

They entered. Mrs. Ashton got them some bread and cheese and Falconer's cupboard supplied its usual bottle of port, to which fare the friends sat down.

The conversation, like a bird descending in spirals, settled at last upon the subject which had more or less occupied Hugh's thoughts for some time. He asked Falconer if he had any theory of the relation between Fenkelstein, Count von Halkar, and Miss Cameron.

''I have been thinking a good deal about it,'' began Falconer. ''It is evident that Miss Cameron possesses a constitution sensitive to emotional and therefore, perhaps, spiritual matters. It is my opinion that it is on such constitutions that the powers of mesmerism are chiefly able to operate. Miss Cameron has at some time or other in her life submitted herself to the influences of this Count Halkar, and he has thus gained a dangerous authority over her, which he has exercised for his own ends.''

''She more than implied that very thing to me.''

''So his will became her law. There is in the world of the mind something corresponding to physical force in the material world. I cannot avoid just touching upon a higher analogy. The kingdom of heaven is not come, even when God's will is our law. It is come when God's will is our will. While God's will is our law, we are but a kind of noble slaves. When his will is our will, we are free children. To return to the point in hand, I recognize in the story a clear evidence of strife and partial victory in the affair of the ring. The count had evidently been anxious for years to possess it, the probable reasons we have already talked of. He had laid his injunctions on Miss Cameron to find it for him, and she, perhaps loving the man as well as submitting to him, had for a long time attempted to find it, but had failed. Probably doubting her sincerity, he followed her to Arnstead where it is likely he had been before, although he had previously avoided Mr. Arnold. Judging it advantageous to get into the house, he employed his chance meeting with you to that result. But before this, he had watched Miss Cameron's familiarity with you and was jealous and tyrannical. Hence the variations of her conduct to you, for when his power was upon her she could not do as she pleased. But she must have had a real regard for you, for she evidently refused to get you into trouble by taking the ring from your custody. But my surprise is that the fellow limited himself to that one jewel.''

''You may soon be relieved from that surprise,'' answered Hugh. ''He took a valuable diamond of mine as well.''

''The rascal. We may catch him, but you are not likely to find your diamond again. Still, there is some possibility.''

''How do you know she was not willing to take it from me?''

''Because, by her own account, he had to destroy her power of choice entirely before he could make her do it. He threw her into a mesmeric sleep.''

''I would like to understand his power over her a little better. Does the influence outlast the hypnotic condition?''

''Undoubtedly, if by condition you mean the state of sleep. For the mesmeric influence is actually quite independent of sleep. That is an accident accompanying it, sometimes indicating its culmination.''

''Does the person so influenced act with or against his will?''

''That is a most difficult question. My own impression is that he acts with his inclination—sometimes with his will, but sometimes against it. This is a very important distinction in morals, but often overlooked. When a man is acting with his inclination, his will can almost be viewed to be in abeyance. Other things no doubt combined to increase the influence in the present case. She liked him—perhaps more than liked him once. She was partially committed to his schemes. And she was easily mesmerized. It would seem besides that she was a natural somnambulist. This is a remarkable coexistence of distinct factors pointing in the same direction which made her, in one sense, an easy prey. But she was torn, especially after you entered the picture, to resist even though she was at times powerless to do so. She warned you to beware of the count that night before you went into the haunted bedchamber. Even when she entered it, by your own account—''

''Entered it? Then you do think it was Euphra who impersonated the ghost?''

''I am sure of it. She was sleepwalking.''

''But so different—such a deathlike look.''

''All that was easy to manage. She refused to obey him at first. He hypnotized her. It very likely went farther than he expected and he succeeded too well. Experienced no doubt in disguises, he dressed her as like the dead Lady Euphrasia as he could, following the picture. Perhaps she possessed such a disguise and had used it before. He thus protected her from suspicion and himself from implication. What was the color of the hair in the picture?''

''Golden.''

"Hence the sparkle of gold dust in her hair. The count managed it all. He willed that she should go, and she went. Her disguise was certain safety should she be seen. You would suspect the ghost. But even in this state she yielded against her better inclination, for she was weeping when you saw her. But she could not help it. While you lay on the couch in the haunted chamber, where he carried you, the awful death-ghost was busy in your room, opening your desk, fingering your papers, and stealing your ring. It is a rather frightful idea."

"She did not take my ring, I am sure. He followed her and took it. But she could not have come in at either door."

"Could not? Did she not go out at one of them? Besides, I do not doubt that such a room as that had a private communication with the open air as well. I should much like to examine the place."

"But how could she have gone through the bolted door then?"

"That door may have been set in another, larger by half the frame or so, which opened with a spring and concealed hinges. There are such places to be found now and then in old houses. But I still do not consider your testimony, on every minute detail, quite satisfactory."

"Why?" asked Hugh.

"First, because of the state of excitement you must have been in. And next, because I doubt the wine that was left in your room. The count no doubt knew enough of drugs to put a few ghostly horrors into the decanter. But poor Miss Cameron! The horrors he has put into her mind and life. It is a sad fate, one that could lead to insanity."

Hugh sprang to his feet.

"By heaven!" he cried. "I will strangle the knave!"

"Stop," said Falconer. "No revenge. Leave him to the sleeping divinity within him, which will awake one day and complete the hell he is now building for himself—for the very fire of hell is the divine in it. Your work is to set Euphra free."

"But what can I do for her?"

"You must teach her to resist and thus foil him."

"How am I to do that? Even if I knew how, I cannot see her, I cannot speak to her."

"I have a great faith in opportunity."

"But how can she foil him?"

"She must pray to God to redeem her tattered will—to strengthen her will to redeem herself. She must resist the count should he again claim her submission (as for her sake, I hope he will). Only then will she be free—not before. This will be very hard to do. His power has been excessive and her submission long and complete. Even if he left her alone she would not be free. She must defy him, break his bonds, oppose his will, assert her freedom, and defeat him."

"I have no power. Even if I were with her I could not help her in such a struggle. I wish David were not dead. You could help her, Mr. Falconer."

"Except I had known her for some time and Providence brought it about, I would do my best. Otherwise I would not interfere. But if she pray to God, he will give her whatever help she needs, and in the best way too."

"I think it would be some comfort to her if we could find either of the rings."

"To do that we must find the count first. I have not given that up, of course."

"Thank you a thousand times," said Hugh. "It is so good of you to take so much trouble on my account."

"It is my business," answered Falconer. "Is there not a soul in trouble?"

Hugh went home full of his new friend. He sat down to his novel, which had been making but little progress for some time. Teaching the Latin grammar and the English alphabet to young aspirants after the honors of "the ministry" was not work calculated to stimulate his sense of invention.

42 / The Lady's Maid

Margaret had gone to Euphra's room with the intention of restoring to her the letter she had written to David Elginbrod. Jeanette had let it lie for some time before she sent it to Margaret, and by now Euphra had given up all expectation of an answer.

Margaret hoped to minister to her, but from what she knew of Euphra she expected anger to be her first reaction. When she heard no answer to her knock, she had concluded that Euphra was not in the room, and she resolved to leave the letter where it would meet her eye. When she saw Euphra and Harry she turned immediately to leave. But Euphra was annoyed by her entrance and now found herself quite able to speak.

"What do you want?" she demanded angrily.

"This is your letter, Miss Cameron, is it not?" said Margaret, approaching her with it in her hand.

Euphra took it, glanced at the address, and pushed Harry away from her. She started up in a passion, letting loose the whole gathered irritability of weariness and disappointment and suffering upon Margaret. Her dark eyes flashed with rage.

"What right have you to handle my letters? How did you get this? It has not been mailed. And open too! I suppose you have read it?"

Margaret was afraid of exciting more wrath before she had an opportunity of explaining. But Euphra gave her no time to think of a reply.

"You have read it, you shameless woman. Impudent prying! My maid never posted it, and you have found it and read it. Did you hope to find a secret worth a bribe?"

She advanced on Margaret till she stood within a foot of her.

"Why don't you answer, you hussy? I will go this instant to your mistress. Either you or I must leave this house for good."

Margaret had stood all this time quietly, waiting for an opportunity to speak. Her face was pale but perfectly still and her eyes did not quail. She had not lost her self-possession.

"You do not know my name, Miss Cameron—of course you could not."

"Your name! What is that to me?"

"That," said Margaret, pointing to the letter, "is my father's name."

Euphra looked at her written address again and then looked at Margaret. She was so bewildered that if she had any thoughts, she did not know them.

Margaret went on. "My father is dead. My mother sent the letter to me."

"Then you *have* had the impertinence to read it!"

"It was my duty to read it."

"Duty! What business had you with it?"

Euphra felt ashamed of the letter as soon as she found that she had applied to a man whose daughter was a servant.

Margaret answered, "I could at least reply to it so that the writer should not think my father had neglected it. I did not know who it was from until I came to the end."

Euphra turned her back on her with the words, "You may go."

Margaret walked out of the room with an unconscious gentleness.

"Come back!" cried Euphra.

Margaret obeyed.

"Of course, you will tell all your fellowservants the contents of this foolish letter."

"Dear Miss Cameron, do not call it foolish. For God's sake—"

"What is it to you? Do you think I am going to make a confidante of *you*?"

Margaret again left the room. No sooner was she out of sight than Euphra sat down, her worn frame exhausted by the violence of the outburst, and began weeping more bitterly than before. She was not only exhausted but ashamed. And to those feelings was added a far greater sense of disappointment than she could have believed possible at the frustration of the hope of help from David Elginbrod. True, this hope had been small. But where there is only one hope, its death is equally bitter whether it be a great or a little hope.

All this time Harry had been looking on in a kind of paralyzed condition, pale with perplexity and distress. He now came up to Euphra, and trying to pull her hand gently from her face said, "What is it all about Euphra, dear?"

"Oh, I have been very naughty, Harry."

"May I read the letter?"

"If you like," answered Euphra listlessly.

Harry read the letter. Then laying it down on the table with reverential slowness he went to Euphra, put his arms round her and kissed her.

"Dear, dear Euphra. I did not know you were so unhappy. It is a beautiful letter. Don't you think that God may read it and take it for a prayer?"

"I wish he would, Harry."

"But it was very wrong of you to speak as you did to the daughter of such a good man."

"Yes, it was."

"Well, you have only to say you are sorry and Margaret won't think anything more about it. She is so good."

Euphra recoiled from making a confession of wrong to a lady's maid. And perhaps she was a little jealous of Harry's admiration of Margaret. For Euphra had not yet cast off all her old habits of mind. So she did not respond to what Harry said, and after he had left her, did not make her appearance again that day.

But at night, when the household was retiring, she rose from the bed on which she had been lying and went to the door and opened it a little way that she might hear when Margaret passed from Mrs. Elton's room to her own. She waited for some time; but judging at length that she must have passed without her knowledge she went and knocked at her door. Margaret opened it a little after a moment's delay, half undressed.

"May I come in, Margaret?"

"Yes, do, Miss Cameron," answered Margaret.

She opened the door wide and Euphra entered. Margaret's rich dark hair fell on her shoulders.

What lovely skin she has, thought Euphra, who realized for the first time that Margaret was beautiful.

"I am very sorry, Margaret, that I spoke to you as I did today."

"Never mind it, Miss Cameron. We cannot help being angry sometimes. And you had great provocation under the mistake you made. I was only sorry because I knew it would trouble you afterward. Please don't think of it again."

"You are very kind, Margaret."

"I regretted my father's death for the first time after reading your letter, for I knew he could have helped you. But it was very foolish of me, for God is not dead."

Margaret smiled as she said this, looking full in Euphra's face. It quite overcame Euphra. She had never felt comfortable in Margaret's presence before, especially after she had encountered the nun in the Ghost's Walk, though she had no suspicion that the nun was Margaret. But this discomfort vanished entirely now.

"Do you, then, know God too, Margaret?"

"Yes," answered Margaret simply and solemnly.

"Will you tell me about him?"

"I can at least tell you about my father and what he taught me."

"Oh, thank you. Do tell me about him—now."

"Not now, dear Miss Cameron. It is late. Let me help you to bed. I will be your maid."

As she spoke, Margaret proceeded to put on her dress again that she might go with Euphra, who had no attendant. She had parted with Jane and did not care, in her present mood, to have a woman about her—especially a new one.

"No, Margaret. You have enough to do without adding me to your troubles."

"Please, do let me. It will be a great pleasure to me. I have hardly anything to call work. You should see how I used to work when I was at home."

Euphra still objected, but Margaret's entreaty prevailed. She followed Euphra to her room. There she served her like a ministering angel, brushed her hair so gently, smoothing it out as if she loved it. There was health in the touch of her hands, because there was love. She undressed her, covered her in bed as if she had been a child, made up the fire to last as long as possible, kissed her on the forehead, and bade her good night.

Euphra cried herself to sleep. They were the first tears she had ever shed that were not painful tears. She slept as she had not slept for months.

When she woke, her first breath was like a deep draught of spiritual water. She felt as if some sorrow had passed from her and some gladness had come in its place. She thought and thought, and found at length that the gladness was Margaret. She had scarcely made the discovery when the door opened gently and Margaret peeped in to see if she were awake.

"May I come in?" she said.

"Yes, please, Margaret."

"How do you feel today?"

"Oh, so much better, dear Margaret. Your kindness will make me well."

"I am so glad. Lie still a while and I will bring you some breakfast. Mrs. Elton will be pleased to let me wait on you."

"She asked me, Margaret, if I wanted you to. But I was too miserable then—and too selfish, for I did not like you."

"I knew that. But I felt sure you would not dislike me always."

"Why?"

"Because I could not help loving you."

"Why did you love me?"

"I will tell you half the reason. Because you looked so unhappy."

"What was the other half?"

"That I cannot—I mean I will not tell you."

"Never?"

"Perhaps. But I don't know. Not now."

"Very well, I won't ask you."

"Thank you. I will go and get your breakfast."

From this time Margaret waited on Euphra as if she had been her own maid. Nor had Mrs. Elton any cause for complaint, for Margaret was always at hand when she was wanted.

Many and long were the conversations between the two girls when everyone else was asleep. And now the teaching for which Euphra had longed sprang in a fountain at her own door. It had been near her all along, but she had not known it, for its hour had not come. Now she drank as only the thirsty drink.

The second night Margaret came to Euphra's room, she said, "Shall I tell you about my father tonight?"

Euphra was delighted.

So they sat down and Margaret began to talk about her childhood, the cottage she lived in, the fir wood all around it, the work she used to do. Summer and winter, springtime and harvest, storm and sunshine all came into the tale. Her mother came into it and the grand form of her father. Every time Euphra saw him thus in the mirror of Margaret's memory, she saw him more clearly than before. Sometimes she asked a question or two, but generally she allowed Margaret's words to flow unchecked, for she painted her pictures better when the colors did not dry between. They talked on far into the night. At length Margaret stopped suddenly and looked at the clock on the chimney-piece.

"I have kept you up too late! I must get you to bed."

"You will come tomorrow night again?"

"Yes, I will."

"Then I will go to bed like a good child," said Euphra, smiling.

The next night, she spoke again of her father and what he taught her. Euphra had thought much about him, and every fresh touch which the story gave to the portrait allowed her to know him better. But what is most worthy of record is that ever as the picture of David grew on the vision of Euphra, the idea of God was growing unawares upon her inward sight. She was learning more and more about his character from the character of his servant. Faith came of itself, and slowly grew.

Euphra began to read the story of the gospel. So did Harry. They found themselves with many questions, and they always applied to Margaret for the light they needed.

Many meetings of this sort did not take place between them before Euphra, in her turn, began to confide her history to Margaret. It was a strangely different one—full of outward events but almost barren as to inward development. It was a history of Euphra's circumstances, not of Euphra herself. Until lately, she had scarcely had any history. Margaret's, on the contrary, was a true history. For even in the midst of monotonous circumstances, it described individual growth and the changes of inner progress. Where there is no change, there can be no history.

And since all change is either growth or decay, all history must describe either progress or retrogression.

But Euphra was now coming to have a history, for the growth process had begun in her. It was proof of her growth that she told Margaret all I have already recorded for my readers. And after she had told it, Euphra was still more humble toward Margaret, and Margaret more tender, full of service, and devoted to Euphra.

43 / Margaret's Secret

Margaret could not proceed very far in the story of her life without making some reference to Hugh Sutherland. But she carefully avoided mentioning his name.

"Ah," said Euphra one day, "your history is a little like mine; a tutor comes into them both. Did you not fall dreadfully in love with him?"

"I loved him very much."

"Where is he now?"

"In London, I believe."

"Do you never see him?"

"No."

"Have you never seen him since he left your home?"

"Yes, but not spoken to him."

"Where?"

Margaret was silent. Euphra knew well enough now not to repeat the question.

"If I had been you," said Euphra, "I should have been in love with him, I know."

Margaret only smiled.

Another day Euphra said, "What a good boy Harry is. But, Margaret, I behaved like a devil to him. I even enticed Mr. Sutherland away from him to me when he was the only real friend he had. I foolishly thought I might possess them both."

"But you have done your best to make up for it since."

"I have tried a little. I cannot say I have done my best. I have been so peevish and irritable."

"You could not quite help that."

"You are kind to excuse me. It makes me so much stronger to try again."

"My father used to say that God was always finding every excuse for us that could be found—every true one, you know."

After a pause, Euphra resumed. "Mr. Sutherland did me some good, Margaret."

"I do not wonder at that."

"He made me think less about Count Halkar; and that was something, for he haunted me."

"Mr. Sutherland loved you very much, Miss Cameron."

"He loved me once," said poor Euphra with a sigh.

"I saw he did. That was why I began to love you too."

Margaret had at last unwittingly opened the door of her secret. She had told her the other reason for loving Euphra. But naturally Euphra could not understand what she meant.

"What do you mean, Margaret?"

"I must confess it," she said; "it cannot hurt him now. My tutor and yours are the same."

"Impossible!"

"True."

"And you never spoke all the time you were both at Arnstead?"

"Not once. He never knew I was in the house."

"And you saw he loved me?"

"Yes."

"And you were not jealous?"

"I did not say that. But I soon found that the only way to escape from my jealousy, if the feeling I had was jealousy, was to love you too. So, I did."

"You beautiful girl. But you could not have loved him much."

"I loved him enough to love you for his sake. But why did he stop loving you?"

"He could not help it, Margaret. I deserved it." Euphra hid her face in her hands.

"He could not have really loved you then?"

"Which is better to believe, Margaret," said Euphra, uncovering her tear-stained face, "that he never loved me, or that he stopped loving me?"

"For his sake, the first."

"And for my sake, the second?"

"That depends."

"So it does. He must have found plenty of faults in me. But I was not so bad as he thought me when he stopped loving me."

Margaret's answer was one of her loving smiles, in which her eyes had more share than her lips.

It would have been unendurable to Euphra a little while before to find that she had a rival in a servant. Now she scarcely thought of that aspect of Margaret's position.

"How is it that you take it so quietly?" she said, looking doubtfully at Margaret. "Your love must have been very different from mine. Indeed, I am not sure that I loved him at all. But you must have loved him dreadfully."

"Perhaps I did. But I had no anxiety about it."

"But that you could not leave even to such a father as yours to settle."

"No. But I could leave it to God. I could trust God with what I could not speak to my father about. He is my father's Father, and so more to him and me than we could be to each other. I loved my father ten times more because he loved God, and because God had secrets with him."

"I wish God were a Father to me as he is to you, Margaret."

"But he is your Father, whether you wish it or not. He cannot be more your Father than he is. You may be more his child than you are, but not more than he meant you to be nor more than he made you for. You are infinitely more his child than you have grown to yet. He made you altogether his child, but you have not given in to it yet."

Euphra made no answer, but wept. Margaret said no more.

Euphra was the first to resume.

"Mr. Sutherland was very kind, Margaret. He promised—and I know he will keep his promise—to do all he could to help me. I hope he is finding out where that wicked count is."

"Write to him and ask him to come to see you. He does not know where you are."

"But I do not know where he is."

"I do."

"Do you?" rejoined Euphra with some surprise.

"But he does not know where I am. I will give you his address if you like."

Euphra pondered a little. She would have liked very much to see him. But now that she knew the relation that had existed between Margaret and him, she shrank from doing anything that might seem to Margaret to give herself an opportunity of regaining his preference. Not that she had herself the smallest hope, even had she had the tiniest desire of doing so. But she would not even suggest the idea of being Margaret's rival.

At length she answered, "No thank you, Margaret. As soon as he has anything to report, he will write to Arnstead, and Mrs. Horton will forward the letter. No—it is quite unnecessary."

44 / Forebodings

Mr. Appleditch had had some business misfortunes, not of a heavy nature but sufficient to cast a gloom over the house, and especially over the face of his spouse who had her heart set on a new carpet for her drawing room. She began contriving ways to procure it nonetheless and thus began to reflect that her two sons were not drawing nine shillings worth a week of the sap of divinity. This she hinted to Mr. Appleditch.

As it would involve some awkwardness to state reasons, Mrs. Appleditch resolved to find some quarrel with Hugh in order to rid herself of him. It was the way she always took, and left her with a comfortable feeling of injured dignity. As a preliminary course she began to treat him with still less politeness than before.

At length, one day she came into the room where Hugh was more busy in teaching than his pupils were in learning, and seated herself by the fire to watch for an opportunity. The boys, rendered still more inattentive by the presence of their mother, could not be induced to fix the least thought upon the matter at hand. Thus Hugh was compelled to go over the same thing again and again without success.

At last he said, "I am afraid, Mrs. Appleditch, I must ask you to leave, for I cannot get any attention from the boys today."

"And how could it be otherwise, Mr. Sutherland, when you keep wearing them out with going over and over the same thing till they are sick of it? Why don't you go on?"

"How can I go on when they have not learned the thing they are at? That would be to build the chimneys before the walls."

"It is easy to be witty, but I beg you will behave more respectfully to me in the presence of my children, the innocent lambs!"

Looking round at that moment, Hugh caught in his face what the eldest had intended for his back—a grimace hideous enough to have procured him instant promotion in the kingdom of apes.

The mother saw it too and added, "You see you cannot make them respect you. Really, Mr. Sutherland!"

Hugh was about to reply to the effect that it was useless in such circumstances to attempt teaching them at all—which was just the sort of excuse Mrs. Appleditch was looking for as the occasion for his instant dismissal. But at that very moment a carriage pulled sharply up at the door and mother and sons darted simultaneously to the window.

"Papa's bought a carriage!" shouted Petie.

"Be quiet, children," said their mother as she saw a footman get down and approach the door.

"Look at that buffer," said Johnny. "Come and see the grand footman, Mr. Sutherland. He's such a gentleman!"

A box on the ear from his mother silenced him. The maid entered with some perturbation a moment later and addressed her mistress.

"Please'm, the carriage is astin' after Mr. Sutherland."

"Mr. Sutherland?"

"Yes'm."

The lady turned to Hugh who, although surprised as well, was not inclined to show his surprise to Mrs. Appleditch.

"I did not know you had carriage friends, Mr. Sutherland," she said, eyebrows arched in disapproval.

"Neither did I," answered Hugh. "But I will go and see who it is."

When he reached the street he found Harry on the pavement, who, having got out of the carriage and not having been asked into the house, was unable to stand still from impatience. As soon as he saw his beloved tutor, he bounded to see him and threw his arms round his neck, standing as they were in the open street. Tears of delight filled his eyes.

"Come, come, come!" said Harry. "We all want you."

"Who wants me?"

"Mrs. Elton and Euphra and me. Come, get in."

He pulled Hugh toward the carriage.

"I cannot go with you now. I have pupils here."

Harry's face fell.

"When will you come?"

"In half an hour."

"Hurrah! I shall be back in exactly half an hour then. Do be ready, please, Mr. Sutherland."

"I will."

Harry jumped into the carriage, telling the coachman to drive where he pleased and be back at the same place in half an hour. Hugh returned into the house.

As may be supposed, Margaret was the means of this happy meeting. For several days Euphra seemed to be gradually regaining her health and composure of mind. One evening as Margaret was going to bed, a knock on her door startled her. Going to it, she saw Euphra standing there, pale as death, with nothing on but her nightgown, even though it was a very cold night. She thought at first she must be walking in her sleep, but the scared intelligence of her open eyes soon satisfied her that it was not so.

"What is the matter, dear Miss Cameron?" she said as calmly as she could.

"He is coming. He wants me. If he calls me I must go."

"No, you shall *not* go," said Margaret firmly.

"I must, I must," answered Euphra, wringing her hands.

"Come in," said Margaret; "you must not stand there in the cold."

Margaret got a shawl to put around Euphra's shoulders and then led her back to her room.

"He wants me. He wants me! He will call me soon," said Euphra in an agonized whisper. "What shall I do?"

As soon as they were back in Euphra's room, Margaret said, "Has this man any right to call you?"

"No, no," answered Euphra vehemently.

"Then don't go."

"But I am afraid of him."

"Defy him, in God's name."

"But besides the fear there is something else that I can't describe—pushing me, drawing me. It is as if I cannot rest till I go, like some demon were shaking my soul till I yield and go. I can't help it."

Trying to soothe her, Margaret said calmly, "It is all right, my darling, you shall not go to him."

"But I must," she answered with despair and then began to weep.

Margaret rose.

"Don't leave me, Margaret," said Euphra, rising from the bed where she lay.

"I didn't mean to leave you for a moment. Lie down again. I am only going to read a little bit out of the New Testament to you."

"I am afraid I can hardly listen to it."

"Never mind. Don't try."

Margaret got a New Testament and read in John's Gospel. After a while she paused. "It cannot be God's will that you go to the count, can it, Miss Cameron? He is not a good man."

"But one does many things that are not God's will."

"But it is God's will that you should *not* go to him."

Euphra lay silent for a few moments. Suddenly she exclaimed, "Then I *must* not go to him. God help me . . . help me!"

Margaret knelt beside her and put her arm around her. Euphra spoke no more. At length Margaret looked at her. She was in a sweet sleep. Rising, Margaret covered her up and then made herself as comfortable as possible to sit by her bedside and watch for her waking.

She slept thus for an hour. Then lifting her head and seeing Margaret, she said with a smile, "Margaret, I was dreaming that I had a mother."

"So you have somewhere."

"Yes, so I have, somewhere," she repeated and crept under the covers again like a child and was asleep again in a moment.

Margaret watched her for another hour and, seeing no signs of restlessness, lay down beside her and soon shared in that repose which to weary women and men is God's best gift.

She rose at her usual hour the next day and was dressed before Euphra awoke. It was a cold, gray December morning with the hoarfrost lying thick on the roofs of the houses. Euphra opened her eyes while Margaret was busy lighting the fire. Seeing that she was there, she closed them again and fell once more fast asleep. Before she woke again, Margaret had some tea ready for her. She rose, looking more bright and hopeful than Margaret had seen her before.

But Margaret watched her intently through the day and saw a change come over her. Her face grew pale and troubled. Now and then her eyes were fixed on vacancy. Margaret saw that the conflict was coming on, if not already begun again. She thought that perhaps a talk with Hugh might comfort Euphra a bit and divert her thoughts from herself. She therefore let Harry know Hugh's address as given in the letter to her father. She was certain that if Harry succeeded in finding him, nothing more was necessary to ensure his being brought to Mrs. Elton's.

Hugh reentered the house. Although Mrs. Appleditch's first feeling had been jealousy of Hugh's acquaintance with "carriage people," by the time he came back in, her consdescension had gained the upper hand.

"Why didn't you ask your friends into the drawing room, Mr. Sutherland?"

"He will return for me when the lesson is over," answered Hugh.

"I am sure any friends of yours that want to call here will be most welcome. It would certainly be more agreeable for you to receive them here than in your accommodations at poor Mrs. Talbot's, a place hardly suitable."

"I am sorry to say, however," answered Hugh, "that after the way you have spoken to me today that I cannot continue my relation to my pupils any longer."

"Ho, ho," retorted the lady with indignation mingled with scorn. "Our grand visitors have set our backs up. Very well, Mr. Sutherland, you may oblige me by leaving the house at once. Don't trouble yourself to finish the lesson. I will pay you for it all the same. The idea of insulting me before the very face of my innocent lambs! And remember," she added, as she pulled out her purse while Hugh was collecting some books he had lent to the boys, "that when you were starving, my husband and I took you in and gave you employment out of charity, pure charity. Here is your money."

"Good morning, Mrs. Appleditch," said Hugh, and walked out with his books under his arm, leaving her with the money in her hand.

Twenty-five minutes later the carriage drove up again. He jumped into it and was carried off in triumph by Harry.

Mrs. Elton received him kindly. Euphra held out her hand with a slight blush and the quiet familiarity of an old friend. Hugh could almost have fallen in love with her again, from compassion for her pale, worn face and subdued expression. Her look also gave him to know that her bondage to the count was still not broken.

Mrs. Elton went out in the carriage herself soon thereafter, and Euphra begged Harry to leave them alone as she had something to talk to Mr. Sutherland about.

"Have you found any trace of Count Halkar, Hugh?" she said the moment they were alone.

"I am sorry to say I have not. I have done my best."

"I am quite sure of that. I just wanted to tell you that I think you will have more chance of finding him now."

Euphra sighed, paused, and then said, "But I am not sure of it. I think he is in London. But he may be on the Continent, for anything I know. I shall in all probability know more about him within a few days."

They continued to talk about the count and the ring. Hugh judged it best to say nothing to her of Falconer. And Euphra, on her part, did not mention Margaret's name, for she had begged her not to do so.

"You remember my speaking to you of Mr. Arnold's jewels?" Euphra asked.

"Yes."

"I wanted to find out through you where the ring was. But I had no intention of involving you."

"I am sure you had not."

"Don't be too sure of anything about me. I don't know what I might have been led to do. But I am very sorry. Do forgive me."

"I cannot allow that I have anything to forgive. But my heart is full and you are welcome to what forgiveness you desire from me."

"Thank you, Hugh," she said with a quiet smile.

They talked until Mrs. Elton, who had made Hugh promise to stay for lunch, returned. When they were seated at the table, the kindhearted woman said, "Now, Mr. Sutherland, when will you begin again with Harry?"

"I do not quite understand you," answered Hugh.

"Of course you will come and give him lessons. He will be broken-hearted if you don't."

"I wish I could. But I cannot, for his father was dissatisfied with me. That was one of the reasons he sent Harry to London."

Harry looked wretchedly disappointed, but said nothing.

"I never heard him say anything of the sort," rejoined Mrs. Elton.

"Nevertheless, it is true. I am sorry he has mistaken me; but he will know me better someday."

"I will take all the responsibility," persisted Mrs. Elton.

"But, unfortunately, the responsibility sticks too fast for you to take it. I cannot get rid of my share, if I would."

"You are too particular. I am sure Mr. Arnold never could have meant that. This is my house too."

"But Harry is his boy. If you will let me come and see him sometimes I shall be very thankful. I may be useful to him without giving him lessons."

"Thank you," said Harry with delight.

45 / The Struggle

As soon as Hugh had left the house, Margaret hastened to Euphra. She found her in her own room, strangely depressed. This appearance increased toward evening until her looks become quite haggard, revealing an inward conflict of growing agony. Margaret remained with her.

Just before dinner, the upstairs bell rang and Margaret went downstairs. Mrs. Elton only detained her a few minutes, and she quickly flew to Euphra's room by the back staircase. Halfway up the stairs she was horrified to meet Euphra, in a cloak and thick veil, creeping down the stairs like a thief. Without saying a word, the strong Margaret lifted her in her arms, as if she had been a child, and carried her back to her room.

Euphra neither struggled nor spoke. Margaret laid her on her couch and sat down beside her. She lay without moving and, although wide awake, gave no other sign of existence than an occasional low moan.

Having lain thus for an hour, she broke the silence.

"Margaret, do you despise me for what I did?"

"Not in the least."

"Yet you found me going to do what I knew was wrong."

"You had not made yourself strong by thinking about the will of God, had you?"

"No. I had been resisting the tormenting inclination to go to him all day and was finally so worn out I could hardly bear it. Then I thought how easy it would be to yield to it—only this once. I thought I might then be stronger to resist next time. I forgot all about the will of God."

"You *must* fight it. All that God requires of you is to try again."

"I will try. Oh, how glad I am that you found me. Do keep watching me, always."

"I will be your sister and servant, Euphra. Anything you like—if you will but keep trying."

"I will."

Suddenly she sprang from the couch with an agonized look on her face and grasped Margaret's arm.

"Margaret," she said in a trembling voice, "could it be that I am still in love with him?"

"No, no, dear. You were haunted with him and so tired you began to give way. That is all. Let me read to you again, Euphra."

The next day the struggle evidently continued and had such an effect on Euphra that Margaret could not help being anxious about her health.

Hugh and Falconer agreed that Mrs. Elton's home should be closely watched so that if she did fall into one of her trances and go to him she could be followed. Once Euphra rose, went to the door, and opened it. But she instantly slammed it shut again and walked slowly back and resumed her seat on the couch. Margaret came to her from the other side of the bed where she had been working by the window in the waning evening light.

"What is it, dear?"

"Oh, Margaret. I did not know you were in the room. I found myself at the door before I knew what I was doing."

"But you came back of yourself this time."

"Yes, I did. But I still feel inclined to go."

"There is no sin in that, so long as you do not yield to it."

"I hate it."

"You will soon be free from it. Keep on courageously. You will be in liberty and joy soon."

"God grant it."

"I am sure he will."

Meantime, Hugh took up temporary lodgings at a public house at the corner of a back street near Mrs. Elton's. He went again to her house, this time to engage the help of a steady old servant who had been very friendly with him. He asked to see the butler.

"Irwan," he said, "has Herr von Fenkelstein called here recently?"

"No, sir, he has not."

"You would know him, would you not?"

"Yes, sir; perfectly."

"Well, if he should call, will you let me know the very moment he is in the house? You will find me at the Golden Staff round the corner. It is of the utmost importance. But do not let him know that anyone wants to see him. You will not be sorry for helping me. I know I can trust you."

"I will do it, sir," answered Irwan, and Hugh felt tolerably sure of him.

Back at his room, Falconer soon came to keep him company. They ordered supper and sat until eleven o'clock. There being then no chance of a summons, they went out for a walk together. Passing the house, they saw light in one upper window only. That light would burn there all night, for it was in Euphra's room. They went on, Hugh accompanying Falconer on one of his midnight walks through London as he had by now done several times before.

As early as was excusable the following morning he called on Euphra. She had not been down yet that morning, but his name was sent up. A message was brought back down that Miss Cameron was sorry not to see him but she had had a bad night and was quite unable to get out of bed. Irwan replied to his inquiry that the count had not called. Hugh returned to the Golden Staff.

A bad night it had been indeed. As Euphra slept well the first part of it and had no attack such as she had had upon both the preceding nights, Margaret had hoped the worst was over. Still she laid herself only within the threshold of sleep, ready to wake at the least motion.

In the middle of the night she felt Euphra move. She lay still to see what she would do. Euphra slipped out of bed and partly dressed herself. Then she went toward the door. Margaret called her, but she made no answer. Margaret sprang up and reached the door before her. Then to her relief she saw that Euphra's eyes were closed. Just as she had her hand on the door, Margaret took her gently in her arms.

''Let me go . . . let me go!'' Euphra almost screamed. Then suddenly opening her eyes she stared at Margaret in bewilderment.

''Euphra,'' said Margaret.

''Oh, Margaret, is it really you?'' exclaimed Euphra throwing her arms about her. ''I am so glad. But I must have been about it again.''

''Come to bed. You couldn't help it. There is not more than half of you awake when you walk in your sleep.''

They went to bed. Euphra crept close to Margaret and cried herself to sleep again. The next day she had a bad headache. This always followed sleep-walking. She did not get up all that day. When Hugh called again in the evening, he heard she was better, but still in bed.

Falconer joined Hugh at the Golden Staff at night. But this time Falconer went out alone, for Hugh wanted to keep himself fresh. Though very strong, he was younger and less hardened then Falconer, who could stand an incredible amount of labor and lack of sleep.

But Hugh was restless and could not sleep. Something would not let him be at peace. So he rose, dressed, and went out. Rounding the corner, he could see Mrs. Elton's house and that the same light they had observed previously was burning now. There was snow in the air. Then Hugh's eyes were arrested by the sight of a man walking up and down the pavement in front of the house. He instantly stepped into the shadow of a porch to watch. The distance was too great and the moonlight too intermittent to see him well, but Hugh thought he saw the man looking up to the windows every now and then. At length he seemed to stop under the lighted one and look up. Hugh was just to the point of trying to get nearer when to his dismay a policeman emerged from another street, and the figure vanished immediately in some mysterious corner. Hugh did not pursue him. If it were the count, Hugh knew his chances of catching him would be slim and that he would unlikely return to a spot he knew to be watched. Hugh, therefore, withdrew once more under a porch and waited. But the man made no further appearance. Hugh watched for two more hours, in spite of the possibility of being accosted by a suspicious policeman. He slept late into the following morning.

During the night, as in the preceding, Margaret had awakened suddenly. Euphra was not in bed. She started up in an agony of terror, but it was soon allayed. She saw Euphra on her knees at the foot of the bed. Her arms were wrapped round one of the bedposts, and her head was thrown back. Her eyes were closed, her face almost deathlike and drenched with sweat. Her lips were moving convulsively in an apparent agony of inward prayer. Margaret watched in anxious sympathy for a long time. Then, longing at length to have some share in the struggle, she rose and went softly to stand behind her, where she lifted up her heart in prayer.

In speaking about it afterward Margaret said that she distinctly remembered hearing, as she stood praying, the measured steps of a policeman pass the house on the pavement below. A few moments later Euphra's countenance relaxed a little and composure slowly followed. Her arms untwined themselves from the bedpost and her hands clasped themselves together, and she continued to pray in the intense silence of absorbing devotion. Margaret stood still as a statue.

In a few minutes Euphra rose to her feet. She turned round toward Margaret as if she knew she was there. To Margaret's astonishment her eyes were wide open.

She smiled a most childlike, peaceful smile and said, "It is over, Margaret—over at last. Thank you."

Margaret looked on her with awe. Fear, distress, and doubt had vanished. Margaret got a handkerchief and wiped the cold perspiration from her face. Then she helped her into bed where she fell asleep almost instantly and slept soundly.

She woke weak and worn, but happy.

"I will not trouble you today, Margaret," she said. "I shall not get up yet, but you will not need to watch me. I have overcome him, I can tell. I got up last night in my sleep. But I remember it. It was like he was dragging me away by bodily force. But I resisted him, praying for strength, till he left me alone. Thank God!"

It had been a terrible struggle and the effect on her weakened constitution doubtful. But she had overcome. In the afternoon Euphra slept again. When she woke she said to Margaret, "Can it be that it was all a dream? Have I been out of my mind all this time? It could not have been me, Margaret, could it?"

"Not your real, true self."

"I have been a dreadful creature. But I feel all that has melted away from me now . . . but how could he ever have had that hateful power over me?''

''Don't think about him now, but enjoy the rest God has given you.''

At that moment, a maid came to the door with Fenkelstein's card for Miss Cameron.

''Very well,'' said Margaret; ''ask him to wait. I will tell Miss Cameron. She may wish to send him a message. You may go.''

She told Euphra that the count was in the house. Euphra showed no surprise, neither fear.

''Will you see him for me, Margaret, if you don't mind? Tell him that I defy him and challenge him to do his worst.''

She had forgotten all about the ring. But Margaret had not.

''I will,'' she said, and left the room.

On her way down she went into the drawing room and rang the bell.

''Send Mr. Irwan to me here, please. It is for Miss Cameron.''

The man went, but presently returned saying that the butler had just stepped out.

''Very well. You will do just as well. When the gentleman leaves who is calling now, you must follow him. Take a cab if necessary and follow him everywhere till you find where he stops for the night. Watch the place and send me word where you are. But don't let him know. Put on plain clothes, please, as fast as you can.''

''Yes, miss, directly.''

The servants all called Margaret ''miss.''

She lingered a little to give the man time. She was not at all satisfied with her plan but could think of nothing better. Fortunately it was not necessary. Irwan had run as fast as his old legs would carry him to the Golden Staff. When he received the news, Hugh's heart seemed to leap into his throat.

''I will wait for him outside the door. We must not have a row in the house.''

''Good gracious! And the plates are all laid out for dinner on the sideboard!'' exclaimed Irwan and hurried off faster than he had come.

But Hugh was standing at the door long before Irwan got up to it. Had Margaret known who was watching outside, it would have been a wonderful relief to her.

She entered the dining room where the count stood impatiently. He advanced quickly, acting on his expectation of Euphra, but seeing his mistake, stopped and bowed politely. Margaret told him that Miss Cameron was ill and gave him her message, word for word. The count turned pale with rage. He made no reply but walked out into the hall where Irwan stood with the handle of the door in his hand, impatient to open it.

No sooner was he out of the house than Hugh sprang upon him. But the count had been perfectly on his guard and eluded him, darting off down the street. Dismayed at his escape, Hugh pursued at full speed. They both passed the Golden Staff at a dead run, and Hugh feared he might lose him with a sudden turn into some unseen alley. But rounding the next turn, the count ran full into Falconer, on his way to Hugh's, who staggered back while the count reeled and fell. Hugh was upon him in a moment.

"Help!" roared the count, hoping for a last chance from the sympathies of a gathering crowd.

"I've got him!" cried Hugh.

"Let the man alone," growled a burly fellow in the crowd, clenching his fists.

"Let me have a look at him," said Falconer, stooping over him. "I don't know him. That's as well for him. Let him up, Sutherland."

The bystanders took Falconer for a detective and did not seem inclined to interfere, all except the burly man who seemed all too ready to make the count's business his own. He came up, pushing the crowd right and left. "Let the man alone," he said in a very offensive tone.

"I assure you," said Falconer, "he's not worth your trouble."

"None o' your cursed jaw!" said the fellow in a louder tone, approaching Falconer with a threatening look. He had apparently been drinking.

"Well, I'm sorry," said Falconer, "but you seem to leave me no alternative. Sutherland, look after the count."

"I have him," said Hugh confidently.

Falconer turned toward the oncoming man who was already on the point of clutching him in what would likely have been a vice-like embrace, for he preferred that mode of fighting. Falconer retreated a step and prepared to defend himself. The man was good with his fists too and, having failed in his first attempt, made the best use of them he could. But he had no chance with Falconer, whose coolness equalled his skill.

Meantime the Bohemian had been watching for his chance, and though the contest did not last longer than one minute, he found opportunity during it to wrench himself free from Hugh, trip him up, and dart off. The crowd gave way before him. He vanished so suddenly and so quickly that it was evident he must have studied the neighborhood from the retreat-side of the question. With rat-like instinct he had consulted the holes and corners in anticipation of the necessity of applying to them. Hugh got up and, directed or possibly misdirected by the bystanders, sped away in pursuit. But he saw or heard nothing of the fugitive.

After a moment the antagonist lay in the road.

''Look after him, somebody,'' said Falconer.

''No fear of him, sir; he's used to it,'' answered one of the bystanders with the respect which Falconer's prowess claimed.

Falconer hurried after Hugh, who soon returned looking very dejected.

''Never mind, Sutherland,'' he said. ''The fellow is up to a trick or two; but we shall catch him yet. If it hadn't been for that big fool there! But he's been punished enough.''

''But what can we do next? He will not come here again.''

''Very likely not. Still, he may not give up his attempts upon Miss Cameron. We must continue to be watchful and diligent. We will find him.''

46 / Margaret

Hugh returned to Mrs. Elton's and in the dining room wrote a note to Euphra to express his disappointment that the count had foiled him. But at the same time he told her of his determination not to abandon the quest. He sent this up to her and waited, thinking that possibly she would send for him. A little weary from the reaction of the excitement he had just gone through, he sat down in the corner farthest from the door. The large room was dimly lighted by one untrimmed lamp.

He sat for some time, thinking that maybe Euphra was writing him a note, or perhaps preparing herself to see him. Involuntarily he looked up, and a sudden pang shot through his heart. A dim form stood in the middle of the room gazing earnestly at him. He saw the same face which he had seen for a moment in the library at Arnstead, shimmering faintly in the dull light. Delight, mingled with hope and tempered by shame, flushed his face as he gradually rose.

She stood still.

"Margaret!" he said with trembling voice.

"Mr. Sutherland," she responded sweetly, smiling.

"Are you a ghost, Margaret?"

She smiled broadly and, advancing slowly, took both his hands and joined them together in hers.

"Margaret . . ." he said again and, trying to continue, found that no words would come. He fell silent as the tears began streaming down his cheeks.

She waited motionless until his emotion should subside, still holding his hands. To Hugh her hands were so good.

"He is dead," said Hugh at last, with an effort.

"Yes, Father is dead," said Margaret calmly. "You would not weep if you had seen him die as I did—with a smile like a summer sunset."

She sighed a gentle, painless sigh, then smiled again.

"Forgive me," said Hugh, "for not writing, for seeming to forget. I . . . I—"

"We are the same as in the old days," answered Margaret; and Hugh was satisfied.

"But, how do you come to be here?" asked Hugh, after a silence.

"I will tell you about that another time. Now I must give you Miss Cameron's message. She is very sorry she cannot see you, but she is quite unable. If you could call tomorrow morning she hopes to be better. She says she can never thank you enough."

The lamp burned yet fainter. Margaret went and proceeded to trim it. The light shone up in her face and she handled the globe delicately. Hugh saw that her hands were very beautiful, not small, but admirably shaped. As she replaced the globe, she said, ''That man will not trouble her anymore.''

''I hope not,'' said Hugh. ''But you speak confidently. Why?''

''Because she has behaved gloriously. She has fought and conquered him on his own ground. And now she is a free and beautiful child of God forever.''

''You delight me,'' rejoined Hugh. ''Another time, perhaps, you will be able to tell me all about it.''

''I hope so. I think she will not mind my telling you.''

They wished each other a good night and Hugh went away with a strange feeling which he had never experienced before. To think of the girl he had first seen at Turriepuffit growing into such a grand, womanly and lovely creature—so strong and yet so graceful! Would that every woman believed in the ideal of herself and hoped for it as the will of God.

Hugh thought about her until he fell asleep and dreamed about her till he woke. Not for a moment did he fancy he was in love with her. The feeling was different from any he had till now associated with those words. It was more an admiration of the woman she had become, mingled with old and precious memories, doubly dear now that she was near him again.

In the morning he went to Mrs. Elton's. Euphra was expecting his visit, and he was shown up into her room, where she was lying on the couch. She received him with the warmth of gratitude added to that of friendship. Her face was pale and thin, but her eyes were brilliant. She did not appear at first to be very ill; but the depth and reality of her sickness grew upon him. Behind her couch stood Margaret, like a guardian angel. Margaret belonged to the day and therefore looked even more beautiful still than by the lamplight. Euphra held out a pale little hand to Hugh, and before she withdrew it, led Hugh's toward Margaret's. Their hands joined. How different to Hugh was the touch of the two hands. Life, strength, persistency in the one; languor, feebleness, and fading in the other.

''I can never thank you enough,'' murmured Euphra. ''Therefore I will not try. It is no bondage to remain your debtor.''

''That would be thanks indeed if I had done anything.''

''I have found out a mystery,'' said Euphra.

''I fear there will be no mysteries left by and by,'' said Hugh. ''But what mystery have you destroyed?''

''Not destroyed; for the mystery of courage remains. I was the ghost that night in the Ghost's Walk, you know—the white one; there is the good ghost, the nun, the black one."

"Who? Margaret?"

"Yes. She has just been confessing it to me. I had my two angels; my evil angel in the count—my good angel in Margaret. Little did I think then that the holy powers were watching me in her. I knew the evil one; I knew nothing of the good. I suppose it is so with a great many people."

Hugh sat silent in astonishment. Margaret, then, had been at Arnstead with Mrs. Elton all the time. It was herself he had seen in the library.

"Did you suspect me, Margaret?" resumed Euphra, turning toward her where she sat in the window.

"Not in the least. I only knew that something was wrong about the house and that some being was terrifying the servants and poor Harry. I resolved to do my best to meet it, especially if it should be anything of a ghostly kind."

"Then you believe in such appearances?" said Hugh.

"I have never met anything of the sort yet."

"And you were not afraid?"

"Not much. I am never really afraid of anything."

The three friends truly enjoyed their visit.

"Come and see me again soon," said Euphra, as Hugh rose to go. He promised.

Hugh dined with Mrs. Elton and Harry the next day. Euphra was unable to see him but sent a kind message by Margaret. He called the day following and saw neither Euphra nor Margaret. She was no better. Mrs. Elton said the physicians could discover no definite disease either of the lungs or of any other organ. Yet life seemed sinking. Margaret thought that the conflict which she had passed through had exhausted her vitality. Had she yielded she might have lived a slave; now, perhaps, she must die a free woman.

Her continued illness made Hugh still more anxious to find the ring. Falconer would have applied to the police, but he feared the man would vanish from London upon the least suspicion that he was watched. They held many consultations on the subject.

47 / The Count

One morning as soon as she waked, Euphra said, "Have I been still all night, Margaret?"

"Quite still. Why do you ask?"

"Because I have had such a strange and vivid dream that I feel as if I must have been to the place."

"I hope it did not trouble you much."

"No, not much. For though I was with the count, I did not seem to be there in the body at all, only somehow near him. I can recall the place perfectly."

"Do you think it really was the place he was in at the time?"

"I should not wonder."

"Could you describe the place to Mr. Sutherland? It might help him to find the count."

"Will you send for him?"

"Yes, certainly."

Margaret wrote to Hugh at once and sent the note to his lodgings, where he was when it arrived. He hurriedly answered it and went to find Falconer; the two arrived at Mrs. Elton's shortly thereafter.

When Margaret met them, Hugh told her that Falconer was his best friend and one who knew London perhaps better than any other man in it. Margaret looked at him full in the face for a moment. Falconer smiled at the intensity of her still gaze, and she returned his smile.

"I will ask Miss Cameron to see you."

After a little while they were shown up to Euphra's room. Falconer took her hand and held it for a moment. A kind of light broke over his face, as if his spirit were smiling, and a tear filled each eye. To understand this look fully, one would need to know his history as I do. He laid her hand gently on her bosom and said, "God bless you."

Euphra felt that God did bless her in the very words.

"I know enough of your history, Miss Cameron," he said, "to understand without any preface whatever you choose to tell me."

Euphra began at once. "I dreamed last night that I found myself outside the street door. I did not know where I was going, but my feet seemed to know. They carried me round two or three corners into a wide, long street which I think was Oxford Street. They carried me on into London, far beyond any place I knew. On and on I walked until I turned to the left beside a church, on the steeple of which stood what I took for a wandering ghost. Then I went on, turning left and right too many times for me to remember till at last I came to a little, old-fashioned court with two or three trees in it. I had to go up a few steps to enter it. I was not afraid, because I knew I was dreaming and that my body was not there. It was a great relief. I opened a door upon which the moon shone very bright and walked up two flights of stairs into a back room. And there I found him doing something at a table by candlelight. He had a sheet of paper before him, but what he was doing with it, I could not see. I think it had something to do with me and why I had gone and how I had known where he was. I tried hard to see the paper, but the dream suddenly faded and I awoke and found Margaret. Then I knew I was safe," she added with a loving glance at her maid.

Falconer rose.

"I know the place you mean perfectly," he said. "It is too peculiar to be mistaken."

"How kind of you not to laugh at me," said Euphra.

"I might make a fool of myself if I laughed at anyone. So I generally avoid it. We may as well get the good out of what we do not understand, or at least try if there be any in it.—Will you come, Sutherland?"

Hugh rose and left with Falconer.

"She seemed pleased with you," Hugh said as they left the house.

"Yes. She touched my heart."

"Won't you go and see her again?"

"Only if she sends for me. There is no need."

"It would please her—comfort her, I am sure."

"She has got one of God's angels beside her, Sutherland. She won't need me."

"What do you mean?"

"I mean that maid of hers."

A pang of jealousy shot through Hugh's heart.

"My dear friend," said Falconer, as if he sensed his feelings, "if you have any influence with that woman, do not lose it. For as sure as there's a sun in heaven, she is one of the winged ones. Don't I know a woman when I see her?"

He sighed with a kind of involuntary sigh.

"My dear boy," he added, "I am nearly twice your age—don't be jealous of *me*."

"Mr. Falconer," said Hugh humbly, "forgive me. The feeling was involuntary. And if you have detected in it more than I was aware of, you are at least as likely to be right as I am."

"Well, we had better part now and meet again tonight."

So Hugh went home and tried to turn his thoughts to the novel he was writing. But Euphra, Fenkelstein, and Margaret persisted in filling his mind instead of the characters in his tale.

At nine that same evening he was at Falconer's door.

"Are you ready, then?" said Falconer.

"Quite."

"Will you have something to eat before we go? It is still early for our project."

This was a welcome proposal to Hugh. Cold meat and ale were excellent preparatives for what might be required of him. By the time the friends set out together, Hugh felt himself ready for anything that might fall to his lot.

The walk was rather a long one, but guided by Falconer they arrived at the place he judged to be that indicated by Euphra. It was very different from the place Hugh had pictured to himself. Yet in everything it corresponded to her description.

"Are we not great fools, Sutherland, to set out on such a chase with the dream of a sick girl for our only guide?"

"I am sure you don't think so, else you would not have gone."

"I think we can afford the small risk to our reputation involved in the chase of this wild goose. There is enough of strange testimony about things of the sort to justify us in attending to the hint, but this ought to be the house," he added going up to one that had a rather more respectable look than the rest.

He knocked at the door. An elderly woman half opened it and looked at them suspiciously.

"Will you take my card to the foreign gentleman who is lodging with you," said Falconer.

She glanced at him again and turned inwards, hesitating whether to leave the door half open or not. Falconer stood so close to it, however, that she was afraid to shut it in his face.

"Now, Sutherland, follow me," whispered Falconer as soon as the woman had disappeared on the stair.

Hugh followed behind the moving tower of his friend, who strode with long, noiseless strides until he reached the staircase. That he took three steps at a time. They went up two flights and reached the top just as the woman was laying her hand on the lock of the back-room door. She turned and faced them.

"Speak not a word," said Falconer in a whisper accompanied by a stern look. She drew back in fright and yielded her place at the door.

"Come in," bawled someone in answer to the knock she had already given.

"It *is* he!" said Hugh, trembling with excitement.

"Hush," said Falconer, and went in.

Hugh followed.

He knew the back of the count at once. He was seated at a table, apparently writing but, going nearer, they saw that he was drawing. A single closer glance showed them a portrait of Euphra growing under his hand. In order to intensify his will and concentrate it upon her, he was drawing her portrait from memory. But at the moment they caught sight of it, aware of the hostile presence, he sprang to his feet and reached the chimney-piece at one bound where he caught up a sword.

"Watch out, Falconer!" cried Hugh; "that weapon is poisoned. He is no everyday villain."

Fenkelstein made a sudden lunge at Hugh, his face pale with hatred and anger. But a blow from Falconer's huge fist, traveling faster than the point of his weapon, stretched him on the floor. Such was Falconer's momentum that it hurled both him and the table across the fallen villain. Falconer was up in a moment. But Fenkelstein lay dazed. There was plenty of time for Hugh to secure the rapier and for Falconer to secure its owner before he came to himself.

"Where's my ring?" said Hugh the moment he opened his eyes.

"Gentlemen, I protest," began Fenkelstein, in a voice upon which the cord that bound his wrists had an evident influence.

"None of that!" said Falconer. "Hand over the two rings or be the security for them yourself."

"What witness have you against me?"

"The best of witnesses—Miss Cameron."

"And me," added Hugh.

"Gentlemen, I am very sorry. I yielded to temptation. I meant to restore the diamond after the joke had been played out, but I was forced to part with it."

"The joke is played out on you," said Falconer. "So you had better produce the other ring you stole at the same time."

"I have not got it."

"Come, come. Nobody would give you more than five shillings for it. And you knew what it was worth when you took it.—Sutherland, you stand over him while I search the room. We may as well get rid of this portrait first."

As he spoke, Falconer tore the portrait and threw it into the fire. He then turned to a cupboard in the room. Whether it was that Fenkelstein feared further revelations I do not know, but he quailed.

"I have not got it," he repeated.

"You lie," answered Falconer.

"I would give it to you if I could," he whined.

"You shall."

The Bohemian looked contemptible now. As soon as he found himself in such a dire situation, the gloss vanished and the true nature came out, that of a ruffian and a sneak. He quivered at the look with which Falconer turned again to the cupboard.

"Stop!" he cried; "here it is."

Muttering what sounded like curses, he pulled out from beneath his shirt the ring, suspended from his neck.

"Sutherland," said Falconer, taking the ring. "Secure that sword and be careful with it. We will have its point tested. Meantime"—here he turned again to his prisoner—"I give you warning that the moment I leave this house, I go to Scotland Yard. Do you know the place? I will recommend the police to watch you, and they will mind what I say. If you leave London, a message will be sent wherever you go, that you had better be watched. My advice to you is to stay where you are as long as you can. I shall meet you again."

They left him on the floor, to the care of his landlady, whom they found outside the room, speechless with terror.

As soon as they were in the square, on which the moon was now shining as it had in Euphra's dream the night before, Falconer gave the ring to Hugh.

"Take it to a jeweler's, Sutherland, and get it cleaned before you give it to Miss Cameron."

"I will," answered Hugh, and added, "I don't know how to thank you."

"Then don't," said Falconer with a smile.

When they reached the end of the street, he turned and bade Hugh good night.

Hugh turned toward home. Falconer walked into a court and was out of sight in a moment.

48 / The End

Hugh took the ring to Mrs. Elton's and gave it into Margaret's hand. She brought him back a message of warmest thanks from Euphra. She had asked for writing materials at once and was now communicating the good news to Mr. Arnold in Madeira.

"I have never seen her look so happy," added Margaret. "She hopes to see you in the evening, if you would not mind calling again."

Hugh did call, and she received him most kindly. He was distressed to see how altered she was. The fire of one life seemed dying out. But the fire of another life—the life of thought and feeling and truth and love, which death cannot touch—was growing fast. He sat with her for an hour and then went.

This chapter of his own history concluded, Hugh returned with fresh energy to his novel. There was the more necessity that he should make progress because of the fact that, having sent his mother the greater part of the salary he had received from Mr. Arnold, he was now reduced to his last sovereign. Poverty looks rather ugly when she comes so close as this. But with a sovereign in his pocket and last week's rent paid, a bachelor is certainly not poverty stricken yet.

But a week passed, and another, then another, and still no financial opportunities presented themselves. At length he reached his last coin. But he would not borrow until absolutely compelled. In the morning he wandered out through the streets, looking through the shop windows, while thinking what he should do.

When he returned he found a letter waiting for him from a friend of his mother, informing him that she was dangerously ill and urging him to set off immediately for her.

When he had read it, he fell on his knees and prayed, "What am I to do?" He scarcely had money for a crust of bread. Trainfare to Scotland was out of the question.

He rose with the simple resolution to go and tell Falconer.

He was not at home. Hugh left his card with the words, "Come to me; I need you."

He then returned, packed a few necessities, and sat down to wait. Within five minutes, Falconer entered. He read trouble on his friend's face immediately.

"What's the matter, Sutherland, my dear fellow?"

Hugh handed him the letter in one hand and his last fourpenny piece in the other. Falconer understood at once.

"Sutherland," he said in a tone of reproof, "it is a shame of you to forget that we are brothers. Why did you not tell me?"

"I would have come to you as soon as the fourpence was gone. Or at least if I hadn't got another before I was very hungry again."

"Good heavens!" exclaimed Falconer. Then pulling out his watch, "We have two hours," he said, "before a train starts for the north. Come to my place."

Hugh rose and obeyed. Falconer's attendant soon brought them a plentiful supper from a neighboring shop. If it had not been for his anxiety about his mother, Hugh would have been happier than he had ever been in his life.

After he had eaten and drunk, Hugh went to take his leave of his friends at Mrs. Elton's. Like most invalids, Euphra was better in the evening; she requested to see him. He found her in bed and much wasted since he saw her last. He could not keep the tears out of his eyes.

"Do not cry, dear friend," she said sweetly. "There is no room for me here anymore. I am sent for."

Hugh could not reply.

"I have written to Mr. Arnold about the ring and all you did to get it. Do you know he is going to marry Lady Emily?"

Still Hugh could not answer.

Margaret stood on the other side of the bed. Her lovely hands were the servants of Euphra, and her light, firm feet moved only in ministration. He felt that Euphra had room in the world while Margaret waited on her. It is not house and servants and possessions that make a home—but loving hearts, hearts that do not grow weary of helping.

"I trust you will find your mother better, Hugh," said Euphra.

"I fear not," he answered.

"Well, Margaret has been teaching me, and I think I have learned it, that death is not such a dreadful thing as it looks. I said to her, 'It is easy for you, Margaret, who are so far from death's door.' But she told me that she had been all but dead once and that you had saved her life almost with your own."

Euphra smiled with ten times the fascination of any of her old smiles; for the soul of the smile was love.

"I shall never see you again," she went on. "My heart thanks you, from its very depths, for your goodness to me. It has been much more than I deserve."

Hugh silently kissed her wasted hand and departed. He found that the world had become a sad, wandering star.

Falconer had called for him. They drove to Mrs. Talbot's where Hugh got his bag and bade his landlady good-bye. Falconer then accompanied him to the railway station.

Having left him for a moment, Falconer rejoined him, saying, "I have your ticket," and put him into a first-class carriage.

Hugh remonstrated but Falconer replied, "I find this hulk of mine worth taking care of. You will be twice the good to your mother if you reach her tolerably fresh."

He stood by the carriage door, talking to him until the train started; he walked alongside till it was fairly in motion. Then, bidding him good-bye, left in his hand a little packet. Going inside, Hugh opened it, and found it to consist of a few sovereigns and a few shillings folded up in a twenty-pound note.

But just before the engine had whistled, Falconer had said to Hugh, "Give me that fourpenny piece, you brace old fellow."

"There it is," said Hugh. "What do you want it for?"

"I am going to make a wedding present of it to your wife, whoever she may happen to be. I hope she will be worthy of it."

49 / Death

Hugh found his mother even worse than he had expected. But she rallied a little after his arrival.

In the evening he wandered out in the bright moonlit snow. How strange it was to see all the old forms with his heart so full of new things. The same hills rose about him, with all the lines of their shapes unchanged. Yet they were changing as surely as he himself. He thought with sadness how all the haunts of his childhood would pass to others who would feel no love or reverence for them; that the house would be the same but would sound with new steps and ring with new laughter. Further thought showed him that places die as well as their dwellers, that by slow degrees their forms are wiped out.

All the old things at home looked sad. He could find no refuge in the past; he must go on into the future.

His mother lingered for some time without any evident change. He sat by her bedside most days. All she wanted was to have him within reach of her feeble voice.

Once she said, "My boy, I am going to your father."

"Yes, Mother," Hugh replied. "How glad he will be to see you."

"But I shall leave you alone."

"God will watch over me." It was the first time he had said the words.

The mother looked at him as only a mother can look, smiled sweetly, closed her eyes, fell asleep holding his hand and slept for hours.

Meanwhile, in London, Margaret was watching Euphra. She was dying and Margaret was the angel of life watching over her.

"I shall get rid of my lameness there, Margaret, won't I?" said Euphra one day, half playfully.

"Yes, dear."

"It will be delightful to walk again without pain."

"Perhaps you will not get rid of it all at once though."

"Why do you think so?" asked Euphra with uneasiness.

"Because if it is taken from you before you are quite willing to have it as long as God pleases, by and by you will ask for it back again that you may bear it for his sake."

"I am willing, Margaret. Only one can't like it, you know."

"I know that," answered Margaret.

The days passed on, and every day she grew weaker. Mrs. Elton was kind; Harry was in dreadful distress. He haunted her room, creeping in whenever he had a chance, sitting out of the way in the corner. Euphra liked to have him near, but she seldom spoke to him, for Margaret alone could hear with ease what she said.

But now and then she would motion him to her bedside and say—it was always the same—"Harry, dear, be good."

"I will, I will, dear Euphra."

One day she said, "I am not right today, Margaret. I seem so hateful to myself. God can't love me the way I feel today."

"Don't measure God's mind by your own, Euphra. It would be a poor love that depended not on itself but on the feelings of the person loved. A crying baby turns away from its mother's breast, but she does not put it away. She holds it closer. In the worst mood I am ever in, when I don't feel I love God at all, I just look up to his love. I say to him, 'Look at me. See what a state I am in. Help me!' "

Euphra laughed a feeble but delighted laugh.

So the winter days passed on.

"I wish I could live till the spring," said Euphra. "I should like to see a snowdrop and a primrose again."

"Perhaps you will, dear. But you are going into a better spring. I almost envy you, Euphra."

"But shall we have spring there?"

"I think so."

"And spring flowers?"

"I think we shall—better than here."

"But they will not mean so much."

"I think they will mean ever so much more and be ever so much more springlike. They will be the spring flowers to all winters in one."

Folded in the love of this woman, anointed for her death by her wisdom, baptized for the new life by her sympathy and its tears, Euphra died in the arms of Margaret.

Margaret wept, fell on her knees, and gave God thanks.

Mrs. Elton was so distressed that as soon as the funeral was over she broke up her London household, sent some of the servants home, and took some to her favorite country home, to which Harry also accompanied her.

She hoped that now the affair of the ring was cleared up, she might, as soon as Hugh returned, succeed in persuading him to come with them to Devonshire and resume his tutorship. This would satisfy her anxiety about Hugh and Harry both.

Hugh's mother died too and was buried. When he returned from the grave, which now held both father and mother, he found a short note from Margaret telling him that Euphra was gone. Sorrow is easier to bear when it comes upon sorrow. But he could not help feeling a keen additional pang when he learned that she was dead whom he had loved once, and now loved better. Margaret's note informed him likewise that Euphra had left a written request that her diamond ring should be given to him to wear for her sake.

He prepared to leave the home whence all the homeness had now vanished. He gathered the little household treasures, the few books, the few portraits and ornaments, his father's sword, and his mother's wedding ring; destroyed with sacred fire all written papers; sold the remainder of the furniture, and so proceeded to take his last departure from the home of his childhood.

50 / The Beginning

Perhaps the greatest benefit that resulted to Hugh from being thus made a pilgrim and a stranger in the earth was that nature herself saw him and took him in. For he did not leave his dead home in haste. He lingered over it and roamed about its neighborhood. Regarding all about him with a quiet, almost passive spirit, he was astonished to find how his eyes opened to see the boughs, the winds, the streams, the fields, the sky, and the snow. When or how the change had passed upon him he could not tell. He beheld in everything about him the thoughts and feelings of the Maker of the heavens and the earth. For the first time in his life he felt at home with nature.

With the sorrow and loneliness within him and nature all around him, it is no wonder that the form of Margaret rose again upon the world of his imagination. Everyone was gone; Margaret remained behind. She had dawned upon him like a sweet crescent moon, hanging far off in a cold and low horizon. Now, lifting his eyes, he saw that same moon nearly at the full. He knew now that he loved her. He knew that every place he went through caught a glimmer of romance the moment he thought of her.

But the growth of these feelings had been gradual—so slow that when he recognized them, it seemed to him as if he had felt them from the first. The fact was that as soon as he began to be capable of loving Margaret, he had begun to love her. He had never been able to understand her until he was driven into the desert. And now, in absence, he began to reflect on the character of her he thought he had known. He saw now that she had always understood many things he was only just waking to recognize. He realized that the scholar had been very patient with the stupidity of the master and had drawn from his lessons a nourishment of which he had known nothing himself. The silent girl of old days, whose countenance wore the stillness of an unsunned pool as she listened with reverence to his lessons, had blossomed into a calm, stately woman.

As he haunted in silence the regions of the past, the whole of his history in connection with David returned on him clear and vivid, as if passing once again before his eyes and through his heart. The birth of nature in his soul, which enabled him to understand and love Margaret, helped him likewise to contemplate with admiration and awe the towering peaks of David's hopes, trusts, and aspirations. He had taught the ploughman mathematics, but that ploughman had possessed in himself all the essential elements of the grandeur of the old prophets glorified by faith.

How good David had been to him! He had built onto his house that he might take him in from the cold and make life pleasant to him. He had given him his heart every time he gave him his manly hand. And this man, this friend, Hugh had forsaken, neglected, and almost forgotten. He could not go to him like the prodigal to his father. He knew David forgave him. But there was one more thing he could do to solidify his repentance. Jeanette still lived, and was David's representative on earth. He would go to her. He would go to see old Jeanette, and visit the grave of his second father. Then he would return to the toil and hunger and hope of London.

So he returned, at last knowing that he, too, was a child of David's Father, great in that humility which alone recognizes greatness and in the beginnings of that meekness which shall inherit the earth. It was with a mingling of strange emotions that Hugh approached the scene of those past memories. The dusk was beginning to gather. The frost lay thick on the ground. The pine trees stood up tall in the cold. The gate was unfriendly and chilled his hand. He turned into the footpath. He saw the room David had built for him. Its thatch was a mass of moss whose colors were now hidden in the frost.

He drew near the door, trembling. He hesitated. Through the kitchen window the glimmer of a fire was just discernible.

He paused, unable to knock.

He would go into the fir wood first and see Margaret's tree, as he always called it.

The evening wind whistled keen and cold through the dry needles of the small, stunted trees. Here and there amongst them rose one of the huge Scotch firs. Toward one of these he walked. It was the one under which he had seen Margaret when he first met her in the wood. To think that the young girl to whom he had on that day given the primrose he had just found should now so fill his mind and his heart. Her childish dream of an angel haunting the wood had been true, only she was the angel herself. He drew near the place. How well he knew it! He seated himself, cold as it was in the February of Scotland, at the base of the tree.

While he sat with his eyes on the ground a light rustle in the fallen leaves made him raise them suddenly. It was all winter and fallen leaves about him. But he lifted his eyes, and in his soul burst a summer of light and warmth.

Margaret stood before him.

She stood a little way off, looking—as if she wanted to be sure before she moved a step. She was dressed in a gray winsey gown, close to her throat and wrists. She had neither shawl nor bonnet. Her fine health kept her warm, even in a Scottish winter at sundown.

She came nearer.

"Margaret!" he murmured, and started to rise.

"No, no; sit still," she said, smiling. "I thought it was the angel as I always imagined. Now I know it. Sit still, dear Mr. Sutherland, one moment more."

Humbled, he said, "Ah, Margaret, I wish you would not praise one so little deserving it."

"Praise," she repeated. "I wasn't praising you, Mr. Sutherland, only appreciating. Next to my father, you made me know and feel. And as I walked here I was thinking of the old times."

She came close to him now. He rose, trembling, but held out no hand.

"Margaret," he faltered, "do I dare love you?"

She looked at him with wide-open eyes.

"*Me?*" she said in astonishment. Her eyes did not move from his. A slight rose flush bloomed out on her motionless face as her lips remained parted but silent.

"I am very poor, Margaret. I could not afford to marry now."

It was a stupid speech, but he made it.

"I don't care," she answered quietly, "if you never marry me." She paused and completed the thought only to herself—*just your love will be enough.*

He misunderstood her words and turned cold to the very heart. He misunderstood her stillness. Her heart lay so deep that it took a long time for its feelings to reach the surface. He said no more but turned away with a sigh, thinking she had spurned his proposal.

"Come home to my mother," she said.

He obeyed mechanically and walked in silence by her side. The love that had risen within him now seemed suddenly to have been dashed apart. They reached the cottage and entered. Margaret said, "Here he is, Mother," and disappeared.

Jeanette was seated in the armchair by the fire quietly thinking. She turned her head. Sorrow had baptized her face with a new gentleness. The tender expression which had been but occasional while her husband lived was almost constant now.

"Mother," he said involuntarily.

She started to her feet, cried, "My bairn! my bairn!", and threw her arms around him, weeping. Hugh led her to a chair and knelt by her side. "Didna David aye say, 'Give the lad time, my bonny woman!'—didn't he say that? Aye, and he ca'd me his bonny woman. An' now ye're come home, an' nothing cud glaidden my heart mair."

Hugh could make no reply. He reached for Margaret's wooden stool and sat down upon it. She gazed in his face for a while, then put her arms round his neck and drew his head to her bosom as if he had been her own firstborn.

''But eh! Yer bonnie face is sharp. I don't doot ye have come through a heap o' trouble.''

''I'll tell you all about it,'' said Hugh.

''Na, na. I know a' aboot it frae Maggie. And God preserve's! Ye're clean perished wi' cold. Let me up, me bairn.''

Jeanette rose and made up the fire which soon cast a joyful glow throughout the room. The peat fire in the little cottage was a good symbol of the heart of its mistress.

She then put on the kettle, saying, ''I'm just goin' to make ye a cup o' tay, Mr. Sutherland. But would ye no tak' a drap oot o' the bottle in the meantime?''

''No, thank you,'' said Hugh, who longed to be alone, for his heart was still cold and confused. ''I would rather wait for the tea.''

He gazed into the fire. But he saw nothing in it. A light step passed him several times, but he did not hear it. The loveliest eyes looked earnestly toward him as they passed. But his were not lifted to meet their gaze. He remained as one in a trance.

''Come, Mr. Sutherland,'' Jeanette called him at length. ''Maggie's got yer own room all ready.''

Hugh rose and Jeanette led the way into the study. Margaret was there. The room was just as he had left it. A bright fire was on the hearth. Tea was on the table, with eggs and oatcakes and flour scones in abundance; for Jeanette had the best she could get for Margaret, who was her guest only for a little while.

They sat down, but Hugh could not eat. Jeanette looked distressed and Margaret glanced at him uneasily. His silence had grown awkward.

''Do eat something, Mr. Sutherland,'' said Margaret.

Hugh looked at her involuntarily. She did not understand his look, and it alarmed her. His countenance was changed.

''What is the matter, dear . . . Hugh?'' she said, rising, and laying her hand on his shoulder tenderly.

''Hoots! lassie,'' broke in her mother; ''are ye' lovemakin' to a man, a gentleman, before my very eyes?''

''He did it first, Mother,'' answered Margaret with a smile.

A pang of hope shot through Hugh's heart. Had he misunderstood?

''Oh, that's the way o't is't? The bairn's in love! Ye're not goin' to marry a gentleman, Maggie, are ye? Na, na, lass!''

So saying, the old lady rather imprudently left the room to fill the teapot in the kitchen.

"Do you remember this?" said Margaret—who felt that Hugh must have misinterpreted something or other—taking from her pocket a little book, and from the book a withered flower.

Hugh saw that it was like a primrose, and hoped against hope that it was the one which he had given to her on the first spring morning in the fir wood. Still, a feeling very different from that throbbing in his chest might have made her preserve it. He *must* know all.

"Why did you keep that?" he said.

"Because I loved you."

"Loved me?"

"Yes. Didn't you know?"

"Why did you say, then, that you didn't care if . . . if I never—"

"Because love is enough, Hugh—that was why."

The complete account of Robert Falconer's life is taken up in *The Musician's Quest*.